ON THE WAY TO MY FATHER'S FUNERAL

ON THE WAY TO MY FATHER'S FUNERAL
New and Selected Stories

JONATHAN BAUMBACH

BAUMB

LOW FIDELITY PRESS

NEW YORK, NEW YORK

Low Fidelity press
P.O. Box 21930 Brooklyn, NY 11202-1930
info@lofipress.com
http://www.lofipress.com

The following stories were published previously in periodicals: "On The Way to My Father's Funeral, He Tells Me His Story," "The Reading," "Men at Lunch," "The Psychopathology of Everyday Life," and "Reverie" in *Boulevard*; "Bright is Innocent: Scenes from an Imaginary Movie" in *Iowa Review*; "Lost in Translation" in *Confrontation*; "Oh, Hum" in *Fiction International*; and "The Villa Mondare" in *Mississippi Review*.

Cover design: Andrew Vernon
Cover painting: "Watching the Unseen" by Harold Baumbach
Text design and typesetting: Ambivalent Design
ambivalent@cox.net
Printed in the U.S.A. by Main Street Rag

Library of Congress Cataloging-in-Publication Data

Baumbach, Jonathan.
On the way to my fathers funeral : new and selected stories / Jonathan Baumbach.
    p. cm.
    ISBN 0-9723363-3-8
    I. Title.
    PS3552.A844O5 2004
    813'.54--dc22

                                        2004022140

For Aurora, a born storyteller.

Contents

I. On the Way to My Father's Funeral

II. from *Babble*

I. On the Way to My Father's Funeral

On the Way to My Father's Funeral, He Tells Me His Story

Are you listening Tommy? Tommy there's this story I have to tell you that will make an absolutely knockout scenario for a film it came to me I was thinking about what the story meant this story that presented itself to me in a dream and it struck me that it could be made into a film that would be right up your alley I want to hear what you think are you listening. The central actor was six years old that's where it starts he had just begun school my father had been out of work for a while and had taken a job moving furniture which was an absolutely terrible job. I was the best one in my class the teacher loved me she absolutely loved me Tommy the teacher she was young and a knockout she encouraged me to draw she thought I was talented she said to my father you're lucky to have a son who can draw like that but you see he always hated my drawings any art he hated anything beautiful was a waste of time to him you're lucky you didn't have a father like that. For my father drawing pictures making anything beautiful was a stupid waste of time in my father's world everything was valued in terms of money if you can sell them you can do them he said I was only six. I want you to hear this I know you can make a film out of it it's your kind of material it's got all the elements you like to use it's a mystery without a solution it's an unsolved case. He thought drawing was a waste of time nothing's a waste of time not even wasting time is a waste of time

3

do you hear what I'm saying. I made mistakes myself don't think I didn't your mother and I came home this one time you were sitting in my chair in the living room bawling as if your heart was broken are you listening the sitter was I don't want to say this the wrong way with Daniel in the car if you get what I mean her boy friend was embracing her you get the picture. They were embracing which is a euphemism for what was really taking place and you were looking on wide-eyed we had to replace her and get someone else none of the girls we got were any good you were only two I needed the time to paint I was just beginning.

The painter Goodkin who you've met he's dead now said to me I have just the gallery for you there's this woman from New Zealand who's handling all the new painters the current thing you see he wasn't interested in the gallery for himself it wasn't important enough but it would be good for me I was just starting out. I had ten one-man shows there I was the star you might say but then I had this problem which maybe you knew about and maybe you didn't I'm calling it a problem for you know what reason but it was more than that. I couldn't paint for a whole year I couldn't complete a single picture I could start a picture I could paint half a picture sometimes even beautifully but I couldn't fin- ish anything. Every painting would self-destruct and I would finish the job which was the only choice left me the painting said put me out of my misery and I was not averse to answering its plea.

•

Driving with Daniel to my father's funeral, trapped in tunnel traffic, a demonstration we would later learn blocking the exit.

•

Listen to what I'm telling you Tommy forget the traffic I lost a whole year of painting I was the one that was lost that year the year lost me I was a missing person. I couldn't paint a picture for the life of me you didn't notice no one noticed but I didn't complete a picture because the reason I painted which was a neurotic reason had been taken away. In the movie you would show the canvas being worked on and then the destruction of the painting the unpainting of the canvas so to speak which is if I'm not mistaken your metier reducing the world to its broken parts. Strokes of white paint blocking out the image on the canvas each stroke effacing a little more of the failed painted image as though some kind of censorship were being enforced before our eyes the painter stifling himself.

I know what I'm talking about Tommy don't pretend I don't. I'm not stupid do you think I am. There are some things I can't forgive I can't I won't forgive being taken as someone of no account because that's the way my father treated me. And that's what you think isn't it you think I'm ignorant because I never finished school but if you listen carefully if you listen to me carefully you'll get yourself a film with what's the phrase they like to use it changes every few years universal application. Something for everyone is also nothing for anyone universality lies in the particular. I'm sure you know what I mean you're not stupid either and Daniel sitting next to you silent as a mouse is the smartest of us all. I was not an athlete I was not a scholar I was none of those things by which achievement is measured but I could draw like an angel. You inherited my eye Tommy everything else except one or two other traits not all of them admirable came from your admirable mother. The story I have to tell you is going to interest you if you give it a chance if you don't give into cynicism it's going to interest you because it's your story too. What was I talking about the scenario for your next film the life of the painter the lives of the painter the whiting out of the failed painting the return to the illusion of nothing I say the illusion of because what was effaced you see was still there it was always there there is no such thing as nothing. I destroyed each painting just before it was finished because the painting would not allow itself to be what I intended for it. The painting had a way of destroying itself I was only its complicit agent nothing is everything. Your mother who was a saint you know what I mean selfless she was selfless to a fault denying herself even basic creature comforts which could be maddening also ignored you to look after me which is why we've never been close Tommy you resent me because I took the teat from your lips and put it in mine.

This is a confession I'll deny on my death bed you never heard it here and that includes you too Daniel if you happen to be listening in. My first therapist who had a directive approach whose fee I paid with paintings instead of money did me no good and did me some disrepair left me as he found me an unfunctioning painter though his confidence in his professional skills I can tell you suffered as a result. He begged me not to leave him can you believe that I was the patient on whom he saw his reputation as a healer depending Dr. Winsocki was his name. You follow my instructions you'll paint again I give you my word he said my professional word my word as a healer of course he didn't use the word healer they don't but that was the ticket. Thank God I had the strength to leave him I went to Goodkin's analyst Goodkin was completing two paintings a week and gave Dr. Barrensin credit whether deserving or not. Dr. Barrensin said what I needed was a second wife because your mother was more like a mother to me than a wife which I think you know though I never talked about it to you that way before I couldn't she was your mother too. What he gave me you see which is what he also gave Goodkin was permission to break the rules something I didn't dare do otherwise I mean God I felt would strike me down if I did anything like Goodkin was doing without His permission you see what I'm saying? His point which I didn't understand right away are you listening Tommy I wish you had a pencil and could take this down was that art was my mistress and that I felt guilt at getting away with it my being successful ten one man shows in twelve years I was the star there it had stopped me from functioning had broken me down.

When he suggested I take a second wife an unmothering wife a mistress is what he meant I almost laughed in his face. The last thing I wanted to do was be unfaithful to your mother who had put up with so much from me over the years your mother was a wonderful woman a saint something she always hated to hear me say. As it turns out the last thing is always the first thing which I can tell from looking at your films is something you know. Even if I wanted to do as he said where do I look how do I do it without hurting your mother which I promised myself I wouldn't ever do. Where do you work? Barrensin asked me. I have a studio in the house I answered and I understood what he was getting at by his question. To have your mistress in my case it was art in the same house as your mother by which I mean my wife I was you see asking for trouble. So what I did which was what Barrensin had in mind for me was to rent an outside studio it made your mother unhappy but I had to do it I was a basket case my life you could say my life as a painter which was my real life depended on it. You of all people can understand that Tommy you've had three or four wives yourself I only had one. It so happens that Goodkin's girl friend had a sister I think she may even have been a twin her name was Martha and she came to my studio during lunch hour she worked in the neighborhood my studio was a floor below Goodkin's in the same building on Fifteenth Street I took you there once or twice. A simple person not beautiful (your mother when she was young was a beauty) not profound not a great reader of books not educated but a good heart.

Years later she married Pinchinn who was the framer who framed my pictures a Sunday painter in those days who after he married Martha many years after had a retrospective show at the Whitney I'm digressing. Barrensin was a quack I don't think he even had a degree his diploma on the wall had the look of something sold at Woolworth's he was an out and out fake but he got results. After I started seeing Barrensin I slowly got better the guilt went away though I had more reason do you see what I'm saying to be guilty than ever before.

•

The air was suffocating, horns barking complaint like trapped dogs. The progress so infinitesimal, we seemed to be going backwards while standing still. The blaring of horns, that was almost the worst of it, the raging sound which had no purpose but to exacerbate the general torment.

•

Tommy, are you getting this down this is the film you were born to make you came into my studio while I was painting I didn't hear you come up behind me you were two years old you jabbed a pencil a stub end of a pencil you had been carrying around into the canvas I was working on and destroyed the painting you ruined it completely the painting you see was your rival for my affection.

I didn't understand that until Dr. Winsocki he was the shrink I went to before I put myself in the hands of that quack Barrensin he pointed it out Tommy you irreparably ruined the painting it was a still life of two apples of different stature a corncob pipe a blue cup and an orange it was my first fully achieved painting and I beat you for destroying it I'm aggrieved to say. I felt terrible about it when it could not be undone but

Winsocki pointed out that it was an understandable reaction which I'm not saying makes it right but does it
do either of us any good to say I'm sorry so long after
the circumstance is beyond remedy. Wait a minute I'm
confusing the time frame that happened before I developed this block and couldn't paint are you listening
before I rented the studio on 15th Street before Martha
who was no beauty who was not a tenth as beautiful as
your mother made me feel I could make an acceptable
painting again. My early work as you know was somber
I used muted colors the painting's beauty was a critic in
Art News wrote its own indelible secret. And Barrenzin
or maybe Hedges I forget which said why didn't I try
painting with brighter colors. I did a portrait of Martha
and Mary together in shocking reds one was crimson
the other burnt umber I called it twins and the painters as well as almost everyone who came to the studio
were knocked off their feet the Carnegie Museum in
Pittsburgh bought it. It was at that time that Goodkin
was getting tired of Mary the other sister and suggested
that we make a switch even though Mary was the pret-
tier of the twins though not as pretty as your mother I
said absolutely not. Then he began to send Mary down
to the studio when Martha wasn't there she asked if I
would like to use her as a "life" model I don't have to tell
you what that is so I don't have to say any more than
I've said. Up until the arrival of Martha who had been
Barrensin's idea of therapy for me I had grown up in a
puritanical household a pleasure-denying household I
was in awe of girls and to tell you the truth somewhat
afraid of them which is to say afraid of my carnal drives
are you listening Tommy does it make any sense I was
always faithful to your mother. So I started conjugating with Mary too once in a while when the heat was
turned off in the building and we needed body heat to
get warm. So what Goodkin did was tell Martha that
I was sleeping with Mary saying therefore she should
sleep with him to even the score Martha told me that's

what he said and she told him he was a liar she didn't believe I was sleeping with Mary it was the craziest thing she wouldn't believe it even when Mary told her it was true I was sleeping with her once in a while. Finally Goodkin got his way with Martha and Martha wouldn't talk to me again she would kick the door of my studio whenever she went by though she had to admit the red painting I did of the two of them the two sisters was a beauty the best painting anyone ever did of the two of them together.

•

Possibility of not making this event is unthinkable and therefore daunting. The one positive sign: We moved the length of a car in the past minute.

•

I don't grieve about my behavior with these women Tommy your mother who was without blemish the best wife any of us had she didn't deserve such treatment that's the most undeniable thing in all of this. Your mother didn't know or never let me know if she was privy to what was going on I sometimes believed she knew and kept it to herself like a thorn in her heart mea culpa mea maxima culpa. She kept after me to give up the studio and work at home as I had but it was obvious even to a blind man and I'm not talking about art reviewers here that I needed to be away from home at that time in my life if I was to paint anything of value I began to paint in the brightest colors in burnt oranges and hot pinks the work freer and more expansive whoever came to the studio then mostly other painters was simply bowled over by what I was doing. But I don't have to tell you there's always a price to be paid. Mary who had been passed on to me more or less Goodkin's idea of a trade was a more skilled lover than Martha but

Martha had other qualities that mattered to me more Martha had a heart and Goodkin and I Goodkin was my best friend at the time had a falling out over Martha we never fully made up. One time we even came to blows in his studio and I bloodied his nose and he said to me Hudson you're an old and valued friend but after today I never want to have anything more to do with you you can have Martha back if she means that much to you. Tommy you used to like to go to Goodkin's studio he always had some candy for you do you remember he was one of the three or four best known painters in America at that time. One of the top five at the very least. He was already doing what was years later called abstract expressionism and he had a trademark which I never had a willful choice he had made when he decided that it was important to him to be famous are you listening? You never say a word Tommy I don't know whether you're hearing anything I say son I'm telling the story for your benefit and for Daniel who is my favorite grandson.

•

Moving along again at quickening pace in fits and starts, I could see a scarf of light on the wall of the tunnel up ahead where it veers to the left. Momentarily, the traffic comes to a complete halt in a concert of squealing brakes.

•

Goodkin was restless Tommy it was his nature to covet what he didn't have when he tired of Martha he threw her over and took up with another girl who was even younger than the twins the new girl friend who eventually moved in with his wife it was a huge house in Long Island her name was something like Dot she was better educated than Mary or Martha and cute as a button a painter herself though without talent. The upshot of which was that Martha came into my studio heartbroken you were there at the time you were staying with me do you remember it was a holiday from school one of the presidents' birthdays or more likely Rosh Hashona or Yum Kippur some holiday anyway I had set up an easel for you and we were doing the same still life I still have that painting oranges a banana and a blue ashtray with a burning cigarette when Martha who looked like something the cat dragged in her eyes raw from crying came by to ask if I could use a life model meaning herself and I said another time because you were there you were eight or nine at the time do you remember. Then she told me that Goodkin had thrown her over and that she was sorry she had left me because I had always treated her well and that she thought she might be with child (she was wrong about that) and she was sick and she didn't know where to turn etcetera etcetera. I took out my wallet and was counting out a few bills to give her I didn't have that much when her twin Mary came in and saw me giving money to Martha Mary was the jealous type and as you can imagine she made a monstrous row.

It would make a terrific passage in a movie the sisters who both had foul mouths going at each other with this kid which was you looking on in wonderment. Mary accused Martha of selling herself for money and Martha said that Mary was a whore because she was sleeping with both of us which wasn't exactly true and Mary said there goes the kettle calling the effing pot black and you were at your little easel painting away I couldn't imagine what you were making of it all. Eventually they quieted down and said what a pretty boy you were and they kissed you do you remember you were blushing Tommy and they said I think it was Mary who said it she was the talker of the two she said they liked boys better than men they were through with men. When they left I said I want to make a pact with you Tommy this is just between us not a word to your mother and you had this strange look on your face I'll remember this to my dying day you gave me this look as if I were speaking to you in a foreign language one you never studied in school. I was sorry it had happened when you were there the two girls coming in like that and making a rumpus I told Barrensin about it though it may have been Graver at that time and he said don't worry Hudson children have the capacity to shut out what they don't want to see and you would deal with it when you were old enough you see I was not unconcerned. The most important thing was Barrensin said or Graver if it was Graver was that I was painting again and that I had a more joyful palette that was the term he used joyful and that it was time for me to move to a gallery with other painters of the same stature where I would have to be satisfied with being less of a star so I moved to the Cathgart Gallery which was more prestigious than Art House and was on the street floor with a big storefront window. They had a roster of stars and I had to wait a year and a half for a one-man show though I had more than enough new work I had enough work for two shows I was learning I suppose to be a small fish which was Barrensin's banal phrase and though I never said so at the time it had been a mistake to leave Art House Barrensin didn't know art from shinola and I actually sold less at Cathgart except for one show which sold out and I couldn't afford to keep up the outside studio so I had to move back into the house move my studio back into the house which made your mother significantly happier I can tell you than it made me.

•

Shortly after we begin to move again the car two cars ahead, a black Mercedes, decides to change lanes and is bumped by the oncoming car which hits its horn at the moment of contact muffling the sound of the actual hit.

The bumped car is turned slightly sideways occupying part of both lanes.

•

When I asked you not to mention Martha or Mary in front of your mother Tommy my intent was to protect your mother who was always the most important thing to me not to put you in a false position which is what your disturbed reaction indicated. You took it into your head that I deliberately compromised your loyalties I had put you in a position where you had to choose between caretakers between your mother and myself which was the last thing I promise you I had in mind. I respected the fact that you were your mother's son as well as mine but you imagined your loyalties to your mother would be compromised if you obeyed me and I will concede that it's possible I didn't have the right to ask that of you who can say. I think you resented it too my asking you resented the women though you were too young to understand that it had nothing to do with your mother these women were the lubricating fluid that made my motor as an artist run I did it so I could work. Whatever you want to think of me I was not without moral values whatever it seemed. Your mother I can't say it too often was a saint an absolutely wonderful person she always came first with me. I know what you're thinking son you're thinking he's telling me this story this dream that he remembers as his life but where's the film he promised me. A film is like a painting except the images are fluid that's the difference one image passing like sleight of hand into another you think I don't know what I'm talking about I've seen all your films Tommy I'm your biggest admirer which doesn't mean I have to like them all equally as though they were your children a sad commentary on the frivolous nature of affections one always has preferences. I have to confess when you started making films you had just graduated film school in California and came home you stayed with us do you remember in your old room when you told me what you were doing I said how could machine-produced images be art I never pulled any punches Tommy which was not the best way to get people to like you but whether people liked me or not has always been the last of my concerns. I once told you wherever large sums of money were involved compromise which is death to art was the order of the day do you remember my saying that. But I have to admit I'm willing to admit that I was wrong about the medium of film when in an artist's hands. What you did Thomas when it all came together was to make the intellectually obscure emotionally available don't deny it you make action films about the clockwork of the inner life which is why I'm offering you this scenario for your next film. If I have other motives ulterior or otherwise they'll all come out in the same wash. I want to move the scene now to Provincialtown Massachusetts I'm changing the name of the town because art deals in fictions it's where we have this summer house we've gone to this is the fifth year. You're fourteen or fifteen ages never meant anything to me and I'm the same age I ever was I have this peculiar obsession which plays an important part in the story every painting I make I destroy I destroyed them all every picture I painted devolved at some point into the mirror image of my own death I can't explain it in any other way I am painting out of some unconscious repository the inner configuration of my own disintegration and death does that make sense to you your camera would have a field day with it. The work scares the hell out of me and I can't look at it once I know what it is I have to destroy it I paint over it and it becomes the background of the painting that follows it but that painting becomes another version of the one under it and the process repeats itself. I can't eat I can't sleep my own reflection in the mirror begins to resemble the buried image of death on the canvas and I have this absolutely terrifying feeling you can't imagine that the inescapable prophesy of my death walks in my shoes with me. The doctors can find nothing wrong but doctors only deal with physical illness each reprieve they offer me gives me a moment or two of relief which lasts only until I find myself peering into the mirror of the latest painting I'm trying to solve and I have the same terrible and terrifying recognition I am painting the portrait of my death something no one else can see because the painting looks superficially like something else what can be the reason for it the feeling of utter hopelessness returns. Resurrection I use that word advisedly as I am not religious and not Christian though I have always been attracted to the idea of Jesus resurrection presents itself in the form of this rich banker's wife who wanted to take private drawing lessons with me she was dark-haired and built like a model which is the type I always went for her husband who managed some bank said how much would I take to do her portrait and since I knew he had a lot of money and valued things in accordance with their monetary value I asked him twice what I usually got for a portrait though I would have done it for free if she had asked me herself. It wasn't the affair which in measurement of time was an eye-drop in the universe it wasn't that or that alone which made it possible for me to make an acceptable painting which made it possible for me to continue my life but and I don't want you to take this in the wrong way or think of it as sentimentality which I despise Tommy as much as you do but it was falling in love with this woman the self-reclaiming feeling of that and not the carnal activity that saved me. It was she who made the first move who came after me who fell in love with me first this beautiful striking girl who was ten or fifteen years younger than your mother. What happened had nothing to do with your mother whom I didn't stop loving it was more like being in a room without air and taking oxygen in order to breathe her husband the banker loved the portrait I had done of her it was a knockout do you remember it and he wrote a check to me for a hundred dollars more than I asked I tore it up the check it wasn't painted for money it was painted because it had to be painted and there's no value you can put on that. I tore up the check and I could have used the money and gave them the painting I told the banker maybe he learned something from it that the painting was worth more than money so I wasn't going to charge him for something that was priceless. He knew then I could see it in his face that Jeanette his wife and I were intimate he knew beyond a shadow of a doubt that we had been amorous there's another story attached to the first one which in terms of the kind of films you like to make may be the foreground scenario a mixed metaphor but I think you get what I'm trying to say. There's a particular image I have in mind I see it in terms of its formal qualities the unfinished portrait on the easel the face roughed-in in charcoal the live subject of the painting at the foot of the easel conjugating with the painter like an adoration this is very important to understand Tommy we celebrated the painting the achievement of the painting by performing our amorous theatrics at its feet. And then you came to see me this is the other story the separate story the parallel story whose connections the film will have to devise for itself. You said to me Dad don't take this the wrong way mother is very unhappy about all the time you're spending with Jeanette maybe it's a good idea to not do this portrait if it's going to make mother unhappy do you remember your saying that to me which made me angry you were off base I thought saying that to me I sent you away I was stern with you because I couldn't tell you the truth I was ashamed of the truth and you were only fourteen. When I said that mother doesn't need you to protect her that she can protect herself that I'm here to protect her you said go to hell as if you wanted me dead on the spot which was like sticking a knife in my chest and I threw you out of my studio I felt justified.

A few days later this man comes in the house I see the two events as inextricably connected and he tells mother that you touched his young daughter in a sexual manner his manner offensively self-righteous. They're just kids mother said they all play around together it's really innocent it's nothing to make a fuss about. Your mother defended you said she found it hard to believe you would actually do such a thing you were a well-brought up boy anyway it was just child's play. The man was not in the least placated and he said he wanted to talk to me which he did the next day after I got home from my session with Jeanette I mean that as it sounds. I was not as tactful as mother that's not my line I told the bastard that you were an innocent kid and that his daughter was probably the aggressor in whatever happened she was a very flirtatious child and if it worried him he ought to keep his daughter under surveillance. He left in a rage threatened me with the police we very nearly came to blows you know how I get with bastards like that when they get out of hand. He said like father like son and he slammed the door and I opened it after him and I said don't ever come back here unless you want your face rearranged I wanted to break his jaw with my fist. The next day I think it was the next day we got a police summons for you to appear in juvenile court which I'm sure you remember it drove me up the wall. I had to hire a lawyer though I was broke at the time I had given away Jeanette's painting without remuneration I was at wit's end and when the lawyer interviewed you you told him the same thing you told us that other kids had touched her between the legs but that you hadn't. The lawyer who was a local fellow it made sense getting a local fellow he didn't seem to believe you were telling the truth he said if others touched her and not you why did she mention you to her father. You said you didn't know you sat there like a stone in his office you were holding everything inside I know how you got but he couldn't tell he thought you were being brazen. The lawyer said to stay in the house not to go near the girl until the case was adjudicated right now it was her word against yours but the sheriff was looking to see if he could get another witness to testify against you. Frankly I didn't know what to believe your mother said you never lied but that was your mother she saw you as perfect she would say that regardless. My intuition about this Tommy I never said this to you before was that you had deliberately got yourself into a situation that would make it impossible for me to continue seeing Jeanette that made me enraged with you and at the same time you kept everything to yourself you wouldn't tell us anything I was at my wit's end you were spiting yourself actually putting yourself in jeopardy to get back at me for what I was doing to your mother. Then the lawyer called to say the other side had turned up another witness a girl from the same group a friend of the one who accused you she was willing to swear she saw you touching the girl whose name I no longer remember that put our situation in the darkest light. That was the final straw even our own lawyer didn't believe you he advised that you admit you had done what she said but to say it was all part of a game all the kids were playing he wanted you to be contrite and promise you would never do it again you refused you absolutely refused.

The judge that had your case the lawyer told us was a church-going Catholic with a moralistic bias particularly in areas of sexual malfeasance the worst possible adjudicator for a case like yours. In the middle of this horror the only thing I could think of was what could happen to you the very worst thing that could happen some kind of curtailment of freedom your life ruined our family life irrevocably deformed then Jeanette called at the house and said she wanted to see me immediately it was urgent could we meet somewhere. I won't go into what I said to her your mother was in the room at the time and I had to pretend I was talking about the portrait so as not to hurt mother in any way. I arranged to meet Jeanette at the new coffee and dessert place we all went to that summer I believe it was called the Double Pot it only lasted one season. She was sitting in the back of the restaurant when I got there drinking a hot chocolate with marshmallows on top a repellent sight. I feel so bad for what you're going through she said and wish I could be with you to ease your pain she was a very passionate person a poet as well as a fledgling painter. Out of the corner of my eye I noticed the father of the girl he wasn't the real father he was the mother's boyfriend the bastard who had gone to the police about you I noticed him enter the shop. If I had a gun in my hand I would have shot him through the heart Tommy without a second thought that's what would have happened if wish and action lived in the same pocket. Jeanette was saying that she was leaving her husband which meant nothing to me I was concerned with what to do about the sonofabitch whose presence in the coffee shop seemed a taunt at the misery he had brought down on our heads these feelings converged on me unexpectedly and I put my face down on the marble table the ice cream parlor table and suddenly the floodgates broke open. Jeanette didn't understand what was going on she said Hudson sweetheart this has nothing to do with us my decision to leave Lewis is mine and mine alone of course you made me see something of what I was missing in that marriage I don't want you to feel any obligation because realistically you have none. When I lifted my head after a while the first thing I saw was the ceiling fan like the shadow of some poisonous spider spinning overhead it made me dizzy I was still having trouble catching my breath. Then I saw where Jeanette was looking and the man was standing there the boyfriend of the mother of the girl he was standing over me. I thought he meant me some harm and I didn't have the strength at that moment to fight but he had this rueful look on his face and was just shaking his head he wasn't even the real father of the girl but the boy friend of the mother who had a habit of changing partners with each turn in the weather he just kept shaking his head in this rueful manner and then he said something under his breath I couldn't hear and walked quickly away looking back at the door as if he thought I might be coming after him.

•

The driver of the car that had been turned around got out of his Mercedes after the other driver said something to him that offended him. "I'm going to kick your ass," the other man, who was dressed in an expensive-looking three-piece suit, said in a barely audible voice.

•

Tommy you make movies that present themselves behind a mask this is something it took me a long time to figure out by mask I mean disguise the movies allow you to understand them as fragments of some larger entity that exists only as a fictitious conjecture I have some paintings like that and I flatter myself that what you do has some connection to what you learned from me how could it be otherwise do you see what I'm saying. If I have other motives in telling you this story then I have other motives in telling it nothing is untainted. I took you to the courthouse do you remember it was eight in the morning we had to shake you to get you out of bed mother of course went too do you remember it was to the judge's chambers in the back of the courthouse building and they interviewed the girl she took an oath on the Bible was God at home at the time I remember thinking they interviewed her step by step about what happened between you for years it stayed with me it felt to me as if I was the one facing judgment. She had this sanctimonious look on her face but

I couldn't help noticing I was aware of this throughout the charade she was holding back a smile why didn't the judge notice you didn't see it because you were looking at the backs of your hands the girl was smirking. While the girl was going through her paces the girl's mother who was sitting across from her next to their lawyer the mother was moving her lips like a ventriloquist. I could have smashed them both. I touched your lawyer's arm to point the smile out to him it was a giveaway didn't he see didn't the judge see the whole charade was exposing itself before their eyes but the lawyer told me to be quiet he was a corrupt functionary he wasn't interested in justice being done. It was all I could do not to stand up and denounce them the sad smirking girl her whore of a mother the salacious judge our dimwitted cynical lawyer the whole corrupt charade but mother mother could always read my mood she had her hand on my shoulder. The boyfriend the woman's boyfriend he wasn't the girl's real father he knew what was going on he was a heavy drinker a year later he took his life he was regretful I could see it in his eyes he had done the whole thing for her his girlfriend the girl's mother she had made a pass at every man in the community he knew it was wrong. The other girl the other witness they were supposed to have was not there that was a relief. Our lawyer spoke next said the kids had not been properly supervised and that what had been described was an outgrowth of the unsupervised games the kids play. He said you were sorry it had happened and that you had given him your solemn oath that it would never happen again. The woman was staring at you and cursing you under her breath her boyfriend had to restrain her. Then the judge asked you if you would come up on the stand and answer a few questions you didn't move. The judge motioned to our lawyer and they stood next to each other talking quietly I was trying to listen in I thought the bastard whose fee we were paying would betray us in a minute if he saw it as being advantageous to his career. Then the lawyer came over to where you were sitting and he said Tommy I need you to answer this one question for me then we can all go home he had two questions though he said one. You heard Ilanna's testimony before the court is it true that as part of a game and because that's what you thought was expected of you that you touched her in her private place as she testified. You said nothing and he repeated the question with some elaboration saying I know you told me of your remorse and your regret but you must also testify before the court this is just a hearing not a trial. You said Yes under your breath not looking at him and then the judge asked you to repeat your answer in a louder voice they spared you nothing and you said Yes again the bastards spared us nothing. Then the judge said because of your age and because you seemed to feel remorse for what you had done which he labeled Indecent Assault he was going to put you under a year's probation and review the case again in a year's time subject to your behavior whatever they have a standard phrase for it during the intervening period. After that we went back to our summer place and you closed yourself in your room you barred the door do you remember I told mother we were going home the next day to begin packing and she said she already had and if it were up to her she would be on the road just as soon as we had cleaned up the place. I wanted to say something to you I was sorry I had yelled at you I stood outside the door of your room and spoke to you I don't know if you heard me you didn't answer you could have been asleep it was absolutely quiet behind your door I said Tommy I am aggrieved that this had happened that I reproached myself for it though I had done nothing that wasn't in your best interests that we had done precisely what the corrupt lawyer had advised that it was over now and we would not come back to this shameless place the next summer or even the one after that though we had been coming here without cease for eight years. You didn't talk to me in the car on our trip home you would only make monosyllabic replies when anything was said to you. You were punishing me you meant to punish me though I wasn't the one who had created the problem. I left Provincial town which is not its real name without even saying goodbye to Jeanette without even seeing her again if nothing else you had gotten your way in that regard.

•

Straightening itself out, the Mercedes pushed ahead, the traffic able to move again at inconsequential speeds.

•

For the longest time, Tommy, for several years as I remember whenever we were in the same room, you would give me this malign glower if looks could kill you would have bombed me back to the stone age which was General LeMay's prescription for the North Vietnamese it wasn't just toward me that you held a grudge you were a kid with a chip on his shoulder I said to mother what can we do with him he doesn't talk to anyone. Then we heard from your school that you hadn't been there for three weeks they thought you were terribly sick what could they think you had always been a good student you always went to class I never went past 7th grade but I didn't have your advantages. I was painting again at home I was putting together a show mother was teaching we couldn't supervise you every moment we did our best your mother was a saint.

When the official at the school the principal or assistant principal I forget which now asked you where you went when you weren't going to school you shrugged your shoulders you said in the mildest possible voice you weren't learning anything at school so you thought you'd take a vacation I was there with mother and we both laughed at that the assistant principal couldn't

understand what kind of people we were she recommended you see a psychiatrist anything that wasn't banal was thought to be crazy. It was the next day I was
telling Goodkin the story of your disappearance he was
at my studio looking at my new work and one thing led
to another he was talking about how he bought himself a movie camera as a way of altering the way he
saw landscape and he offered me the camera for you or
sold it to me I forget which Goodkin always had a price
but since he no longer had any use for it he suggested
that I try it when Goodkin had a new idea everybody
had to taste it. When I gave you that camera it was a
Bolex wasn't it the best money could buy you began
to talk to me again it did more good for you than that
children's shrink that quack Barrensin had us send you
to Mrs. Podge was her name do you remember it was
your first camera I was passing on the baton so to speak
though in another sense if you gather my meaning I
never gave it up. When I gave you that Bolex camera a
primitive piece of machinery by today's standards you
could make pictures with it but it had no sound mechanism you became my heir. I'm losing my thread here
it was Barrensin's idea that I talk to you about what
happened with the girl that summer not to bury it so
one day I asked you we were at the Modern Museum I
asked you if you had talked to anyone about what really happened I had my own theories. You said if I told
you my theories, you would tell me yours meaning I
assumed you meant you would tell me what took place
but you meant something else I was buying you lunch
in the Modern cafeteria and Jeanette who I hadn't seen
since the summer was sitting in the courtyard just across
from us. You noticed her presence she was a handsome
woman Jeanette even before I did and I would wager
all the money I have that you took her being there you
know what I'm saying in the worst possible light.

•

Reaching the lip of the tunnel, we move out into the light two cars at a time. Free at last.

•

When Jeanette came over to the table, Tommy, you simply flew out of your chair you were the first to see Jeanette approach it happens I was facing the wrong way at the time and your chair seemed to eject you you simply fled the room. You were forcing me to make a choice either you or Jeanette either I listened to what Jeanette had to say and I let you sulk off or I assuaged you and abandoned Jeanette left her alone at an abandoned table which I think you know would have been unconscionable behavior. To my mind what I did was choose you both by letting you know you couldn't bulldoze me do you hear what I'm saying I wasn't going to let you jerk me around by your sulking off every time something went on that wasn't part of your scenario you were making obscure movies even then. What's his problem Jeanette said and I told her you were protective of your mother that you thought you had to protect her because I had let her down and she said Jeanette was nobody's fool that that was absolute nonsense. What was really going on she said was that you were competing head to head with me. Well contrary to what you were prepared to believe I made no immediate arrangement to see Jeanette that was over for me even though she had come to my table expressly to tell me she had broken completely with her husband the banker and was living in New York all alone she had this tiny apartment in the village two tiny rooms with a kitchen folded into the living room wall even so I made no attempt to see her though an invitation was offered that was difficult to refuse.

When I came home mother seemed aggrieved with me you must have mentioned seeing Jeanette at the Modern she wouldn't tell me what was amiss when I inquired about the sour look on her puss and then she slapped me across the face that was the only time. Well I was the pariah that was my role and you were the accuser and mother who slapped my face mother was the one who put up with everything and held us all together by her ability to forgive I couldn't believe she slapped my face. You know the way a recovering alcoholic will keep a bottle in the house to show that he can control himself in the face of temptation I was that way with this woman Jeanette I kept her number in my wallet and I didn't call her once not once for a whole year at the same time it couldn't be said that mother and I were getting on surpassingly well and you were going through your teenage angst you were silent and bitter and whenever I asked you if you wanted to go somewhere with me you would always have some excuse why you couldn't. One time you showed me a little film you had made with Goodkin's camera and I was I admit this too honest with you which was not in the short run a way to improve relations between us the truth never wins any friends but all my life I said what was on my mind I was never afraid to tell the truth even to my own disadvantage maybe always to my disadvantage my point is and this is something Tommy I've had on my mind to say to you for the longest time I had no faith that art could come from a machine a camera is a machine how could it art is a human endeavor if I'm wrong I'm wrong. The uninformed viewer tends to admire paintings that seem difficult to achieve which means in most cases that the painter had failed to make a painting and could only offer in its place the transmography is that a word of his labors the manifest portrait of a failed process. Art makes the most difficult seem the most simple which is something you know or your films wouldn't be any good you solve the problem of the material and the work's difficulty disappears the illusion of the work is its simplicity that is the most difficult thing to do to give the illusion of an impossible assignment being absolutely simple to achieve. You see

son I'm confessing this to you I may have been wrong
in thinking that the machine which is what I call the
camera moving or still the machine no matter the brilliantly stupid sophistication of its technology is merely a
recording instrument and how could I believe in its art-
making powers without despairing of my own primitive
atavistic activity. Your first films which I criticized with
the best intentions seemed to me wrongheaded because
they asked to be judged as art which I saw at that time as
contrary to possibility. I have no capacity for diplomacy
you asked me whether I liked your film and I said if you
remember the only truth I knew that it hadn't reached
the level in which questions of good or bad become
significant. I meant that as encouraging even pointed
out one shot that showed promise I had no intention
of hurting your feelings but my criticism served to further embitter you against me. Tommy in our family we
didn't know how to be kind to those closest which is
why we spent our lives pursuing art instead of going out
to make money which was the norm in other families. I
had a show that year which sold out the second or third
day of its run the reviews which I'm the first to admit
were written in a language only paint could understand
they were unusually attentive and laudatory *Art News*
called it a major show and it nearly killed me that was
the show you made a point of not seeing even mother
was upset with you and for mother the sun rose and set
on your navel. It was my most successful show and I
was beset with symptoms of illness dizziness palpitations
chest pains cold sweats and the medical doctors could
find nothing wrong they called it anxiety. I got into a
fight with the dealer Henry Stimpson I don't remember
what about I think it was politics all the capitalists in the
art world in those days were communists and I quit him
cold as a result took all my paintings back and this was
one of the three best galleries on 57th Street Goodkin
said I was crazy. So after this big success after selling out
my show which was perceived as a major show I got

myself in a position where I had no representation. Now I had left this smaller gallery run by this woman from New Zealand Amelia Dickinson to go with Stimpson at Cathgart she had given me my start I had ten one-man shows with Dickinson and some people in the gallery world had this idea this was told to me by Goodkin that I was not to be trusted.

When I started to look for a new dealer I had a string of people come to the studio to look at paintings there was an unspoken prejudice among the dealers against taking me on. I went around to all the major galleries and I got the cold shoulder the line they gave me was that their calendars were filled up I already had most of a new show painted they kept saying they were sorry but it would be a disservice to me to take me on and not be able to give me a show for two years or more when I had all this work ready to show which I accepted the first few times but when you get the same line from five or six dealers you know something unacceptable is the order of the day I would have used a harsher word than unacceptable if my grandson weren't in the car with us. I ended up signing on with a gallery that was even less prestigious than Dickinson's because they promised me a show in three months but I left them after Goodkin told me they had no standing in the art world Goodkin had another idea for me he knew the scene like the back of his hand and he had talked to some dealers who were friends of his on my behalf I was without a gallery for what turned out to be two years. None of the front-line galleries would handle me and it made no sense to go to a dealer who handled lesser painters after my successful show at Cathgart did it make any sense though I ended up doing just that I went to this new gallery Nuit et Brouillard that Jeanette was connected to and I was their first show. It couldn't have been a bigger mistake the people who ran it knew less than nothing about art and not a blessed thing about how the art world functioned they had no clientele and then the partners stopped talking to each other they took no ads they didn't know the first thing about running a gallery and that's the positive side. The negative side is that they sold two paintings not through any talents of their own mother's father bought one the other was by an important collector who had been to my studio they ended up paying me about a third of what I had coming and then went out of business my show was their first and last. I felt this is what I had coming to me my reward for mistreating mother for being an indifferent father to you for leaving Miss Dickinson who had started me out etcetera etcetera etcetera. I don't remember a time when I was any happier I was using color like Bonnard like no one had ever used color before unimaginable combinations to tell you the truth I was astonishing myself. Painters came to the studio and said Hudson you're doing revolutionary stuff this is dazzling stuff they were envious as hell these guys who were showing in the best galleries and getting top dollar they were jealous of the kind of freedom being unsuccessful allowed at least that's what they said praise didn't cost them anything. I think looking back on it that they could say these things to me because they perceived me as being out of the race. When I left Stimpson because I felt slighted I can't remember now what it was even about I had unwittingly taken myself out of the race do you see what I'm saying I had elected not to have success. It was a half-conscious choice Tommy I couldn't do both I couldn't make a success that was my gut feeling and still continue to paint the pictures I had to paint is that sour grapes. Tommy this could be a movie showing how perceived failure may be the only real success Cezanne never sold a painting in his lifetime but who's going to be the arbiter who's going to say failure is really success and commercial success represents artistic failure that's the theme of the movie I'm offering you that's the truth of the culture but who's going to believe it. Mother wanted you to go to a college with a high-priced pedigree you were in your last year of high school but I told her the city schools were every bit as good and we were broke as usual broker than usual so there wasn't any other choice. I didn't want to disappoint you but that was my role that was our relationship I wanted you to earn your way to learn to be self-reliant. I didn't want you to turn away from me even so I was a better father to you than my father ever was to me I know though you're sometimes accepting of me that you've never forgiven me why should you not forgiving a father comes with the territory of being a son. Still I have to say I won't forgive you Tommy for holding a grudge against me for not forgiving me whatever it is that needs forgiving for such a prolonged time for half a lifetime it seems what did I do to you that couldn't be forgiven?

•

We are stuck for two light changes at Canal Street, which is always villainous to cross. We have ten minutes at most—they run these funerals like clockwork—to get to the chapel at 79th, which means there is no longer any margin for further unaccountable delay.

•

Tommy son domesticity was not what we knew how to do you and I we didn't know how to limit ourselves to one person which in marriages is thought to be the basic unit such amorous excess being the cause of dire misadventure in our domestic lives I'm referring to your alliances here Tommy you've had more than your share of unfortuitous luck in this regard for which I know the reason. It was that business with the young girl the summer you were fourteen. The girl betrayed the understanding you had between you don't deny it. You don't deny it by informing her parents that you put

31

your hand on her privates and you had to abase yourself before a corrupt judge some local political hack there was nothing your mother or I could do to get you off subsequently it became a pattern in your life you know it's true the evidence is irrefutable you believed that any girl you struck up an alliance with would in the last analysis betray you which happened because it was bound to happen. Take Louise for example Louise adored you you know this is true I commented to mother when you were first together how she couldn't take her eyes off you when you were together in a room she positively adored you but you didn't know how to treat her you were careless of her and so you let her take the controls which I happen to know she never really wanted which is what I told you at the time you let the whole thing get out of hand because of guilt so everything ends woefully. There were at least three times that your mother asked me to leave and she was absolutely in the right to ask but I refused to go and by refusing I kept my marriage a going concern because I knew with an inner certainty that your mother didn't want me to leave she did at the moment but not in the long run do you see what I'm saying. The same was true for you with Louise I know what I'm talking about you made the mistake of taking her at her word Tommy which was the last thing she wanted you to do it was just guilt anyway your passive behavior your letting her take charge the two of you would still be married today if you had listened to me you know what I'm saying is true. Why would she call me up tell me that why would she confide in me if she didn't believe that I would intercede that was her message to you the call to me was the message I was the letter carrier and you chose I'm sure you had your reasons not to get it for which I blame myself though why should I. I have no way of knowing beyond guesswork what you said to Louise in private it's not my business to know though I could make an educated guess I only know what Louise confided to me with evident sincerity. The things she told me about herself I believe absolutely why would she lie she wanted my good offices she wanted me to stop you from taking her at her word you put too much power in the word that's why the rank-and-file audience has no patience for your films. I did this beautiful portrait of Louise which caused you to wash your hands of me which was a blindness on your part if you look for blame you find it I felt strongly about Louise my best portraits you know this is true are all of mother. Had you stayed with Louise at least the portrait one of my better portraits as you've acknowledged though I don't need anyone to tell me when I do a first rate piece of work it would have stayed in the family. I did the painting of Louise for you not against you as you were ready to believe I did it to show you another way to look at Louise you forget how to see the people closest to you I wanted to show her to you with the blinders off this was at a passage in your life when you couldn't see your wife any clearer than you could see what was coming up behind you. When I painted her there were only two short sittings so I had to work very fast I made a point of observing her through your eyes you'll laugh at this but why would I lie. I thought when you looked at the finished portrait you would remember having seen her in such and such a way that it would restore her to your sight once and for all. Instead it got you angry at me you wouldn't even look at the portrait which is ironic because it was your comprehension of Louise I had painted this was a fleshly sexual Louise your Louise not mine but the end result was that you threw up your hands at both of us. I think Louise knew what I was doing because she didn't like the picture either not at that time though now she says to me Hudson it's a masterpiece. Most of the time I was too busy to pay sufficient attention to you I'm talking about when you were small art is the most ungenerous and jealous mistress in trying to be the opposite of my father who was a tyrant plain and simple I became my father you always become your own worst enemy particularly when you make a point of going the opposite way. The occasions I did pay attention to you I mean I wasn't always neglectful you had a better father than I had it was taken as the wrong kind of attention I'm talking about the business on Cape Cod with the girl the truth is I never believed you were innocent I confess that now so my support which was dishonest only made matters worse and you've never forgiven me for that never and I can't forgive you for that either for being so embittered at my attempt to help I won't forgive that.

•

Stoplights are out of phase—one is permanently red—as we move in a chaotic crush of traffic toward the entrance of the West Side Drive. We have five minutes to do twenty-two blocks, find a parking space, and get to the chapel. Seven minutes actually—the digital clock in the car, as I remember, is two minutes fast.

•

Tommy I've seen all your movies everyone of them at least once some three times I may even be your greatest admirer because I didn't get them at first and learned by repeated seeing to understand their inner mechanism so when I say what I'm going to say I want you to know I know whereof I speak. Film you know this is true has more in common with painting than with theater which is a moribund medium in our age film is a bastard form which doesn't make it any the less wonderful but its most significant paternity comes from the visual. Didn't Hitchcock say that talk in a movie is just one of a number of background noises I remember reading that somewhere my point is you became a filmmaker because your father was a painter an avoidance of footsteps though really in fact the same devious path.

You are my heir whether you like to think of it that way or not that's why I've taken it on myself a presumption you are thinking but without presumption there is only banality so I've presumed as your father to give you this undigested material to regurgitate into your next or post-next movie. When you make something from next to nothing which is the province of art it requires shutting everything else out it requires shutting yourself out from those closest to you wives and children friends lovers all betrayed in the wake of the so-called creative process do you see what I'm saying. There is no compromise for the artist art will allow no compromising which is no apology I did my best but which leaves us I don't have to tell you in the position of being negligent therefore despised by those who have the misfortune of sharing our lives. We're despicable people outside the context of our work this is not to be construed as an apology despicable because everything and everyone else is secondary or tertiary you know what I'm saying everything is tertiary to the grand scheme the life's work and for what? Tommy son the truth is and if you and I don't know it I can't imagine who does the truth is I don't know what the truth is anyone can lead a good life whatever we mean by that but not everyone can make a good painting yes and no. This is a confession of doubt of which I've told no one but you and maybe one or two of my analysts a confession I take back and deny lord of hosts father son and holy ghost as soon as the words are out of my mouth and out on their own. Everything in my life is subordinated to making paintings to painting as arrestingly as talent and skill allows everything and that's the way it had to be if there was a choice nobody told me what it was mother came second you came second even I came second only the work came first.

If hell wants him your old man is packed and ready to go I don't believe there's any torment out there worse than life. We've made the same mistakes you and I Tommy you let Louise get away which meant I won't spell it out Daniel knows what I mean always the ones that matter most get hurt you'll say it was her doing and I won't presume to dispute what you think you know but there might have been a last minute healing of differences if the right medicine were offered. You have even less capacity for compromise it's the theme of your movies than has your quote irascible unquote old man it's the hidden message of each movie you've made compromise is the betrayal of self compromise is sellout which is something you learned not to my credit at my knee which brings me to the real story which is the competitiveness that has defined and scarred our relationship. First of all I had your mother you didn't have a chance there and I didn't share her sufficiently I was always in your way I was always her first concern for which you could never forgive me. Mother loved you in her way but I had exclusive rights to her I owned so to speak the franchise which was not something I understood in its moment and I can see now how that jaundiced feelings between us you saw me as the enemy I was the enemy. In turn you broke my heart. You let me know that anything I did for you was insufficient and proceeded from motives mired in bad faith. And then there was that journalist who did the magazine story on you who came to look at my work she was a knockout wasn't she the one who came to see me in my studio we became friends that made you upset with me. We were living in New Rochelle then in the big house which had an outbuilding I used as a studio it was a house the outbuilding in its own right I knocked down the walls to make three rooms into one we had crazy neighbors on both sides. She came into my studio it was on a Saturday and I had just done some terrific new work and she walked around looking at the paintings without making comment then she turned around and looked me in the eye and said Hudson I'm overwhelmed. I said to her in response I didn't know her from Adam had only talked to her a few minutes on the phone I said not half as overwhelmed as I am. She was the kind of person that you felt right after you met her for the first time that you'd known her since God knows when. I had no way of knowing that there was anything but a professional relationship between you and this woman Jacqueline O'Hare can you believe it I'd forgotten her name you were still married to Louise at the time and I had no inkling that anything was untoward between you believe me I had no such knowledge which is not to say I could swear it would not have happened I'm being as straight with you as I can. And you never told me a thing you never said Dad there's another woman in my life another wife and her name is so and so you never concerned yourself to tell me the last thing I wanted was to give you another reason to hate me the last thing. Then again she was not an easy woman to say no to as you know she had exceptional charm she knew how to look at my work she understood that painting had to do with the materials used and not the rendering of subject she had taste she understood what I was trying to do and where I succeeded and where I didn't we were fast friends from that first meeting in my studio in New Rochelle from the word go. It was a friendship for the most part kept alive through correspondence we were in the same room four or five times at most I was not in competition with you for her Tommy that was the furthest thing from my mind I promise you. You called me on the phone do you remember that time you said Dad if It's true that you've been rutting with Jackie O'Hare I'd as soon as throw you out a window as look at you again that may not have been your exact words but that was the gist of what you said I said I won't confirm or deny and then you wished me off to hell. Your wishes did the trick I won't deny that a son's wishes have powerful wings I did my turn in hell at your behest which I no longer think about which no longer matters though I want it understood here that you've misread my intentions toward you from beginning to end.

●

Traffic seems to part like the Red Sea after we move on to the West Side Drive. I can't help but be aware that in a minute or so they will be ushering our sea of mourners into the chapel. Even if I speeded up and risked being stopped, we would not get there in time.

●

You never told me where we're going Tommy you have to keep me abreast of the latest news is this a funeral you're taking me to or some exhibition you think I might enjoy I no longer can tell the difference. You know I haven't been getting out of the house the way I used to mother and I used to go to the galleries every Saturday rain or shine sometimes 57 Street sometimes Soho I felt it incumbent on me as a painter to keep in touch. What I was looking for I think was my own work on the walls the satisfaction of still being part of the scene so instead I invited renewed disappointment mostly everything was counterfeit and noisy or derivative in shameless ways competing for attention on the basis of false plumage was that what shunted me from the scene this self-serving witless cleverness these weren't galleries Tommy they were brothels. I won't ask as I'm assuming you already told me and possibly it's not conducive to my wellbeing to know so I'm not going to ask whose funeral it is we're rushing headlong to as if there were no tomorrow I just want you to tell me son it isn't mine. It isn't that I'm afraid to die I'm ready as I'll ever be and as unready also I've almost completed my life's work I have a will in the hopper I've painted most of what it's in me to paint I've had a good life a life full of necessary pain your mother was a saint to put up with me. All the best painters of my time the ones that left their immortality behind are dead and gone asleep in the earth with the beatitudes all my fellow shmearers have departed the vale it would be churlish of me to refuse to enter their ranks it's only this and it's the only thing that keeps me from bowing out gracefully it's only that my work isn't yet finished there's more to do I'm still learning for God's sake I still haven't learned all I need to know to make a good painting I won't leave this is a promise to Daniel who is my favorite grandchild until I am able to copyright the formula for making a beautiful painting and there is no formula from which to make art your grandfather won't leave I'm talking to Daniel now Tommy until he has completed his life.

•

Moving from the car to the chapel in a maze of rain, a bouquet of invisible weeds in my mourner's hand.

•

Tommy you want all to come together at the end which you know is coming everything that begins comes to an end life is a continuum you want everything to come together all the disjointed parts so your life becomes a complete story it becomes art that's what I had in mind when I started to tell you this scenario. Am I absolutely wrong in thinking that there is no sense of history in our time none each morning the world wakes up re-born all our yesterdays I'm paraphrasing Shakespeare Daniel revised to justify the moment's vulgar perception of itself by vulgar I mean dishonest. We are probably not much worse than any other time only our quotient of self-loathing pitches to a higher decibel because we have not allowed ourselves a past we have murdered the past by putting the best spin on our worst acts if it sells it's good it doesn't matter that most everything is shoddy everywhere you go people are living in the street we have unsalvageable holes in the ozone how brilliant to make it all seem for the best. You know what I'm saying Tommy what else is left but to say the truth we live in the age of puffery and shoddy goods our cars self-destruct our detergents pollute the air our government deforms the truth history is just another falsified product sold us by the people in charge a carcinogenic lie something that will kill us only after we vote for it if it makes money you can do it know what I'm saying all our wrongdoing wrapped in the latest Christmas paper by which I mean bogus sentiment exaggerated feelings official fakery that's why son I have nothing to say at the end no regrets no wisdom no apologies no avowals of paternal love I did my best which wasn't good enough but who's to say what's good enough. Art in my unacceptable view is all there is it's my story and you are my footsteps. I'd be a liar if I told you I wasn't afraid to die what is oblivion but hell.

●

Our entrance into the chapel five perhaps ten minutes late evokes turned heads, unspoken communications of grief. The service waits, frozen in place, until we find our seats in the front row. At that moment I realize that this event is my father's funeral. Hudson is dead. Hudson, who in his relentless survival had promised us that he would go on forever, is dead. I'll have to say a few words. I will say, I cannot say, that there were things my father did for which I have never forgiven him. I cannot forgive him. I will not, I have not. I will say, I cannot say, I was never able to love him. The words echo in my head. Never. Able. Love. Him. Can that be said? ... As we hurry down the aisle my knees give out and Daniel, who is alongside me, throws his arms around me at the last possible moment to keep me from falling.

Men at Lunch

It took him five years to discover that his wife was getting it on with his daughter's best friend's father, a man he played poker with on Friday nights, a man with a history of failed bluffs. And it was not that the devious couple went out of their way to deceive. Their involvement with each other was so continually in evidence he found it difficult—all but impossible—to believe they might have something to hide. That was the explanation he gave to his friends for his five years or more of blindness and inaction. We said we had thought he knew, which was our excuse for not having said anything. And then, strictly speaking, it really wasn't any of our business.

How had he missed the point for so long? It was that, the failure to see what was obvious to everyone else, that troubled him even more than the fact of his wife's long-term deception. Once a week for five years she had been fucking this neighbor, this friend, and he had let it go by as if it were not anything out of the ordinary.

Whitlock and Schiller, who went to graduate school together at Stanford in the seventies, tended to meet for lunch whenever their busy schedules allowed. Schiller, a therapist and author, had for some time now been collecting case studies of denial for a definitive book on the subject. Whitlock, a magazine journalist, took pleasure in offering his friend provocative stories for "the book," the latest being the one about the evasive man with the unfaithful wife. Schiller took no pains to hide the fact that he was unimpressed.

"So what else is knew?" the therapist said. "Whit, I have more stories of domestic betrayal than I can possibly accommodate, which is not to say I don't appreciate your sharing this little parable of misery with me. The infidelity of a loved one is the second most common form of denial."

"Makes sense," said Whitlock. "There's more to the story, Max, if you want to hear it."

Schiller sighed. "Five plus years is a long time for your friend to deny. It's like holding one's breath, hoping against reason the air will eventually change for the better. I didn't mean to seem to belittle your story. It's just that my plate is overfilled with cases of sexual betrayal. Whit, when you say that the wife and the lover were obvious, how do you mean that exactly?"

Whitlock seemed in no hurry to continue, took a forkful of his linguini putanesca, chewed it delicately. He spoke before his mouth was fully cleared. "Speak of the devil," he muttered, lowering his head. "It never fails."

Schiller was watching a juggler in a clown costume just outside the restaurant. "What never fails?" he asked. "In the long run, everything fails."

Whitlock leaned forward and lowered his voice. "The man we were talking about is sitting with his wife about five tables over to the right. Don't look."

The exhortation not to look was more seductive than the juggler's next trick which were meat cleavers of an exceptional size. Schiller fixed a glance at the man (the man he assumed was the man) with the provocatively unfaithful wife. He was small boned and elegant with a wispy beard. The wife was dark with a pouty mouth, intense, marginally attractive and very probably depressive.

"It doesn't surprise me that he stayed with her," Schiller said in a voice that seemed to carry across the room. "Deniers are notorious forgivers."

"Are they?" Whitlock said, amused at his friend's pedantry, lowering his voice. "I guess to forget is to forgive, huh?, though in this case there were also other factors."

"The pattern is predictable," Schiller said, looking off as if reading a cue card in the distance. "Even after the evidence was undeniable, even after his wife confessed to the affair, your friend in question came to terms with the news by allowing himself to believe that the affair meant nothing to her. As it pleased him to see it, his wife's affair was just a means of gaining his distracted attention. By putting himself at the center of the scenario, his role became more powerful, less pitiable. And why not?" Schiller looked to Whitlock for confirmation.

The juggler rotated two of the cleavers from hand to hand, while the third seemed to float in the air over his head, a perpetual threat. How does he do that? Schiller wondered.

"Close but no cigar," Whitlock said.

"Not absolutely on the mark?"

"Let's let it drop, Max," Whitlock said. "Tell you the truth, this is making me uncomfortable. I have another story for you that might even be more appropriate for the book."

"What am I missing?" Schiller mused. "Was it that your friend was also having an affair? Is that the other element in the equation?" He moved his glance between the juggler in the street below and the inexplicable couple Whitlock had pointed out. "Sexual betrayal is just another form of oedipal displacement."

Whitlock nodded at the evasive friend who, absorbed in conversation with his wife, gave no indication of noticing him. "He doesn't want to acknowledge me," he whispered to Schiller. "He senses we're talking about him."

Schiller laughed. "He doesn't see you, Whit. He doesn't know you're in the room. He doesn't want to know. It's all part of the same pattern."

"You think so?" Whitlock said. "Could be he needs glasses."

"I'm only telling you what you already know," said the therapist. "What's your other story?"

"My other story? Yes. There's this woman, a friend of a friend—all right, the wife of a friend—who had a drinking problem it suited her to pretend didn't exist. After she fell down a flight of stairs, admitting nothing (hey, no problem, just the stairs acting up again), she announced she would give up drinking if it would relieve her husband of anxiety. The husband said, yes, it would make him feel a whole lot better. What she did was stop drinking in public while increasing her secret consumption. It wasn't so much that her various stashes of vodka gave her away, though the husband couldn't help but run into them from time to time. It was the change in her behavior that drinking induced that exposed her deception. Her personality changed radically after a few drinks, she became gratuitously belligerent and her speech tended in subtle ways to slur. What I'm saying is it was obvious to anyone who had even the slightest acquaintance with her that the woman had had her fix of vodka. And of course vodka has an odor, despite misinformation to the contrary. The official line, however, that both husband and wife held to unwaveringly was that the wife had given up drinking. Someone would offer her a drink at a party and she would say, 'I'll have some seltzer if you have any, or Perrier.' No one was fooled, yet everyone around was complicit in her self-deception."

"Do me a favor, Whit," Schiller said. "Go up to your friend and say hello. I want to see how he reacts to seeing you."

Whitlock got up, then changed his mind and sat down again. "These happen to be real people," he said.

"Had I known my friend would appear, I never would have told you his story."

"Is he less of a real person when he's not in the room?" Schiller asked in his therapist's voice.

"Yes," Whitlock said. "Because he remains anonymous."

"I acknowledge your point," said Schiller.

Whitlock's muted rebuke and Schiller's muted apology produced an awkward silence between the two friends. Schiller continued to glance at the man with the wispy beard who seemed locked in life-and-death conversation with the probably depressive woman presumably his wife.

It was Whitlock's turn to stare out the window. The juggler was standing on his head, an inflatable pillow set under him, and rotating three orange tennis balls with his feet. The first time he tried it the balls got away, and scattered into the crowd, provoking anxious laughter. Was it accident or part of the act? As soon as the crowd accepted the fact that the trick was not doable, was meant as self-parody, the juggler got it going. The balls fluttered awkwardly off his toes and it didn't look as if he could keep them in the air for more than a few seconds. But minutes passed and the balls continued to dance aloft.

"I'd like to interview him for the book," Schiller said. "Do you think he'd talk to me? I'll do my best to keep you out of it."

"Absolutely not, Max," Whitlock said. "And how are you going to meet him without bringing me into it? Anyway I have on good authority that the man's story is common as dirt and will not fit on your overcrowded plate."

Schiller wore his misunderstood look. "If I overstated, Whit, I apologize," he said. "Seeing them together is different from hearing their story without context. There's something about the way they relate that moves the hell out of me. I don't dispute your facts, but my intuition tells me there's also something else going on. Look how intense they are together. They are talking about something that doesn't matter as if it was the most important thing in the world."

One waiter cleared the table while another refilled their coffee cups.

"To get out of the restaurant," Schiller said, "we have to go by their table. There's really no way to avoid them." He signaled the nearest waiter—there had been different ones working their station at different times—to bring the check. The waiter ignored or misread Schiller's pantomime. Moments later, another one from some other quarter served them their check on a tray. Schiller produced plastic before Whitlock could reach for his wallet, a gesture which only seemed to enhance the journalist's displeasure. The juggler had completed his routine and was passing a hat among a fast-dispersing crowd.

On the way out, Whitlock stopped to say hello to his friends, Norman and Louise Hartman. Schiller standing behind him like a shadow while they chatted, waited for his introduction.

Three months had gone by the next time Schiller and Whitlock met at The Owl Pastaria for lunch. It had been an eventful period particularly for Whitlock, who had separated from his wife of fifteen years. Schiller had little to report beyond the continued progress of his book on denial. They talked briefly about the World Series, which had been delayed by an earthquake ("Even God was bored," Whitlock said), but they were New Yorkers and a west coast World Series held limited appeal.

"I'm sorry to hear about your marriage," Schiller said. "I always liked..."—he fumbled for the name— "Phyllis."

"Felicia," said Whitlock.

Schiller hated to be corrected, which is to say hated to be found in the wrong, a problem which six years of back-to-couch analysis had hardly altered. "Do you want to talk about it," he said, looking away.

"My therapist has heard all I'm going to say on the subject," Whitlock said, smiling grimly to show the humorless Schiller that he meant it as a joke.

Schiller's mild amusement at Whitlock's remark was exaggerated into a small silent partial laugh. "Whatever you do," he added, "don't deny your pain, Whit. Go with it."

"I take it everywhere," Whitlock said.

"You do," Schiller said, "but you don't always know it."

Whitlock changed the subject. "Did my friends, the Hartmans, make your book?" he asked. "Was there space on the overfilled plate?"

"Not exactly," Schiller said, looking evasive and cryptic at the same time.

Whitlock paraphrased. "No, but yes."

"Your friend, Norman Hartman, represents approximately a third of the male subject in the chapter called 'Betrayal Denied'."

"Which third of him did you use?" Whitlock asked. His eye wandered to the window to see what street theater was being offered that day. There was a man in a polar bear costume being tied with metal chains, his accomplice telling jokes as he assembled the locks.

The waiter came to take their orders, which momentarily rescued Schiller from the half-truth he was about to offer.

Whitlock sniffed the air with his journalist's nose for hidden news. "You interviewed them, didn't you?" he said, pointing a finger.

Schiller shook his head in private gesture, a denial he saw no point in making overtly. "I did interview them," he said, the smile on his lips pleased with itself. "Deniers, as you might imagine, make very poor interviewees."

"You sly devil," Whitlock said as if it were a compliment. "How did you manage it, Max?"

"After we split up, I went back to the restaurant to recover a book I had left at the table," Schiller said. "The book was gone, but it gave me an opening to approach the Hartmans again. I asked them if they had seen anyone go by with a paperback copy of a novel called *City of Glass*. One thing led to another."

"Wait a minute," Whitlock said. "I don't remember you having a book with you."

"No? Then I was mistaken about the book," Schiller said, his swallowed smile seemingly aimed at the man in the polar bear suit who was making a melodramatic effort to escape his chains. "Anyway, it was a device I learned from you, Whit, if you remember. You pretended to leave something behind to get a follow-up interview with the parents of that preppie kid who killed a girl while making love to her."

"So I taught you to be unscrupulous, Max," Whitlock said. "My friends' mothers used to say I was a bad influence. But you, Max, that's a different story. If the shrinks of the world don't set us a good example, what on earth's the use of them?"

"The Hartmans invited me to have a cup of coffee with them," Schiller said. "They seemed eager to have a third party at the table. You know what they wanted to talk about?"

The crowd cheered when the polar bear broke through his chains by expanding his chest muscles and grunting forcefully.

"They wanted to talk about you," Schiller said. "They said they were concerned about you, Whit."

"You guys have a word for that," Whitlock said. "Displacement I believe it's called."

Schiller nodded, pinched the bridge of his nose. "Yes, that was my take on it too," he said. "It nevertheless took me by surprise, pal. It was not what I was prepared to expect."

"And why should it be?" Whitlock said, unwilling to hide his annoyance at the turn in the conversation. He hated to be left out, particularly so when he was the subject of the news being denied him.

Schiller let the silence extend itself. "I know what you're thinking, Whit," he said, "but I can't tell you. What the Hartmans said to me was in confidence."

"Bullshit," Whitlock said in a voice that turned heads.

The man in the polar bear suit was prancing about outside with his bear head off, razzing the crowd. Without his bear head, he resembled the man whom Whitlock had observed juggling balls with his feet during his last lunch with Schiller at The Owl Pastaria. Schiller presented an unruffled front. "I'm sorry you're upset," he said. "But as a journalist, Whit, surely you understand I have no right to divulge information told to me in strictest confidence. If you were in my shoes, you would do the same."

Whitlock felt his hands clench. He had a tendency, he had been told, as if he needed corroboration, to fly into rages at negligible provocations. The fact is anger disabled him. He had things to say that scrambled about in his head, words that refused to form themselves into sentences. He thought of pouring his mostly filled glass of water over Schiller's head.

Schiller was adept at reading angry faces, also adept at forestalling violence. He sensed that Whitlock was close to doing something they would both regret. "I'm grateful to you, Whit, for putting me in touch with the Hartmans," he said. "I'd like to mention you in the acknowledgements when the book comes out, if there's no objection."

"I'll bite," Whitlock said. "What was it that worried the Hartmans about me?" His voice was clamorous and seemed to fill the restaurant. "I want to know what was said, Max. We're not talking about national security here."

Schiller wore his severest look. "Get hold of yourself, Whit," he whispered. "You're out of control. I'll tell you this much: The Hartmans are very fond of you. Their concern was prompted by affection."

Whitlock crossed his arms in front of him, felt on the edge of losing control, just as the man in the polar bear costume and his assistant wandered into the restaurant.

The street entertainers were locked in discussion with the hostess, who seemed offended by their intrusion. Schiller continued eating while Whitlock took a series of deep breaths. When he felt his anger recede, the journalist uncrossed his arms, an elbow or forearm overturning his water glass.

Schiller struggled to escape the stream of liquid moving relentlessly in his direction, but inertia held him back and he paid the price. His pants were already soaked by the time he evacuated his chair.

"It was an accident," Whitlock murmured.

"There are no accidents," said Schiller, daubing at his pants with a napkin. "Deniers carry a lot of anger around with them."

"Look, what I really wanted to do was pour it on your head," said Whitlock, belying his remark with a disarming smile.

Schiller meticulously dried off his seat before reclaiming it. As if it had been orchestrated, a crew of waiters appeared and replaced the wet table cloth with a fresh one that had a bleached-out red stain on Whitlock's side.

"Felicia says I'm unconscious," Whitlock said as a form of apology when the waiters were gone.

"Forget it," Schiller said, still damp at the crotch, mildly amused at the turn of events despite his discomfort.

The man in the polar bear suit and his assistant sat down at the table directly behind theirs. As soon as they were seated, the entertainers began to juggle between them whatever was on the table—silverware, salt shaker, pepper grinder, napkins, menus, a balled-up red and white striped sock.

"You've known more about this than you've let on, haven't you?" Whitlock said.

"In a sense," Schiller said, studying his plate as if the missing context were hidden somewhere in the morass of his pasta. "Did you have something specific in mind?"

"You knew all along that the story I told you may have had as much to do with me as it did with the Hartmans," Whitlock said.

The polar bear pretended the knives were getting by him, plucking them out of the air behind his head, which is to say also behind Schiller's head.

"Then who are the Hartmans?" Schiller asked. "Why did you bring them into it?"

Whitlock shrugged. "They brought themselves into it," he said. "I hadn't thought of them, or hadn't known I was thinking of them, until they showed up in the restaurant. Their appearance was fortuitous. I knew their marriage was in trouble, though I could only guess what their story was."

Schiller turned around to observe the two men juggling behind him, then he moved his chair away from the line of fire. "Whit, how long have I known you—twenty-two years? Even so, I never know when you're being serious," he said.

"I thought you saw right through people like me, Max," Whitlock said, a touch of irony in his tone. "When you made that remark about deniers being angry people, which I know is on the money, I took it as a signal you were giving me. Max knows, I said to myself, but he doesn't want to embarrass me with his knowledge. I'm the kind of guy who thinks shrinks know everything."

Schiller processed the various data available to him and came to the same conclusion he had come to before. "Whit, we know, some of us, some of the time, when we're being put on," he said. He looked at his watch, said that he had a patient in fifteen minutes and had to run. When the check arrived, Whitlock claimed it.

Schiller had turned in the completed manuscript to his publisher by the next time they met for lunch at The Owl

Pastaria. He was no longer in the market for unusual stories about denial. Whitlock had moved back in with his wife, though rumor had it that their reconciliation was on shaky ground.

"I see you're wearing a different pair of pants," Whitlock said.

Schiller looked bemused; he had forgotten the incident of the spilled glass of water, finessed his confusion by changing the subject. "Are things better with you?" he asked.

"Much better," Whitlock said in automatic response. "The same but different. And you?"

Schiller laughed. "What do you mean the same but different?"

Whitlock thought about what he meant but no language introduced itself. "You know, don't you, that the Hartmans have split up?" he said. "A tacky business at the end, nasty."

The news seemed to worry Schiller. "When was this?" he asked. "You're not putting me on again, are you?"

"When have I ever put you on, Max?"

Schiller looked away. "Whit, I think there's something competitive going on between us," he said. "No. Let me put that another way. I think you resent the ostensible authority invested in my role as therapist."

Whitlock nodded. "That may be true," he said. "Max, for someone whose profession it is to help other people, you're inordinately self-involved."

"It's good that you can say that directly to me, Whit," Schiller said, speaking in the voice of concern. "I appreciate how difficult it is to confront someone who has been an old and distant friend. The reason I haven't been in touch with the Hartmans, as it turns out, is that they've been a red herring in all this. It was not their story you told me but yours."

Whitlock did an exaggerated double take. "Max, when I told you that in the first place, you accused me of putting you on. Remember? You can't give me back my own story and claim it as yours."

It was Schiller's turn to be angry. "This is unworthy of you, Whit," he said, tight-lipped. "This is no longer amusing."

Whitlock looked out the window to divert himself from his irritation with his friend, but there was nothing to see. The street entertainers had not yet arrived or had taken the day off. "Believe what you want," he said. "My memory of what went on during our previous lunch is absolutely clear."

"Just listen to yourself, Whit," Schiller said. "That's all I'm going to say. Just listen to what you just said." He raised his finger to make a further point, but let it drop. "I'm done."

Their lunches were served, but neither made a move to eat. Eventually, Schiller lifted a forkful of tortellini to his mouth and held it there a moment, hostage to a false intention, before returning it to his plate.

"Sure," Whitlock said. "Sure you're done."

Schiller censured his friend with a disapproving stare.

"Max, do any of your patients ever get better?" Whitlock asked him.

Schiller seemed encrusted in some mirror image of willed dignity. He took out his wallet, threw some money on the table and got to his feet. "Fuck off," he whispered.

Whitlock wore his scapegrace grin. "That's unworthy of you, Max," he said. "Don't be an asshole. Sit down and finish your meal."

A waiter came by to ask if everything was all right.

"Everything's the way it always is," Schiller said, easing himself back into his seat.

Whitlock was the first to break the extended silence. "Look to your left," he said. Schiller turned his head on cue. Two women were going by, being escorted to their table by one of the hostesses.

"What about them?" Schiller asked.

"The dark one—don't you recognize her?—it's Louise Hartman."

Schiller didn't at first, didn't see what he wasn't looking for. He got the larger picture in the following moment. The two women were intimate, were apparently a couple, which was a new wrinkle on the Hartmans' situation.

"So the daughter's friend's parent she was having the affair with was the mother," he said, pointing his finger at Whitlock. A further perception flashed like the shadow of lightning across his face. "The other one isn't Felicia, is it? I don't remember exactly what she looks like."

Whitlock pointed his finger back. "There is no resemblance," he said. "Does this mean you have to redo the chapter called 'Betrayal Denied?'"

"The particulars matter less than the overall dynamic," Schiller said, looking behind him as if errant cleavers might be flying in his direction. "We all deny to a certain extent," he confessed. "If my wife ever had an affair, I don't know that I wouldn't resist knowledge that might be painful to me."

"You never know," said Whitlock, "until, as it turns out, you don't know."

"Five years ago," Schiller said, "my wife had a brief episode with someone whose identity I never discovered. It ended in less than a year. I chose not to let her know I knew. That was when I began my research on the book."

"Did you forgive her?" Whitlock asked.

Schiller sighed, looked away. "I became kinder to her," he said. "Whit, how much of your story was really about the Hartmans and how much about you? I'd appreciate the truth."

"The truth is, I was being creative," said Whitlock. "I was trying to give you a good story for the book. The truth is, it's all true. I mean, it's all true, isn't it? One way or another."

Schiller nodded, said if there were time he would redo the chapter, "Betrayal Denied", but the book was already in galleys. He had an original theory about women who moved from men to other women, which he outlined in brief. Whitlock told him of an article he was writing on a riot that took place in Florida four years before, in which almost all the basic causes of rioting in our time were manifest.

Gradually the subject changed to baseball. Schiller and Whitlock, both of whom were Mets fans, exchanged conjectures on the forthcoming season. Pieces of the puzzle were missing, Whitlock said, a shortstop who could hit his weight, a major league catcher, an appropriate centerfielder. Schiller, on the other hand, was generally content with his team's prospects, said he wouldn't be surprised if this wasn't the year they won it all. Whitlock shook his head in amusement at his friend's capacity for self-deception. The discussion moved to basketball and an analysis of the failure of the Knicks to live up to expectations. Too many coaches, said Whitlock. Too much dependency on one player, said Schiller. Even after their plates had been long cleared away and coffee cups refilled for the second perhaps third time, they lingered over sports talk, the conversation of men.

When the two friends said goodbye at the door—the street entertainer, whose late arrival had gone unnoticed, was juggling flaming batons—they shook hands and talked of doing it again soon, which was their usual parting line.

Schiller went one way; Whitlock went the other. Life on the New York streets moved, or didn't, in its odd and mysterious ways between them.

Bright Is Innocent: Scenes from an Imaginary Movie

This is the way it usually happens. Our man, who toils in the creative trenches for a state-of-the-art advertising firm, who's inoffensive and untested, sophisticated to a fault yet surprisingly innocent, with a socialite mother who can maim you with a wisecrack, finds himself mistaken for a notorious secret agent. He gets up from his table in the Russian Tea Room to phone his overbearing mother at the very moment the real agent is paged by the people trying to trap him. Once he is mistaken for this ostensibly dangerous figure, a man of a thousand faces, a man who may not even exist, Jonathan Bright's life is irremediably altered. He becomes a figure adrift in an irrational universe, living by his tattered wits. An inescapable succession of improbable adventures awaits him.

Two men with guns discreetly displayed approach him as he is getting into a phone booth and direct him outside into a waiting limousine. They identify him as a Mr. Phillip Levy. The more he insists that he is not this Mr. Levy, the more his captors are convinced that he is exactly the person he says he is not. When he tries to leap out the car door at a red light, they laugh at him for behaving like an amateur.

"You are one funny guy, Mr. Levy," the short one says.

"You are two funny guys to think I'm Mr. Levy," says our man.

He is taken to an elegant country estate belonging to the famous criminal lawyer, defender of lost causes, Wilfred Cog, where he is grilled by an over-civilized white-haired man with an English or vaguely German accent.

"What is your assignment, Mr. Levy?" he is asked. Bright senses that if his captors don't get what they want, his life is not worth a hill of beans or a plugged nickel, whichever is less. What an impossible situation for an innocent man to find himself in!

Still he tells them nothing, a man unwilling to give up state secrets even if he has none to give, playing to the hilt the false role (while denying he is who they say) he has unwittingly inherited. With his ad-man's sense of the absurdity of all human transactions, he makes up stories for his captors that, though credible in some ways, are basically impossible to believe. Amused by Bright, they nevertheless talk of drowning him in a bathtub or pouring whiskey down his throat and taking him for a one-way ride to nowhere. If they are only trying to scare him, which he factors as a possibility, it is the one thing they have done so far in his regard with some measure of success.

He wakes up the next morning, hungover, in an unfamiliar room, a smoking gun at the foot of his bed, a dead body lying in the center of the room like its own tracing. He is awakened by a pounding on the door and a persistent voice calling, "Police. Open up. Police. Open up."

What to do. He knows himself to be an innocent man caught in a maelstrom of misunderstanding so he climbs out of bed and opens the door. The police knock him down and handcuff him and read him his rights. "Wait a minute," he says. "Would I have opened the door for you if I had killed this man?"

"The criminal mind will go to any length to disguise the nature of its crimes," says Sergeant Black. "Don't give us any more trouble, Mr. Bedford, or you'll be adding resisting arrest charges to those already on your docket."

"My name isn't Bedford," says Bright/Levy. "It looks like you low-rent Sherlocks have got the wrong man."

The two policemen are flustered for a moment or so and check the information they have been given from headquarters. Wouldn't you know it, they are one smudged digit off on the room number. In their zealousness, they have forced their way into the wrong hotel room and abused the wrong perpetrator. Since this is not their case, not at the moment, they remove Bright's handcuffs and give him ten minutes to get his life in order.

Our man puts on shoes and socks, a coat over his pajamas—there isn't time to get fully dressed—and hurries out of his hotel room, which is on the twenty-ninth floor. How did I get here? he wonders. It is not a question he often asks himself. Crisis has deepened him in a myriad of barely perceptible ways. His plan is to go home, take a hot shower, change his clothes, call his office and his mother and perhaps even a lawyer, but as he steps out of the elevator he sees one of the two men who had kidnapped him the day before.

He slips back into the elevator, bumping into (in both senses) a slightly tarnished attractive blond woman getting in at the same time. "This may sound crazy," he says, "but there's a man in the lobby who'd like nothing better than to drown me in a bathtub."

"I wouldn't be at all surprised, Mr. Levy," she says. "Your picture's on the front page of almost every, newspaper in America."

The woman, for her own reasons which are yet to make themselves known, offers to hide him in her room until the worst of the heat is off. "How do you know I'm not dangerous?" he asks.

"I don't," she says, "but I've never run from danger before and I'm not going to start on your account." Her room turns out to be on the 30th floor just above his former room—an odd coincidence, which makes him distrustful.

When Maria is out on an errand, he calls his office to explain his absence and is told by his own secretary that he can't possibly be who he says since the real Jonathan Bright happens to be working at his desk at the moment.

"Darlene, your left breast is slightly higher than your right and you have a beauty mark on your right buttock," he tells his secretary.

"Oh my God," she says. "Who told you that?"

"The other man is an imposter," he says. "The reason I'm not at work is that I've been mistaken for a spy and framed for a murder."

She hangs up or they are cut off from another source. Before he can call back, there is a knock at the door—two knocks in impatient succession. "Is everything all right in there, Miss Carlyle?" a man's voice calls. It sounds like Sergeant Black.

"Everything's fine," he says in unconvincing imitation of Maria Carlyle's voice. "If you'll excuse me, I'm taking a nap."

"Don't answer the door for anything, Miss," the voice says. "There's a dangerous character running around the hotel and someone spotted him exiting the elevator at this very floor."

"Thank you for the warning, boys," he says in his improvised falsetto.

"Something's wrong in there," he hears the one who's not Sergeant Black stage whisper. "I think he's in there with her."

He presses his ear to the wall to get the sergeant's response, but the only thing he hears is troubled breathing and footsteps toward or away. What to do—that persistent question. Bright shaves himself with a woman's tiny razor, then dresses himself in Maria Carlyle's clothes. He's never done anything like this before, but his picture is in the papers and everyone seems to be looking for him, and he's always wanted (secretly of course) to get in touch with the feminine side of his nature.

One of the policemen, the one who is not Sergeant Black, is lounging in the hall with his back to him. While Bright (in women's clothes) is waiting for the elevator, the cop looks at him, does a double take, and turns away.

The high heels get to him—he has never worn heels before—and his ankles begin to wobble in a telltale way as he click-clacks through the lobby to the exit: "New shoes," he says jokingly to an old woman he passes. "Not broken in yet."

As he is hailing a cab—pursuers emerging from every shadow—a police car drives up and asks the woman he appears to be where she thinks she is going.

"To work," he says, which is the wrong answer.

"I think you better come with us, doll," the vice squad cop says. "We know you've been working the hotel. We've had our eye on you for some time."

"You have the wrong girl," our man says with genuine outrage. "Just who do you think I am?"

"Be a good girl, Mary, and get in the car," the cop says. "Spare us the innocent act, sweetheart."

At that moment, Maria appears, says, "What's going on here? What are you doing to my sister?"

After some negotiation, and some extended studying of Bright's face, the police decide that they may have made a mistake. "Let us see some identification"; they say.

For a wild moment, Bright thinks of whipping out his penis, but of course that's not what they mean by identification.

Maria covers for him. "You must have left your purse in the hotel room," she says. The police get bored with the complexities of the discussion and decide to leave, though not without warning him/her to stay off the street.

Maria and Bright go back into the hotel and into the Grill Room (where lunch is being served), at the very moment someone coming out of the restaurant is assassinated with a knife.

As chance would have it, the blood-stained knife ends up in Bright's left hand. "Stay away from me," he/she says, backing out of the restaurant. There are screams. Someone points a finger at him/her, the real murderer, an assassin in Cog's employ. "Cherchez la femme," he yells, slipping out the door while the crowd turns its attention to the odd looking woman with the knife. In the commotion, someone knocks Bright's wig off, which creates a gasp of desperate surprise. Bright punches a man trying to hold on to him and gets out the door just in time to see the real murderer, Hermann, a man with a face like a barber's razor, get into one of the cabs that hang around outside the hotel.

Bright gets into the next cab and instructs the driver the way they do in movies to follow the cab just ahead. Maria stands in front of the hotel calling something to him he is unable or unwilling to hear. She is shaking her head, indicating that his rushing off this way is only going to make things worse. As he follows the cab in front, Bright becomes aware that his cab is being followed in turn by an unmarked (he assumes) police car. The lead cab, aware of being followed, makes a couple of unexpected turns, hoping to lose its pursuer.

Bright's cab, not to be left behind, too late to make the second of the two abrupt turns, crashes into a telephone pole.

Two months later, our man wakes in a hospital bed with no memory of a past. He wakes at four ten in the afternoon in a strange room as if he had just been torn from the womb. The afternoon nurse, a light-skinned black woman named Helene, addresses him as Mr. Willow.

At five o'clock, the doctor comes by to see his progress. "Good to have you among the living again, Willow," he says. "We've had our worries about you, fella. How do you feel? Any discomfort?"

"Head," Willow says, unable to locate a second word to follow the first. In truth, he has what feels like a toothache at the back of his head.

"Hurts?" The doctor asks. "I wouldn't be surprised."

The next day he receives a visitor, a woman in a business suit he has no recollection of having seen before but whose manner toward him suggests long term intimacy.

"Darling, you can't possibly know how pleased we all are to have you back among us," she says, sitting on the side of the bed. "Is there anything I can do for you, Chance?"

"Get me out of here," he says.

"The doctor says you can leave the hospital in a week to ten days depending on your progress," she says in a voice that strikes a nerve of irritation. "And then of course you'll have to talk to the police."

"Get me out of here," he says again.

She leans toward him, puts her head in whispering distance of his, and between them they hatch a complicated escape plot. The next visiting day she will bring him a doctor's uniform. Meanwhile he is to pretend to be too weak to get out of bed so as not to arouse suspicion. He does not tell her of his apparent amnesia or of the pain at the back of his head, the weakness in his legs, the deep sense of foreboding.

He does ask one question: Why should the police want to talk to him? Oh the usual reasons, she says, telling him nothing, there are loose ends that need to be tied together in cases like this. Loose ends? You know, loose ends, as if it all weren't too obvious for words. She calls him Chance, which is probably a nickname, long or short for something else.

She returns two days later with a set of neatly pressed doctors' whites in an unmarked shopping bag.

In the intervening two days his memory has improved sufficiently for him to know that his name is not Willow. The woman, who is almost beautiful and almost young, is no one he remembers knowing, but she seems fond of him so he goes along with her plan for his escape.

The stenciled name on his uniform is Dr. Levy, which strikes a chord. Even after they escape together in her metallic blue Dodge Polaris, he has no clear idea of how he should behave toward her, what's expected and what's not. She takes him to a cottage outside the city, a place only a handful know about, she says, where he will be safe while he convalesces.

There is a closet full of men's clothes at the cottage, of a style so fashionably anonymous and nondescript they seem to have been tailor-made for an amnesiac. "This is the best I could do on short notice," she says, holding out a double-breasted blazer for him to try on. It all happens so quickly, the escape from the hospital, the drive to the country, the room by room tour of the cottage which is to be his temporary home, the not quite right multi-course gourmet dinner she prepares for him, that none of it quite registers as experience. It is as if he were watching the life of someone else, someone like himself, on the bigger-than-life screen of a movie theater.

When she announces after dinner that she has to get back to the city (or else what?), our man wonders if there's anything he can do to change her mind. "When will I see you again?" he asks. "As soon as it's safe to return," she says, which tells him nothing. They work out a code so he'll be able to tell, when the phone rings, whether it's Maria on the other end. Otherwise, as a matter of perhaps excessive precaution he's not to answer.

He's almost glad when she drives off so that he can do some detective work and find out who she is and who he is and what they might be to each other. On a kitchen table, he discovers a picture postcard (a reproduction of the Mona Lisa) sent from Paris to a Ms. Anne Laurie, a name that strikes only the most distant echo of familiarity.

It is the usual tourist message—saw this and that, loving Paris, had furtive sex on the Champs Elyses. So usual that he wonders if the message isn't some kind of code. The card is signed with the initial W. Before he can explore further, exhaustion reaches him and he falls asleep on one of the living room couches.

A noise wakes him. Someone is in the house with him, in an adjoining room, and is rooting around in an impatient heat. Whoever it is must have already been through the living room, which is the first room you enter, and either had chosen to ignore Chance or had not noticed him, hunkered down on the couch in the shadow of the dark room. The second possibility he sees as the more likely.

When the phone rings, the intruder answers from the kitchen. Chance overhears the following conversation. "I found it," an unplaceably familiar voice with a faint German accent rasps. "I'm going upstairs next to see if there's something else... Don't call again. I'll be in touch after the house is torched."

When he hears the intruder go upstairs, our man gets off the couch and goes outside into the steely night air. His first impulse is to get away and with that in mind he gets into the black car parked down the road from the house. His plans are in constant variation. There is no key in the ignition which precludes his immediate escape so he hides himself in the back, a wrench in his right hand, waiting for the intruder, whose name he seems to remember as Wilfred Cog, to return.

Chance falls asleep, waiting. He wakes with a start the moment the engine of the car starts. The wrench is under him and to get it he has to raise his legs without calling attention to himself. As the intruder lights a cigarette, Chance, balanced on one knee, brings down the wrench on the back of the other's head in a glancing blow. The intruder, cursing in German, turns toward him, but Chance gets a better swing at him the second time, connecting with a blow that leaves Wilfred Cog slumped like a rag doll against the door.

Five minutes later Chance has rolled the body out of the car and is starting to go through the man's pockets when he notices that a fire has started in one of the upstairs rooms of the cottage. He leaves Cog, whom he assumes is dead, and goes to see what he can do about saving the house.

At first the fire is localized to one bedroom on the second floor. Chance finds a bucket in an adjoining bathroom and fills it with water, flinging the water at the flames, repeating the process several times to no useful result. The fire outpaces his efforts. After calling the fire department, he goes back to the black car except the car is no longer where it was.

What a disaster! By the time the fire trucks arrive, the house is burning out of control. Lying on his belly in the field, watching the flames gradually decline, Chance remembers his name as Phillip Levy. When after several hours the fire trucks leave, Levy/Willow returns to what remains of the cottage and calls the almost young, almost beautiful woman, who may or may not be Anne Laurie, from the melted kitchen phone still hot to the touch. He reports what has happened in understated detail, giving her a description of the intruder. She is her usual cryptic self on the phone, advising him to make himself scarce until she gets there.

Waiting for her, Levy goes through the rubble looking for clarifying detail, finds an address book which he puts in the pocket of his borrowed pants. Then he hears several cars drive up and he has the impression, looking out from the charred remains of the cottage, that the field is on fire. What he sees are the flashing lights of five perhaps six police cars.

A voice blares from a bullhorn. "WILLOW, WE KNOW YOU'RE IN THERE. COME OUT WITH YOUR HANDS ABOVE YOUR

HEAD AND I PERSONALLY GUARANTEE YOUR SAFETY. THIS IS
SERGEANT BLACK REPEAT SERGEANT BLACK SPEAKING."

Seemingly moments after this announcement,
before Levy has decided on a course of action within
severely limited alternatives, bullets fly through the
shattered house like a plague of locusts. What now?
He lies in a crawl space behind the stairs waiting for
the gunfire to exhaust itself.

Periodically, the bullhorn announcement returns,
but the blasts of gunfire follow within twenty seconds
of its conclusion. Even if Levy/ Willow (and which is
the real self?) were ready to give himself up, there is
not enough time for him to get out of the crawl space
and through the front door before the firing resumes.
When they warn him that they are about to charge the
house, he crawls out an opening in a back wall into a
garage whose existence he hadn't noted before. There is
a moped in the garage and though he has never driven
one, he drives off on it into the dense backwoods as if
he had been riding one all his life.

Someone spots him (wouldn't you know it?) and
two police cars come after him, but the woods resist their
entrance and the cops are forced to pursue on foot. And
then our man, looking over his shoulder, crashes into a
tree stump. The fall, as falls will, jogs loose much of his
buried memory (like seeing the beginning of a movie in
which you already know the outcome), and so he knows
who he is again as he stumbles through the dense brush
away from unseen pursuers. He is Jonathan Bright, one
of the top copywriters in the business, a man with a gift
for the falsely sincere persuasive phrase, who, through
misunderstanding and malice, has become hopelessly
estranged from his former life. Bright's only concern at
this point is to prove his innocence and clear his name
and see the world made a safer place for the comings
and goings of innocent men.

On the other side of the woods, he comes to a dirt
road which leads him to Wilfred Cog's country house,

the place to which he had been abducted at the beginning of his adventure. In fact, Cog's black Mercedes—
the one Bright regrets not driving off in when he had
the chance—is parked in the adjoining carport. The
other car parked conspicuously out front, the metallic
blue Dodge Polaris, is also familiar. It is the car he was
taken in by Anne Laurie (AKA Maria Carlyle) when she
helped him escape from the hospital.

So, armed only with his pay-as-you-go wit, Bright
has reached the apparent epicenter of the conspiracy
against him. One of Cog's henchmen, the one called
Werner, approaches Bright as he is going through the
glove compartment of the Polaris. Bright sees him just
in time and takes out Werner, who had been his particular nemesis during their earlier encounter, with a
punishing right hand, a fortuitous gesture of desperation, to the side of the head.

Bright ties Werner up and stuffs him in the trunk
of the car, arming himself with the thug's Smith and
Wesson revolver. He also comes up with a miniature tape
recorder that he finds in Maria's glove compartment, a
means, as he sees it, to clearing his name. Just when
it looks like Bright is about to transcend his long siege
of adversity—he has been sneaking around the house
peering into windows to get the lay of things (there is
a portrait of Hitler done in a Gilbert Stuart mode on a
back wall)—Cog's other henchman, Hermann, gets the
drop on him from behind.

So Bright is led once again at gunpoint into the
hands of his enemy, Wilfred Cog, who is sitting in
a thronelike chair in his study, wearing a bandage
around his head the size and scope of a turban. "A
pleasure to meet you again, Mr. Levy," says Cog. "I
fear our friendship, which I had counted on so much,
will never blossom. Unfortunately, you have become
superfluous to my plans. I no longer have need of that
information you once, even as your life depended on
it, refused to give me."

It is shocking to Bright that a man as apparently clever as Wilfred Cog still hasn't gotten his name right, still persists in mistaking him for someone else. He takes a new tack. "What if I told you everything I know," he says. "Would that make a difference?"

Wilfred Cog looks at his watch. "Pity I don't have more time," he says. "If I weren't assassinating your president in a few hours, it might be amusing to hear your sad story, Mr. Levy. Might be, yes?"

At a signal from Wilfred Cog, Bright is bound and loosely gagged and hustled into an almost pitch-black basement room. Someone else is in the room with him, someone he can't see, someone whose presence is only announced by the sound of breathing. A woman's voice says, "They're going to burn the house down when they leave. We have about twenty minutes to get out of here before they torch the place."

Bright crawls in the direction of the woman's voice and when they connect awkwardly in the dark, she pulls his gag free with her teeth, which amounts to their first kiss. There is no time to ask why she betrayed him to the police. In no more than ten minutes they are out of their bonds and in five minutes more they have discovered a small, nailed shut window, leading to outside the house.

They have almost dislodged the window when they are interrupted by the sound of footsteps coming down the basement stairs. There is no time to plan a strategy, barely time for Bright to take up position behind the door. The door opens abruptly and the beam of a flashlight intrudes on the almost perfect blackness of the room.

"I have come to say goodbye in person," says the voice. It is the ineluctable Wilfred Cog himself. Cog moves the beam of light in a slow arc from one side of the basement to the other without discovering either of its occupants. "You are probably wondering what I have in store for you. To tell you the truth, for the longest time I had nothing in mind. Only to do the right thing, the necessary thing. To reward faithfulness and to punish betrayal." When the flashlight focuses its attention on the partially dislodged window, Cog discontinues his monologue. "Problems," he sighs and backs off, closing the door without relocking it. Bright hears Cog ordering his henchmen to search the grounds. "Shoot anything that moves," he says. "The time for subtlety is past."

In the next few moments, several things happen almost at once. Cog, carrying an attaché case with the viscera of an assassin's rifle inside, gets into his car and drives off. He leaves a moment before a team of his people begin their systematic search of the grounds. It is also the moment that the police, pursuing Bright on foot, arrive at Cog's country house. One of Cog's men, the notorious Hermann, panics and fires at the approaching police. Challenged, the cops take cover behind hedges sculpted in the shape of swans and fire back.

Maria, it appears—we have only her own word to go on—is a double (perhaps triple) agent working for the U.S. government which explains, or seems to explain, the vagaries of her behavior vis-a-vis Bright. Loyalty to country takes precedent over concern for the life of an innocent man.

Maria and Bright kiss for the second time. As before, as always, there is no time to lose, though personal matters—love perhaps—tend to slow things down. Bright slips out of the house unnoticed and into Maria's car, drives around the back where Maria waits for him. As she is getting into the car, a random bullet probably from one of the team of police hits her in the most circumstantial way, glancing off the door of the car and into her skull.

Bright has started driving away before he realizes that Maria has been hit, goes about a hundred yards down the road before coming to a stop. "Are you all right, darling?" he asks when she slumps against him. Her silence is his answer.

He carries Maria out of the car and back toward the house. The fighting has mostly stopped—occasional shots here and there echo like after-thoughts. Virtually everyone is dead or critically wounded. Before he can get her into the house, a second group of police arrive led by the indefatigable Sergeant Black.

Bright ignores Sergeant Black's command to halt and carries Maria into the house, putting her down on the orange and ivory Ming dynasty rug in the front room. The phone lines have been cut so he can't dial an ambulance, which is his first idea. He refuses to believe, has cut himself off from believing, that Maria is dead.

Sergeant Black follows him inside. "A lot of people have been looking for you, Bedford," he says.

"Well, it looks like you've found me," says Bright/ Levy/Willow/Bedford, who even in the midst of possible tragedy, has not lost his capacity for the playful retort. "While you've been hounding an innocent man, Wilfred Cog is on the loose preparing perhaps at this very moment to assassinate the president of the United States."

The police doctor comes in and after examining Maria Carlyle, places a sheet over the body. "She won't be running any more stop lights," he says.

Black plays with his moustache. "I admit we've made a few mistakes along the way, Bedford. I freely admit to some misapprehensions, but we've got the business straight now. Wilfred Cog is in custody—we picked him up not five miles from here. The republic is safe for one more night. Case closed."

"If the case is closed, then you no longer want me," Bright says. "I can go back to my unexceptional life if it's still there to go back to."

"Sure, you're a free man," says the sergeant, moving across the room to discuss something in private with one of his men. "Take off, old man. Get lost. Hit the road."

The abrupt change in his status confuses Bright. He lingers a moment. He has been too long on the wrong end of the fox hunt to give up his role of injured innocence without second thoughts. Walking toward the door, he has an odd premonition (a part of the puzzle is missing) and prodded by intuition, he turns back. And just in time. He discovers a gun pointed at what had been his back, cocked, primed to fire. Fortunately, there is also a gun in his own hand, the one canceling out the other.

"I might have known," says our man.

"Don't you trust anyone?" says the sergeant.

The standoff lasts three minutes perhaps five, at which point (and for reasons which may soon become clear) Sergeant Black withdraws his gun. In the next moment a man identified as the notorious Wilfred Cog is brought into the house by two government agents for questioning.

Bright is astonished. This Wilfred Cog is several inches shorter and perhaps ten years younger than the Wilfred Cog who had tried to kill him. "This is the wrong man," he says. Astonishment pervades the room.

The government agent, one Phillip Levy, assures our man that this indeed is the real Wilfred Cog, hotshot lawyer, defender of lost causes. If true, the real one is less credible than the imposter. Bright takes advantage of the general confusion and rushes out of the house and down the road to Maria's metallic blue Dodge Polaris—someone has to stop the senseless murders—and the adventure, such as it is, continues. The case surrounding our man is in a state of permanent irresolution.

Phillip Levy and his men follow after him in their unmarked government car, hoping to arrive at some point of clarity. Once again Bright is a wanted man.

There is no point of clarity, merely the mechanism of pursuit and empty discovery. There are more chases to come in this case, more instances of mistaken identity, more murders, more delusory solutions to murder, more willful destruction of property, more questions without answers, more enigmatic assassins, more almost young almost beautiful women (who may or may not be spies), more betrayal, more lost love. All the wrong people (only the wrong people) will be caught and punished, the inevitable happy ending a deceptive waystation, an accommodating illusion to permit us to go on to more of the same: more deaths, more fast automobiles, more dimwitted spying, more incomprehensible secrets. And Bright, who is our man, who is innocent (he believes) of everything, is caught up in this hectic continuum, misperceived and disbelieved, wanting only to understand why him of all people, which is the one thing, among all the wisdom disappointment has to offer, he will never find out.

French History

Jack blamed the excursion to Vaux-le-Vicomte on Harry, whom he aspired with virtually no success to dislike. On the other hand, he knew it was his mother's project, that Harry had merely arranged the tiresome trip to make points with Lily. Whatever, the foreign correspondent was the third irrelevant stranger in his mother's life since his father had disappeared in Nepal seven years ago. Jack had managed to get rid of the first two interlopers without showing his hand. He didn't doubt that Harry, a semi-famous magazine journalist and good-natured buffoon, would be more difficult to unseat.

This trip may have been his mother's idea, but Harry had been making a meal of it on the drive over from Paris. There was this mystery, Harry told him, involving the king, Louis XIV, and the lord of the chateau they were visiting, a man named Fouquet, that remained unsolved. Jack nodded in acknowledgment, his mind wherever distraction would take it.

"You're going to love this chateau, Jack," his mother said, making one of her teasing faces. She rested her hand on Harry's shoulder. "I interrupted you, sweetheart," she said.

Jack had become an expert in pretending to listen, in picking up the odd phrase here and there and making passable sense of it all. Harry was gassing about how Fouquet gave "this knock-your-eyes-out feast" at the place they were visiting—the original menu on display—as a demonstration of his loyalty to the boy king. Nevertheless, a few weeks later, the guy ("our guy," as Harry called him), was lured away from his castle on a false errand and arrested by the king's soldiers.

"As a matter of fact, the musketeer that took him in was d'Artagnan himself," Harry said. "You know who d'Artagnan was, don't you?"

"Is this fact or supposition?" his mother asked, winking at Jack.

"Trust me," Harry said. "I know this stuff. I have a degree in French history. There was this trial that lasted four years in which our guy was finally found not guilty. Now here's the kicker, Jack. Although the jury cleared Fouquet, the king refused to release him from prison."

"I suppose kings are allowed to break the rules," Jack said. He had lost track of Harry's argument, had been thinking of hanging out in the car while they visited the castle. "So what exactly is the mystery, sir?"

"Darling," his mother said, a nervous laugh interrupting her thought, "the mystery has to do with why the king arrested Fouquet in the first place. Isn't that right?" The question was addressed to Harry, who had missed the turnoff to the chateau and was looking for a place to turn around.

His mother, to whom he was devoted, had her unacknowledged faults. She had this annoying talent, for example, for fixing the unbroken. Rather than say what was on his mind, Jack enclosed himself in the private sound of his walkman.

"This is it, guys," Harry said, driving into a parking lot, which had only two other cars.

"The other tourists are keeping a low profile today," Jack said.

The manicured grounds, which was the first thing he noticed, had an endless aspect, the eccentric hedges like rows of squat soldiers.

"Why don't we make a game of it?" Harry said to him in a confidential whisper as soon as they were out of the car. "Let's see who can come up with the most convincing take on the mystery."

Jack noted that Harry had set himself the task, doomed to humiliating failure, of winning over his girl-friend's son. For the moment, it seemed a redeeming flaw. "Maybe the king felt that our guy was showing off," Jack said. "I mean, look at this place, sir. It's an advertisement for self-importance. The king figured that whatshisname was in need of a lesson he wouldn't soon forget."

"I like that," his mother said. "I think that's a very good way of explaining it."

"That's a hell of a lesson," said Harry. "You deprive a man of his freedom for the rest of his life because he overdid it as a host."

"If that's the way you want to look at it," his mother said.

"You know if I were in Louis's position," Jack said, "I would have done the same thing."

"Would you?" his mother said. "What a tyrant I've raised."

"Wait a minute," Harry said. "There was another factor. There was this rival minister, Colbert, who insinuated himself into the king's confidence. It was Colbert apparently who convinced the young king that Fouquet was dangerous. In some versions of the story, Colbert is perceived as the villain. But who knows what goes on behind closed doors?"

"Hey, not me," said Jack.

His mother, who walked between them, said teasingly, "It's lucky that poor Colbert was around to take the blame."

"You're giving your sympathy to the wrong man," said Harry.

"If I am, I am," she said.

Jack was glad to see that there was actually a restaurant on the grounds. "Am I the only one who's hungry?" he asked.

"Yes," his mother said. (Harry, standing behind her, shook his head in denial.) "We'll eat after we see the chateau. Besides, it's too early for lunch, isn't it?"

"Some of us think it's never too early for lunch," Harry said, glancing at him as if they were in some kind of conspiracy against his mother.

Nevertheless, they walked toward the chateau as if there were no other choice possible. Harry went through the motions of resisting his mother's willfulness, but it was his MO to let Lily get her way. His mother, who was otherwise not a bad person and reputed to be beautiful, would drive you crazy if you didn't do what she wanted.

The tour started in an enormous square space, larger than their entire Paris apartment, with mirrored doors, called The Entrance Hall. Lily effused a sigh of admiration, as soon as they stepped into the room. Jack looked away out of embarrassment.

•

Jack imagined his mother catching her reflection in one of the mirrored doors and feeling confirmed in her sense of herself, while also being just a slight bit disappointed. In the same glance, she caught Harry's burly reflection ambling by into history. When Jack appeared momentarily, she was struck by his strong resemblance to his father, which pleased and disturbed in equal parts. These were inadvertent thoughts, for which she felt no enduring responsibility.

Harry was regaling Jack with some story (perhaps one of his foreign correspondent anecdotes) she couldn't quite overhear. Jack had a fixed smile on his face, seemed spectacularly not amused.

Lily wanted to see everything. She enjoyed imagining herself living in other people's houses with other people's things. Elegance on this scale was pleasurable to visit but could be oppressive, she suspected, if you had to live up to it all year around. Browsing through the family portraits, she found herself confronted by a painting the size of a photograph of the enigmatic Nicolas Fouquet himself. It was an arrogant face; she disliked him on sight. She called the others over to show them the portrait.

"Would you buy a used car from this man?" she asked Harry.

"They all look kind of self-important in their portraits," said Harry.

"He looks kind of sly to me," Jack said.

"That's what I think too," she said. "It's not a face that I would want to trust."

"For God's sake," Harry said, "give me a break."

"I'm going to walk ahead," Jack said. "I hope that doesn't offend anybody."

"Goodbye," she said, waving him on, missing him the moment he was out of the room. Feeling the need to do something, she slipped over to Harry and put her arm around his waist.

"I just had this funny idea," Harry said. "What if Louis, who was used to getting whatever woman he set his sights on, had coveted Fouquet's wife."

"That's very funny," she said, and giggled. "I don't know why I think it's so funny. What made you say that?"

"I'm like the government," Harry said. "I create nasty rumors to divert you from the real issues."

"I don't really know what that means," she said. "Harry, I want this to be fun, okay? Don't try so hard with Jack."

He seemed annoyed by her remark, and moved ahead into the next room. Lily followed him, but not right away.

There was a loud German couple with two small children ahead of her so she hurried through the second room, which was of small interest anyway, into the Great Gallery. Harry's back awaited her.

"Have you seen Jack anywhere?" she asked him.

•

Fouquet was on the grounds with the landscape architect, Le Notre, overseeing the construction of an artificial lake when one of the servants came out with a note from his wife.

The servant did an exceptionally adroit tumble in the grass before giving him the message. "I tumble for you," the note said.

•

Looking out the window of Fouquet's Bed Chamber, Harry didn't notice Lily come up behind him. "Don't you just love it here?" she whispered to him. Jack knew the voice so well he could mimic it in his head

"I know what you mean," Harry said.

"What do I mean?" she quizzed him. "Sometimes, sweetheart, you seem to say things just to be agreeable." She gave him an ambiguous poke with her elbow.

The over-stylized gardens reminded Harry of a French film he'd seen a long time ago, whose forgotten title might come to mind eventually. "You mean," Harry said, choosing his words carefully, "that this strange place has a kind of comforting familiarity."

"Oh you're so smart," she said, and kissed him. When he reached for her, she squeezed his hand and then seemed to dance out of his reach.

It was in Madame Fouquet's closet where they caught up with Jack.

"I've seen everything already including the banquet menu," he said. "I'm on my return trip."

"I'm impressed," she said, admiring him as if he were one of the artifacts on display, "but you might get more out of it if you didn't rush through. This is a part of your tradition."

That was a veiled reference to his disappeared father being French. It amused Jack that Harry, whose business was none of it, jumped in to defend him. "That's not fair, Lily" he said. "Jack takes in whatever interests him,"

"If I'm wrong, I'm wrong," Lily said.

"Mother, you're wrong a lot more than you know," Jack said.

•

Madame Fouquet had a premonition. "Nicolas, we were in the garden," she said, "and a snake not common to these parts, came out of a tree and wound itself around your throat. It took away your power of speech. I pleaded with it to let you go, but it ignored me and dragged you into the woods. Although I followed the snake, I couldn't find you again once the snake had taken you from me."

•

Lily was studying the ceiling mural in the Room of the Muses. "This is what I think," she said. "I think the king came to Fouquet's banquet to test his host's loyalty, and Fouquet failed the test. Whatever the former Minister of the Treasury thought he was about, the ostentatious display of his wealth, some of which was probably stolen, revealed him as an arrogant man who felt himself superior to the king. The loyal Colbert, much maligned by present company, confirmed Louis in his perceptions. By taking Fouquet down, Louis sent the message that the king in name only was now the king in fact." She rested her case by taking Harry's hand.

"I like it," said Harry, "up to a point."

"I couldn't disagree more," said Jack.

•

"What can you possibly disagree with?" his mother asked him. They were waiting, he and Harry, for his mother to finish studying the intricate mural of the nine muses, which covered the entire ceiling of the Room of the Muses. "I didn't say anything controversial."

Jack, thinking of himself as a poker player who had not yet looked at his cards, smiled cryptically.

"Well, Jack," Lily said, "if you have something to tell us, we're all ears."

Jack had been secretly hoping that Harry would take his turn ahead of him. "When I'm ready," he said.

"Oh you're a difficult child," she said, her hand on her hip. "So when are you going to favor us?"

"After lunch," he said, "or possibly during lunch."

"He's telling us," Harry said, looking at his watch, "that his muse needs to be fed."

As they walked to the restaurant, Jack wondered why his mother didn't ask Harry for his version of the Vaux-le-Vicomte mystery. He could tell that Harry, who had this phony self-assured manner, was just dying to be asked. Perhaps, after all, his mother wasn't interested in Harry's story. It didn't do to overstate the perception, but he sensed that, of the two of them, his mother mostly preferred him.

•

For the first five years of his imprisonment, Fouquet's wife wrote to him at length every day without exception. "I am with you," she wrote. "We will be together no matter what."

When she missed a day in the sixth year, Fouquet was pained by the sudden absence of her voice. "She forgets me," he told himself. "I know now what it means to be alone. I am isolated forever."

•

When they got to the restaurant, which was housed in a remodeled 17th century barn, Lily had lost her appetite. She settled for a bottle of Evian and an orange.

Both Harry and Jack ordered the steak/frites lunch from the 68 franc prix fix menu. While Lily was chatting with Jack, Harry, who seemed increasingly irrelevant, inserted himself into the conversation. "Don't you have something to tell us?" he asked Jack, pieces of the ropy steak he was chewing making an unscheduled appearance between his teeth.

Jack hung a french fry from the corner of his mouth like a cigarette to steady his nerves. "Louis was just this kid, this fat over-indulged kid," he said, "which is the way Fouquet thought of him, a king only because of accident of birth. After Louis's father dies—the kid is like, what, five—he has a long wait before he is old enough to take over. Still, he knows he's the king and he grows up studying for the role, waiting his chance. He gets it finally, okay? when the sleazy cardinal, who's been running France, dies. To assume power, he's got to show the other dudes out there that he has no fear. So he takes on his most powerful rival, the self-important clown, Fouquet. By imprisoning the guy who has tried to show him up, Louis gets rid of the major threat to his authority and shows anyone who has his eyes open that this king is not to be messed with. Not a bad move for a kid."

"That could be a winner," Harry said.

Lily rolled her eyes. "I'd be eternally grateful if one of you smart guys would tell me how Jack's version is different from mine."

•

"I am the State and the State is me," Louis said, standing before a mirror. Colbert hung back in the shadows, mouthing the words with his lips mostly closed like a ventriloquist.

•

Harry's turn came when they were walking the center path of the grounds under the hot sun. You could tell from his hunched shoulders that the foreign correspondent knew that he had fallen out of favor. Lily, who was in one of her moods, was ignoring him. Unless he did something brilliant to reestablish his credibility, the game was lost. Harry was history.

"First of all, I think Nicolas Fouquet was one of the good guys," Harry said as they walked between two rows of giant hedges. (Were they listening? He intentionally kept his voice low to bring the others toward him.) "He had made some compromises in his life that he was not altogether proud of, but he was not corrupt. There's an important difference between corruption and compromise. Cardinal Mazarin was corrupt; Fouquet was ambitious. To survive, our guy was obliged to look the other way while Mazarin picked the country's pocket."

Lily interrupted. "I don't understand what you're saying, sweetheart. If an American politician did what Fouquet did, you'd certainly call him corrupt. Wouldn't you?"

"Not the same thing," said Harry.

"How come?" asked Jack. "I mean, the way you describe it, he sounds corrupt."

Harry, who had stopped smoking, who had not smoked in two months, lit the cigarette he carried with him as a demonstration of his willpower. "You have to take context into consideration," he said. "Mazarin was an absolute ruler. Fouquet had been appointed by him and was his second in command. To confront Mazarin would have been virtual suicide. Anyway, when Mazarin died, Fouquet had more actual power in France than the king. It followed that the king would eventually perceive our guy as a rival. Colbert, who was a lesser minister under Mazarin, manipulated the king's competitive feelings toward Fouquet. So Louis, who was already prejudiced against our guy—perhaps they were too much alike in their preoccupation with things beautiful—took Fouquet's gesture of loyalty the wrong way. My guess is, Louis had made up his mind to eliminate Fouquet even before he attended the banquet. He was abetted in this decision by the devious Colbert, that nasty piece of work, who had been urging this dishonorable course of action from the start. The rest, as they say, is history."

Lily clapped her hands in mock applause.

"I think Harry's is the hottest," Jack said. "How much further do we have to walk?"

"My two men," Lily said, apropos of nothing. "Jack, don't you think the gardens are very beautiful?"

"I guess so," Jack said. "The thing is, I'm not really into beautiful gardens."

Lily laughed, while Harry, his poise in disarray, tucked in his shirt.

•

He knew how it would be done, had imagined it from the first days of his imprisonment. There would be two of them, the jailer and an accomplice—someone Fouquet knew and was disposed to trust. They would be friendly, share food and drink with him, offer the latest gossip. When he was off his guard, lulled into a false sense of security, one of them would slip behind him and pin his arms while the other stabbed him in the heart or strangled him with his thumbs. That he had survived 19 years in prison was an indication only of the king's cruel patience. One day, when he was least expecting it, they would murder him. Perhaps it would happen while he slept. His last dream would be his last moment of realization. He would hardly know it was happening.

•

They were on the road again, making their way back to Paris. Harry was driving, Jack plugged into his walkman in the seat next to him. His mother, for unadvertised reasons, had chosen again to be in back. Even with the windows open, it was hot in the car. An extended silence predominated.

"How are you doing back there?" Harry asked.

"I'm okay," she said. "I have a slight headache. I know the two of you don't like going on these trips. It would be easier for me if you did."

"Hey, I had a good time," Harry said.

"You're a good sport, I'll say that," she said. "I mean, you go along with things, Harry, but that's not the same thing as enjoying them. Or do you think it is?"

Jack removed his headphones to pick up on the fight he hadn't anticipated but felt responsible for setting in motion.

Harry's body language suggested discomfort. Jack sensed that the least useful thing he could do for Harry was defend him. "Mom, why don't you get off his case," he said.

"I wasn't on your case, Harry, was I?" she asked.

Harry didn't answer.

"It feels to me as if the two of you are on my case," she said. "All I said was that I thought that Harry had been a good sport." She reached over and squeezed his arm. "Thanks for taking us on this trip you really didn't want to do. ...are you sulking?"

"Let him be," Jack said.

"I don't understand what's going on," his mother said. "Why are the two of you angry at me? I thought we had a very nice time today. Did the two of you enjoy yourselves at all?"

"We had a very nice time," Jack said.

"Is that true, Harry?" she asked. "Did you have a nice time, sweetheart?"

"Uh, huh," Harry said. "I had a sweetheart of a time."

"To tell the truth, I don't believe you," she said, "but it doesn't matter."

"Why the hell don't you believe me?" Harry said. "Why the hell would I lie about something like that?"

"I'm not going to get into this," she said. "It's true, Harry that you say things you don't mean so that people will like you. You go out of your way not to offend. You know that's true."

"Why is it we only fight when Jack's with us?" Harry said. As he increased the speed of the car, it was as if a wind were blowing the rolling French countryside away from them.

"This isn't a fight," she said. "I'm feeling very fond of both of you at the moment."

Jack had his headphones on and was grinning to himself.

•

The new jailer, a burly man with ruddy cheeks, a man more cultivated than his predecessor, brought him an extra beer with his lunch. They talked about the theater. Too much spectacle, not enough heart, said the jailer. All anyone's concerned with is being in the moment. A distant alarm sounded in Fouquet's head.

That night, Fouquet had a feverish dream (had the beer been poisoned?) in which Colbert, on his own authority, ordered his death—the killers in silhouette, impossible to identify. When he woke there were two men, dressed in black, sitting across from him on a bench. They were playing cards.

•

He followed Lily into the kitchen and said his piece. "If you don't love Harry, why do you stay with him?" This was a memory. Or something. They were still in their rental car, a Renault Encore, making their way back to Paris. Lily was preparing dinner, Harry away somewhere on an assignment. They were in the car, Harry driving in silence, Jack in the seat next to him, listening to a Talking Heads tape, his eyes closed.

"Of course I love Harry," she said with some vehemence. "I don't know where you get the idea that I don't. I'm extremely fond of Harry."

Jack made an incredulous face. "Come on, mom," he said. "You treat the guy as if he came to read the gas meter and overstayed his welcome."

She giggled. "I do not," she said.

"Okay, I'm wrong," he said.

"I get irritated with him sometimes—I don't like it when he denies his feelings—but I don't not love him. Of course, it will never be the way it was with your father."

"Okay," he said. "What do I know about it? I'm just a kid." He turned his back on her but didn't leave.

They were stuck in traffic, a single line of cars barely moving, the sun behind dark clouds.

"You may be precocious," Lily said, "but there are a lot of things you don't understand about adults." She was slicing tomatoes and she cut her finger. When she let out a cry, Jack spun around in surprise. She was holding the finger over the sink, the blood dripping on the white porcelain in small dots like some kind of coded message.

"I'll get a band aid," he said.

"They're on my list of things we need," Lily said. She put her finger in her mouth and sucked on it. She was both smiling and crying.

The blood seemed to speckle her lips, reminding him of a figure in a vampire movie that had scared him when he was younger. Rising from her perch, Lily seemed to float into the sink as if an unexpected breeze had moved her. Jack rushed over and helped her into one of the two kitchen chairs. "I wasn't going to faint," she said.

They were driving through a small French village that seemed untouched by the last hundred years—his mother had her hand on Harry's shoulder.

"Don't move," he said. Jack went into his room and returned with two strips of cloth from an old tee shirt, with which he bandaged Lily's finger.

"You take good care of your mother," Lily said, her other hand caressing his face. She started to say something else but stopped herself. "You go set the table, Jack. I'll finish fixing dinner."

•

Fouquet insisted on knowing what these men in black were doing in his cell, playing cards. The bigger one, who was the new jailer, said never mind, they were there to tend to him in his illness.

"What illness?" Fouquet asked.

"I'm not actually a surgeon," the jailer said, "so it wouldn't help for me to give you an answer."

•

"I cut my finger," she said to Harry, who had returned from wherever he had been. "Jack bandaged it for me."

Harry held her bandaged hand in his two hands as if he were holding a bird with a broken wing. "You have the most graceful hands," he said.

She put her other arm around Harry's waist, kissed his ear and whispered something unintelligible to him.

Jack watched them from his place on the couch in the combination living/dining room. "Are we eating soon?" he asked and got no answer. "If not, I'm going to my room to listen to my music." He stood up, expecting his mother or Harry to tell him that dinner was imminent, but they were involved in their own murmuring chat to his total exclusion. One minute he was a presence in their lives and in the next he was no one. He took refuge in his room with the door closed, and turned on the stereo, raising the volume by degrees so that the room became his headphones and the music shut out everything but his secret presence inside it. The two men in black approached Fouquet—the smaller one was carrying what looked like a dirk, the jailer held a thick cloth in his arms. They had reached the outskirts of Paris. In five days he would be fourteen—it was time to become his own person, get out from under his mother's skirts. He raised the volume on his walkman—his mother was pecking Harry on the cheek. It's just a dream, my friend, the jailer said. Fouquet refused to close his eyes. Inside the blast of the stereo, which seemed to shake the walls, was a shimmering silence that enveloped him. Inside that private place, he was the one in charge. The cloth pressed itself over his mouth and nose, something foreign lodged itself in his chest. Patience, Harry said to himself, as he was about to curse a driver who had forced his way in front of him. He could feel his life slip like a magician's trick through the narrow opening in his chest. I'm dead, he thought to himself, remembered thinking. None of it mattered. The adult game around him had no enduring consequence. The future, if there was going to be any, belonged to him.

The Psychopathology of Everyday Life

As my marriage deteriorated, I became increasingly distracted with my patients, drifting into fantasy, confusing details and names, falling into private obsession. I found myself identifying with the mistreated lovers of certain women patients. One, in particular.

There was an untherapeutic harshness in my voice as I pointed out to Melinda Goldhart that her behavior toward the boyfriend she complained endlessly about was provocative and self-fulfilling. Don't you see, I threw at her like stones, the man behaves badly because you want him to behave badly.

She shook loose a tear. I was supposed to feel sorry for mistreating her. Instead I felt annoyance, wanted to shake some real tears out of that calculating soul. I was also aware—dimly—that these feelings were inappropriate, that I was behaving unprofessionally, that I was out of control.

Why do I go on like this?

This is not a confession but an investigation into feeling. I am imperfect.

Melinda's parents had refused all authority, had pretended to Melinda that she could do anything she liked. They had offered her a world without boundaries, a dazzling chaos. Every step was a step off a precipice into space. The simplest act for Melinda engendered paralyzing anxieties.

When Melinda first went into treatment with me she

rarely talked during the therapy session. She withheld speech willfully, talked to me in her head, as she later reported, but could barely articulate a complex sentence in my presence. She was afraid of exposing her secrets, she said. We tried different arrangements to make her feel less vulnerable. For awhile we sat with the backs of our chairs together. She worried when she couldn't see me that I had gone away, or was reading a book, or had gone to sleep.

What are you doing now? she would ask from time to time.

Why don't you turn around and see for yourself? I said.

She sometimes turned, sometimes didn't.

The same or almost the same conversation repeated like an echo. The repetition seemed to comfort Melinda like the routine of a game. I know it lulled me into a sense of false comfort. The routines we established between us broke down the feelings of strangeness, created a bond of familiarity.

We moved our chairs into a whole range of configurations. That too was part of the game. We could do or say anything in my office, I wanted her to see, without any real danger.

If I was Melinda's parent in the sense that she imagined me as a parent, I was also much of the time a fellow child with her.

When Melinda began to talk in our sessions she talked nonstop, the words coming out in barrages like machine gun fire. She alternated between silence and prattle, the talk a disguised form of silence.

She sometimes talked to me as if she were talking out loud to herself.

In most of her relationships, Melinda felt herself to be the victim, though in fact she tended to be the controlling one. She rarely allowed herself, despite her pretense that it was otherwise, to be not in control. A way to control situations, while at the same time not feeling responsible for her life, was to make herself appear to be a victim.

A victim needs a victimizer to complete the circle.

Melinda had been dating the same man for five years—she was twenty-three when she came to me—a man she complained about whenever his name came up in the conversation. He was insensitive to her feelings. She was repelled by much of his behavior and—this a recurrent obsession—his odor. The repulsion was uncharacteristic. Melinda was not ordinarily squeamish and was subject to few sexual taboos.

Why did she continue to see him if he repelled her?

She tended to ignore questions in areas of confusion or ambivalence, would take recourse in silence. It embarrassed her to admit there was any question she couldn't answer.

On the evidence it appeared that she continued to see the man in order to complain of his failings. He was her occasion for grievance.

Sometimes she would say no more than a dozen words in an entire fifty-minute session.

I didn't urge her to speak, not at first, not directly. I knew from our first session that to ask something directly of Melinda was to be denied. Why did I know that?

I want to be part of your life, she told me on one occasion. I want you to think of me when I'm not here.

Sometimes I do, I said. I think of all my patients.

She mumbled something.

What? ... What?

It's cold in here, Yuri. Would you turn of the air-conditioning please. I'd appreciate it if you would consider my comfort once in a while.

You sound as if you're talking to a servant, I said.

I don't think you like me, she said. She had a sly smile on her face.

If you don't think I like you, why are you smiling.

Melinda pushed the corners of her lips down with her fingers. Am I ugly? she asked with a slight stammer.

You haven't told me why you were smiling, I said.

I wasn't, she said, covering her mouth with her hand. When she took her hand away her tongue shot out at me. Are you angry, Yuri? I don't want you to be angry with me. She raised her eyes which had been averted.

You're a tease, Melinda, I said. That makes people angry.

Fuck you, she said, shouted it at me.

Her outburst, because it seemed so uncharacter-istic—she had always been exceedingly polite in our sessions—shocked me. My first impulse was to order her out of my office. I wanted to punish her for of-fending me. Fuck you, I said in return.

Her face broke. I won't be talked to that way, she said. You have no right to say that to me.

You handled that very well, Melinda, I said.

She smiled joyously through her tears, wiped her cheeks with the back of her hand like a child. Oh thank you, she said.

We moved in these sessions between war and se-duction, different faces of the same aggression.

Her accounts of experiences with the man she re-ferred to as her boyfriend were unvaryingly unpleasant. It worried me that I was encouraging her to disparage him, that I had a personal stake in her negative feelings toward other men.

•

I mention my difficulties with Melinda to Adrienne who says, under her breath, that my misunderstanding of the girl is symptomatic.

I ask her to explain this unflattering description but she is in another room, her attention focused elsewhere. When I persist she says, What do you really want?

Human contact, I say.

Adrienne laughs without amusement, laughs wryly, laughs with some measure of disdain.

Melinda protested again and again that I didn't like her, that it was only because I wanted her money that I continued to see her.

I tried different responses, admitted on one occasion that I sometimes found her unbearable. My remark brought a smile to her face, a look of triumph.

She denied that she was smiling.

We were facing each other that day at my insistence. The denied smile persisted brazenly.

Did I say that Melinda was seductive? Have I mentioned it anywhere?

I wish I had a mirror so that I could show you your face, I said. Even as you deny it, you continue to smile.

You too, she said, her smile opening like a blossom.

I traced my lips with an imaginary finger. It was possible that our unacknowledged smiles mirrored one another.

I felt the strongest impulse to say something hurtful to her. My feelings must have expressed themselves in my face because she blanched, seemed almost to tremble.

I have this feeling, she said, that this is the beginning of the end of our relationship.

I was trembling, though I didn't know why, did and didn't. I was conscious of wanting to assure her that I had no intention of dropping her as a patient and conscious of withholding such assurance out of anger.

She turned her chair halfway around. You want to be rid of me, she said.

I'm your therapist not your lover, I said.

I had a dream about Melinda, a seemingly literal dream, not all of which I remembered. I wrote it down as soon as I awoke in a notebook I used to keep at bedside for just that purpose.

There is, I discover only one chair in my office. The

other chair, the patient's chair, is at some shop being reupholstered. Why hasn't it been returned? Melinda comes in conspicuously late and asks indignantly where she is supposed to sit.

I offer her my seat. She remarks that I am still in it.

It surprises me to discover that what she says is true. I am sitting in the very seat I offer her. It is wide enough for two, I say. At this moment I can't be sure whether the ostensible patient is Melinda or Adrienne. She shakes her head coyly. I beckon to her with a finger. We are both standing. The chair is between us. It is not my office any longer but a bedroom, a room I had as a child. I point out the view from the window. The overgrown garden, the porcelain cupids, the huge cherry tree just coming into blossom.

She says she admires the tree, though she is unable to believe that it actually produces cherries. Why would it want to? Her breasts press against my back as she makes this pronouncement.

She says the nipples of her breasts are real cherry buds.

I am leaning out the window trying to find a bud on the cherry tree to prove the tree's identity. There are no buds, only faded blossoms.

I bring in a handful of crushed petals. These are cherry blossoms, I say. Melinda giggles, says not really.

Just take my word for it, I say. This is a cherry tree. It produces sour cherries. I take a bud from the tree and hold it out to her.

She puts my fingers to her lips, says poor man. I notice that there is a red stain on the back of my hand.

I've always wanted to taste your blood, she says.

You're a liar, I rage. That's your blood. That's female blood.

Today was the first time Melinda talked about her boyfriend, Phillip, by name.

She valued Phillip most when he ceased to be available. It was the pattern of their relationship. Melinda would mistreat Phillip, would reject and torment him until, provoked beyond endurance, he would stop seeing her. At that point she would decide that she was in love with him and plot obsessively to get him back.

When Phillip would return to her, as he did, she would feel contempt for him again as if such yielding were a failure of character. Any man foolish enough to love her was unworthy of her love.

I pointed this out to her, but for the longest time she refused to acknowledge it.

I tended to respond to Melinda's complaints about Phillip as if they were complaints about me.

As an aspect of this identification, I found myself intensely attracted to her. Was this counter-transference or something else?

•

Melinda told me of a dream in which I appeared in the guise of a teddy bear named Swoosh whom she held in her arms while she slept. That's all she offered of the dream.

I said the best way to remember dreams was to write them down as soon as you woke.

She pouted, said that most of her dreams were crazy and that it embarrassed her to think about them. The first three buttons of her gauzy blouse were open and I could see the lacy top of her pink undershirt. My impulse was to look away, but I didn't. I was almost certain that she wasn't wearing a bra.

I don't have to tell you my dreams if I don't want to, she said. I have a right to privacy. Do you tell everything? I don't know anything about you, do I? She turned her chair halfway around to offer me a view of only half her face.

Her gesture enraged me out of all proportion. I'm

not going to let you do that, I said, getting to my feet.

Don't you dare touch me, she said.

When I took a step toward her she gasped as if in fright and shifted her chair part of the way back toward its original position.

Put your chair back the way it was or I'm going to discontinue the session, I said.

She grudgingly moved her chair back into position, sulked.

I returned to my seat with an assumption of dignity, felt relieved that she hadn't tested me further.

Though I don't like it, Yuri, she said, it's good for me to be treated that way.

How do you feel I treated you?

Your face is flushed, she said. Are you blushing?

I repeated my question, had to repeat it several times to get a response.

I don't understand what you're asking, she said, not quite repressing a smirk.

Tell me what's so funny.

I can't, she whispered, lowering her eyes. I'll tell you when I know you better.

Our sessions had the quality on occasion of lovers' quarrels.

When I finally went to see Leo Pizzicatti after several months of procrastination I was in a state of intractable depression.

I sat down, somewhat disoriented, thinking myself in the wrong seat.

Adrienne won't sleep with me, was the first thing I said, which was interesting because it was not what I planned to say.

Leo seemed pained on my account, profoundly sad, which I immediately recognized as a projection.

I have the sense that I am making this up, recreating a scene out of a mix of memory and imagination. The ugly paintings on the wall, the tacky plastic furniture, the refusal to lay claim to style. There are a few inconsequential changes in his office (or maybe it's just a lapse of memory) but in matters that count nothing has changed.

I talk about Adrienne despite my intention to avoid that subject, get lost in a maze of evasion.

I came to talk to you about a counter-transference problem I'm having with a woman patient, I say with about ten minutes left in the session.

Are you fucking this patient? he asks.

I laugh nervously at this abrupt perception, feel exposed and defensive. I'm not fucking anyone, I say.

Are you feeling sorry for yourself?

I am close to tears, though unaware of feeling sad. She wants me to fuck her, I say.

And you can't turn her down? he asks. Does she have a name, this patient? Yuri, you look as if you want to cry.

I deny it, but the tears come in the wake of my denial. I refuse to cry, cover my face with my left hand, feel the tears prick my fingers. Just a minute, I hear myself say.

I've never fully worked through the feeling that it is unmanly to cry so I suffer embarrassment at breaking down. I remove my hand as if to say it's really nothing, a momentary aberration, but the crying continues and I am unable to speak.

When the fit is over, when I come back to myself, I begin to talk to Leo about my mother, though I have no new insights into that relationship. What's the point of my telling you this? I ask him.

He removes his pipe, says nothing, puffs coded messages in smoke.

I know the answer of course. My relationship with my mother is a paradigm of my relationship with all women. My mother thinks I'm perfect, I say.

I should say something about that, not so much what I said to Leo which is in a certain context, within a shared realm of assumptions, but say something about my mother, what she's like, how I experience her. Last week I lost her at the Metropolitan Museum of Art, couldn't find her for almost two hours. It is symptomatic. She had ways when I was a child of being there and not there. When she was missing we split up to search for her—Adrienne and Rebecca taking the first floor while I went upstairs. It was as if she had been claimed by some black hole. When she finally made herself available—she just seemed to appear—my mother refused to acknowledge that she had been lost. What I didn't mention to Leo was that while I was searching for her, I had the urge to take off and leave her to her disappearance. I felt—how should I put it—burdened by the oppressive presence of her absence.

Two facts. My mother lost in the tombs of the Metropolitan Museum, Melinda sitting with her back to me.

Sometimes in bed in the morning, Adrienne would see something in my face and say, What?

I am wary these days with Melinda, take a distant and paternal tone in our sessions. She comments on my apparent disaffection, says it hurts her that I no longer care for her.

Her left breast is slightly higher than the right, I notice. The disparity touches me, takes my breath away.

Her new phase is less confrontational. She seems to court my sympathy, wants me to be pleased by the progress she is making.

Am I getting ahead of myself? I have fallen into disorder, have lost the thread of events.

It is another time. The question comes up at an unexpected moment. Do you find me attractive? she asks, looking sagely skeptical, aware of performance.

What did I tell you the last time you asked? I say.

I can't trust your answer, she says, looking up shyly under hooded eyes. How could you say no? I mean, you're trying to build up my sense of self-worth.

It's not what she says (do I even remember it as precisely as I pretend?), but the unspoken context we share.

I ask her if there's some way I can prove to her that I find her attractive.

The question enlists a sly smile and a delayed shrug. There are six minutes left in our fifty-minute hour. I know that the next time we meet, which is two days from now, we will fuck. I have made an oblique offer and she has given oblique acceptance.

Reading over what I have written, I can see how melodramatic, even pathological this all sounds. I knew what I was about to do was unethical and at the same time I felt driven to do it. I felt the need to bust loose from all the invisible restraints I had placed on myself, to take what I had previously considered unacceptable risks. And maybe, said arrogance in its nasty whisper, it would do us both some good.

I was resolved that it would happen once and once only, a demonstration of my attraction to her, and then we would use it as an area of exploration in her therapy. I have a predilection for being defensive so I will stop myself here to say that whatever the extenuating circumstances—I am imperfect, I am human—I am fully responsible for what happened with Melinda.

Outside of my professional commitments, I am a man of obsessive urges, sudden fixations, deep pockets of need. I have never learned to put off having the things I want. My toleration for frustration is small. I sometimes, out of the blue, ache with undefined longing. Unaccountable things fill me with desire.

I barely slept the night before, was in a revved-up state the next morning. Rebecca took note of it, said, Daddy's in a silly mood.

Adrienne made an acerbic remark, disguised as good-natured teasing. You used to be funnier, she said, withdrawing herself, fading out of the picture.

Having decided on a course of action, I gave my attention to logistics, the where and how of the matter. The idea of making love to her in my office, on the couch or on the rug, gave me pause. Yet I couldn't very well take her to a hotel without trashing the therapeutic situation altogether.

And then just before she was scheduled to arrive, I had a change of heart, decided not to pursue the matter further.

When she didn't show up on time—she was not usually late—I assumed she wasn't coming, assumed further that she had decided to break off treatment with me. I felt rueful.

I am not very observant as to what women wear—it is the effect rather than the details that catch my attention—but I was aware that Melinda, when she made her belated entrance, was wearing a red dress with black velvet trim. She didn't sit down, stood alongside her chair as if keeping it company. My sense of her was that she was glowing, that she was absolutely radiant.

I disguised my anxiety in exquisite self-possession. Her reality testing may have been weak in other circumstances, but Melinda understood my intentions in the full flower of their confusion.

There is no point going on with this, recounting how we got from here to there.

We used the seldom-used analytic couch for our transaction—I was glad to find some service for it—then spent what remained of the hour talking about what it was like.

It was like: good for me. Like that.

I remember her saying this much: I feel, you know, that I've corrupted you.

With the putting on of my pants, I moved back into the role of therapist. What makes you think you're so powerful, I said.

I can get any man I want, she said, blushing. I got

you, didn't I?

Is that how it feels to you?

I feel used, she said. I feel that you've taken advantage of me. I feel that you don't really like me. Not really like me. I feel that you shouldn't have done what you did. I feel that I've ruined everything. I'll never get well after this. Her eyes filled with tears.

I maintained an appropriate distance, performed my role as it suited me to perceive it.

The next three sessions followed a similar pattern. Melinda would arrive late, offer a perfunctory greeting, then lie down on the couch with her skirt above her knees. Although it had been my conscious intent not to continue the physical relationship, I had no heart to deny either of us its melodrama. The sex was perfunctory, took place, we pretended, for the sake of the discussion in its wake.

What feelings did it excite? For me, it excited a sense of shame, a moderate, not unbearable sense of shame. For Melinda: I no longer thought of Melinda's feelings as apart from mine. I was collaborating with Melinda's fantasy, proving to her that she was capable of winning her therapist's (ergo father's) love. Can that be right? I am something of a literalist. I was not, despite the evidence of my behavior, lost to blind urge.

If I didn't stop the sexual contact, it is because I don't want to stop, was getting something from it that outweighed its disadvantages. It gave me a sense perhaps of power and accomplishment. Is that it? I'll have to revisit my notes.

I have the revived illusion that if I can say the right thing to Adrienne, she can't help but love me again or recognize that she hadn't stopped loving me. The words don't come, refuse to announce themselves, though the illusion itself sustains me.

I feel surges of passion for Melinda when she isn't there, particularly when she isn't there, my need for her complicated by her actual presence.

Melinda misses her appointment, leaves a garbled message with my answering service about some prior commitment. I feel vaguely needy for the rest of the day, lack energy, doze during one of my sessions at the hospital. My inattention seems to go unnoticed. The patient is a lingerie fetishist. I could put a mannequin in the room with him and he would go on with his obsessive story.

Henry told me that when he had an affair with a patient he felt so guilty he expected to be pulled out of his bed at night—he once actually heard footsteps—and be carted off to jail.

I have a dream the next night of dying, wake in a state of grinding anxiety, barely able to breathe. I haven't felt this vulnerable since the early days of analysis—my first analysis. (First analysis=First love.)

Melinda comes in, coughing, huddled over, removes her scarf and coat and, without acknowledgment of me, begins to talk about an experience with her boyfriend, Phillip. No reference is made to what's gone on the past three—three or four—sessions with us. It's as if I'm hardly in the room with her, as if she's talking in a dream.

I listen to her in an analytic way, try to pick up the real issue of the monologue. She is putting me in an intricate double bind. If I admit to feeling jealous, I lack the appropriate distance to deal with her problems, disqualify myself as her therapist. If I am not jealous, it indicates that I don't care for her sufficiently. My impulse is to pull down my pants and take her on the floor while she babbles on about Phillip's fear of making commitments.

Why are you telling me this? I ask.

She blinks her eyes with mock innocence. What do

you mean, Yuri? I don't understand what you're asking.

You know very well what I'm asking, I say. Something is going on with us that you're conspicuously avoiding.

She pouts childishly, flutters her hands. Are you saying that all I can talk about here is you?

Melinda, why did you miss our last session?

I was sick, she says. You'll say it's hysterical, I know, but the fact is I had a splitting headache. I almost didn't come today. I had to drag myself here. I just don't know what I'm doing here. I have no idea.

Why did you come today?

She shrugs, starts to say something and doesn't. Because I'm in love with you, she whispers.

Leo has no answers for me, refuses to give advice, though I can tell from his face that he is worried about me. I can tell from the sorrowful pinch at the corner of his eyes that he suspects I am lost. I grieve for the person he sees.

Another therapist couldn't have helped her as much as I had, I say.

His mouth moves into a smile that is gone the moment I perceive it. You see the sex, do you, as part of a therapeutic program?

I no longer believe in therapy, I shout at him. If I had any courage, I'd give it up and do something more honorable.

Yes? What would you do? What is the honorable profession you have in mind for yourself?

If I gave up practicing therapy, I say, I think I'd give up psychology altogether.

If you do, you do, he says, as if my defection from the science of the soul were not a serious issue.

Leo is unimpressed with my threat to give up the faith, and I am disappointed that he has no solace for me, come away from the session unimproved.

He doesn't tell me, as he might, that I am making a serious mistake. It is what I want from him and what he refuses to give me.

(Headline in the *New York Post*)

I was having difficulty sleeping through the night. I would wake periodically and look at Adrienne asleep or pretending to be asleep, turning in her sleep. I would move from back to side, from side to back, hoping to send tremors of my presence to her, to wake her to affection after this long sleep of rejection and denial. When I moved she also moved. When I turned toward her she would turn away as if there was some mechanism between us that had gone awry.

I looked at her sleeping form (her feigned sleep perhaps) and thought of the things I might do to her, was unable to separate the sexual from the violent. Pain short-circuited awareness. The moment I got in touch I was out of touch, lost to feeling, dead to myself. I imagined Adrienne in a fatal car crash, or crushed by the wheels of a train, or snuffed by a sniper's bullet, or falling in slow motion from a high window. I suffered her loss, mourned her death as she slept next to me (or pretended to sleep) blissfully unaware. I was in a fever of madness.

I feel myself in some kind of helpless limbo, some deadly inertia. I talk to myself as though I were a robot. Move your ass, I say. Sit, will you? Stand. Move to the right. Left, huh? Turn now please. Do something. Why aren't you moving? The answer is: I am. From outside and only from an exterior vantage is there the illusion of paralysis.

I go alone to the Virgin Islands for a week, a way of getting myself together, lie impatiently in the sun. I read detective stories and psychology journals, keep a fragmented record of my thoughts and feelings, interior dialogues, the story of my soul. It worries me that for seven days not once do I concern myself with the well-being of my patients. Melinda barely touches my consciousness. I consider at times not returning, going somewhere else, starting over. The truth is, I am homesick.

When I get back, Adrienne and Rebecca embrace me like a returning hero.

I feel a constant buzz of unwanted news in her presence. We talk only to transact the business of the house, act as if the other were a moving shadow, a false image.

Melinda comes for another week, for two weeks, for three, seems eager to please, talks of the improvements in her life. I suggest that she see another therapist and, to my surprise and disappointment, she agrees, without further discussion.

It is the same thing, the same experience, the same silent presence, the same oppressive house, the same feeling of hopelessness. Despite appearances, despite the extent of our dislocation, I am convinced that the deepest ties of feeling between us remain unbroken.

I decided to write down the story of my marriage as a means of investigating its peculiarly contemporary neurotic pattern.

For months after Melinda leaves treatment with me, I feel the pull of her attraction—a tug on the sleeve of feelings from an invisible hand.

I made arrangements for her to see someone else, a therapist I knew only by reputation. She refused my choice.

After that she isn't available when I want her, except on those occasions when she is, Melinda choosing the occasions. And then not at all. My need for her when she is not available is twice (is ten times) what it was when she was there for me.

She tells me in a letter that I was the best therapist she ever had. I am both amused and made anxious by

The Relationship

They talked about it as if it were a separate entity in which they were both circumstantial participants. Why isn't the "relationship" working? they lamented. What can be done to make the "relationship" work? Whose fault is it that the "relationship" has lost its upward mobility? The relationship lived with them like a hypochondriacal out-of-work uncle, too emotionally fragile to leave the house.

Maybe it was more like having a talented child that offered continuous disappointment.

The relationship visited specialists, was offered the best emergency treatment money could buy. And yet it sulked, it listed, it had no grace.

Jake held Joan, who was a perfectionist, responsible for the battered condition of the relationship, though withheld this divisive opinion except when provoked beyond normal endurance.

Joan for her part blamed Jake openly for everything that had gone wrong, though not in her heart, never in her heart. The blaming, as she saw it, was the extending of a hand, the earliest stages of negotiation.

Jake and Joan, between them, had sole proprietorship of the aggrieved relationship in question.

They talked of a trial separation. Such talk was almost always in the air, a form of threat and counter-threat, a line drawn in the sand. One or the other would always back down when push came to shove. Accommodations would be made, short-lived, self-defeating compromises. A trial separation, they each feared, would produce an irreparable crack in the relationship. And that, for both, was the one unacceptable thing.

—We stay together for the sake of the relationship, Joan told her friend Annette. When we're alone in a room together we no longer have anything of interest to say.

Jake, who was a tax lawyer, focused all his energies on improving his position. Joan wrote short fictions and ran a small real estate business out of her kitchen. She could feel her humble ambition growing a little each day, getting larger and more unwieldy, kicking up its heels. It was already, this burgeoning ambition, too big for the two-bedroom apartment she shared with the chronically oblivious Jake.

They talked of moving to a larger place, but while their relationship was so precarious, it seemed unwise. Or so everyone said, anyone who had an opinion on the matter. As if anyone else's opinion mattered.

Joan looked at houses on her own, wanting to find the perfect living situation before bringing Jake into the picture.

With each house she inspected, the question she asked herself was, How would the relationship do in surroundings like this? It was not always easy to know. Above and beyond the increasingly insistent needs of self, a stress-free situation for the relationship and a woodsy backyard were her first priorities.

Finally she found the right house, though it was not at all the one she imagined herself looking for, and she brought Jake along to secure his approval.

Jake acknowledged that the house had considerable charm and that its location couldn't be more favorable. Nevertheless, he saw no reason to rush into something that smacked of permanence. —Don't you think buying a house like this will put a lot of pressure on the relationship? he asked. It could raise unacceptable expectations.

His response neither surprised nor disappointed. Joan laughed off his objections. —We will have greater opportunity for privacy, she said, and that I'm sure will create a more nurturing environment for the relationship.

—Think of making a big move like this, he said, and then discovering that nothing has changed or things have changed for the worse. The one thing the relationship doesn't need is another major disappointment.

—That's just reasons, she said, coveting the house now, wanting it more than she was willing to let on. The stained glass on the second floor had been indemnified in memory, the period details, the wideboard wood floors.

—If it means so much to you, he said, I won't stand in the way.

Not good enough, she thought, but getting there.

The matter went undiscussed for the next three days, secreted itself in the silence. In the meantime, Joan's passion for the house seemed to lose some of its ardor. Wanting something too much could only lead to heartbreak.

Joan had already projected herself into a state of desirelessness when Jake suggested one morning that they take another look at the house.

—Why don't you go without me, she said, the decision made in a flash of disregard.

—Does that mean you've changed your mind about the house? he asked.

—Something like that, she said.

A few days later when Joan inquired about the house she was told that it had gone to contract with a buyer who had seen it once and snapped it up. She suffered the news like intimations of fatal illness.

Another house appeared on the market that seemed possible for them, but it was inferior to the first so she let it pass. Jake, bitter experience had taught her, was an unwavering partisan of keeping things as they were— unless a context of desperation prevailed.

She raised the ante. –I want a separation, she said the next morning over breakfast.

–I'll move out as soon as I can find a place, he said.

–I'd rather be the one to leave, she said. I don't see this as a trial separation. I see this as the real thing.

Jake understood the game they were playing and that it was his role in the present charade to call Joan's bluff.

Her friend Annette offered Joan her apartment while she was away and about two weeks after Joan had announced her need to separate, she packed a small suitcase and left. Jake made no difficulty, though he was not enthralled at Joan going away.

Two days later Jake got a call from a woman he barely knew who was an acquaintance of Joan's in the real estate business. The acquaintance, Madge, said that Joan had been going through bad times, not leaving her bed and having these crying jags. Jake was amazed to hear this news. Joan had seemed so cool and determined when she walked out the door. Jake said he would do what he could to get her to come home, though he was beginning to get used to her absence.

When Jake called and asked Joan how she was doing, she said in this cool voice that she was doing just fine. –You know when you focus on problems really hard, Jake said, solutions you never dreamed of before begin to offer themselves. Could we get together to talk about some new ideas I have about the relationship.

Joan hesitated with her answer, said she didn't see the point really, but if that's what he wanted, if that would make him happy, she would meet him for dinner after work.

A few days later they were back together in the same house, both feeling aggrieved and defeated.

Jake resumed an affair he had been having with a woman in his office, a younger colleague, also married.

Joan had a one-night stand with a client she had been showing houses to for more than six months.

Jake and Joan were nearing the 10th anniversary of their relationship when they came to see me at my offices on the upper east side.

I was not the first marriage counselor they had consulted, nor the second. They each had one failed marriage in their checkered pasts and knew what it was to lose something you once valued above all else.

Jake, who had been a lifelong Democrat, was thinking of voting Republican in the presidential elections. If he couldn't change his personal life, he would settle for changing the drift of the country.

Joan had begun to pocket inconspicuous items from the houses she showed prospective buyers.

Was there anything positive between these people, some vestiges of affection to draw on. Joan said she had stopped loving Jake three years ago to the day. It had just happened. Love had slipped out the back door without even putting on a coat. She had no recollection of what had provoked such disaffection.

Jake, for his part, said he had never stopped loving Joan but that he found it virtually impossible to be faithful to her.

For all that, they had an aggressively active sex life, which was unexpected. They made love two or three times a week on the average. Often, as it turned out, when they were angriest with each other. Their worst fights resolved themselves in sexual abandon. This was one of the few issues in which their stories corresponded.

Angry sex is not the best kind of sex, I told them, though even the wrong kind of contact is a hopeful sign. Where there's passion there's life.

Joan talked about her crying jags. —I get these feelings of being absolutely alone in the world and I feel desolated, she said. I feel inconsolable.

They talked about themselves and about the relationship but never about the other. Jake tended to say very little, was opposed, he said, to indulgent self-revelation.

I met with them Tuesday mornings at 9:15 for a period of approximately three years. Though things at that point were not significantly improved (I sensed a slight turn for the better somewhere on the horizon), they discontinued the mediation process. Joan notified me by phone the day before a scheduled appointment that they were both agreed that it was time to try something else.

A year later I ran into Joan in a restaurant having dinner with another man. I was prepared to pretend I hadn't seen her but she waved at me and I acknowledged her by waving back. She looked more than usually haggard, her spectacular blond hair piled on her head in a tight bun.

—Who's that? my wife asked me.

Before I could answer, Joan was standing alongside our table telling me about the changes in her life. She was with another man now, as I could see, but she and Jake had become better friends after their break-up than during the difficult years of their marriage. —Our relationship has never been more satisfying, she said.

—How so? I asked.

—It's no longer under all this pressure we put on it to work, she said. Jake and I always more or less liked each other. The relationship just couldn't function under the pressure it must have felt to succeed.

—What's Jake up to? I asked.

—Same old, same old, she said.

Two days after this chance meeting, Jake called me at my office. —What did Joan tell you about me? he asked.

—Only that you and she had become better friends, I said.

—Did she say that? he said. I sensed some belligerence in his tone.

—Is your assessment different? I asked.

—What would you say, he said, if I told you I hadn't talked to Joan in five months.

—I would say that your respective versions of the situation are disparate in the extreme, I said.

—There is no longer a relationship, he said. There's no point in pretending something exists that doesn't.

I didn't know what to make of such conflicting reports and we ended the conversation with Jake making an appointment to see me early the next week. An appointment as it turned out he never kept.

Joan appeared in the waiting room at the very time Jake had been scheduled to arrive which I took at first to be a remarkable coincidence.

—I have an appointment with someone else, I told her.

—I know who you have an appointment with, she said. Your scheduled appointment couldn't make it and asked me to take his place.

Such exchanges were of course not acceptable practice, but this did not seem the time to make an issue of it.

As soon as Joan took the seat I offered her, she began to cry uncontrollably. This was one of her characteristic jags and I knew from experience that it was virtually impossible to cut it short.

I sang to her while she cried, a lullaby I vaguely remembered my mother singing to me. It went something like: "Hush little baby, don't say a word. Mama's gonna buy you a mocking bird. If that mocking bird don't sing, mama's gonna buy you a diamond ring."

The next thing I knew Joan's crying had turned itself into semi-hysterical laughter.

—I miss the relationship, she said, laughing, coughing, tears running from her eyes. Whoever told you you could sing.

—Have you discussed this with Jake? I asked.

—Your singing? she said. No.

—Would you like me to arrange a joint session between you? I asked.

She took a tissue from the box on the table and blotted her eyes. –I don't think it would be appropriate, she said. Given present circumstances. Do you know what I mean?

I did of course, though I made no indication of it. She was referring to her relationship with the man I'd seen her with in the restaurant. –What would you like to see happen? I asked.

–I want to see Jake as unhappy as he's made me, she said.

Jake went into the hospital to have an operation on his knee. When Joan heard about it through a mutual friend, she sent flowers and a note wishing him a quick and total recovery.

Jake showed me the note (he was still walking with a cane at the time), professed not to understand its intent.

–Why can't it mean what it says? I asked.

–Because she doesn't do things that way, he said. If she really wanted to get back together, she knows all she has to do is call.

–Why do you assume she wants to get back together? I asked.

–What else could it mean? he said. She's obsessed with the relationship even in its absence.

–If she called and said, Jake I want us to be together again, would you take her back?

–That would take some time to sort out, he said. This is not about giving in to her every whim.

–Listen to yourself, I said.

–She's not going to ask, he said, so the question of what I do or don't do is beside the point. And besides there is no relationship left to save, absolutely none.

It was not my part to bring them together, only to help them determine what they wanted independent of the other.

Both wanted to resume the relationship under ideal circumstances whatever those might be. Neither, insofar as I could tell, was interested in going back to the way things had been. The standoff that prevailed offered little hope for Joan and Jake continuing together. That was my professional judgment.

I barely heard from either of them for the next several years, each pursuing a life apart from the other. And then, as happens, I lost touch with them altogether. It was not as if they were my only failure. They were merely the most disappointing and incomprehensible of my failures. Jake and Joan, and I say this in the kindest possible way, were the kind of people who seemed to take pleasure in frustrating one's best hopes for them.

What follows I learned from several sources and is as true as such hit-and-miss researches allow. Twelve years after their final separation, Jake and Joan ran into each other by chance at a book publishing party. (Why be coy about it? It was a party for a book called *Two on a Match: Should This Relationship Be Saved*, a text on Couples Therapy I had worked on for 15 years.) Anyway, Jake and Joan both showed up for the party, both in their late fifties now, Joan in particular significantly altered. They approached each other warily—to that much I was witness.

It was one of those: Is it you? Is it actually you? Yes. Yes. Yes. A tentative embrace, followed by a more enthusiastic one. Yes. After the first awkward moment had passed, they stood huddled together chatting, trying to hear one another over the hubbub of the crowd. Joan had put on weight, her face reconfigured in the transaction, her gray-streaked hair in a middle-aged bob, while Jake, who had been ill, was now the gaunt one.

Jake suggested they move to a quieter place, and Joan said, what a good idea, but then she remembered she had come to the party with her husband and courtesy required not running off without telling him first. They searched for the husband but he was not to be found, so they forgot about him, losing themselves once again in catching up.

When the husband emerged he was eager to leave and Joan said she wouldn't mind if he went on without her.

–Do you want me to leave you the car? he said.

–No, she said, I want you to take it.

She may have lost her figure, Jake mused, but not her high-handed manner. He admired her decisiveness, her insistence on controlling events.

He didn't tell her he was dying, which was his own unconfirmed judgment in the aftermath of illness.

–I've never seen you look so handsome, she said.

They didn't leave the party so much as the party left them, emptying out at the assigned time except for the usual stragglers, people with no place in particular they wanted to go. At some point, they had the room almost to themselves which was when they chose to make their silent departure.

They went to a nearby bar, though both had been on the wagon, and nursed a split of champagne between them. At midnight, Joan mentioned that it was past her bedtime and that she ought to go home.

Jake said, –And then what? When will I see you again?

–Whenever you want to, she said.

–I want to keep you in my sight, he said. I know from experience that to let you leave is to lose whatever remains of the relationship forever.

–You never tried to get me back, she said, touching his hand to disarm the cutting edge of her remark.

Jake tended to think she was right, though his memory of the time was clouded over with the baggage of pain and regret. –If I hadn't tried, for which I make no excuses, it was probably because I knew you would turn me down, he said.

–You had no way of knowing that, she said sternly. I don't think you ever had the faintest inkling of what I wanted.

For the moment, his exaltation at seeing her again, the woman in his life he had never relinquished, turned on itself. He was ready to take her home to the husband she had dismissed like an unworthy question. —It is getting late, he said, laying his Amex card on the bill.

Joan studied her hands, smiled to herself with knowledge she was not willing to share with him. —I can get a cab, she said.

—It would make me happy to drive you home, he said.

—It'll be easier for me to take a cab, she said, planning her separation from him as if it were a military retreat from a failed campaign. Please don't insist.

—What good would it do me if I did, he said.

—This has been a wonderful evening, she said, taking his hand. Don't spoil it with recriminations. I was so pleased to see you again, Jake, I really was.

How quickly they had recapitulated the past. Jake retrieved his hand from under hers and stood up. —We'll find you a taxi, he said.

—Let's say goodbye here, she said. All right? All right, dear?

Her calling him dear stung his heart, left him feeling as if he had spent much of his life standing on one leg.

When he sat down again he felt he was gradually lowering himself into some kind of bottomless pool, chains around his ankles, a weight of stones in his pockets.

She kissed his cheek quickly, more of a peck than a kiss, then hurried out of the restaurant, her coat over her shoulders like a cape, two fingers holding it together at the throat.

They had not exchanged phone numbers and he had no idea how, if ever, he would get in touch with her again. No doubt there were ways.

He hunkered in his chair until the head waiter asked him to leave. —I can't, he thought to say, but he could and did, floating like a sleepwalker to his car.

He let himself in and started up the ignition without first swathing himself in his seat belt as though getting away was a matter of some urgency. The engine raced and abruptly died. It gave him a moment to collect himself, to tote up the evening's credits and debits.

He let himself imagine Joan in the taxi being chauffeured to her apartment. She was caught as he was—he could feel it—in the vast frightening pull of the relationship, the tides that bind. When he closed his eyes he could read her thoughts. She was trying to explain away as a ghost of the past the inexplicable thing that held them both in its whirl.

Her choices were clear, though irritatingly limited. She would either have to make a point of never seeing Jake again or give up the traces of her present life. She had the driver take her once around the block before dropping her off, which settled nothing.

The sound of a passing drunk talking to himself made Jake aware that he was sitting alone in his car on a dark street. He triggered the engine, made sure that all his doors were locked. Joan remained vivid to him for as long as she sat in the back seat of her taxi or even, arriving home, as she trundled over to the building she lived in with her husband. He envisioned her wayward back as if he were standing across the street with binoculars tracking her every move. Once she entered the building, however, and resumed a life that had nothing to do with the relationship they shared only in memory at this point, he lost sight of her. It was as though she had disappeared into a void, had ceased to exist. When the heavy door, the outside door, rang shut behind her, he could see nothing beyond the ornate facade (a suggestion of sardonic gargoyles in the molding), a failure of the imagination that estranged him from the relationship forever.

For Joan's part, as she turned the key in the lock to let herself in, the relationship, frail and tremulous in the best of times, barely able to get out of its own dogged way, nipped at her heels unshakably.

Lost in Translation

1.

This is not the first time that Louise is not behind me when I have every reason to assume she is. I force myself through the crowd and triumphantly board the awaiting boat when I spin around, stung by a premonition, to offer my absent wife a hand.

I am a reluctant and disagreeable traveler, attached to home, which is Boston, like something rooted in cement. I have certain routines that sustain me. It is almost always at my wife's urging that I go anywhere at all.

Louise likes to travel—as if one part of the world were any different from any other—and most of the time I go along, not wanting to be left behind. I look around the boat for a familiar face, someone on the same four-country tour, but oddly there's no one in the front cabin I can remember having seen before. We are always in a place it seems where English, the only language that understands me, is not the verbal currency of choice. Some of the locals speak a word or two, but what they mean and what they say is never quite the same thing.
    I ask them to stop the boat to give my wife, who is still not in the picture, an opportunity to come on board. But they are in a hurry or don't seem to understand my

request. "It won't hurt to wait a few minutes, will it?" I say to the man who has me by the arm.

For a while now Louise and I have been fighting as if something immense and unseen depended on the outcome, not fighting exactly but arguing, the issues trivial and unmemorable. Who's right, who's wrong. What to do next. Where to go, whether to go. We each tend to take the other side, anything not to agree.

Inevitably, one of us is in the wrong.

I think I see Louise in the distance, waving her arms at the boat. "I'll wait for you at the dock," I call to her, but I can tell from the look on her face that the noise of the boat's engine has made white noise of my words. I have no way of knowing if the next boat is going to the same destination.

Some official person takes my arm and ushers me out of the first cabin into the second where all the seats are taken. Wherever it is I am, it is, it seems, the wrong place.

After three days in Prague or is it Helsinki, I tell Louise I am ready to go home. "Do whatever you want," she says. "I'm going to finish the tour with our group. I'm not going to sacrifice my pleasure to your killjoy moods this time around."

"Do you understand English?" I say to the woman sitting next to me, who is dandling a two- or three-year-old on her lap. She smiles at my question.

"This is the last trip I'm going on with you," she says when I make a lame joke about the airline food. "The absolutely last time. You have zero capacity for having fun." I whistle with worked-up cheer at her remark.

"Do I know you?" I ask a familiar looking man, who has been staring out a window at the seemingly endless expanse of water. I give him my name. He says something in a language that might be German or Swedish and then returns to his view. I take a seat in the third cabin, the only one available, next to a woman holding a small complaining child on her lap.

We're on this two-week four-country tour, Louise and I, visiting (as Louise likes to say) unexpected places. As usual, I have stopped paying attention and I can't say for certain what unexpected country I'm in at the moment.

I doze for what may have been an hour, what may have been five minutes, and dream I am going home, waking to find myself on a fast-moving boat, a hydrofoil I believe it's called, it moves through the water as if it were threshing wheat, next to the smiling woman with the unhappy child. She is talking to me animatedly, with evident concern, in her incomprehensible language.

Perhaps it is intuition but after awhile I begin to make some rudimentary sense of what she is telling me. Her husband, Sergei or Sczcerbik, has left her for a younger woman, perhaps a younger man, but she is hoping that his abrupt defection is a temporary move and that he will return to her and their son in the near future.

Only yesterday, I stood in front of a glass-enclosed painting of a black square that had an entire room of an unimaginably large museum all to itself. "I don't get it," I say to Louise. "That's the point," she says, her face turning red with embarrassment.

I encourage the woman, speaking the few words I have picked up of her language, to continue to believe her husband will tire of the folly of his seemingly incomprehensible defection. "He will come back to you," I insist. "How could he not?"

"I wish that you were the man in my life," she says to me, "and not the scoundrel I foolishly took to my heart."

"Sergei?" I say.

"Yes Sergei," she confirms.

"My name is Joshua," I say in my crude version of her language.

"Son also Joshua," she says, repeating my name like a mantra, pleased with the coincidence. "It is my favorite name."

"What's your name?" I ask her.

"No," she says. "I not know you that well."

"How well do you need to know me to tell me your name?" I say. And then I remember that I had considered giving her a false name as a way of protecting my real self.

"I will whisper it in your ear," she says. But when she does, I am unable to decipher the sounds. "Now you know," she says.

Now I will never know.

The trip seems longer than I had been led to expect and I ask my companion how much more there is to go.

"You ask the same questions little Joshua asks," she says. "I always tell him we will get there when we get there when we get there."

Soon after this exchange, she gets up, planting little J on my lap, and disappears. I tell him a story to occupy him, but he squirms throughout, looking in every direction for his mother's return. I also get anxious after awhile, musing on the idea that the two of us have been abandoned.

The other Joshua has just about settled down when his mother returns.

Tanya, which is the name I have chosen for her, has some disturbing news. The boat has changed its destination for reasons that no one in authority will make known.

Later I learn that the captain and crew of the boat have decided to defect. Defect from what to what?

I have no way of getting word to Louise.

When we get off the boat, we are lined up in double file by a group of soldiers carrying rifles over their shoulders at what appears to be a bus terminal. I have momentarily lost Tanya and the other Joshua. "Is there a boat going back?" I ask my neighbors.

I am unhappy being herded wherever it is they plan to take us and I step out of line to test my options. "I am an American citizen," I think of saying, but I don't imagine any of the people around me much care.

At this point a bus shows up and my colleagues pour in, using both the front and back doors. When the bus pulls away a handful of us are left on the sidelines.

Tanya comes up to me. There are tears in her eyes. She is alone. "Joshua is on the bus," she says. "I thought I was right behind him, but the door closed in my face."

I wait with her for the next bus, but an hour passes and nothing arrives, Tanya becoming increasingly frantic. She slaps her face, tears at her hair.

There are seven of us remaining at the terminal. An older couple returns to the boat, reducing our number to five.

Finally, a second bus comes and I board with Tanya, who has been inconsolable. The bus takes us to a warehouselike enclosure where, after some frenzied consultation—Tanya is required to produce a photo—mother and child are reconciled.

As I have no passport to show—it is in my wife's purse—I am escorted to a back room for further questioning. The problem is I don't understand the questioning (the translator seems to share my difficulty) and the questioners don't understand my answers.

Tanya comes in at some point, carrying her child, and listens to the interrogation. "Nonsense," she says to them. "This man is an American and he's with me."

The detective Ugo's face lights up after Tanya says her piece. "You have two choices," he says (through the translator's intervention): "Go back where you came from at your own expense. Or stay with Tanya until we can do a background check."

"He will stay with me," Tanya says, not waiting for my answer. "Tell them, Joshua, that your decision is to stay with me."

As I see it, this is a pivotal moment (what in baseball is called the turning point of the game) and I mentally review my options before answering. I have some currency in my wallet from at least two of the countries we have visited so I can probably afford the ride back to wherever our tour group was going.

"If he stays with you, Tanya," Ugo says, "I am satisfied."

So the matter is settled without my saying a word.

2.

I have been living for 3 months now with Tanya and her son in a hill town in one of the former Soviet republics, waiting to hear if my identity has been confirmed.

The only correspondence I have received is a letter from Louise's lawyer—how he got my address I have no way of knowing—with a form for me to sign releasing Louise from all marital obligations.

I'm still not sure whether my new life with Tanya and Joshua is an improvement over the old. I imagine myself to be happy though slightly bored. The language gap has made for a number of misunderstandings. For example, Tanya has gotten it into her head that I like to be smeared all over with bacon grease before lovemaking, which is only a partial truth.

One day Tanya's former husband, Sergei, comes to visit, bearing flowers and miles of attitude. "What is this man doing here?" he asks the walls, apparently unwilling to confront me directly.

Little Joshua explains that I am under house arrest in Tanya's jurisdiction as an alien of unknown origins. His explanation is news to me as is his hitherto unrevealed capacity for complex statement.

"Tell the alien," Sergei says, "that he has worn out his welcome in this house."

Joshua is in the process of repeating his father's remarks verbatim when Tanya intercedes. She orders Sergei out of the house, pointing to the door in a melodramatic way.

Sergei makes a point of refusing to leave, insisting that he has as much right to be in the house as Tanya, that his father's government connections made possible the purchase of the house.

His protest made, he storms out, threatening something my limited vocabulary is unable to access. For some time afterward, everyone is miserable.

One day word arrives via messenger that my identity has been established. The only thing is, that the name they have on my temporary ID card is not quite mine, though it shares some of the same letters.

"Doesn't matter," Tanya says. "What difference does it matter what they call you so long as you can leave the house."

I don't leave the house for the next two days and I can see that Tanya is disappointed in me. So on the third day, though I am still not ready for what's out there, I take a walk through the neighborhood.

The houses all seem so interchangeable and I have neglected to write down the number of Tanya's house that I have trouble finding my way back. Anyway, I do know the house is an attached grayish-green two-story and has a similar brownish green house to its right. There is also a smaller two-story gray-green house exactly across from it, so I should be able to identify the right structure once I'm correctly positioned.

The thing is, these blocks of houses are so much alike, I don't seem to be able to position myself on the right street. So I sit down on a bench in the small park that abuts our neighborhood, trying to remember the name of Tanya's street. Not that I could recognize it in print—they use a different alphabet—if it were right before my eyes.

Eventually, I think, Tanya will come looking for me so it is probably best if I stay in one place. I won't begin to worry until it becomes dark, which is usually about two a.m.

I spend the night on the park bench, most of the night, am forced to disembark when a local cop rousts me, saying something that sounds like come back later.

The streets seem different in the dark and I walk around for awhile, hoping to find Tanya's house through the radar of happy accident. I wonder why she hasn't come looking for me and it strikes me that her urging me to take what seems at this point a fateful walk had been her way of excising me from her life.

Why, Tanya?

I'm not even sure how to pronounce the name of the place I'm in—I believe it is one of the former soviet republics–or how to negotiate the currency, though it doesn't matter much since I have none of it. But then turning the corner, I come on what appears to be an ATM machine.

An hour later, I am sacking out in a narrow room—the kingsize bed reaches from wall to wall—in a small, faceless hotel. I have barely fallen asleep when someone knocks on the door.

A woman comes in, introduces herself and proceeds to undress, standing with her back to me in what I take mistakenly to be a gesture of modesty.

When she turns around—a big woman with a prosperous stomach—her arms crossed over her breasts, she is as naked a sight as I can remember looking on outside of my dreams.

I don't know what to make of her presence, which at the moment is an unwanted intrusion. We explain ourselves in our separate languages to neither's satisfaction.

I pantomime my need to get some sleep, which seems to confuse her further. "Leave it to me," she says in English, waving off my apparent objections.

"Leave what to you?" I ask.

"To me," she answers, sticking out her tongue in ambiguous gesture. "To me. Okay?"

When she unbuckles my belt and slips my pants off, I assume this is prelude to oral sex, which isn't what I want at the moment. But then I think, what the hell, I have put up with worse.

Instead she takes the big toe of my right foot in her mouth and sucks on it with a tenacity that impresses and frightens me.

While she is sucking my toe, I close my eyes and catch a few z's, back my way into a dream. I am walking on an unpopulated street with a much younger woman, holding her hand, wondering if I ought to confess my real age. Perhaps she already knows how much older I am and it doesn't matter.

The street that we are strolling on ends in a cul de sac and we reluctantly reconfigure our route.

"Okay?" the woman in my bed asks.

"Okay," I say and hand her one of the bills I have stashed under the pillow.

She returns the bill, puts on her underwear, and lies down along side me in the bed.

"I'd prefer being alone," I say, but not so I can hear myself say it, and I drift into the sequel of the previous dream, find myself walking with a slightly different younger woman on a slightly different street.

I discover in the morning that it was the understanding of the concierge that I had ordered a woman with my room—it is one of the services of the establishment. My protests to the contrary go ignored, though the woman—the one who came with the room—disappears without a word.

Approximately an hour later, the woman returns carrying a tray (balancing it with one hand) with some breakfast on it—a runny white omelet, a slice of brown bread, a hard red pear, and a cup of tea.

I drink the tea, which is unpleasantly strong, and leave the food untouched. Tears run down her face.

I apologize for rejecting her food, dress myself in yesterday's clothes and leave the woman who is sitting cross-legged on the bed eating the breakfast she had offered me.

The moment I step out into the street, young Joshua comes running toward me. "Please come back," he says. "While you were gone, my mother's shitty boyfriend moved back in."

"That's no way to talk about your father," I say.

I follow him back to Tanya's house, have to run after a point to keep up with him. The hotel where I had been staying turns out to be two and a half blocks away.

A numerical code opens the door (or should) and the boy tries the combination three times with no success. Finally, he bangs on the buzzer, irritated at his failure. Some time passes before Sergei opens the door. I expect to be turned away, but he steps aside graciously to let me pass.

Young Joshua asks Sergei what right he had to change the combination. Tanya's husband gives the boy a gentle kick in the pants as he goes by.

I am struggling at this point to imagine a role for myself in the present household.

"Kids," Sergei says, winking at me.

"You didn't need to kick him," I say.

Sergei pokes me in the chest with his finger. "Understand this," he says. "Whatever I do is something I need to do."

I doze off on the living room couch, awaiting Tanya's return. If she wants me to leave, I tell myself, I will go without an argument.

"Oh God," Tanya says when she sees me lying on the couch. "I thought you were gone forever."

It is too embarrassing to tell her that I couldn't find my way back so I merely assert the self-evident. "I'm back," I say.

"No," she says. "You're not." She has her hands covering her eyes when she makes this statement.

I offer to leave, though I make no effort to get up from the couch, which she probably takes as a mixed signal.

Tanya shouts something at me that I don't understand.

While all this is going on, I notice out of the side of my eye that Sergei is standing in the coat closet, the door ajar, watching us.

"You have official ID, Joshua," Tanya says. "Any time you want you can return to your former life."

For all my resolve, I am ready to break down and plead with her to let me stay. I pull my hair to remind myself that it is important to keep my dignity no matter what.

"Go," she says. Then she relents and says, "Don't go."

Little Joshua is sent to his room. Sergei closes the closet door.

"I'll do whatever you want me to do," I say.

"Whatever?" she asks. "If I tell you go to the moon, you'll go to the moon?"

"I have already gone to the moon for you," I say.

She leaves the room in tears then momentarily returns with what I take to be new resolve.

3.

Louise meets me at Logan airport with her lawyer in tow, or so that is the impression I take away. When I ask him if he has anything new for me to sign, he gives me what I take to be a condescending look.

Later, it strikes me that he is not her lawyer at all but the new man in her life.

He sits between us in the taxi we take to my house—the house I've shared with Louise—in Waban, which is a suburb of Newton, itself a suburb of Boston.

I am invited like a stranger into my own house. "You've lost weight," Louise says before offering me a seat on our black leather couch.

Louise has cut her hair short, I notice, though I withhold comment. The other man, the man I mistakenly thought was her lawyer, takes a large suitcase from the hall closet and puts it down in front of me. I notice out of the side of my eye that Louise is shaking her head at him.

"You never wrote," Louise says. "How could I know you planned to return? You sent no word."

"We packed your stuff for you," the man says. "I don't want to rush you, but you can see there's nothing for you here."

I don't want to seem a poor sport, but the house I am being asked to vacate is half mine, so I get up, list in the direction of the door, then slump back in my seat. I look over at Louise to see what her face has to say.

What it says, or rather she says is, "All right. Franco and I will find another place for tonight if that's how it has to be. Is that how it has to be?"

Later, after they are gone, I think of some of the things I might have said and didn't. I might have said, "There's room in the house for all of us." For all that, I am glad they are gone, though not without a mild pang of guilt for having driven them away.

Instead of sleeping, I spend the night rehearsing the events that have brought me to my present predicament.

Louise and I had, in the strictest sense, not been getting along.

During a tour, I push ahead, which is my way, and board a boat—the wrong boat it turns out—leaving Louise temporarily out of the picture.

The boat bypasses the tour stop and ends up in another country.

I begin a new life there with the woman and child, Tatiana and Joshua, who had been seated next to me on the boat.

Tatiana's former husband, Sergei returns in my brief absence—I have gone for a walk and gotten lost—and I find myself odd man out.

I leave as if discharged from paradise for some incomprehensible sin. I fly to London by way of Frankfurt as if each distraction in my life required a detour.

I borrow money from a former editor and have a brief guilt-ridden liaison with his wife before returning to my former life almost a year after I had inadvertently wandered like a cloud into another.

I am pleased to return to the states, filled with a sense of new possibility, until the actual fact of my return and the discovery that Louise, the woman I've lived with for 16 years, has replaced me with this thoroughly unpleasant lookalike.

The new man in her life is the lawyer she has hired to protect her from the implications of my possible or inevitable or unlikely return.

My choices, as I see them, are to try to win Louise back—a high risk possibility—or to take my misery elsewhere while maintaining a semblance of dignity.

Meanwhile, the government of my country talks of conducting a holy war against a country it alone perceives as unreclaimably dangerous.

While trying to choose between two almost equally unacceptable choices, I consider what my life—what remained of it—might have been like if I hadn't run away from the foreign place that had taken me in.

4.

I run a booth in the flea market behind the Church of Death and Disfiguration, selling faux artifacts from my adopted country's renounced past.

I do a patter in English with a Slavic accent which American tourists find particularly endearing.

It keeps me out-of-doors in the warm weather and offers ample opportunity for meeting people. The best part of the job is inventing stories about the various items I have for sale, giving each its own peculiar exotic history.

Of course when the cold weather arrives, I can no longer work my stall so I end up staying home, looking after Joshua while Tanya goes off to her job designing knockoff Parisian clothes for a major department store. A few private students come to the house to study English with me, but most of them are too poor to pay my fee so I let it slide.

The winters are long and dark and I begin to drink to ward off the onset of depression. After awhile, I talk to myself for companionship, which doesn't go unnoticed by the government official that follows me everywhere.

Fortunately, my reputation as a "character" makes my drunken behavior relatively acceptable. Sometimes the official that haunts my steps copies down in a notebook fragments of my drunken monologues.

At some point a certain native wariness natural to this part of the world—thought of by unsympathetic outsiders as paranoia—comes to the fore and I am brought into government headquarters for questioning.

I am asked to explain the ambiguous implications of my drunken monologues, which have been translated into the local dialect and re-translated for presentation.

Though I don't recognize virtually any of the remarks attributed to me, I make an effort to explain them, to assure my interrogators that I am loyal to a fault.

I watch Ugo's implacable face as the translator they have assigned to me makes my remarks accessible to him. His stern, slightly dim-witted look never varies. At one point he smiles at the ornate ceiling fixture and bangs his fist on the table.

The questioning goes on for several hours—it is mostly the same question rephrased (What am I doing in their country?)—and I become increasingly articulate with each elaboration on my original answer.

When I leave I am almost certain that I have allayed their suspicions, which is what I tell Tanya on my return, a remark that produces a wan disbelieving smile.

The next day I am arrested, kept in jail for two days, then put on a plane back to the states.

There is no time to notify anyone of my impending return.

It is lonely coming home with no one at the airport to meet me.

I am taken into custody by airport officials—my replacement passport has my name misspelled—and questioned about the reasons for my extended stay in the former Soviet republic.

In this case we are speaking the same language, though it seems to make no difference. Under the new security regulations, the head woman says, they are required to hold anyone who seems in any way suspicious.

When they talk of sending me back to where I came from, I remind them that I am an American citizen.

I am asked to recite "God Bless America," though under stress I block out the opening and offer "America the Beautiful" instead.

When Louise comes down to the airport to identify me—it takes awhile to reach her, she is not at her desk at work the first time they call—they reluctantly and with notable regret let me go.

5.

We are lazing in bed on a rainy morning, when Louise says, "I saw an ad in the *Voice* for a summer tour of Eastern Europe for less than it would cost to go on our own. What do you think? That sounds like fun, doesn't it? Doesn't that sound like fun? This may be our last chance to see that part of the world. ... Well?"

I say nothing, hoping to out wait Louise's enthusiasm.

"Do it for me if not for yourself," she says.

And that's where our story begins.

Oh, Hum

Yes, she said, this world was just one gag after another. If somebody wrote up her life, nobody would ever believe it.
—*Lolita*, Vladimir Nabokov

Henry Luftman, who was this famous guy in his own right, terminated my regular treatment so we could, as he put it, take my therapy to the next level and have "the special thing" we were destined to have. Gag city, right? The illustrious shrink, I later learned, did the dirty deed with most of his former female patients (and maybe some male ones too) as a kind of graduation gift. With this kid, he just kept on giving and giving. The high-rent, doctor-prescribed nastiness between us lasting almost as long as the therapy itself.

Politics never turned me on (though I had a secret thing for Ike), but the first time I did the special thing with Luftman was a day in November 1963 that a lot of people in New York (and maybe elsewhere) thought would be the end of civilization such as it is. Luftman's over-zealous missile was the only one, to my limited knowledge, that kicked ass that day.

For a while there, falsely assuming I was his one and only lovable patient, I thought I had won the brass ring. He was so distinguished, my therapist-lover, so dishy, so brilliant, so sweet-talking (he actually whispered the 'L' word in my ear), so obviously top of the line. And I, poor thing, so honored beyond my merits, well I must have been worthier than I knew. Hadn't I been singled out by this higher being who, having tended my wounded spirit in his professional capacity, knew me inside and in so to speak. Being so honored had to improve my under-achieving self-esteem. So what if I didn't actually like Dr. Luftman all that much. I couldn't let mere personal considerations get in the way of the larger picture. I was being loved (the whispered word made flesh) and healed and whatever all at the same time. So what if my lover never wanted to appear with me in public and charged me (at reduced rates of course) for our special thing. If I didn't pay, he told me, the therapeutic value of our transaction reduced itself to almost nothing. Besides, old Aaron, who otherwise offered no benefits to his employees, was footing the bill. Did Henry know that? I wonder.

Subsidized as I was, I could only afford my exalted fucking with the great man on a once a week basis.

I can't really say I felt broken-hearted when Dr. Luftman cut me loose. It wasn't half as crummy as when Q banished me from Duk-Duk ranch. Weeks before I got my termination notice, I had been thinking of stopping on my own, but I couldn't bring myself to tell him.

—Dolly, all things beautiful must have a beginning and an end, Henry said in his calming voice moments after we had concluded our weekly session on the analytic couch. That's what makes them complete. Only complete things are truly beautiful.

—What are you saying? I said, though I knew exactly what he was saying.

—I promise you the loss will be much more painful for me, love, I can promise you that, he said, but the right thing for me to do at this point is let you go. The illusion of two tears slipped down his noble cheek.

—I guess that means it's over between us, I said with foolish calm, wanting above all to behave well.

–I wish more than anything it wasn't, he said, but we both know it has to be.

We shook hands, I forgot to pay him, he forgot to ask and I went home. It took about two hours for the news to work its way into my system. Then I got drunk and moaned and threw things and let loose a lot more than two tears. The next morning, I decided that the real closure of my therapeutic experience would be the day I paid him back.

I'd rather not tell you what I ended up doing to him and see that pursed look of disapproval on your face, though I must say revenging myself on the bastard in the way I did certainly improved my view of the relationship as a whole. Depraved creature that I was, I thought at first of getting together with some of his former patients and bringing charges against him for malpractice, but that seemed merely pissy. I couldn't make him jealous as I did Ray and Aaron because I knew—who was I kidding to think otherwise?—that Luftman didn't care all that much about me. So I was patient (not my usual style) and waited for a really delicious inspiration.

The perfect revenge fell into my lap about six months later. As a consequence of a one-night stand with a lapsed member of the cloth, I contracted a social disease. It was a mild form of the disease and not noticeable in any obvious way to the uninformed. Ashamed, I told no one and lied my head off in elaborate ways to avoid sex with Aaron, who was the only one in my life at the time for whom excuses were needed.

Interesting: Aaron had put me into therapy in the first place to "work through" what he thought of as my sexual inhibitions.

Of course you know what's coming, right? I phoned Dr. Luftman, whom I hadn't seen in a while, and said I needed to talk to him. He asked what about, can you imagine? I said I wouldn't dream of discussing it over the phone. An appointment was set up at my old time for the following week. He called to cancel the night before with an excuse so unlikely I would have been ashamed to use it myself. Our meeting was postponed a second time. I sensed the famous shrink wasn't too anxious to see me again. He knew my history, knew I could be a tad vengeful when I felt misused. In fact, his secretary, whom he usually dismissed before our meetings, was in the anteroom when I arrived. It seemed almost heroic that he didn't have the harridan frisk me before allowing me access to the inner office.

I was wearing the sexiest of the designer children's outfits Ray had bought for me in Paris. It was what I wore, I thought (though I turned out to be mistaken) the first time we did "the special thing" on his analytic couch. There was no point being seductive with Henry Luftman. Come on to him and he will turn you down every time. He wanted you to want him, but what really turned him on was the persuading power of his authority. When he was hot for you, he would let you know that resisting him was this neurotic reaction. In reality (he explained it with his usual panache), you desired him so much you were afraid to open yourself to the "chaos of passion."

So I played it cool, seemed to struggle against what any brilliant therapist could tell was foremost on my unconscious mind.

My performance of course was wasted on him. Dr. Luftman had his own agenda. As soon as he saw that I meant him no harm, that I had no hidden weapons, he sent his secretary home and invited me to lie down on the analytic couch. Then he kneeled next to me and while caressing my hair, asked me if I missed our times together as much as he did.

–Before I could answer that, I said, I would have to know to exact specification how much you missed them.

–Perhaps I could better make my point if I showed you, he said.

—I don't know, I started to say, and was never given the chance to complete my thought. Herr doctor, the prince of doc-ness, had his mouth on mine, was perched over me, before my consent, which I hardly would have denied him, could be actively offered.

My focusing on the consequences of our one-shot special fuck made the occasion more blissful than most of its predecessors.

—I feel so much better, I said to him as I was getting ready to leave, handing him my payment so as not to lose the therapeutic advantages of our session.

He kissed my hand and clicked his heels in a kind of military salute. Dolores, he said, you're one of my five all-time favorite patients.

I was a little disappointed in my ranking, having imagined myself all these years as everyone's favorite child.

After not hearing from my seducer for several months—I had been expecting a furious phone call—my satisfaction with my revenge lost a little of its luster. Was the godlike shrink immune to social diseases? Or maybe there were so many others doing the special thing on his couch, he hadn't glommed on to me as the culprit. Or what?

I thought of sending him an unsigned Get Well card, something classy from Hallmark, though after going through racks of cards at Brentanno's and finding nothing appropriate to the occasion, I gave up the idea.

Not knowing the outcome of my revenge was getting me down.

I called Luftman's secretary, using a phony name, and requested an appointment and was told that the doctor had no open time.

—That's hard to believe, I said. The harridan said that if it was an emergency, she could give me a referral. I said, Look, never mind.

That convinced me that something was out of order in the shrink's life. Luftman once told me that the most exciting time for him in the therapist-patient relationship was the first meeting. I happily assumed the worst.

I must seem like a dreadful person going on like this about another person's misfortune. All I can say in my behalf is that the whole point to vengeance is getting pleasure from your enemy's grief. I happen to think it's very American.

Finally, it was Aaron, who had published the last of Luftman's books (the one not even the reviewers liked) that brought the news. Some former patient, a woman my age who had been an actress in porno movies, was suing Doctor L for sexual harassment and for transmitting a venereal disease. Luftman, according to Aaron's source, which was one of the New York tabloids (the headline was "Shrink Caught With Pants Down"), was not available for comment.

There were follow-ups in the tabloids for the next two or three days, including a categorical denial from the doctor who, it was reported, had been hospitalized for "exhaustion" and then the story died. There were interviews in the papers with a few former patients who seemed to have reason for concern that they had not been informed that their therapist, if such was the case, was harboring an infectious disease.

When someone from the DA's office called and asked if Doctor Luftman had ever made sexual advances toward me, I said absolutely not. Give me a break, okay? What was between us, in my humble opinion, was none of their effing business. Even in my most spiteful days, I never turned anyone in to the police.

The thing about getting even is that there is nothing to measure it against beyond your own feelings of satisfaction. When I looked into my heart, I could see I was still unsatisfied.

So I ended up doing something so crazy that I have difficulty believing that it happened even when I know absolutely that it did. The idea, if you could call it that, came to me when I saw Dr. Luftman strutting his stuff on public television.

I was already beginning to see Ray again, which is another story. We met for lunch every now and then and traded insults as a kind of offputting flirtation.

Anyway, after I saw Luftman on television, as full of himself as always, the sore on his lip covered over by a band aid, lying through his teeth, I felt my revenge hadn't amounted to much. It was confusing because I had done this awful thing to him and I was almost sorry (so she says) and at the same time it didn't feel to me I had evened the score. Go figure.

It would be just dumb to play another nasty trick on him. Even I knew that. I thought if I could see for myself what the disease had done to him, see it up close, I would be satisfied and my revenge against Dr. Luftman could be put to rest.

Anyway, that was the genesis of what I think of as my Wanda ploy. The problems I faced were obvious. If I was going to get close to him, I would have to come up with a totally convincing disguise. I mean, fake that he was, he was no fool and he prided himself on being brilliantly perceptive.

I started with this witchy fright wig I had around, something I had borrowed from Beardsley and never returned, and I decided I would make myself over as an older woman. My real talent, if you could call it that, was as an actress, although I never did all that much with it in a professional way. So I got myself up with make-up and padding and such to look like a woman over seventy. When I finished and studied the results in the mirror, the only recognizable thing about me were the eyes. The eyes, God help me, were Charlotte's. I looked amazingly like my mother as the old woman she never lived to be.

After I had the disguise down to perfection, I created a voice with the barest suspicion of a European accent. The voice spoke to itself in the mirror. The disguise walked around the neighborhood unrecognized. It bought a notebook from John's Bargain Store and a wedge of Monterey Jack from International Cheeses. When I got home, I had a Tom Collins and some cheese on cracker and wrote my character's history in a notebook. It took awhile to get the various and sundry details not to contradict one another. The important part was that at thirteen my character had been analyzed by Freud in Vienna and in the process had her virginity taken from her, poor thing. I knew enough about it to create a semi-believable history. Not only had I read Henry Luftman's kick-ass book on Freud but I had also read a memoir of a woman who had been (or claimed to have been) a sexually abused former patient of Sigmund F. It was a book—I had screened it in manuscript—that Aaron had considered publishing and then decided against because he was afraid that if it turned out to be a hoax, it would be so embarrassing.

My character initiated a correspondence with Dr. Luftman, by praising his Freud book to him from the position of having been a patient of Freud's who was harboring a dark secret. About a month later, Luftman wrote back saying he had been ill but that he was now feeling improved and would like to meet with me to hear my story.

After I read his letter over a few times, I developed an advanced case of *pieds fois*. I had my act together so to speak but I worried that he would ask questions that would burn holes in my story.

So I wrote back some BS about not being all that well myself and that when I felt better I would get in touch and blah blah blah. At that point, I was ready to forget the whole dumb business and get on with my pathetic life. A few days later, I received another letter from him, the pages oily with charm, offering to come and see me at my place if I would be kind enough to accept his visit.

I didn't answer. Luftman was persistent and wrote again asking if he might have my phone number and offering an unspecified honorarium for my story.

I was always in need of money and the honorarium, I confess, sorely tempted me. What to do? I wrote back, telling him that he could send a list of questions to me and I would answer them insofar as failing memory allowed. My life was such, suggesting unmentionable depths of horror, that I could not relinquish my privacy even for someone I admired as much as the brilliant Dr. Luftman. Within a week the questions arrived. I wrote out the answers in my character Wanda's voice, inventing details when necessary. I was so pleased with myself until I reread my handiwork. My answers would never get by Henry. You know the expression, it takes one to know one? Without a doubt, the fraudulent shrink would see right through my fraudulent character to the ventriloquist within. It was clear to me then that to pursue the game any further was to claim a nasty comeuppance of my own.

Be that as it may, I was not about to give up the ghost that was Wanda without one last effort. One of my jobs at Aaron's was to keep a record of manuscript submissions.

So I looked up the phone number of the woman who had been a childhood patient of Freud's and called her on the pretext of wanting to discuss her book with her. I took her to lunch at Luchow's which was a really nifty place in those days and asked her in the course of an apparently casual conversation versions of the questions Luftman had asked me.

There was no reason for Wanda, which is not her real name, to spill her guts to me and she was somewhat hesitant at first to answer the more intimate questions I threw at her, though in the end she told me everything I needed to know.

I was totally sure she was authentic—she was so shy and inarticulate, her English barely available—but

I learned, alas, years later that she was a pathological liar. She was so convincing. I mean, who wouldn't she have fooled. The character I created for Luftman was modeled on Wanda with some personal flourishes of my own added on for dramatic effect.

So. Even though I knew there was no chance of getting away with it, I made a deal with Luftman for slightly more than the generous sum of money he had originally offered and wrote out answers to his questions using Wanda's "life" as my source.

To make the exchange, we arranged to meet like movie spies on a park bench on the Fifth Avenue side of Central Park. As soon as the agreement was made, I knew I didn't dare face the prince of doc-ness in my tacky disguise. Yet when the time came, good trooper that I was, I got into my makeup and costume and, after a few last minute final touches, headed to the park. I wasn't drinking all that much then, but I had a flask of vodka in my purse, which I drew on in the back seat of the cab for courage.

I consoled myself with the idea that there was nothing further he could do to hurt me and that what I was doing was anyway a trial performance before an interested audience of one. It was a way of finding out, right?, what kind of actress I might have been.

Doctor L was there ahead of me sprawled on a bench, wearing as prearranged a yellow cashmere scarf, a copy of one of his books (turned to his photo) on his lap. I pretended to be uncertain as to who he was, walked by him a few times, hyperventilating, barely able to catch my breath.

–Is that you, Wanda? he said, peering over a copy of The New York Times. Come join me in my office (meaning his bench). So I did and we sat a few minutes next to each other, Henry chatting me up, Henry charming the birds off the trees. I assumed this was a form of test—was I for real or not?—and so I let Henry do most of the talking. I figured the less I said, the less likely I was to give myself away. I was so into it, I was seeing him with Wanda's eyes and thinking, If only I was thirty years younger.

–You are so familiar to me, he said at some point and I thought, somewhere between relief and terror, Now that you've been found out, kid, what do you do for an encore?

Whatever you do, I said to myself, stay in character.

–You are familiar too to me, Wanda said. You are so like my baby brother Andrei who was such an original young man.

–You made love to him, didn't you? he said, this sickly-sweet smile on his face, covering over the aggressiveness of the remark.

Offended, Wanda sputtered with outrage. How dare you, she said, voice cracking. –How dare you, sir.

–Trust me, Wanda, Henry said. You've repressed the memory but I promise you the wounds are there, half-healed, festering. The telltale scars give away your secret. What I'm telling you, dear, you know as well as I do.

My world-weary character sighed, asked for the money promised her so that she might return to her cluttered, womb-like apartment. –Andrei loved me only as he should, she said.

–I didn't mean to trouble you, Wanda, the bully said, squeezing my hand. What I was doing was speaking to you in Freud's voice, not mine. Do you see?

–I am puzzled to tell you truth, Wanda said.

–I'm not at all surprised, he said, making no move to hand over the money we had agreed on to be paid in cash. He looked again at the scribbled pages that had my answers to his questions and shook his head. Wanda, he said, dear Wanda, you are a sly one.

Wanda gave him a sly smile as if she thought his veiled insult was meant to be flattering.

The sleaze-ball wagged his finger at me and repeated his aggression. –Your answers are of no use to me, he said. Why should I pay for something, Wanda, that has no value to me?

Wanda could think of no good reason beyond the reason that gentlemen were supposed to honor their agreements, though who was I to complain about the indecency of others. I chose to hold my tongue. I was so angry that if I said anything I'd probably give the game away.

Henry Luftman took two twenties from his wallet and held them out to me. —For your trouble, he said.

—Please to give back my answers, Wanda said.

—They're nothing, he said, waving the sheets in the air as if he was about to throw them away.

Nothing to you maybe, Wanda said. To me, they are my life.

He returned the twenties to his wallet and he took out a hundred dollar bill, which he seemed to dangle before me. —Trust me, dear, this is much more than your answers are worth. I offer it to you in deference to your straitened circumstances.

The hundred was considerably less than the amount we had agreed on and Wanda, who showed more character than the actress who played her, refused with some reluctance to take less than her due.

Despite his expressed contempt for the worthless document I had prepared for him, it didn't take any psychoanalytic training to see he was not eager to give it back. He returned his wallet to his coat pocket, rubbed his hands together and stood up. His lips were pressed together in motherly disapproval. It was all I could do not to laugh at him. The slippery fraud was about to walk off with the story of Wanda's life as if he didn't know he had it stuffed into his coat pocket inside the folded-up *Times*. I reminded him in a small sad voice of his impending theft. Luftman was sweating profusely and he had to hold on to the bench to keep his balance.

We settled finally on half the amount he had originally offered to pay for Wanda's story, provided I left him my phone number in case further questions emerged. I wrote Wanda's number (not a real one of course) on the back of one of his cards, and we went our separate triumphant ways.

About two years later, the revised edition of Henry Luftman's Freud book came out. It had a chapter on Wanda, who was presented as one of Freud's unacknowledged failures, a woman who was sexually abused by her father and older brother and, while in analysis with him, by Freud himself. According to Luftman, Freud had sex with Wanda because he had been unable to reach his teenaged patient in any other way, so deeply had she blocked her experiences with her father and brother. In the act with Freud, she called out her father's name, which confirmed Freud in his thesis concerning her. Wanda made some apparent progress after that, but it turned out to be illusory. It didn't help that Freud continued to sleep with the girl after the act no longer had the excuse of therapeutic purpose. One possible reason offered for Freud's unethical behavior was that Wanda's father had stopped paying for the treatment and the sex was extracted as his compensation for continuing the analysis. Luftman thought it more likely that Freud had developed a fixation for the girl and couldn't stop himself. As an adult, Wanda (in Luftman's revisionist version) lived a double life, a respected scientist by day and the absolute queen of tarts by night.

Since Wanda was in a way me (I mean, I had invented her, wouldn't you say?) I felt that Luftman's distorted version of Wanda was in its way a portrait of me. Though the man was a fake and a clown and an abuser of trust, he was also, I believed, a kind of genius. He had seen through me without knowing he had taken my measure. After rereading the Wanda chapter, I got down on myself in a way you wouldn't believe. I'll tell you I felt more shamed than in the early days on the road with Hum when I saw my depravity mirrored in the glances of nosy strangers. I was a distinguished assistant in a respectable book publishing firm by day and a slut—let's not mince words—when out in the world on my own. I needed someone to tell me that I wasn't half as bad as the portrait my worst feelings about myself had drawn indelibly. So I gave a copy of Henry Luftman's book to Ray and asked him to read the chapter on poor fallen Wanda.

Poor fallen Dolores! The nights I wasn't seeing Aaron or Ray, I tended to frequent singles bars, get sloshed, and end up in bed with the best available loser. This nasty routine started in a small way about six months after I came to New York and was going on in full flower at the present. Up until I read Dr. L's take on Wanda and recognized myself in her portrait, I had a romantic view of myself as this wild person living life to the fullest.

Before he gave me his council, Ray asked me why I was interested in getting his take on Wanda.

–You tell me first, I said, not wanting his answer softened in any way.

–Wanda is a case, he said, of a woman who has been brutalized by others and holds herself responsible.

A cartoon light bulb went on over my head. –So she kind of punishes herself to even the score.

–Something like that, he said. So what's your investment in this?

I removed his arms which had been encircling me and was about to invent a useful lie when something impelled me to tell him the truth. –Wanda, *c'est moi*, I said, hanging my head.

Now anyone else would have said, What are you talking about?, but not Ray. He understood immediately what I was getting at without me filling in the dots. –That's sad, he said. It breaks my heart that you think so, Lo. Whatever truth there is in it, you know it's not the whole truth, don't you?

Though he was being so nice, I would not be comforted. I was only thirty-one and I already had had more lovers twice over than most women had in a lifetime. I spoke my thoughts out loud. The most meaningful thing I could do with my life would be to give up sex.

—I think that's a bit extreme, he said, his notable hard-on at this juncture making his advice seem insufficiently disinterested.

The more I thought of it, the more it seemed to me that totally giving up sex was the only way I could save myself. —I'm sorry, Ray, I said, but I can't see any other way of becoming a person that even someone of your unbending standards might respect.

Ray looked mournful, but he didn't try to argue me out of my decision, which I thought deserving of some kind of reward. I took his face in my hands. —We could make this one the last one before my resolution goes into effect, I said.

—I'm honored to be the last meal before the fast, Ray said, but if you really mean what you say, Lo, I'd like to donate, although reluctantly, my last opportunity to the cause.

It always pissed me off how understanding the man was.

Before I could begin my new improved life, which I'd already entered into in my head, I had to make peace with the old. Aaron, for one, was still out there. Though I was no longer working for him, we were getting together about once a week sometimes for sex, sometimes just for dinner or talk. When I told him I meant to clean up my act, he said he'd like to clean up his too. Then he added, —I suppose I'm too old and set in my ways to become respectable.

—Well, the last thing I'd do is try to convert you, I said, and we had a laugh together over it.

Then he said in this shy voice, I think of you as my daughter, Mona.

I mentioned, didn't I?, that Aaron liked me to call him Daddy Warbucks as foreplay to our foreplay. The first time I had said it jokingly, but it pleased him so much it became part of our routine.

–Oh God, I said. If I were your daughter, we'd both be in a lot worse trouble than we already are.

Hey, there were a few more last ones with Aaron and some others (alas) before the girl closed up shop once and for all. It wasn't that I had gotten religion overnight, though it would have been nice, I thought, to be born again. I had just gotten fed up with being the fastest article in the neighborhood of make-believe.

The hardest thing to give up were the one-night stands that were so much part of my routine, I didn't know what to do with myself without them. I had no women friends in New York. Well, none who were just friends. My oldest pal, Mona (whose name I had taken) had married a Frenchman and moved to some suburb of Paris, and the only times I heard from her were in the middle of the night via frantic phone calls whenever she felt herself grievously misunderstood.

I tried staying home at nights, even bought myself a TV, but it was a lot less fun, I have to say, than going to singles bars. So from time to time out of habit or neediness, I lapsed into old ways. I set myself limits, I did. I would not go out hunting more than once a week, a rule I kept to as much as I could. I was slowing down in the nocturnal activities department with the long range goal of finding a more socially acceptable way of occupying my idle hours. I might even have gone back into therapy had the experience with Luftman not cured me of putting my problems in the hands of a higher power. I had set my will, such as it was, on cleaning up my act without outside intervention. The pity of it was, it just wasn't happening. One morning, I realized that six months had passed since I made the decision to give up sex and, for all my resolve, I was as far from succeeding as when I started.

The six month anniversary of failure was the low point for me. My will to continue the probably impossible, high-minded regimen I had set myself was fading fast.

I was on the way to lunch, feeling like something on the underside of someone's shoe when I heard my name called not Mona but Lolita by a familiar male voice. I thought, my God it's Humbert. In the frame of mind I was in, anything was possible. It turned out to be Henry Luftman who I had had a nightmare about the night before, though it was like two years since I had seen him.

He asked me where I was going and I said, To lunch, and he said, Have it with me. I said no a few times but either I was speaking a totally foreign language or there was a problem with the translation. He led me by the arm into this classy French restaurant, Café Chauveniste, and I went along, believing all the time that I was offering total resistance. Everyone in the restaurant seemed to be about ninety. I suppose I could have gotten away if I tried harder but Luftman was impressively forceful.

The creature was being agreeable and I let myself forget for a few moments here and there what a snake he was. He entertained me with stories of weird behavior, inside stuff that he had no business letting out. And he was flattering in this noblesse oblige way he had—it was like getting a gold star from God. He told me that I was looking more devastating than ever and that in all his years as an analyst, I had been one of his three favorite patients. I was moving up the ladder.

–Who were the other two? I asked him.

He winked at me, the cad, then leaned over and whispered in my ear, Come over to my office after lunch and I promise to give you a complete report.

I couldn't think of any reason to say no, though I knew there was one somewhere locked in the back of my mind and I ended up walking with him the three blocks or whatever it was to his office.

–I have to get back to work, I told him the moment we reached his building.

–Call in and say you've met an important author who wanted you to look at the manuscript of his new book, he said. Your boss will be pleased that you're so enterprising.

I knew I didn't want to do this, but I was unable to find the words to tell him. The next thing I knew I was inside his office, bending over the phone. I took in my old therapeutic torture chamber in a glance, horrified at myself for being there. –You've got new curtains, I said, holding off the inevitable.

–Make your call, he said, leaning up against me from behind, kissing my neck.

–Wait a minute, I said (the receiver was in my hand), didn't I read somewhere that you had some nasty social disease?

He was on the other side of the room, pretending to read his mail, and he laughed unpleasantly. Unless I miss my guess, you've been similarly blessed, he said.

Alarms went off inside my head. I put down the phone and walked to the door in what felt, in my anxiety to get out of there, like slow motion. Luftman, who had this devilish leer on his face, stayed where he was, made no attempt to stop me.

–You don't deny it, do you? he said.

–I do deny it, I said under my breath. As I scampered in slow-motion toward the door, my feet seemed to sink into his plush two-hundred-year old gold brocade Chinese rug as if it were sand.

–It was an indecent thing to do, he said. Unworthy of even you.

Unworthy of even me? I couldn't believe he had said it. –You disgusting creep, I shouted at him. And I went on from there endowing him with every insult I knew, each one truer than the last. My tirade, which went on and on (the light seemed to fade behind his window after awhile) finally exhausted itself. I then became aware of myself standing knee deep in his rug, my back pressed against the door, bawling as though I were the baby the candy had just been taken from. I didn't have the strength to turn around and leave the room. I swear I didn't.

When I was finished, Henry, who had been seated, leapt to his feet and applauded. −Bravo, he shouted. Baby, you took us all out with that aria, all of us, Humbert, Q, Dick, Ray, Aaron, the lot of us. I'm proud of you, Lo.

−Yeah? I said in a choked voice.

−Yeah, he said.

−Really? I felt my mouth twisting into a smile.

−Really, he said. I don't stand up and clap for just anyone.

−I'm so moved, I said.

−Good, he said. You should be. He opened his belt and let his pants fall gracefully to his ankles. He was wearing off-white boxers decorated with red skulls. −Now let's fuck, he said.

I got out of there. You bet.

Courtship

Sometimes you find yourself in the same airless place whichever way you choose to turn. Usually when that happens there's a woman involved—beautiful (or so you think), dangerous (bodies strewn in her wake), and indifferent to your crazy need for her. Whatever the evidence, that's not precisely my story.

That's the opening of a detective novel the poet Nicholas Lyme has been unable to complete.

What Nick does more or less—more more perhaps than less—is who he is not. He is a poet, who under the pressure of financial need (there are alimonies to be paid, college tuitions, children to be supported), has taken to writing genre novels, mystery and detective principally, under three different names. The fallen is his most enduring subject, the fallen world, the pains and beauties of moral imperfection. His heroes, such as they are, take on the coloration of the gray urban landscape they're doomed to wander until death (really authorial prerogative) dials their number. They are hardly better than they have to be, though more than good enough for the soiled world they ransom their souls to redeem.

You come on Nick in the midst of writer's block, something he's never suffered before, but which has held him by the collar now for almost a year. Actually, he's been banging away at his near antique Underwood portable, turning out seven to ten pages a day, keeping one word ahead of the next, one sentence ahead of its pursuer. He is writing close to his usual amount, but nothing survives the wary second look he gives his pages at the end of the day. It is worse than writing nothing, he believes. He has on his desk the manuscripts of three unfinished books, two of which are barely more than half along.

It is during this fallow period in his life that he is tapped for grand jury service. As a self-employed person, he is possibly eligible for an exemption, but he chooses instead to take on his civic obligation with grudging good grace. There are also other considerations. He needs a change of air, needs desperately to get out of the house. And there is the odd chance that the non-fictional thing—what we call real life—will inspire a fictional counterpart.

Nick is an incorrigible enthusiast, a child in adult disguise, which means disappointment sleeps in the sleeve of his coat. To keep out of tendency's way, he comes to grand jury armed with a notebook, which he jots in during the down time between cases. To occupy the idled imagination, he supposes his fellow jurors as characters in a detective novel with the usual baggage of unspeakable pasts and buried crimes. Of the 23 jurors in the cramped, almost square room, all but a few seem harmless, domesticated to a fault or burnt out, but Nick nevertheless invents dark undersides to each, dangerous secret selves.

The real-life cases have their intriguing aspects in the early going, or so he is determined to believe. What he gets off on most is the way the alleged crime reveals itself through the ritual Q and A between assistant district attorneys and rehearsed witnesses. It's like getting back to the basics of story telling.

He enforces privacy while pretending to be congenial in superficial ways, says, "Good morning, fellow indicters" when he enters the room and "Catch you tomorrow, amigos" when he leaves. The rest of the time he hides out in the sanctuary of the imagination while true life crime buzzes harmlessly about the room.

That is, before he loses his heart to the timid, married femme fatale, at least ten years younger, seated to his left. He names her Medina, a woman seemingly respectable to a fault who had done unforgivable things under another identity in some dark past. The name she introduces herself by is Esther.

"Are you keeping a record of the cases?" Esther asks hesitantly on their fourth day of service, a reference to his secret notebook jottings. "I don't mean to intrude."

"As a matter of fact," he says, "I'm not."

He barely notices her until her question invades his concentration. By public standards, she is more plain than pretty, faded blue eyes behind thick-lensed glasses, medium-length mousy brown hair, but there is something in her face—intelligence perhaps, inner beauty, generosity of spirit—that leaves him for dead.

Esther is a high school creative writing teacher who has never heard of him, not as himself, nor as any of his pseudonymous secret selves.

from Nick's Journal

I found out that she was a teacher when we lunched together at a denatured Chinese restaurant called China Lagoon the last day of the first week. Like many shy people, she tended to silence or chatter. We discussed the more puzzling cases that came our way. Why, she wanted to know, did I vote against indicting the confessed murderer who kept his victim's body in the trunk of his car for over a week.

I had uncharacteristic difficult explaining my reasons. "I'm not usually a bleeding heart," I said, "but I thought the guy had suffered enough."

"The quantification of his suffering is not the issue here, is it?" she said, a stern rebuff delicately offered. "We're supposed to make our decision on the facts of the case alone."

I laughed, which seemed to fluster her, and again I struggled to explain myself, told her I was laughing at the idea that the worked-up evidence of the ADAs could be characterized as facts.

My explanation didn't conciliate, failed its intention. I resisted the impulse to apologize, said instead that I was impressed with her openness, that her face seemed to register her feelings like the most sensitive of seismographs.

"I have no idea what you mean by that," she said, averting her eyes. Then she put her hands over her face as though to cover her nakedness. That was the precise moment I fell in love with her.

When I apologized for intruding on her privacy, she peered out at me from between her fingers. "I have difficulty with intimacy," she confided from behind her hands.

While we were talking, I noticed a woman who resembled a witness from a case we had heard that morning come into the restaurant with three other women. On the basis of her testimony we had indicted a defendant on two counts of sexual assault. The woman and her friends seemed inappropriately giddy.

"If that's Ms. Contreras," I said, gesturing with my head at the laughing woman at the adjoining table, "we've been had, kid."

Esther put on her glasses, glanced skeptically at the presumptive Ms. Contreras, and her face registered a flash of outrage. "I know it looks suspicious," she said, "but we don't know anything really."

I knew as I drove up the winding driveway to the Hubley estate that I would not get there in time. A gun shot, hollow as an echo, resounded from somewhere at the top of the hill. The dowager, Medina Hubley, who thirty years ago had been the notorious matricide, Miranda Culvert, and had silenced five people to sustain her secret, a secret which included the murder of her first husband and marriage to her son, had avoided the embarrassment of public exposure by taking her life. She had had a good run and now it was over. I was just one of many that had been taken in by her seductive charm. That was my punishment at the end. Her twisted life had been hers.

Esther is occupied with *The New York Times* when Nick comes in on Monday after a long, unusually desolate weekend in which he ran a low grade fever, slept badly, and dreamed of making ruinous irreparable mistakes in a variety of life-and-death situations. He mumbles hello, but gets no answer. Even after he sits down next to her in his usual seat, his presence goes unacknowledged. He says nothing, pretends indifference, waits for her to make the next move. When the court stenographer appears, signaling the beginning of the work day, Esther glances at him and glances away, a secret blush rouging her cheeks. Nick decodes the message and takes heart.

For the rest of the morning, a series of unmemorable, seemingly interchangeable cases—most of them gun possession—parade their desperate circumstances before Nick and the others.

from Nick's Journal

As we were filing out of the court house for lunch break, Esther said she had some shopping to do and would grab a sandwich along the way. When I indicated a willingness to keep her company, her face registered distress.

"If you rather I didn't come along, Esther, I won't," I said.

"I'm not handling this well," she sighed. "My plan was not to spend all my time with you during break, but I don't seem to know how to say no." She kept her hands out in front of her as if she were holding at bay some invisible force.

We walked around fecklessly, looking for a restaurant that spoke to our disparate hungers, our time dissipating. I had my hands in my coat pockets. Our arms seemed to brush as we walked.

We ended up at a poisonous Mexican dive called El Gringo—the food so bad even the in-house roaches seemed to dine elsewhere—and we both ordered the special (two tacos and a burrito) and when they took away our plates the food seemed to have expanded rather than diminished. Out of a desire to impress (what else could it have been?)—perhaps it was just nervousness—I told her I had become a mystery writer because I felt that almost everything about the human condition was mysterious, which is why I tended to be skeptical about the cases presented to us.

In response she told me about going with her two girls to the Museum of Natural History and the younger one getting lost for almost an hour. Her daughter's mystifying absence made her unbearably anxious, she said, laughing nervously.

When it was time to return, we walked back to the courthouse with our heads down, surrendered like escaped prisoners to the authority of the system. Esther, who had been smoking nervously, stubbed out her cigarette.

When the smoke cleared, Medina was holding a gun in her hot little hand and pointing it carelessly in the direction of my heart. Medina, you're making a mistake, I said. I'm your only friend, and you've already got my heart. I didn't hear her reply. An explosive shot from an open transom just above our heads made white noise of Medina's last words.

Nick studies the witnesses with a wary eye as they go through the ritual paces of their rehearsed testimony. When he senses someone is lying, he insists on the witness being called back for redirect. That doesn't always ingratiate him with his colleagues, who tend to believe any person charged with a crime is more than likely guilty of something or other. The system has its reasons, all but Nick seem to hold as faith, no matter how obscure or unfounded or dumbfounding those reasons appear.

So Nick takes it as his task to plead for defendants who the rest of the jurors, Esther sometimes included, find unequivocally indictable.

from Nick's Journal

While we were ambling along, looking or not looking for some place to have our lunch, Esther said to me in a hushed voice, "You know you're an impossible person. Are you always this way?"

Her admonishment, gentle as it was, had the impact of a slap. I made a remark about being inspired by her presence, which evoked a secretive smile. We kept walking until we found an unoccupied bench alongside a playground and then we sat down.

"Hey, let's not go back," I said.

"You're kidding," she said. "Where would we go? There's no place for us to go."

"We could go to a movie, Esther," I said.

"They'll indict us for dereliction of duty," she said and unsuccessfully withheld a grin. When her remark registered, I nearly fell off the bench laughing. Then Esther broke up. Then I started laughing again, which set Esther off, which set me off, and so on. At some point—it was inevitable—we fell into each other's arms.

When they find themselves inside the courthouse, Nick says, "One of these days, kid, we're not going to come back from lunch. You know that, don't you?"

"Maybe I won't have lunch with you ever again," she says.

She has a smile on her face when she makes this pronouncement, but the next day she doesn't have lunch with him, doesn't show up for service, just isn't there.

In her absence, the day seems to move in reverse. During break, Nick asks the foreman if he knows why Esther is out. The black, former marine colonel, drummed out of the corps for treason, says come to think of it he heard something to the effect that there was some kind of crisis at home. "It might be," he says, "that they released her from the rest of her obligation."

So Nick does some detective work, looks up her last name on the juror sheet, and during afternoon break he calls information (after waiting 15 minutes for a pay phone to free up). Her number is unlisted.

Nick returns to the jury room in a funk, angry at himself for not getting Esther's number when he had the chance. He contests nothing the rest of the afternoon, his attention span about the length of a hiccup. "You look like death warmed over," the child molester on his right says while he is obsessing on what to do to get through the rest of his life (forget the week and a half more of grand jury) without this woman.

On Friday, Nick arrives ten minutes late, anticipating another long pleasureless day of rubber-stamping the will of the state. He doesn't dare expect Esther's return, but there she is in her usual seat, acknowledging his arrival by looking away. He doesn't ask where she has been, though he is more than curious, doesn't tell her he had expected never to see her again. "I couldn't get through this without you," he says as though it were a witty remark.

"I thought you might be pleased to have a respite from my chatter," she says.

They whisper like school children during the morning's run of interchangeable cases, one desperate nastiness beginning to seem much like another. One of the ADAs, impatient with their childish behavior, actually stops in mid-sentence to rebuke them with a amused stare.

from Nick's Journal

When we were dismissed at 5:20, I walked Esther to her subway, which was a different one from mine. I reached for her gloved hand, which she let me hold for about nine seconds. "I'd like to see you on Saturday," I said. "Is that possible?"

"I don't see how," she said, scribbling her phone number above the headline on *The New York Times*. She handed the paper to me as if entrusting an important document. As I walked away, I imagined her hurrying down the steps of the subway, creating as much space between us as possible. When I glanced back, she was almost exactly where I left her, fiddling in her purse for a metro card or a token or a gun.

Expecting the worst, I stepped into the Hubley's bedroom and was only slightly disappointed. There was the body of a woman on the floor that was not intended as part of the decor. It was Medina and a few feet away, equally dead, was her husband, Antonio, who it turned out was also her son. The story wrote itself. Antonio, who had left a trail of carnage behind him to protect his mother's secret—at least six killings, probably seven—had shot himself to avoid retribution. Medina in turn had slit her wrists and then, with whatever strength she had left, shot herself in the chest. The whole sorry mess made me regret my brief involvement in their lives and the unsavory career I had chosen to pursue. I stood with my back to the wall for about ten minutes, bracing myself, before I was ready to call Sergeant Hives at homicide to make my report.

Nick doesn't call her on Saturday. He makes a point of not calling her on Saturday, which makes the urge to call all the stronger. He writes all day, writes a possible ending to a book about an unnatural involvement between a mother and a son he had for a long time been unable to resolve. In the evening, he takes his sometime girlfriend, Constance, to dinner and a movie. Constance comments on his distraction, which he explains away as tiredness.

On Sunday morning, he goes for a drive to clear his head, parking at a plug a few doors down from her limestone house. After an hour or so of uneventful vigil, he dozes in the car and dreams. A telltale tap on the window steals his dream from memory.

After she scolds him for parking at her doorstep, Esther gets into the passenger side of his Saab and slumps down. "Where are you taking me?" she says. Nick pulls abruptly away from the curb and drives off in no particular direction. He expects her to insist on being taken home, but she remains uncharacteristically silent.

"When I left this morning, babe, I had no intention of coming to see you," he says in the voice of one of his private eyes.

"No one has ever called me 'babe' before," she says. I don't know whether to be pleased or insulted. Since you're here you might as well come in and meet my family."

"Would that be awkward?"

"The situation is already that," she says. "If you like, you can take me to D'Agostino's—that's where I was going—or some supermarket in another neighborhood. It might be better to go some place where nobody knows us."

Nick sees their story momentarily from the vantage of an outsider reading it on the page and the discovery he makes is that the male character seems like a jerk. So he finds his way back to the parking space at the plug two doors from her house and makes some excuse about having to get home.

"You're humiliating me, sweetheart," she says under her breath. Perhaps he imagines the word "sweetheart" at the end of her complaint.

Why does he keep getting it wrong? he wonders.

from Nick's Journal

I took her to a Key Food in a neighborhood in which neither of us had connections. While she filled her cart, I read to her from *The National Enquirer* about a hitherto unreported epidemic of sexual encounters with Martians in the cornfields of Iowa. The headline read: "Martians Foul Field of Dreams."

When I dropped her off around the corner from her house, she kissed me on the side of the mouth and squeezed my arm before leaving the car.

Esther has made Nick aware that many of the jurors in the room are offended by his resistance to virtually every case brought before them. So when this compelling, four witness affair (plus defendant) comes their way, he is resolved to keep a low profile during deliberations. At first he doesn't know what to think. Two of the police officers tell the same story—they are on a stakeout (its purpose not relevant to the case) and accordingly follow a suspect into a building and order him to freeze. The suspect ignores their command and flees up some stairs, the two cops giving chase. During the exchange of gunfire, a backup police officer, who is the third witness, is wounded. The defendant, who was the suspect in the stakeout, has also been shot. The charges include attempted murder in the second degree and depraved indifference to human life. A gun possession charge has been dropped as the weapon at issue has not been recovered.

The defendant, a tall, emaciated black man wearing shades he refuses to remove despite the ADA's request, is the last to present his story. It is a rare occurrence in these proceedings when a defendant makes a personal appearance. "It is a case of mistaken identity," the man says. "I'm a college student. I've never been in trouble with the pigs before."

The ADA, an overweight, balding white man named Harry Asquith, rolls his eyes during the defendant's testimony. "Why, if you're a law-abiding citizen, as you tell us," he asks, "did you run from the police?"

"The men was white," he says in his uninflected voice. "They be pointing guns."

"Isn't it true you repeatedly fired a gun at your pursuers?"

The suspect, who stands with the aid of a cane during his testimony, says he doesn't own a gun, which moves ADA Asquith to roll his eyes in disbelief once again.

When the floor is turned over to the jury to deliberate and vote, Nick's colleagues, the one's inclined to talk, feel the suspect has minimal credibility.

"Say the defendant is lying," Nick says. "Let's make this a worst case scenario. All the man did, if he did what the police allege, was defend his life."

Nick takes no more than five minutes to argue his case despite interruptions—coughs and yawns—that break his train of thought. At the end, he reminds his colleagues that they are not here to rubber stamp an imperfect, possibly corrupt system.

The jury votes 19-3 (with one abstention) to indict. Nick's impassioned appeal only seems to confirm the others in their opposing positions. The worst of it is that Esther, although with some reluctance, casts her lot with the majority.

from Nick's Journal

We had our first fight during lunch break at the local Thai restaurant, Bangkok Palace, mostly my fault. After lunch, upset at our dispute, we went to a movie instead of returning to the courthouse, sat in the back row, taking whatever contact darkness and proximity offered. Neither of us saw much of the movie, a lugubrious foolishness called *Sleepless in Seattle*. Afterward, Esther said that she knew she had no right to ask, but it would mean a lot to her if I wasn't so contentious during deliberations. She didn't mind my voting against the majority every time if that's the way I saw it, but my monopolizing the floor with farfetched arguments had been a source of acute embarrassment to her. "I know you're trying to be honorable," she said, "but it gives a wholly different impression to those who don't know you the way I do."

I said I would be less contentious, but it was an unfelt concession. Then I said, "How can you respect someone who evades doing what he thinks is right just because you ask him to?"

"Please! " she said.

Nick expects to be reprimanded the next day for missing the previous afternoon and he comes armed with mostly implausible excuses. No one says a word to either of them about their absence—not to their faces anyway. Nick's fantasy is that they are building a case against them and the silence is a ruse to trick them into further damning misbehavior.

No matter his promise to Esther, when he senses that a possibly innocent man has been charged with a crime because the police have been unable to get their hands on the real perpetrator, he ends his self-imposed silence. The vote is close this time, but his side—the defendant's side—loses again.

"You're really impossible," Esther whispers when the vote is concluded, the only words she speaks in his direction all afternoon.

The next day he meets her on the courthouse steps going in and they embrace in their bulky winter coats. "Are we still friends?" he asks.

"I don't know what we are," she says.

from Nick's Journal

In my dreams I found myself in the role of misunderstood defendant denying the commission of crimes for which I secretly knew I was responsible. I woke from these dreams in a state of painful disorientation. I am innocent, I wanted to say, but there was no one to hear me out, no one to whom it mattered, and besides it was a lie.

For the final day of Grand Jury, Nick gets himself up in an unpressed suit and retro tie, feeling a bit like a character in one of his detective novels. Esther shows up, looking apologetic and uncomfortable in a dark wool dress and heels, gold bird pin in elegant repose above left breast. In a busy morning, five defendants are indicted. They go for lunch at Francesca's, which has white table cloths and signed photos of mostly obscure movie stars on the walls. Nick orders champagne and puts together the text of a prior life, from whose glossy pages he gives her a rundown of the highlights. Two failed marriages, two grown children, three books of poems, five detective novels, a half-life suffused with guilt and semi-literary aspiration. Esther has difficulty talking about her life, but her generosity in the end exceeds all expectations.

Esther married her second boyfriend when she was nineteen shortly after she had broken up with the first who had been her great love, had married while in flight from a flood of feelings that seemed to threaten her sanity. The marriage had been shaky in its early years but time had strengthened it, and in a little more than a week, in nine days to be exact, she and her husband would commemorate 18 years together. The pictures she shows him of her girls, who are fifteen and nine, who are beautiful in their plainness, stop his tongue. Her life is thick with reality, inviolable.

So he doesn't tell her at their last lunch any of the things he wrote in his head, wrote and rewrote, rehearsed and memorized.

The afternoon limps along, prolonged by ritual. Nick glances at Esther from time to time, catches her glancing back, holds her briefly with his eyes. The jury is released at a few minutes before six, and after shaking hands with the others, who seem to forgive him his passionate pursuit of self-involved justice, he walks with Esther to her subway. They shuffle their feet in the cold as prelude to saying goodbye.

They stand in the cold at the subway entrance, crowds of people filing by them, with nothing to say. Platitudes hang like frozen breath in the air. "I really have to get home, Nick," she says, holding out her gloved hand, which he takes and reluctantly returns after his borrower's rights have run out. An eternity passes in a fraction of a second—he hugs her awkwardly—and then she merges with the crowd pouring down the steps. He doesn't stay around to watch her descent.

from Nick's Journal

I walked away for a half block, then trudged back, shouldered my way down the stairs to the dungeon of the subway. Impulse spurred me, mindlessness, a vague feeling of entitlement. I had no intention, nothing on my mind beyond seeing her one last time. After that she could resume her life as if I had never entered it. When I finally located her, she was moving at the center of a crowd into the open doors of a train. I fought my way down the last flight of steps to the platform, losing sight of her in my haste, and squeezed my way through the doors, which were in the process of shutting. I had a self-deluded moment of unalloyed triumph.

As the train started to pull away, I realized that Esther was not in the car—she was still on the platform, her head slightly turned as if she was waiting for some-one unexpected to intercept her. I banged on the glass of the door to get her attention, but she was occupied with the prospect of the someone approaching from be-hind and she didn't look my way. I never found out if it was disappointment or relief she experienced at not being intercepted, saw only my saturnine reflection in the murky door window as the train hurtled through the netherworld between stations. I talked to her in my head, said I understood why we couldn't go off together and start a new life. We had already been indicted into the life we had been living and we were required to stand trial indefinitely.

Esther talked back in my imagination. "Nick, I have loved ones, you understand, waiting for me."

Loved or unloved, Nick is also going home, but not just yet. For the moment at least, he is imprisoned on an overcrowded train, a wordsmith (and grand juror) dressed like a low-rent detective, in love with the wrong woman, heading nowhere he needs to go.

It didn't matter that I loved her. A woman who would kill for even the best of reasons was not likely to wear well in the long run. I had second and third thoughts even as I phoned the law to come and get her. She pleaded with me to look the other way, then resigning herself to the fact that her charms would get her nowhere this time around, she asked in a plaintive voice for one last kiss. It seemed a small thing to do for someone who would probably go away for 20 years, but as I leaned forward to kiss her something intractable came down against the back of my head, teaching me once again the same lesson I had never learned. That she didn't shoot me when she had the chance was the one positive surprise in all this. She had vanished into air by the time I came to and I doubted I would ever see her again in this lifetime. Medina had done unforgiv-able things but she wasn't all bad. My survival was testimony to that. I was still on the planet, still around to kick my dust in the bully's face. Rubber-legged and sore-hearted though I might be, I was breathing and mostly in one piece. To claim title to anything more in this vale of shadows was the quixotic province of imbeciles, thieves and angels.

That's it, Nick tells himself. That's the way it has to end.

Past Perfect

An arbitrary last minute decision brought Tristram Schwartz to a publishing party in a cramped upper west side apartment to celebrate a writer he didn't know and had never actually read. His connection to the writer was his agent, Mary Dodson, who also represented the other, and she had made a point of urging him to come. He had originally thought to take in a movie, but the timing was bad—the movie was three hours long and the party, which he had thought to avoid, seemed preferable to staying home. Tris figured he'd hang out a half hour or so, make the rounds, and find someone there to join him for dinner. The least of his expectations was that he'd run into a woman he had been crazy about 30 years ago and hadn't seen since.

Holding a flute of champagne above the wall-to-wall crowd like an Olympic torch, he was half listening to a conversation about the decline of civility in small town America when he noticed over the speaker's shoulder a tall, silvery-haired woman in a spectacular black suit, observing him with a wry smile. He nodded at her in gratuitous acknowledgment, and she winked in return. A socialite type, she was not someone he was likely to know and he could only assume she had mistaken him for someone else. Tris tended at times to be confused with a sanctimonious, high profile trial lawyer who specialized in controversial cases. He wondered if the lawyer was ever mistaken for a twice divorced culture editor of a middle of the road national affairs magazine.

A few minutes later, the woman who imagined she knew him, appeared mysteriously at his side. That he hadn't seen her approach gave him an unpleasant frisson. –I'm Tris, he said. He held out his hand, which she ignored.

–I know who you are, she said. You probably won't remember—I'm sure you won't, in fact—but you once promised you would never forget me.

–How can you be so sure that I have? he said, considering the possibility that she was putting him on.

–Okay. What's my name?

The moment she appeared at his side a name came to mind, but the coincidence was too unlikely and he withheld the perception. –Don't tell me, he said.

–My lips are sealed, she said, the seriousness of her demeanor mocking him.

She was charming, but too self-conscious about it, he decided, and there was something self-satisfied about her that put him off. Clearly, she had once been immensely compelling. He found himself admiring her sangfroid, while resenting her sense of entitlement.

–You don't remember me, do you?

He studied her almost beautiful face, which seemed to fade in repose, and the same troubling name came to mind as before. –I confess I don't, he said... You're not Molly Lief by any chance, are you?

For an extended moment, she didn't respond, her face blank, and then, as if a curtain had lifted on a performance, she smiled. –I was beginning to doubt my own existence, she said.

Once her name was in the air between them, he remembered her abbreviated dance through his life. It was at a wedding, his friend Richard's wedding, a long time ago, that they met for the first time and it was true, as she claimed, that he had once told her—he had been very young and fairly desperate when he made the pronouncement—that he would never forget her. He even remembered certain details of the wedding itself as if he were watching an old dream on videotape playing in slow motion in his head.

Richard and Laura had written their own vows and Richard, wearing glasses Tris didn't know he owned, read his statement from note cards in a high-pitched voice. –When Laura and I broke up for the third time, I was absolutely sure it was over between us. I know Laura felt the same way because it was almost a year after our third break-up before we even talked to each other again. One of us called—it was me actually—to break the silence. And the other, which had to be Laura, said, You don't know how much I was hoping you'd call. And then I said, You don't know how much I was hoping you'd say that.

The woman standing on Tris's right made a sniffling sound and he noticed out of the side of his eye that tears were streaming down her face. –You all right? He heard himself say.

She put a finger over her lips to silence him.

Annoyed at her rebuke, he turned away, but momentarily he found himself glancing at her again. She had a slightly off-center face and her nose was aggressively long—perhaps the red from the crying made it seem so—but she had the kind of charismatic presence certain actors have only in front of the camera. For the moment, he was her camera and he was so entranced by her charm it took an act of will to look away. Even when he looked elsewhere, anywhere else, she was there, her shimmering image in his mind's eye. –I'm in love, he joked to himself, exorcising the demon before it took hold. The translation of his feelings seemed to pass through three or four obscure languages, losing intelligibility in the process. The message he allowed himself was proprietary. –I want her, said impulse.

–She's taken, he was later told by Richard's mother who had come up to him after the ceremony. –She's living with someone—a man named Reede, I believe. And Tris had not even asked at that point. Was there something in his face that conveyed the question? That they all seemed to know he was pursuing her made it somehow easier as if it wasn't his choice to behave badly but merely the nature of the character he had been assigned to play.

–Molly, you nearly drowned us all in there, he said to her after the ceremony was over.

She laughed, which gave him a rush of pleasure. –When a woman cries at a wedding, you're supposed to look the other way, she said. I seem to identify with everyone at weddings—bride, groom, maids of honor, caterers, mothers, former lovers.

–And there I was identifying with you when you were crying, he said.

She squeezed his arm. –You weren't really, were you?

He managed by switching the table cards to sit next to her during the dinner and they hung out together, even danced a couple of times, at the reception that followed.

Afterwards, expecting to be turned down, he invited her to have a drink with him, which she accepted as if she'd been hoping he'd ask. The fact of the boyfriend had come up earlier, reference to his being in Chicago on business, though no mention had been made of him since that initial establishing of her unavailability.

A rapport had been struck between them, a kind of misleading ease, and Tris thought to himself, –This is just a flirtation, nothing is going to happen.

–You look very much the same, she said to him. It's odd, isn't it, that it's taken all these years to run into each other again.

–Why don't we go someplace for a cup of coffee, he said. I think there's a Starbucks around the corner.

–There's a Starbucks around every corner, she said. Anyway, my husband's coming in a bit to pick me up.

–Look, I have to ask, he said. Is the husband you're meeting the guy, what's his name, Reede, the guy you were with when we met.

–My husband's name is Tom, she said.

–And whatever happened to Reede?

–I can't imagine, she said. At some point obviously we broke up. I don't remember the circumstances, though I suspect I was the one who walked away.

–Why didn't you let me know? Tris said. Hey, I hung out at the phone for months, gave up eating and sleeping, waiting to hear you had broken with Reede.

–And why don't I believe that? she said. When I decided Reede wasn't what I wanted, I suppose I assumed you had also moved on.

Tris's agent, Mary Dodson, came over, said, appropriating his arm, that there was someone interesting she wanted him to meet.

–I'm meeting someone interesting now, Tris said, introducing Molly.

–Do what you have to do, Molly said. We can talk later. I'm not going anywhere.

Tris let himself be led away, was introduced to an editor named Doris Gaines he had met before when she was working for another publisher. She now had her own imprint and was, said the editor, looking for new work.

–I really liked your early stuff, she told him. The book you wrote about the first world war, what was the name of it again? It stayed with me for the longest time. If you have something on the way, I'd love to have the opportunity to look at it.

He was working on a novel, his first, set in the near past, about an ambitious man plagued by indecisiveness, and it seemed years away from completion, but he thanked her for the compliment, and promised to think of her when his new book was ready to show.

Tris moved on under the guise of getting himself another glass of champagne, retracing his steps to see if Molly was still around. There was no sign of her and he stayed in place for awhile in case she returned. When he finished his champagne, which he hadn't really wanted, he wandered through the adjoining two rooms, assuming with more annoyance than regret that the husband, whom he thought of as Reede, had come for her and they had left the party.

He let himself believe that her disappearance—had she run away from him again?—hardly mattered, and he made an effort to talk to other people while glancing around whatever room he was in in the vain hope that she would reappear.

The Village bar they had gone to was noisy and Tris suggested that they move on to his place which was only a few blocks away. When they got to the door of his building—they had been holding hands as they walked—Molly said, –Maybe this isn't such a good idea.

–We can go to another bar instead, he said.

–Well, since we're here, she said, I'll have one last drink with you then catch a cab and get myself home.

As soon as they stepped inside his apartment, they kissed, rattling against the door. He was surprised how open she was to him, and taken aback, almost frightened, at the intensity of his own feelings.

He wished he had made his bed but she didn't seem to notice or mind and afterward when she did bring it up it became a shared joke between them. It wasn't just that the sex was good, there was something else, some compelling illusion of tenderness that seemed to transcend (they both had had a lot to drink to this point) the surviving myths of his past.

When she had gone—he had gotten her a car service at seven a.m.—he felt an unreasonable sense of loss.

He had not expected her to come to his apartment, had not expected her to go to bed with him, and had certainly not expected—Tris was deeply skeptical by nature—that he would wake up in the morning thinking himself enamored with this woman he barely knew.

She wouldn't have made love to him with such abandon if she really were in love with Reede, he told himself. Tris tended to believe what it suited him to believe and so was vulnerable in alternate moments to charges of willful self-deception.

Later in the day, he called her at work, first calling Richard's mother to get the number.

Molly seemed surprised to hear his voice, said it wasn't a good time to talk, that she would call him back when things were less hectic.

Two days passed without a return call and he called again, suggesting they meet for a drink after work. –I can't, she said. The last thing I want to do is to hurt Reede.

He spent hours replaying her response in his head, analyzing its implications. Her remark about not wanting to hurt Reede suggested that Tris was the one she really cared about. His confidence rose and fell like stock market quotes in a shaky season.

He composed a note which he mailed to her at work, regretting its excesses as soon as the mailbox stole it from his hand.

Dear Molly,
You remain with me like internal weather. Tell me you feel nothing for me and I won't bother you again.
Yours,
Tris

–I can't tell you that, she wrote back. And the day after that, he got a note saying, –This is hard for me too, but I can't see you again. I'm committed to another relationship.

She came up to him, holding out her hand. —It was good running into you again.

—I thought you had gone, he said.

—As you can see, I'm still here, she said.

—Why didn't you tell me when you broke up with Reede? he asked, the question surprising them both. Did you think I was unreliable or insincere?

A rumpled white-haired man appeared and Molly introduced him as her husband, Tom.

He was someone Tris had met before though the particulars eluded him at the moment.

—Are you about ready to go? Tom asked her. This seems more like a wake than a party, doesn't it?

—About ready, she said. Getting there.

—I'll get myself a glass of something, Tom said, and moved off toward the back room where an assistant editor or intern was serving the champagne.

—I'm sorry about all the questions, Tris said. When I get obsessive about something, I have difficulty letting it go.

—If you like, she said, we could meet for lunch some time. I don't know how you feel about that. She took an embossed card from her purse and slipped it into his jacket pocket, an unexpected intimacy. Call me, and we'll arrange something.

She had stopped returning his calls and hadn't answered the last two of his notes and still Tris wasn't ready to give up. He tried to put himself in her place. What could he say or do (or not do) that would get her to want to see him again? He could of course go to her place of work and wait for her to come out, but that might be overstepping whatever implicit agreement lay between them. Molly was an honorable person, which he admired, who wouldn't betray a commitment (a second time) unless she was willing to break with Reede altogether. He respected that about her and yet he wanted (almost but not quite desperately) that she continue to be available to him on any terms.

Tris had a way of inventing negative scenarios that sometimes restrained him from acting in his most immediate interests. What if, he mused, Molly broke up with Reede over him and he and she got together and then, as happens when people get to know each other, they fell out of love. He would feel responsible, he would be responsible, for messing up her life.

Despite his resistance to pushing things too far, Tris finally decided to risk waiting for Molly after work. Desperate to be with her again, he saw it as his last and best chance.

They met for lunch at an out of the way Vietnamese restaurant in the East Village, which had been Molly's choice. She was already there when he arrived, looking as self-possessed as ever. They shook hands on his arrival like diplomats from hostile countries.

After they ordered, she said, –Tris, I'd prefer it if you stopped asking me about Reede. He's a footnote in my life, and barely that. As I told you, I don't like to dwell on the past particularly when it's already written in stone.

And it was only the past, or mostly the past, at least in so far as Molly was concerned, that interested Tris. The Molly in front of him was a stranger and probably not someone in other circumstances he'd make an effort to befriend. –Then why did you suggest we meet for lunch? he asked.

–Why do you think? she said, her face turned away when she asked the question.

–If I knew, he said, I wouldn't have asked. It's obvious, whatever our original sympathies, our lives have taken very different paths.

–I don't agree, she said. Don't you find it just extraordinary that after all these years, 29 by my count, that we happen to run into each other a second time. Don't you find that significant? Probably you don't. Do you?

–Sure, he said.

–I'm a little embarrassed to say what I came here to say because I have no idea how you're going to take it.

–Have you been married before? he asked her. I've been married twice. I have two grown children.

–Tom and I have no children, she said. I do have a college-age daughter from another marriage. ... Please! This is hard enough for me as it is.

–Why won't you tell me about your life? he said. I promise that not a word of it will appear in my novel.

–There's really nothing to tell, she said. I'm on the board of a few cultural organizations, museums and such. I do some charity work. I'm an idle person who does what she can to make herself useful. After years of feeling the loss, I've begun painting again, and though I've gotten better, I'm not nearly where I want to be. Tris, if we're going to continue to be friends, you're going to have to respect that I don't like to talk about the past. The only thing that matters, I've come to believe, is what happens next. Does that make any sense to you?

It didn't, but he was not prepared to say so. –Okay, he said. What happens next?

Tris waited almost two hours for her in a persistent drizzle to come out of work. It seemed noble somehow, given the nature of his quest, not to seek cover. Would she be impressed, he wondered, to discover his extended vigil in the rain. For whatever reason, she didn't appear. Perhaps she had seen him from her window and gone out the back way. Anyway, he was soaked and shivering when he got home and he felt foolish and pissed and a little sorry for himself.

He let a week pass and then wrote her another letter, pleading for five minutes of her company, some kind of closure, not mentioning the fiasco in the rain.

There was no answer to his letter. For weeks his obsession with her shaped his life.

He was late for appointments or forgot them altogether, got into a fight with a supervisor at work, broke-up with a woman he'd been dating on and off for eight months. Nevertheless he insisted, whenever the question came up, that he accepted Molly's unavailability, that he was no longer smitten.

The first of their illicit encounters was on a Wednesday at the Plaza, which was Molly's idea—she also suggested that they alternate paying the tab—and they made love, rather warily that second first time, in a well-made bed between elegant sheets.

This was the start of a series of early evening Wednesday liaisons, most of them at the Plaza, a few at other hotels, always, at Molly's insistence, on neutral ground.

One of the conditions of their meetings was that he would not ask her any more questions about her life. On occasion, in the most casual way, she talked about her husband, Tom, mentioned plays they had seen together, movies she had hated that Tom had enjoyed.

Tris never mentioned that he was also married, though separated for over two years. He thought of himself as unattached, but he had a seventeen-year-old son that lived with his wife in Port Washington and that kept ties alive between them that might have long ago dissolved.

Their Wednesday night routine went on for several months and Tris saw it more as a consolation than a pleasure. He liked making love to her but nothing much seemed at stake—it was an interlude that existed outside of what he thought of as his real life. Then one afternoon rather late in the day, she called him at work to say she couldn't make it that night, no explanation offered. It was the first call he had gotten from her at his office at the magazine since the time she had invited him for lunch.

Whatever his public story, Tris had difficulty accepting

that Molly was resolute against spending even five minutes alone with him. And he continued to fantasize about her, imagined her calling to say she had broken with Reede and asking if he was still interested in getting together. After awhile Tris started dating again—a married woman (unhappily married, she said without saying)—and he gradually stopped obsessing about Molly. He meant to ask Richard when he returned from his honeymoon what he knew about Molly's relationship to Reede, but the time came and passed and Tris either forgot about his resolve or was uncomfortable involving Richard in this aspect of his life.

It was not that Molly was the only woman in Tris's life or that he was infatuated with her or that their Wednesday nights together were something he couldn't do without. At least that had been his appraisal of the situation until the moment of her first cancellation. It was human nature, he realized, that when something became unavailable its value became immediately enhanced. So his disappointment at her cancellation was not to be made too much of. He had been aware of resenting that Molly made almost all of the arrangements for their assignations, assuming, correctly as it turned out, that he would go along with her plans. He wondered what would happen if some Wednesday night he decided not to show up.

Instead of course, she had been the first to cancel, and when it happened it took him a fretful hour or two to figure out what else he might do with his unsubscribed night. He chose a local movie—something much admired which he had been saving for just such an occasion—but he walked out before it was over, impatient with what seemed to him its basic dishonesty.

When he thought about their time together, Tris tended to focus on Molly's habit of going into the bathroom before sex to prepare herself, emerging eventually in her elegant black nightgown while Tris waited impatiently under the covers. In their lovemaking, she tended to be spontaneous and often surprisingly uninhibited.

She asked him once what their Wednesdays meant to him, insisting she wanted an honest reply and he had difficulty putting what he felt into coherent language. —I like being with you, he said to which she rolled her eyes. And you? he asked in return.

—It's something I need to do for myself, she said.

—I'm not sure I understand what you mean, he said. What is it that you need to do for yourself? Have illicit sex or have illicit sex with me.

If he tried, he could still conjure up their first night together when they were both in their twenties and she was living with a man named Reede and how her fingers played against his back during sex as if passing some kind of private music between them.

The next week when they got together, he asked her about the cancellation. —My husband was sick, she said. He asked me to stay with him.

He let the news sink in, wondering if he felt jealous of the husband, whose name he continued to think of as Reede.

One night, after sex, when she was dressing to leave, she said, —I think you're getting tired of me, Tris. We need to find another hotel or somebody's empty apartment. What do you think?

—The Wednesday you canceled, he said, my life felt empty. I felt unbearably deprived.

She turned her face away in what he took to be a gesture of contempt.

—That's the first genuinely affectionate thing you've said to me, she said. Tears pooled down her face as they had when she stood next to him at Richard's wedding. He felt a sudden surge of love for her.

—Molly, he said, repeating the name twice as if he were an amnesiac recovering a lost fragment of memory.

He watched her from the bed as she opened the hotel room door to leave. —Tris, will you choose the place for next week, she said, turning back to glance at him. I want you to make the choice.

He imagined he answered but in fact said nothing, watching the door close between them. –I stood two hours in the rain for you, he said to the closed door, then he got out of bed and got into his clothes, making sure ten minutes had passed—they were careful never to leave at the same time—before he left the hotel and returned by taxi to his apartment.

He had dinner with his estranged wife on Friday night and she said maybe they ought to make one more try at living together to see if that was possible or end things cleanly and irrevocably. –Why can't we leave things as they are, Tris said.

–That's just like you, she said. You like everything to remain in limbo. It so happens I know you're seeing someone else. A friend of mine noticed you leaving the Plaza about two weeks ago right after this beautiful woman had left.

To some degree, he had taken on faith that this was the same Molly he had met at Richard's wedding 30 years ago, though some part of him saw the connection as merely circumstantial. But one night—it was the moment she had cried at something he had said—he found that he recognized her and more than that, actually seemed to see her as her younger self. It was as though a spell had been cast that had turned her into an unrecognizable older woman and now the spell had been broken.

To fall in love with her, he told himself, was a sure way to lose her and he made an effort to seem as cool and untouched as she appeared to be to him.

One night she announced, while she was dressing to leave, that she was going to Prague for two weeks with her husband.

–Will you miss me? she asked as if the question amused her.

–Why do you have to go? he said.

–Tom asked me to go with him, she said. It's a business trip but it will be a chance to see Prague.

He got out of bed and came up behind her and put his arms around her. –A hug for the road, he said. Something to last me for two weeks.

She moved out of his grasp before he was ready to relinquish her. –It gives me a start when you're affectionate, she said. I feel you take our Wednesday night fucking pretty much for granted. I suspect while I'm away you'll wonder vaguely from time to time what what'shername is doing in Prague. You're a nice man, Tris, but you're somewhat jaded.

–Am I?

–I like that about you. We couldn't go on the way we are, you know that's true, if one of us lost it about the other.

He was seeing her at the moment as the twentysomething Molly he couldn't bear to let out of his sight and an odd idea came to mind that held him in its grasp. –What if, he started to say but it was just the kind of thing he couldn't say. What if he followed her to Prague and...

He knew to the minute the scheduled time of her return and wondered, expecting nothing, if she would find some way to get in touch. Two days passed before she left a message for him on his home phone, inviting him to call after 10 the following morning.

He finally reached her at noon moments before she had to leave to attend some board meeting she was chairing. –We need to talk about what's going on between us, she said. They made arrangements to have lunch the next day at the same Vietnamese Restaurant they had been to when she had first suggested the affair.

The omens were not difficult to read. They could have had the same meeting at their hotel room at the Plaza and had the same talk before or after making love. The choice of the restaurant was an indication that she was going to end the relationship. His first impulse was to preempt her move by striking first but it seemed a childish gesture despite its obvious satisfactions. But the real question—the one he had evaded all these months—was what did he want beyond keeping things as they were? He didn't know. Ambivalence was at the core of his nature. And even if he did know, even if he was ready to ask her to leave her husband, he would only be inviting, he suspected, further rejection.

The substance of their talk at lunch was not what he had spent a mostly sleepless night anticipating. What Molly wanted was not to stop seeing him but to change the night of their liaison. Wednesdays were no longer possible. Actually, Monday was the only other night she had available. The news brought a mixture of relief and unaccountable disappointment.

As it happened, Tris had a tennis game on Monday nights, which had entailed renting a court for the indoor season. His presence was relied on. Beyond the sense of obligation, it was a great pleasure to him to play.

–Monday night isn't good for me, he said.

–I was afraid of that, she said. There's no way—I shouldn't even ask you this—you can shift things around?

–Not really, he said. What about you?

She sighed. –You have no idea, she said, how difficult it's been for me to see you as I have. I'm asking you to make a sacrifice for me. What is it that you do on Monday nights that's so important?

The imperiousness in her tone annoyed him and though he wanted to make peace, wanted their routine to continue as it was, he felt it a matter of pride to hold his ground. –It's an obligation, he said.

–Yes? To whom?

–I have a regular tennis game Monday nights. There are three other people who rely on me to be there.

–A tennis game? A tennis game! I don't know what to say.

She started to rise and he put his hand on her arm to restrain her.

–Please don't go, he said. We'll find another time that suits us both.

–I don't know that I want to see you again, she said. She moved more quickly than he anticipated or perhaps a willed indifference held him back. In any event, she was out of the restaurant and into a cab before he could settle the bill and follow after her.

They had hardly even fought over inconsequential things before and now they were having their first life-and-death fight. Of course he would give up the tennis for her, but it seemed virtually impossible now to yield to her demands after he had taken the stand he had. She hadn't even bothered to tell him what unbreakable commitments on her part kept her from meeting him on some other night. Hadn't she been unreasonable too? He let a day pass to get some perspective on his feelings and then he called her at home at a time her husband was usually at work. He got her answering machine and mumbled something unintelligible before hanging up in despair.

The next time he called she picked up but her manner was abrupt and she wouldn't stay on long enough to hear him out, though he was aware, even as he was pleading for her forgiveness, that the things he was willing to say were not what she wanted to hear. It struck him when he thought about it that he had more reason to be angry at her than she at him, but such wisdom seemed idle comfort.

A further irony: he pulled something in his back playing tennis and had to take a month off from the game.

And then one day, two months or so after their fight (or misunderstanding, as he saw it), she called him at home. –It's Molly, she said as if he didn't know. How have you been?

–Much better now that I hear your voice, he said.

She laughed at his remark as if she had rehearsed it in advance. –I'm really calling to say goodbye, she said. My husband's firm is moving him to the London office and we leave in three weeks.

–For how long? He asked.

–You never know, she said. It could be forever for all anyone knows.

–Well, he said, I hope it's what you want.

–Thank you for that, she said. As a matter of fact, I'm free next Tuesday night and I wonder if we could meet.

The surprise of her offer left him uncharacteristically silent.

–If you can't make it, she said, that's all right too.

–I can make it, he said.

–Good, she said. I've reserved our old room at the Plaza.

It was not their usual room as it turned out, but the one directly above, which had certain similarities and as such was disconcertingly unfamiliar. Molly was late or Tris was early and it struck him, as he paced the room, that she might not show up. These anxious feelings persisted even after her arrival.

After embracing, and removing their coats, they remained in their clothes for a while, one of them sitting on the bed and the other in an overstuffed chair across the room.

–I'm feeling shy with you, she said. It's not that we haven't seen each other in a while. It's something else altogether. I'm feeling a little frightened, can you understand that?

–We don't have to make love tonight, he said.

–You know, sometimes I don't understand you at all, she said. Is that what you want, to come to the Plaza with me for the last time, not to make love?

He sensed that she was about to cry and he moved to where she sat and knelt beside the chair, the forgotten ache in his back returning to torment him.

–How much I hated you these past months, she said. You can't imagine. I even thought of running you over in a rented car when you were coming out of your tennis club.

When he put his head in her lap she pulled his hair, gave it a painful tug, lifting his head just enough so that she could lean forward and kiss his eyes. –I still hate you, she whispered. I will hate you for as long as we both shall live.

–Those sound like wedding vows, he said.

–Are you making fun of me, Tris? Is that what it's come to?

He lifted her to her feet and danced with her—Molly in her heels, he in his stocking feet—to whatever music the silence provided.

When they finally got under the covers, he noticed from the clock on the wall that they had less than an hour left. He imagined the hour passing, imagined their lovemaking, more tender than usual, though not quite as intense as it had been at its best. He imagined her getting into her clothes, kissing him on the cheek then pulling away while he considered pleading with her to stay five minutes longer. He imagined watching her from the hotel window get into a waiting cab, and drive off to her husband who he perceived as a shadow figure. Then he imagined the two of them, Molly and the shadow husband, boarding a plane for London. Then he imagined getting older and being alone and trying to remember this last night together which had passed so unceremoniously.

It was only then when he already imagined the end of whatever had been between them that they began to make love—they had been holding each other in a becalmed state—and it seemed to him like the first time which he no longer remembered, and so it followed that he could imagine that they were in his old Village apartment in his unmade bed and that it didn't matter that she lived with a man named Reede whom she didn't love, and whatever was between them (their sex at the moment, their angelic selves, their secret divinity) would go on for as long as he could imagine it going on, for as long as consciousness and self-deception and

Window in the Woods

I met the ingenue goddess Janice Pilgrim in a Realms of Film course that I had no business taking. She had been sitting next to me during the screening of *Diary of a Country Priest*, and afterward Professor Weinstein, in his summing up, said that Robert Bresson's great film had virtually no direct influence on American cinema outside of perhaps the recent films of the little known American independent, Thomas Zorich.

"Have you heard of him?" she asked (not so much me as anyone who might have been in my seat) in her little girl's whisper. And I said, "Thomas who?" thinking she knew my last name and had meant the question as a joke, which were both misguided assumptions. Nevertheless she laughed, touching my hand to punctuate her amusement. In the next moment, she had her hand raised to ask the names of the Zorich films inspired by Bresson.

Professor Weinstein had this way of looking at the ceiling when trying to access information that temporarily eluded him. "If you see one Zorich film," he said, "I would recommend *The Window in the Woods*, which is on tape, I believe, though probably not in any of the local video stores."

Janice wrote *The Window in the Woods* in her notebook under the heading: Inspired by Bresson.

After class, wedged together as some ninety students piled out of the auditorium, I asked if she was interested in screening one of the Zorich films.

She treated the question as if I were hitting on her, made an exaggeratedly rueful face, the way small children do before self-consciousness sets in.

"I can get a tape of Window in the Woods—there's no 'the' in the title—if you want to check it out."

She looked away as we walked together. I talked to fill the void, ignored the rebuke her silence intended. "I mean, there's no 'the' before window."

She was a sulky girl, though astonishing looking. I had noted her presence in the class from opening day, very tall, greenish eyes, long straight unwashed satiny blond hair, heartbreaking lips.

A slightly tarnished, over-aged Alice in Wonderland. At some point, we turned into her dorm.

I don't know what possessed me to follow her into her room—it was not my usual style. I had a reputation, at least I imagined I did, for being shy. Waiting for her to ask me to leave, I browsed through her music—her CD's and tapes—thinking she needed better advice, while she rearranged the scarifying mess on her floor to no notable improvement. On her top shelf , I noticed, book ended by Metropolitan Museum of Art ceramic hippos, were paperbacks of *Invisible Cities*, *Notes of a Native Son*, *Anagrams*, *Beloved*, *Cathedral*, and *Gravity's Rainbow*. "I'm impressed," I said.

A smile emerged almost despite itself; sulky girls in my limited experience showed the most beautiful smiles. "Who cares?" she said.

When she finished with her charade of straightening up, she sat down on her bed and began to look through a *New Yorker* which had been on the floor next to her pillow.

I considered leaving without being asked—her inattention was, after all, a form of dismissal—but the B-movie detective I found myself impersonating was not so easily deterred.

When I established myself on her roommate's bed, she glanced up at me in a kind of slow motion, acknowledged my presence with feigned surprise. "If Danitra walked in," she said, "which she won't, she would be seriously put out to find you on her bed." I stood up, surveyed the room, then sat down again. "There isn't another comfortable place to sit."

"Well," she said, expanding the word into three syllables, her brow ruffled to signify the burdens of concentrated thought, "there's Danitra's desk chair which doesn't look too comfortable but you never know, and my desk chair which has stuff piled on it which might be removed but won't, and my bed which has some space left."

Her invitation, though not quite direct, was more or less undeniable. Still, I replayed it in my head three times before daring to take her at her word. Was there something, some hidden context, I was missing?

As I plopped down on her bed, as Janice moved over an inch or so to give the illusion of newly created space, I felt compelled to tell her that I was sort of seeing someone else (as if anyone had asked), which is what I did in a wholly unintelligible, roundabout way, mumbling much of it, a confession so obscure it cost neither of us anything.

And then I sat there rather stiffly until she leaned over, tilted my head back (the way men used to do to women in old black and white movies) and kissed me. "There," she said.

I couldn't honestly say that the kiss displeased me, but since I hadn't initiated it, my sense of self depended, I felt, on making her regret her generosity. "Are you one of those people who are into role reversal?" I asked.

"Look," she said, "it wasn't me who followed you into your room, was it? You like people to think you're a wise-ass, don't you, but I heard you sniffling at the end of the Bresson movie, and don't deny it."

This is the moment in the imaginary movie of my life when the film fades to black.

When the camera returns to Janice's room, we are still mostly clothed, though decidedly disheveled, and I was saying that I had work awaiting me in my room.

If I didn't get away, I knew (I had a history of such) that I would do something to ruin what was already more pleasure than I needed.

"Just don't ever lie to me," she said, dismissing me with a half-hearted wave. And then as an afterthought, "My name's Janice Pilgrim, what's yours?'

My name is Daniel Zorich.

2.

When the tape of *Window in the Woods* arrived—his father had sent it by Fed Ex—Daniel was in the throes of one of his periodic migraine headaches, and was lying in bed with his eyes squeezed shut. He had just broken up with Bonnie—it was less stressful than keeping the secret of his relationship with Janice from her—and he was already having second thoughts. Bonnie had taken his decision with such good grace, had even offered to remain friends if that's what he wanted, had even loaned him her VCR so that he could watch the tape of his father's movie (with Janice, which she didn't know). Even at his most resolutely honest, he was not wholly free of deceit.

The headache passed as it does only when you think it never will, and he invited Janice Pilgrim over at 11 for a showing of *Window in the Woods*.

Waiting for her, he had two beers in the useless pursuit of calm. She was already five minutes late.

The first and only time he saw the film he was sitting with his father in a closet-sized screening room in LA. That was a few years after his parents' divorce and he was not feeling especially sympathetic.

Impatient, he turned on the VCR, inserted the tape, put his 13" Sharp TV on Channel 3 and waited another two minutes, evading anxiety (or love) through forced marches of oblivion, half-listening to a CD of Tom Waits, the growl coming from an open door across the hall.

The film came on before he was ready for it. The first image was the glint of human eyes in a near dark enclosure, followed by the sound of a figure scurrying invisibly, and then the impenetrably dark room began to spin as though perceived through the eyes of some-one whirling himself around. Then the room slowed down and the perspective was revealed as coming from a figure lying on his back. After a moment, a flicker of dusty light appears from somewhere above. And the unseen figure, a child it now seems, lets out an incom-prehensible sound.

At this point, hearing Janice's footsteps, Daniel pushed the Pause button and froze the image. As the door to his room opened, he was having trouble catch-ing his breath.

They watched the first half hour of the movie, then ended up making love while the images flickered be-hind them on the 13" screen. After sex, after the movie was shut down, they got into talking about their par-ents' divorces. Janice said that she liked to think that her parents had broken up so that she and her older sister, whom she had never been able to stand, could find a subject they could finally agree on. Daniel told Janice that he had no idea his mother and father were not perfectly matched until the harrowing last month or so before they separated when demons seemed to have taken possession of them both.

3.

I had just turned fourteen when my Dad moved out. In the next few years, he got married again and divorced again and made another film and lived with a woman or two he never got around to marrying. That may not be totally accurate, but that's the subjective reality, and that's the one that makes sense to me.

After the break-up, my father moved to California where he had been staying anyway much of the time. He had put together his own production company, a co-op of sorts made up of people he had been working with, which he called "Of No Redeeming Social Value Productions." With his own company, which he went in to debt to create, he would have (he said), if the possibility existed beyond metaphor, total artistic freedom. The first film my father made wholly under his own auspices was the one my teacher had mentioned as inspired by Bresson, *Window in the Woods*. From my skewed vantage, having seen Zorich first, Bresson seemed the inspired follower.

When Thomas Zorich first moved to California, he would fly back and forth, spending a weekend with us every two weeks or so. I remembered the visits as awkward and frenetic, overfilled with predetermined activity. Also, my father tended to be distracted and distant during these whirlwind appearances as if only his outward presence had made the three thousand mile trip while the rest of him stayed behind to work on whatever film or woman preoccupied him at the moment.

The visiting years (back and forth) had the quality for me of shadows that vanish when the lights go on. One day, my Dad was home writing his screenplays and taking me to movies, and the next he was living in California with another family. In real time, several years actually intervened between those two crucial days but I had no recollection of what I had been doing when they went by. I must have been in some unmapped other place, dreaming of something else.

The period of dreaminess and confusion ended with the discovery that my father was a marginal person in my life. The visits to New York dwindled and then stopped. Once a year, usually in the summer, usually for a period of three weeks, I flew out to LA with

my sister to visit my dad and his new family. The new
wife, Kristina, who had a daughter of five or six, took
us in like poor relations. Kristina was a scriptwriter and
model, at least those were the titles given her when she
was presented to us for the first time. I was something
like fifteen and a half and Nancy seventeen (entering
Oberlin in the fall) at our first meeting and we were no
doubt a small bit unaccommodating. Still, in my view,
that didn't wholly justify Kristina's view that they we
were badly brought up urban savages in need of her
post-hippie, new wave, civilizing hand.

My father seemed terrifically glad to see us for a day
or two, but business—the pre-production of his movie—occupied him for large portions of our visit, which
means we were thrown, unmediated, into the authority of Kristina's bizarre domesticating regimen. Not that
we were defenseless—no doubt we were as big a pain
to Kristina as she was to us—but we hadn't come three
thousand miles for the pleasure of being barely toler-
ated intruders in Kristina's house. In Kristina's house,
you were obliged to take off your shoes when you
came in and put on paper slippers. We tended to honor
the custom by its breach and were reproached mildly,
though constantly, for repeated offenses. Kristina was
unfailingly mild in all things except where her daughter, Omega-Sunshine (I had forgotten her name until
this moment) was concerned.

Kristina tended to wear a black miniskirt and a tight
purple T-shirt with the inscription, THINK FUN, which
Nancy, who had a highly developed sense of irony, professed to admire.

"If I bought a T-shirt like yours," Nancy asked her,
"would I think fun too?"

Impervious to thorns, Kristina smiled serenely. "Not
necessarily," she said in her high-pitched, mild voice,
"though it might be a step in the right direction."

Omega-S tended to hang out with us for as much as
we'd let her which I guess, looking back on it, wasn't

all that much. She was an intuitive, laconic kid with a penchant for tantrums, which Kristina used to deal with by rational appeal. Her loopy method, which she never deviated from, her insistently mild appeal to reason, showed, to my limited observance, a zero rate of success, and the screaming would go on each time until the relentless Omega-S exhausted herself. I liked the silent blond child, who had some charming ways, but the tantrums wore on us all like sandpaper scraping the soul. And it was through Omega-S finally that Kristina got at us with our father.

One afternoon, as we were returning to the house from a walk on the beach (I was carrying Omega-S on my shoulders), I noticed Kristina in her purple T-shirt coming toward us from the opposite direction. As soon as I saw her, I lifted Omega-S from my shoulders and returned her to earth without first declaring my intention—I had the idea that Kristina would think piggy-backing her was dangerous—and the child insisted on being returned to her throne.

"We'll do it again later," I said.

"Now please," Omega-S whispered. In the next moment—Kristina was probably still out of earshot but approaching in her laid back, determined way—the child went into her number. When Kristina reached us, she was screaming and flailing in her characteristic way.

"What happened?" Kristina said in her concerned, mild voice.

"She's having a tantrum because my bro wouldn't put her back on his shoulders," Nancy told her, not bothering to hide her irritation, hands over her ears.

"She must have gotten over-excited," Kristina said, then she pleaded with Omega-S to calm herself for her own good, promising her extra helpings of her favorite sugar-free organic desert. When the wailing increased in volume, Kristina reminded her how exhausted she got when she went on this way, how little fun it was for any of the people who loved her. Omega-S, possessed by shrill demons, seemed oblivious to her mother's appeal, punctuated the screaming with a little spastic dance of agony. Then Nancy took over. She stepped in front of Kristina and grasped the flailing kid firmly by the arms. Then she put her face into Omega-S's and shouted at her in a voice that pierced through the screaming. "WE'RE ALL TIRED OF THIS SHIT, OMEGA. YOU BRATTY PAIN IN THE ASS. ENOUGH! SHUT. YOUR. MOUTH. THIS. INSTANT."

The screaming trailed off and stopped. Omega-S had a glazed look as if woken abruptly from a confusing dream.

"How dare you!" Kristina said in unrepressed anger. Lifting her silent child from the sand, she hurried off toward the house like the wronged heroine in a Victorian melodrama.

"That was brilliant," I said to Nancy, who merely shrugged.

That evening, after dinner, in which hardly a word was spoken at the table (Omega-S, who usually ate with us, was kept in her room), my father, looking more amused than angry, asked us to come into his study for a talk.

"I thought you were all getting along so well," he said as soon as we had taken seats, "and now this happens."

"Do you want to hear our side?" Nancy asked.

"I'd like to think we're all on the same side," he said.

"Whether you think it's deserved or not, I'd like you, both of you, to apologize to Kristina."

"Like hell I will," said Nancy. "Sorry."

"Why don't you ask your wife to apologize to us," I said.

"Come off it," my father said. "Do you deny that you provoked one of Omega-Sunshine's tantrums?"

"Isn't that what they call a leading question?" Nancy, who planned to go to Law School when she graduated college, asked.

"I'm not saying you did anything wrong," my father said. "I'm asking you as a favor to me to make an apology to Kristina."

"I don't need this," Nancy said. "I'm flying back to New York tomorrow and I'm never coming back here again."

"If Nancy goes, I'm going with her," I said.

My father sighed, studied the far wall like an actor trying to read a cue card that was held upside down. This was clearly not the movie he was prepared to direct. "It would make me unhappy if you left like this," he said, "but if you feel you can't stay, I'll take you to the airport the first free moment I have and put you on the next flight to New York." Then he asked us to sleep on the decision and see how we felt about it in the morning.

We agreed to nothing.

In the morning, Nancy was as resolute as ever and I found myself caught up in her momentum.

Dad accommodated our decision to leave without further argument, took us to the airport in his Volvo wagon after an abbreviated breakfast, Kristina and Omega-S tagging along in the silent car. There was no time to reconcile our differences. Omega-S hugged us; she was the only one. Kristina gave us one of her dispassionately reasonable lectures on our prospects with herself and Tom in the future, and we boarded our plane and flew out of our father's life for another year.

4.

The next July, Daniel visited alone. Nancy, true to her word, remained absent and unforgiving.

The second visit started promisingly. On his first day in California, after a surprisingly warm greeting from Kristina, his father took him to his production studio where the editing of *Window in the Woods* had been going on apparently for several months. In a screening room that had no more than ten seats, they watched a rough cut together. There was no real ending to the version he saw; the screen just went blank at some unexpected time. Two different endings had been shot, his father told him, and neither had been right. When Daniel's opinion was solicited, he withheld comment, not wanting his father to see that his presumed knowingness was mostly bluff.

Daniel didn't see much of his father after the first day of the second visit. Figuring out how to end the film, or something else not readily defined, kept the filmmaker occupied. There were evenings in which he didn't come home for dinner and even a few in which he didn't, for whatever reason, return at all. Daniel hung out with Kristina and Omega-Sunshine, went swimming, went to local movies, took walks along the beach, went to Disneyland, which out of snobbery he had avoided the summer before. In the beginning, it was just a matter of making the best of a disappointing situation, but after a while something else, something it embarrassed him to think about, began to happen.

In his father's absence, after Omega-Sunshine was asleep, hanging out on the back porch so as not to miss the spectacular sunsets, he and his stepmother got in to talking about their childhoods. Kristina told him how her father used to hit her with a belt when she was small for mostly incomprehensible transgressions. He had wanted her to be perfect, she said. Not quite sure how to respond, Daniel found himself telling her that she had come a long way in that regard without her father's inappropriate guidance.

"You have a good soul," she said and leaned over (they were on one of those porch swings called gliders) and kissed him on the cheek.

It was after the kiss that he began to have fantasies about Kristina, unprecocious sexual fantasies, 16-year-old stuff. It was odd how she seemed so detestable one summer and so desirable the next. Embarrassed at the disloyalty to Nancy it implied, he began to wear paper slippers in the house, not only to avoid Kristina's mild reproaches which had become perfunctory and unimpassioned, but actually to please her.

"My father's a lucky man to have you," he told her on one of their back porch evenings, which earned him a second kiss and an abbreviated hug.

"You're a handsome guy," she told him. "You're going to break a lot of girls' hearts before you're through."

He blushed and offered a modest stammering denial.

It was about that time that his father took him out to lunch at a celebrity, mostly groupie, hangout (he referred to the place as a "scene") in one of those interchangeably glitzy tourist towns that bordered Hollywood. He apologized for not having spent as much time with him as he had hoped, and told him about the decision he had come to concerning the ending of his film, identified with brief bio the starlets in the room (none of whom Daniel had heard of before), asked him how he was getting on with Kristina. Not wanting to give away what he sensed were unacceptable feelings, Daniel understated their improved relations. "I can understand that she's not your type," his father said.

Then a dark-haired woman, excruciatingly thin and notably serious, marched over to their table and joined them as if she had been expected. His father introduced them, but Daniel, taken aback by her unannounced presence, didn't catch the name. The intense woman and his father dished some technical talk back and forth about *Window*, as they called it, about some problems only partially solved. He figured that she worked on the film in some capacity (his father referred to her once as a second set of eyes), but there was something else too and he didn't know what he knew until months later when his father was living with the woman (Sarah

Bliss) in New York and he recalled their lunch together. The something else was that they were in sexual thrall, probably already lovers, and he sensed that about them, though their talk was mostly confined to an entity outside themselves called *Window*.

When he went home to Kristina (and Omega-S), not knowing exactly what he knew, he sensed that he had betrayed them in some thoughtless way. The filmmaker was home for dinner that night too and he was loving to Kristina, who seemed to all but melt at his touch. They went out together for the evening and Daniel baby-sat, at Kristina's request, for Omega-S.

He read her a good-night story and then a second, but she wasn't sleepy, and refused to stay in bed, so they ended up watching videos on the big screen TV in his father's study until very late. They watched The *Wild Child*, which he had seen once before when he was too young to understand it, until Omega-Sunshine finally fell asleep, and he carried her into her own room and put her to bed. The instant, it seemed, her head touched the pillow her eyes shot open and she began to scream. Daniel went into a panic. Kristina would come in at any moment and blame him for her daughter's tantrum, and hate him again as she had the summer before. He sat for a while on the edge of the screaming kid's bed with his back to her, staring into space, in some kind of numbed, oblivious state. Then, unable to confront her as Nancy had, he held the flailing child tight against him, whispering, "There, there," over and over and over again.

Eventually, he must have fallen asleep because the next thing he knew he was lying pressed against Omega-Sunshine, his sometime sister sleeping like a baby. He woke, discombobulated, having no idea what time it was or where he was or whose bed he was occupying. There were voices in the house coming from another room, hushed strident voices more penetrating than shouts. He heard Kristina say, "Tom, I have not the slightest idea any more where you're coming from and that's the truth." And his father saying something meant to calm that he couldn't quite hear.

"Fuck off," Kristina whispered, and momentarily the door to Omega-Sunshine's room opened, Kristina entering on a shaft of light like some angelic embodiment. She didn't see Daniel until their eyes met virtually inches apart—he had been getting out of bed in a kind of dreamlike slow motion—and she let out a frightened groan at discovering him.

He expected Kristina to be angry at finding him in her daughter's bed, though at the same time he couldn't imagine why. Instead, she smiled to see him, offered her hand to help complete his journey from bed to floor and then (maybe because like the mountain he was there) she put her arms around him, hugged him with more apparent affection than he could handle. His insistent hard-on was his only conversation. When she relaxed her hold, he escaped from the threat of love and got himself out the door.

He found his father in the kitchen drinking red wine and they filled the silence with conversation they had already had two or three times before. Kristina appeared in the doorway and announced that she was coming down with something and was going to sleep in the guest room Nancy had used the previous summer. At first, the announcement alarmed Daniel—Nancy's old room was the room closest to his.

"Sleep with me," his father said to her, more plea than demand.

"I don't want to infect you," she whined, withdrawing her head.

His father got up to go after her, but almost immediately changed his mind and sat down again. "Women!" he said under his breath, shrugging off his exasperation. And then as if more man talk was in order, "Daniel, why don't we catch a Dodger game before you have to go back to New York."

"I haven't been following baseball the last couple of years," he said, which was not wholly true but felt like the gesture he needed to make.

"Well, maybe I'm more childish than you," his father said.

Daniel said he would think about the game and excused himself to go to sleep.

The announcement that Kristina would spend the night in Nancy's room had been made, it flattered him to believe, as a coded message between them, the answer to the inadvertent proposition of his hard-on. Was she supposed to come to him or was he supposed to go to her? He left his door ajar to signal his availability and waited, recalling her hug in Omega-Sunshine's room, which replayed itself in the tape loop of the feverish imagination.

By virtue of three months and twelve days and one brief semi-satisfying experience with this girl Rachel in his history class, Daniel was no longer a virgin. That didn't mean he was fully prepared to take on Kristina who had just turned twenty-nine, and was movie star beautiful, and was his father's wife. Still, if she offered herself, he told himself, he could pull it off. He dozed from time to time, riding the waves of sleep like a porpoise. The noises that woke him periodically were always false alarms. Finally, he heard real steps and the opening of a door. His father, he realized, had let himself into Kristina's room. Waiting for him to leave, he tumbled into a soundless sleep. When he woke in the morning— Omega-Sunshine came in to wake him—his father was in the kitchen making breakfast.

I tend to think of that night as a kind of turning point in my life. When I saw Kristina wander into the kitchen in her torn Japanese kimono, her yards of twisty blond hair in some ratty, sleep-tossed configuration, I was no longer out-of-my-mind in love with her. It was like recovering from an illness in which a dim memory of the fever still remains.

"How did everything come off last night?" she asked with her back to me.

"Come off?"

"With Omega-Sunshine," she said as if no other context permitted itself. "You fell asleep in her bed if you remember."

I recited the events of the evening, the two stories, the videos, the game of Clue we played, everything up until and not including the tantrum.

"You're a good brother for a little girl to have," she said in her laid back California voice. I could think of no corresponding compliment to offer in return.

The rest of that summer offered more and less of the same—an ongoing idyll of intimacy punctuated by erotic false alarms. I finally went to the Dodger game with my father, who got us box seats behind third base from some producer friend of his. We had to leave at the end of seven with the Dodgers four runs behind (they actually came back to win) because my father had an early evening dinner commitment with, as he evasively put it, "a business associate."

When Kristina said "I'm going to miss you" to me at the airport—my father was in the Men's Room at the time—she gave me an extended hug, something like the one in Omega-S's room, but this one was goodbye rather than hello.

"I love you like a brother, Daniel," she said, which seemed to confuse even further the geography of our relationship. The word "brother" tangled on her tongue.

I love you too, I wanted to say, but instead mumbled some platitudes about having enjoyed my time with her.

"Sometimes feelings get confused," she whispered.

When my father's company moved to New York in late October—he had mentioned the possibility in an off-handed way at the Dodger game—it signaled the end of his marriage to Kristina. I thought it likely that Kristina would write to me—the letter I sent her had been returned "addressee unknown"—if only to let me know where she was. I was fully prepared to help her out in whatever way I could, though no specifics, outside of the untaken next step our hugs prefigured, came to mind. From time to time, I checked the Personals on the back page of *The Village Voice*, which seemed an ideal letter drop for someone of Kristina's sensibility. If I tried hard enough, I could imagine among the coded, often desperate love messages in The Voice was Kristina's disguised acknowledgment of the unspoken unspeakable between us.

"Do I remind you of her?" Janice asked.

5.

Sitting alone on his bed—Janice has just gone off to class—Daniel is watching the movie his father completed during the last of his California visits. The first time he played the tape, he and Janice got into messing around on his couch, Janice going down on him, the movie remaining on throughout as imponderable counterpoint. Something about his father's odd movie had put Janice in a sexy mood. Now, giving *Window in the Woods* his almost undivided attention, he can hardly imagine what that had been all about.

The last time he was in New York, his mother said in a rather casual tone that as he got older, he seemed more and more like his father.

"How so?" he asked, and got no more than a distant, knowing smile as his answer.

The film focuses on a boy of about seven who is kept prisoner by his grave, silent guardian in a cabin in the woods. The cabin has one window which is a foot or so higher than the child's eye level. In addition to a shabby mattress on the dirt floor (the child's bed), there is a wooden box that the boy uses as a chair. After an extended period of sensory deprivation, the boy discovers that by standing on his toes on the wooden box he can see outside his room.

The boy spends as much time at the window as he can physically bear, standing on his toes on the wooden box, craning his neck to look out. Everything he sees delights him: a field of wildflowers; the scurrying of a snake; a swarm of insects; the sudden appearance of a deer. A ragged girl passes one day, hurries by not even glancing at the cabin. With the passing of time, she becomes a familiar awaited presence, almost always alone, often oblivious to what's happening around her. One day a vicious-looking scavenger who has been by this way before, ambushes the girl and rapes her. The watcher lets out a cry, which is a sound we have not heard him make before. It is not clear but perhaps the cry, which drives away the rapist, saves the girl's life. A month or so later, the boy observes another man, even scruffier than the first, rob and murder the one who had raped the girl.

Years pass and the boy's guardian, a figure seen mostly in shadowy silhouette bringing food to the boy, lies on his death bed. Before he dies, he gives his housekeeper the key to the cabin in the woods and with it the secret of the boy's presence there. When the housekeeper releases the boy from his prison, he is no longer a child. She takes him in and cares for him in his father's house—the guardian turns out to have been his real father—teaches him a few basic words so that he can communicate his needs. She also dresses him in his father's clothes as a means of civilizing him, but the boy tends to roam the woods, returning to his former prison at every opportunity. Even though the door to the cabin is permanently unlocked, the grown boy (he looks about 18) likes to stand inside, looking out the window as if the world makes sense to him only from this circumscribed perspective.

6.

One day I found in the Voice Mail Box the message I imagined I had been waiting for. It read: "I miss you, my soul mate, my brother, my son, my unrequited lover, my friend. Have I lost you forever? When you flew away, a piece of my heart went with you. Lancelot please contact your Guinevere." I studied the notice, reread it until I could almost hear the voice behind the prose. During one of our evening talks, Christina had told me that *The Once and Future King* had been her favorite book as a child. So I spent a couple of days, composing an answer, taking care to say what I felt but not to overstate it to the point of scaring her away. "My view of what happened is very different from my father's," I wrote. "When I see you again, which I hope will be soon, I'll tell you what's in my heart." Of course, I received no answer. The message had obviously been meant for someone else, had been just another false alarm between us.

7.

One day, for no apparent reason, he murders the housekeeper, cuts her throat while she sleeps, steals her money, packs his belongings into a small valise and leaves. He travels by foot across the countryside, spending the night at various places along the way, motels and private houses, leaving a trail of gratuitous slaughter behind him. His manner is impassive and, on the few occasions when it is necessary to talk, gruffly polite.

Walking through one of the interchangeable towns on his road, he recognizes the girl he had seen from his window, now fully grown, and he follows her to a small hotel where she works as a chambermaid and part-time prostitute. Using his guardian's name, he takes a room at the hotel. After he showers and shaves and dresses himself in a suit and tie, he seeks out the desk clerk and asks to have the chambermaid, Marie, sent to his room. When she comes in, he is sitting on the bed with his back to her. She stands over him until he turns around, asks him what he wants in a shy, businesslike way.

"I want what the others want," he says.

At this point, she recognizes him as the strange man who had been following her. "No," she says. "You scare me."

He gets up from the bed, moves to the window and stares out at the empty street. The girl turns to leave, takes two steps toward the door but then stops herself.

"Have we met before?" she asks him.

He says nothing, seems to nod his head imperceptibly. As he stares out the window, an unmarked police car drives up to the hotel, and two plainclothes detectives get out.

"I'm going," the girl says, but she makes no move to leave.

As if drawn by a magnetic force, she moves slowly toward him. Her hand touches his shoulder and he lets out a cry, which echoes the sound he made years back when he watched her from his cabin window being attacked. Marie's face registers astonishment as the film gradually fades to black, the cry continuing long after the screen is dark.

Reverie

The next time we meet is in another country—Paris, as a matter of fact, the city of love (or is it light?)—at my brother's wedding to your half-sister. In the intervening three years, during which I publish my second book (a modestly reviewed meditation on war called *The Lion's Share*) I think of you no more than five or six times. From the moment I discover you, I try to catch your eye, but you never turn in my direction, seem occupied by the details of the ceremony or perhaps preoccupied in private reverie.

At the reception that follows, one thing or another keeps me from approaching you, an ongoing intention unobtrusively thwarted. I have the sense on no evidence beyond the fact that circumstance never brings you close to my side that you're willfully avoiding me.

I am the only one of my brother's family present for the occasion and, from what I can make out, one of the few Americans at hand. You are there with several people, perhaps one of them your husband, and appear to be an intimate of the bride. It is only later that I discover that there is a family connection as well—you share, or so everyone says, the same absent father.

For a moment, I catch your eye and wave and you make an ambiguous face at me in return, mocking, petulant, self-parodying, impossible to decipher.

I begin to wonder if it is really you and not some uncanny look-alike when the bride's mother sidles up to me and asks if I would be so kind—the request elaborate and, under the circumstances, unrefusable. She is asking me to dance with her.

It is not what I want to do and I make an awkward excuse or two (bad hip, naturally clumsy), which she steadfastly ignores, before leading her on to the floor.

"My name is Madeleine," she says in barely accented English. "I want to hear much about you. Are you a true person like your *frere*."

What can I say? Whatever I come up with is bound to seem either boastful or self-deprecating or some embarrassing combination of the two. "The question that had been on my mind," I say, the first of several mistakes I make that evening, "is whether the mother is as beautiful as the daughter and that is already answered before I ask it."

"*Je ne comprends*," you say. "I am or I am not?"

"You are of course," I say.

"*Oo la la*," you say. "Certainly not. It is a cruel compliment because so patently false and insincere." All this is said as if she meant something else—not easy to say what that else might be—altogether. We finish the dance in relative silence, and I have the sense that I have disappointed Madeleine's expectations.

"*Merci, monsieur*," Madeleine says when the music has stopped. "Thank you, Donald's brother, for indulging the whim of an older woman."

"My pleasure," I say and Madeleine laughs as if we shared some private joke, and waltzes off, aware of an audience, to greet whoever's next on her agenda.

I spot you at one of the hors d'oeuvres tables and I come up on you from behind and wait with willed patience for you to acknowledge me.

"Not here," you say without turning around. "Later."

"When?" I ask.

"Go away," you say, and I do.

It comes out while I am paying my respects to the married couple that the bride is your half-sister on your father's side and that the two of you have become fast friends on short acquaintance.

"I'm sorry your dad couldn't join us," the bride says.

"He's also sorry," I say to which my brother, standing behind the bride, rolls his eyes.

The reason our father is not at the wedding is because my brother is not speaking to him, but apparently that is not the story in circulation.

Madeleine appears and asks me if I need a place to stay for the night and I have trouble remembering if other arrangements were made and I say I don't know.

"Of course you'll stay with us," Madeleine says. "I'm not sure who else I've committed to, but we'll find out soon enough."

Dinner comes first and I drift off with what appears to be an insider group which includes Donald and his bride, Madeleine and her fourth husband, Bruno, and you and your date among others. You still have not quite acknowledged me.

During dinner at trendy Soixante-neuf, it strikes me that I left my overnight case in the closet of the reception hall or perhaps in the trunk of a taxi en route to the restaurant. My anxiety at its loss slips away after my second glass of wine.

Just as the dessert course arrives, as if it were their cue, Donald and Lola slip off on their honeymoon. When they are gone, Madeleine, who is at the head of the table, gives an audible sigh of relief.

Then I find myself sitting on a jump seat in an overcrowded taxi with Madeleine and Bruno, you and your date (whose name I understand is Roget) traveling to Madeleine's house in the 13th arrondisement.

When we arrive, there are some other wedding guests waiting at the door to whom Madeleine has also promised lodging for the night. We congregate in the living room to wait for our assignments.

A mathematical problem ensues. There are four guest bedrooms in Madeleine's charming, somewhat cluttered house, and nine people to accommodate.

It makes sense of course to award the bedrooms to the couples, which leaves me, the only single on the scene, odd man out.

"I have a perfectly comfortable folding cot," Madeleine says, first in French then in English. "The question is, where do we locate this cot?"

"I appreciate your concern," I say, "but it's no problem for me to stay at a hotel."

"I will take it as an insult if you leave," she says, "and I am not one, I promise you, quick to forgive."

To avoid seeming difficult, I offer to spend the night on the living room couch.

"I wouldn't think of it," Madeleine says. "Not at all. I will put a screen between us to give you intimacy. You will stay in my room."

"I think you mean privacy," I say.

"Do I?" Madeleine says. "Of course."

Everyone by this time has gone off to their assigned rooms except you and your date. During the preceding conversation, you have been browsing through the bookshelves that line the walls with the kind of concentration that seems to shut everything out so I am taken aback when you turn and say, "As always, Madeleine, you are too kind for your own good. This is your house and you have a right to be comfortable in it. So let me make a counter suggestion."

"Such as?" Madeleine says, perplexed as we all are by your unexpected intervention.

"We can just as easily install your lovely screen in the room Roget and I will be staying in," you say.

"I wouldn't hear of it," Madeleine says. "The matter is settled."

"Really, Madeleine," you say, "it makes no one happy to have you martyr yourself. Roget and I would be pleased to share our room in your lovely house with Donald's brother."

The debate between the two women goes on for longer than needs to be described and I watch like a spectator with only a marginal rooting interest in the outcome.

I am uncomfortably aware, though I have no idea of the history behind it, that the two of you have no love for one another.

At some point, Roget comes over to you, puts his hand on your arm and says in French—the following an estimate of his remarks—"This is Madeleine's house, dear, and the decision where a guest will be put up should be hers to make." He says this in a quiet voice but you push him away and whisper what I imagine to be the French equivalent of fuck off.

Roget turns to me and shrugs.

"*Oo la la*," Madeleine says. And then, turning in my direction, adds, "You decide please."

The narrow-eyed stare she gives me has a different message altogether. It is as if she is daring me to refuse her and if I dare, I fall beyond the pale of her forbearance. She will not, perhaps never, forgive me.

"Whatever you decide is fine," I say, trying to occupy an ephemeral middle ground that probably does not exist.

"Then it is decided," Madeleine says, "I'll get the cot for you and some linen." She sweeps out of the room in modest triumph.

Roget seems relieved, but you ask him, virtually order him, to go to the kitchen and get you a glass of white wine.

He hesitates before leaving, seems troubled, considers refusing you, but decides to postpone whatever scene he will eventually make.

And then for the first time that evening, we are alone. Everyone else has left the stage.

"Look," you say, "this has nothing to do with us, I want you to understand that, you and I are through as we both know, this had to do with Madeleine."

"Yes?"

"Yes. Madeleine has a sweet tooth for younger men. She is a notorious man eater. I stood up to her to protect you from an embarrassing situation."

"I don't see why you think I need protecting," I say. "Besides, Bruno will be in the room, won't he?"

You shake your head, impatient with what seems to you my willed innocence. "They have separate rooms," you say, not looking at me, watching the door for Madeleine's return. "Don't you see what's going on? Are you so totally oblivious?"

Unwilling to understand the intensity of your concern, I nevertheless thank you for your trouble on my behalf just as Madeleine returns.

"Your bed is made up," Madeleine says, making a point of saying bonne nuit to your back as you leave.

Madeleine's room is not as large as I imagined it, but there is a six foot high Japanese-style screen between her plush queen-sized bed (which she makes a point of showing me) and my austere single. A well-appointed private bathroom, which includes a bidet and double sinks with gleaming faucets is on my side of the room.

I wait a few minutes to let Madeleine use the bathroom, but when she doesn't appear after about 10 minutes I take my turn, following my usual routine except for the addition of a mild sleeping pill and get into my cot, which is reassuringly comfortable. Your warning makes a brief appearance in my thoughts. Before I know it, before I can obsess about the difficulty I have falling asleep in other people's beds, I have fallen asleep.

I have fallen asleep.

I have fallen asleep.

The third of my dreams has to do with rescuing a woman in some historical movie (of indeterminate

period) who I discover tied to a tree in the bois de bou-
logne. "Only a man pure of art has the power to free
me," she says.

And yet I have been the one chosen to untie her. Is
it possible that I have been mistaken for someone else
and so arbitrarily put into a false role. I look for a sharp-
edged stone to cut her bonds.

The woman, who is dressed in tatters, laughs mock-
ingly at my efforts. "If you are the right person, all you
have to do is kiss the hem of my robe and my ropes will
untie of their own accord."

I hesitate. Which of the tatters represents her robe,
I wonder. "And what will happen if I am the wrong
person?"

"We will both die," she says. "I hope you understand that I am speaking metaphorically."

How can I determine whether I am sufficiently pure
of art, whatever that means. A kind of inertia or paralysis holds me as I try to assess the potential negative consequences of the good deed I am asked to perform—like
what is a metaphorical death?—when I hear footsteps.

"What the hell's holding you back?" the woman
says, then adds something in a language that is not one
of mine.

Is it possible to be aware of dreaming or is that an
inherent contradiction? I find, unexpectedly, a Swiss
Army knife in my right hand pocket and I use the first
blade to release, which turns out to be a bottle opener,
to cut the woman's bonds, spilling the smallest possible
amount of blood.

She rubs her wrists, then puts her arms around my
neck and mumbles in a grudging tone of voice something about being forever in my debt. "You have a kiss
coming," she says. "Where would you like it?"

I am embarrassed to say what I want, and she laughs
and says, "All right, dummy, then I'll make the choice
for you." The next thing I know we are on the mossy
ground together, rolling around, struggling for position.

It is at this point I usually awake, but tonight the dream insists on playing itself out.

When I open my eyes at first light, I am shivering and sweating, my covers in a sprawl on the floor next to the cot.

I drag myself up to go to the bathroom, but the door is latched from the inside so I return to my cot. Exhausted, I try to go back to sleep—that is, I shut my eyes—but the urgencies of my bladder become the more crucial concern.

So I put on the gray suit I wore at the wedding—my overnight case lost—and go off to find an unoccupied bathroom. The first two I try are, like my own, latched from within and I begin to consider other alternatives.

Then I remember there being a closet with a toilet in it right off the kitchen and I work my way down two flights of stairs. In the dark, nothing seems quite like it was in the light. Somehow I manage to find myself inside the closet-like enclosure. With the door closed and latched against my back, there is barely room to stand.

After peeing, I rub my hands against the sides of my pants, then comb my hair with my fingers. When I step out of the bathroom after a serious struggle with the latch, the light is on in the kitchen and Roget in his overcoat is sitting with his back to me, drinking coffee from a mug the size of a soup bowl.

Looking over his shoulder to take my measure, he offers me a scornful smile.

"*Bonjour*," I say.

"*Ca va*," he says in return.

The amenities out of the way, he finishes his coffee in silence.

The coffee pot is one of those plunger types I have no idea how to use, but I stumble around self-consciously opening cupboards. "Where does she keep the coffee?" I ask him.

Roget seems not to hear me or perhaps not to understand the question.

He is washing his coffee cup when you come into the kitchen and say something to him in French—the inflection suggests a question—which he answers, or seems to, without turning to look at you.

Roget pushes open the side door, the door that comes off the kitchen, makes no attempt to button his coat, and disappears from the scene.

You walk to the window and look out after him, tracking his progress, or so it seems.

"What was that about?" I ask.

You ignore my question, retreat to the table in a defeated posture, slump into the chair farthest from mine.

"Are you all right?" I ask.

"No."

"Is there something I can do for you?"

"Absolutely not." You keep your face turned away.

I take sips of my coffee and wait my turn, my patience running out before the coffee turns cold. After awhile, after my cup is drained, I get up and announce that I am going back to my room.

"Don't you leave me too," you say.

"Did Roget leave you?" I ask. "The impression he gave me is that you asked him to go."

You raise your head momentarily. "Is that what he told you? Whatever, it comes to the same thing, doesn't it? The fact is he's gone."

I sit down at the table, honoring your request, leaving an empty seat between us. After a moment, you take the seat next to me and put your head on my shoulder. And then I put my arm around you—where else can it go?—and your body stiffens almost imperceptibly.

And that's the way we are, trapped by the flashbulb of the imaginary onlooker's imaginary camera, when Madeleine discovers us, sitting cheek to shoulder at the kitchen table.

She makes a point of not looking directly at us, asks the room if anyone—we are the only two in the kitchen—would like some breakfast.

She has, I notice, put her long gray hair in an over-elaborate bun, a designer chopstick seemingly holding it in place.

"I almost never eat breakfast," I say.

You seem about to speak, but instead get up from the table, nod to me, and leave the room.

"She knows I didn't want her here," Madeleine says. "It's no trouble, you know, for me to make something for you. I'm one of those woman who enjoys to challenge the kitchen. And so what are your plans for today? What would you like to do with your day?"

I have no plans, which is to say I had planned to return home as soon as it seemed appropriate to leave. At the same time, I have a kind of anxious unobjectified foreboding. I want desperately to get out of the kitchen, but I am unable to come up with an acceptable excuse to take off.

"Before you go," Madeleine says, "there's something I feel I should say, if you knew me better you would know this is not my style to criticize, but somebody, some friend should tell you this for your own good. I say this very reluctantly because I believe there is some good in her too. I suppose there is good in everybody, but who knows."

Then she goes on to tell me this extraordinary story about you, insisting on her reluctance to give out this information while of course giving it out in profusion. According to Madeleine, there is an unsolved mystery in your past, a former husband who died suddenly under, as she puts it, a dark cloud. Though nothing was ever proved, there were those who thought that you had arranged his murder, or possibly even committed the murder yourself.

"I for one don't believe she's capable of murder," Madeleine said, "no more than any of us, though for an American she's extremely subtle. In any event, I like you too much not to let you know what you might be facing. I know with my own eyes that you are sweet on her so don't deny it."

Later in the day, when you drive me to the airport, you ask in a casual voice if I had sex with Madeleine when I spent the night in her room.

I don't see that it is any of your business, which is what I don't say or at least don't say aloud. Instead I ask if it's true that you had been married and widowed since the last time we ran into one another.

"Well, did you or didn't you?" you say.

"Why do you care?" I ask.

"That means you did, doesn't it? What a helpless innocent you are. Frankly, I'm embarrassed on your behalf."

My suspicion is that the woman in the dream was Madeleine and that what happened between us extended beyond the dream. Nothing is certain, however. "You were married before or you weren't, which is it?" I ask.

We drive another twenty minutes in silence when I realize the road we are on is not going to Orly and ask, as anyone might in my position, for an explanation.

"I was wondering when you'd notice," you say. "There's a totally charming cabin in San Remy, isolated from virtually everything, that I've been invited to use. I was in no mood to go alone so I thought I'd kidnap you if you have no objections."

I look at my watch. My flight to JFK leaves Orly in an hour and fifteen minutes. "How far are we from the airport?" I ask.

"Too far to walk," you say. "Look, I promise you it will be different this time. If you prefer to go to the US by yourself to going to San Remy with me, I'll drive you to Orly. Deal? Either way, you have to tell me you didn't sleep with my sister's mother."

"I didn't sleep with my sister's mother, I mean your sister's mother," I say.

"I don't know whether to believe you," you say. "Can I believe you? How can I? Do I even want to believe you? Do you even care whether I believe you or not."

"I'd appreciate it if you'd take me to the airport," I say, a gesture at reclaiming some pretense of dignity.

You pull over onto the apron and stop the car with a jolting screech. I expect you to ask me to get out of the car, which I plan to refuse, but instead you stare (or look blindly) ahead as if your image were paused, and say nothing for more time than I know what to do with.

When I look at my watch you unfreeze long enough to glance in my direction. "It's disgusting to always want to know the time," you say. "If you live in the moment, you have no need of a watch."

It may be true that I almost never live in the moment, though I have always aspired to make the necessary adjustment. On the other hand, living in the moment does you no particular good when you have a flight to make.

A police car pulls off the highway and stops about fifty feet behind us. A few minutes pass—it seems like no time at all—but no one emerges from the vehicle.

"There's some dope in the glove compartment," you say. "When they stop you in France, they tend to search the car. I don't know what will catch his attention more, rushing off or staying put."

"We're probably better off returning to the highway," I say.

"You think?"

"We're less conspicuous as part of the general traffic, don't you think?"

"You make the decision."

"Let's go," I say and we pull back onto the highway, sliding in front of a paper goods truck that honks its horn at us.

"Even when I was with others," you say, "it's always been you."

After a moment, I turn around to see if there's anything to concern us coming up from behind.

Years later, when we meet at a party given by people neither of us have met before, we go off together into the coat room, which is also the master bedroom, and endeavor to catch up. At some point the discussion turns to the confusing events of our brief time together in San Remy.

"It was kind of you to come with me," you say. "I'm sorry I behaved like such a bitch. Look, I never wanted it to happen the way it did, but I have to say it—You got on my nerves."

"Did I?"

"It was all my fault I'm sure," you say. "It was a difficult time for me as you know. A man I was crazy about, a man totally undeserving, dumped me." We are sitting on a pile of coats a foot or so apart and you offer me your hand.

"I thought I was the one that owed you an apology," I say.

"You were always so nice to me," you say. "Really, you were too nice—that was your problem. I've always had trouble getting on with men who were nice to me."

I have trouble reconciling the image of niceness with the sense of myself I carry away from that strange period in my life. "I behaved unconscionably in San Remy," I say.

"Not at all," you say. "I understand perfectly why you felt you had to get away."

"I should at least have left a note, some kind of explanation," I say.

"The fact of your absence was explanation enough. You realized I was putting minute doses of poison in your food. Do you think I didn't understand that? Why wouldn't you run away? I just wonder you had enough strength to walk by yourself to the next town."

"I left you the car because I was sort of hoping you'd come after me," I say.

You retrieve your hand and use it along with the other to cover your face. "I can't believe you wanted me to come after you. Why would you? Why would you possibly?"

For the moment, I let the conversation die, feeling with some desperation the need to get away, the need to escape further explanation. When I fled the cabin in San Remy, I recall, I had been feeling a little weak in the legs, a light sweat on my forehead, my stomach in minor turmoil. All pretense. The illness was just a ruse on my part to throw you off. I didn't want to have to explain my need to be on my own. I had so thoroughly internalized my sense of being desperately ill, my body accepted the implications as though they were real. I even collapsed a few times while running.

"I just wanted to see how far I could take it," you say, your hands still over your face. "You may not want to believe this, but I never intended to go all the way. I want you to believe that. I really do."

I get up from the bed, leaving my coat somewhere in the pile, and edging my way through the crowd, nodding to the woman I had exchanged smiles with earlier in the evening, exit the party, summon the elevator and, without waiting for its arrival, scramble down nine flights to the lobby and then into the street, crossing my arms in front of me as a stay against the shock of the night air.

For the first block or so, I walk briskly, but then as I near the subway, I slow down as if all this desperate hurrying had tired me out. In fact, I avoid going into the station and continue to walk downtown perhaps to the next stop, which is eighteen blocks away, the streets quiet, almost deserted at this time of night. The moon in a crescent phase, offering a gesture of light as if coming from behind a closed door.

I must have walked fifteen blocks in all when I glance behind me for the first time and see, or imagine I see, some incalculable distance away, a shadow figure running toward me, holding up something, some offering, a coat perhaps. Deciphering my perception costs me no more than a moment or two. And then I pick up my stride, continue on my way, my urgency unabated, but as in a dream I suddenly feel the poison flash through my veins, the microscopic doses retarding my progress in imperceptible ways and I sense that before long, before I reach the entrance to the next station of the subway—I've waited a long time for this—I will be caught by whoever is coming up behind me (it is always you), prepared to accept whatever comes next.

The Villa Mondare

1.

A few days before Wheeler was scheduled to leave Boston for the Villa Mondare in the Lake Magiorre district of northern Italy to begin a five week almost all expenses paid residence as a scholar, his wife of ten years, Flora, without advance warning, left him.

His wife's abrupt departure after so many difficult years together unnerved Wheeler, made him feel unfit for the company of strangers, so he called the sponsoring agency, the Holden Foundation, to postpone his arrival for at least five days.

His request for a delay was received with no great enthusiasm.

It was not encouraged, he was told, the spaces at the Villa in great demand, a long list of people waiting for a cancellation.

"A family problem, an emergency," he heard himself saying when the silence at the other end threatened his already fragile equilibrium, "which should take three or four days to put to rest."

Wheeler flew to Milan in an unprepared state three days later than previously arranged.

Nothing had been settled at home except that his recently estranged wife, Flora, would not be joining him at the Villa, would not be joining him, so she said, anywhere ever again.

Wheeler had been to Italy once before, though not to this part of Italy, had spent three days at a conference in Rome twenty years ago and had been robbed by a team of professional pickpockets, which had undermined an otherwise positive trip.

A limousine picked him up at the Milan airport—a limousine for him alone—and took him on narrow picturesque roads, ancient stucco houses like jewels set into the sides of cliffs, to his elegant accommodations at the Villa Mondare, which was just outside the town of Tuamo on a dramatic hill overlooking the lake.

The astonishment of the views from the windows and balcony of the spacious room they had ushered him to eased his sense of dislocation, let him feeling if only for a moment or two that some unsought grace had entered his life.

He unpacked, showered and changed, put on his public face and went to the East Terrace, as advised, for "apperitivi," which preceded lunch.

The other scholars and their spouses gathered around him to make his acquaintance and, for an extended moment, he knew what it was to be celebrated by an unknown public.

What had happened to delay his arrival? his new-found friends, his crowd of well-wishers, wanted to know.

Almost everyone was older than he was—five, ten years older—and they were all, with one interesting exception, in residence as couples.

The exception was a single woman of perhaps thirty-five, small, dark, intense, painfully private, a visual artist with the unlikely name, Serena Swan.

She was the only one who hadn't come up to him on the terrace to introduce herself, which had the effect of making him more aware of her than anyone else.

(Was it a conscious device? he wondered.)

The others were friendly and solicitous like a family of uncles and aunts, seemed barely distinguishable to him on first introduction.

There was a sanitary engineer, a Sovietologist, a president of a university, a rocket scientist, an Incan specialist, a composer of computer music, a Romanian literary scholar, a famous criminal lawyer, an ecologist who worked for the government, a deposed leader of a small Asian country, a philosopher from Harvard, and an avant-garde visual artist among others.

For his first meal, he was obliged to sit next to the high-spirited director of the center, Marco Antonelli who questioned him about his difficulties in arriving and the nature of his work.

Wheeler was forthcoming and evasive.

His wife had taken ill, he said, the first explanation to come to mind, an innocent enough lie, a marginal truth.

"Will she be joining you?" Antonelli asked.

Wheeler said it depended on her health and whether she could get away from her job.

In the accelerating derangement of his personal life, Wheeler had lost contact with his project, his book-length study on domestic violence in primitive cultures, a study he had been collecting odd bits of data on for more than a decade.

So when Antonelli, out of hostly obligation asked about it, he found himself explaining his project in the language of his application, which had stuck in his mind like a frozen computer file.

His book was made of narratives, he said, was meant to be suggestive rather than conclusive.

But what did Wheeler mean by "primitive cultures"?

Primitive in the loosest possible sense, said Wheeler, no longer fully sure what he meant, mountain people, the uneducated, the illiterate, people who live far from civilization.

Antonelli, who had a sly wit, made a joke about Wheeler interviewing one of the gardeners who, years back, had strangled his wife for a seemingly negligible provocation, the man a wonderful gardener, tender with plants, devoted to the soil.

Wheeler didn't know how to reply, mumbled, "Well, maybe I'll make time to talk to him."

"He speaks no English," said Antonelli.

"My Italian is rather primitive," Wheeler confessed, abashed at the failing, "restaurant and guide book stuff."

"He won't even talk to me," said Antonelli.

Wheeler slept in the afternoon, feeling slightly feverish, postponed visiting his studio which was in an outbuilding somewhere on the estate's extensive grounds.

The next morning—the beginning of his first full day—Wheeler slept through breakfast.

At a little before eleven o'clock—he was not even sure he had set his watch to the right time—he took his briefcase and the xeroxed map they had given him and set off into the woods to establish a presence in his studio.

Once he got caught up in his work, he thought, he might be able to let go of this obsessive feeling of loss.

The Tower studio, which took him ten minutes to reach, was a fifteenth century stone building equipped with two catty-cornered desks, an IBM Selectric on one and paper, pencils, ribbon cartridges, three ballpoint pens, four pencils, paperclips, whiteout, hole puncher, erasers, pencil sharpener, and two bottles of mineral water on the right-hand corner of the other.

Wheeler sat down at the desk without the typewriter, opened his manila folder of notes and jottings, felt closed-in and reopened the outside door.

While he was shuffling through his papers, a bee found its way into the small enclosure and buzzed about in a rage of frustration.

Waiting in vain for the bee to find its way out, Wheeler poured himself a cup of mineral water (one of several graces provided for him) and leaned on an elbow.

From his narrow window, the waters of Lake Magiorre, glistening in the sun through a scrim of leaves, looked like multi-colored tinted glass.

As he was leaving the studio for lunch, a small figure jogged by without a word—intrusive in her silence—on the path outside his door, wearing a red tee shirt with the black-lettered inscription, "Woman in Motion."

At lunch he found himself sitting next to the jogger, Serena Swann.

"I don't believe we've actually met," he said, holding out his hand and offering his full name, Henry Adams Wheeler.

Serena had her eyes down, head turned away, as if painfully shy or lost in contemplation or studying the poker hand of bread sticks in front of her.

Her continuing silence provoked him to talk, which she attended to without verbal response, a conscientious wordless listener.

He found himself telling her things about his life he had given away to no one else: his sense of incompletion at Flora's departure as if a piece of himself had torn itself free and floated away.

He had no idea why he was exposing himself to this stranger, though that he had, and that she seemed receptive, intensified his attraction to her.

The middleaged woman on his left, a Romanian scholar doing study of 19th century Transylvanian heroines, interrupted Wheeler's monologue with a question about Wheeler's belated arrival.

"All that matters," he said abruptly, "is that I'm here now."

When he turned back to his sympathetic listener, she was in apparent conversation with the man on her right, Lucien Karamazov, a world famous Sovietologist, a man capable of decoding tomorrow's headlines.

Feeling betrayed and somewhat disheartened (he had bored her with his self-involvement), Wheeler made no further attempt to engage Serena.

After dessert and coffee had been served, as he was getting up to leave the table, Serena seemed to say to him from behind her hand, "Don't lose heart."

Wheeler walked away without looking at her, considered that it was possible that he had misheard her, that she couldn't possibly have said what he thought he heard, though it echoed in his head with a nasty authority.

He made a pit stop at his elegant room, took a couple of aspirin and sat down with a detective novel by Jim Thompson the previous guest had left behind, planning to begin work in earnest at the Tower after a few minutes of rest.

He read two pages of the book, the second page twice.

It was 4:30 when Wheeler woke, feeling better if still slightly feverish—the sweat like ashes on his forehead—the prospect for an afternoon of work diminishing by the minute.

An alternate plan formed itself: Why not use the time before dinner to explore Tuamo, which he had only seen from his terrace, and to get himself a gellatto—his throat a little sore—and maybe even take a ride on one of the ferries that seemed to come and go from one distant lake village or another at ten minute intervals.

Wheeler stopped at the second gellateria he passed, the one on the steps going down to the ferry docks and was assessing the ice cream on display in the glass showcase when he noticed someone familiar out of the side of his eye a few feet away, her back to him.

Hoping to escape without being discovered, he ordered a cone of something called nociolla by pointing to it, the whole transaction made through gesture.

He was walking down the steep stairway to the lake front, in a self-congratulatory mood when he felt a cool hand on his arm, and heard a woman's teasing voice saying, "You made a wise choice."

"Garbo speaks," he said.

She rolled her eyes up in mock exasperation and said, "I don't talk while I eat and I don't talk while I fuck, capice?"

She accompanied him down the steps or perhaps he accompanied her.

"Look, they don't approve of guests getting romantically involved," she said, touching his arm, taking that liberty, "which was made apparent a couple years ago when some guy was caught in the room of a woman who wasn't his wife and was sent home the next day."

"I'll be careful not to let that happen," he said.

She took two gliding sidesteps away from him and said, "That's an obnoxious thing to say."

Resisting the impulse to apologize, he said, "You like to think of yourself as an outrageous person, don't you?"

She shook her head in smirking denial, said, "Are you so prickly all the time?"

"I am boringly even tempered," he said.

"Just so," she said, entertaining a private smile.

They walked down the steps side by side (arms brushing) to the parallel street below that ran alongside the lake.

Who was following whom? he troubled himself to wonder.

They made their way to the ferry docks and tarried at the schedule posted out front, all in fuckless silence.

It was implicitly arranged: he would take his maiden (so to speak) voyage with her on the ferry leaving for Terrarosa in a little over five minutes and return (it was ten after five at the moment) on the 6:20 or 7:15 boat, the latter making dinner a close call though not impossible if they walked up the 295 steps from town to Villa at a brisk pace.

Wheeler bought two round trip tickets to Terrarosa, and they boarded the ferry which had just arrived and unburdened itself, taking seats upstairs on the right side, which was less populated than the left, all of which was done with barely a word spoken between them.

"There are gardens in Terrarosa that require visiting," she said, "which is what you have in mind, I suppose."

"I'm always game for a good garden," he said, aware that their legs were touching and that it was she who initiated contact.

The Terrarosa Gardens were a seven minute walk from the ferry dock, Wheeler taking note so as to assess the latest they might stay and still get back in time for dinner, Serena mildly amused at his diligence.

The gardens were virtually flowerless, not what he expected, all huge overhanging palms and cunning paths.

Serena gave full concentration to the exotic landscape while Wheeler went through the motions of looking, out of patience with the outside world.

At some inevitable point, he moved on ahead. When he looked back some minutes later, not to let her get too far behind, she was not in the picture, which made him anxious though he couldn't imagine why.

He knew he wasn't responsible for her, but he felt responsible.

Wheeler retraced his steps, took a subsidiary path on the left that ascended to a higher level—the only place she might have turned off—and he hurried along hoping to overtake her.

He was out of breath when he reached the top of the hill and, finding no sign of her in either direction, he shouted her name into the void.

An old man, shovel in one hand, burning stub end of a cigarette in the other, turned his way.

Wheeler asked in his guidebook Italian if the man had seen a young American woman go by.

Flicking his glowing stub to the ground, the old man considered Wheeler's question as if it presented some hidden metaphysical problem.

"Signorina Americana," he said at last, holding out empty hands, "notta here."

Wheeler rephrased his question to make it clear he was asking if she had been there, had gone by there on her way to somewhere else.

The old man shook a gnarled finger at him, a look of bemusement on his face, then he said something Wheeler didn't understand and made a backhanded gesture which indicated (or didn't) that he take the turn to the right.

Fifteen minutes later, having lost himself briefly in a simulated rain forest, Wheeler found himself back at the center path about fifty feet further on.

He completed the tour of the gardens then retraced his steps to the entrance, which was also the way out, hoping to find Serena waiting for him.

He asked the attendant, whom he recognized as the woman who had sold them their tickets to the garden, if Serena (describing her) had come through.

Although she spoke English and had been chatty with them earlier, the woman seemed to misunderstand his question.

When he asked again if Serena had passed through, the woman said she had just come on duty, which Wheeler knew to be a lie, though he could think of no reason for her dissembling.

After another failed search, he took the 7:15 ferry back to Tuamo, showered, put on the obligatory jacket and tie and arrived at dinner without appetite just as the soup course was being served.

Serena, sitting five seats away on the same side of the long table, ignored his inquiring glance.

Wheeler fulfilled his obligation to the meal, argued with the energy specialist on his left about what might be done to head off the uncertain possibility of global warming.

At midnight there was a knock on his door, which he reluctantly left his bed, slipping on pajama pants— he had been lying in the nude on top of his blanket, the night still—to answer.

Standing facing away, hands on hips, Serena whispered, an insinuating smile on her face, "Is it too late?"

He said it was, said where the hell were you, I was sleeping, I'm going to sleep, goodnight, and yet he was pleased she had come to his door,

"Sorr-ry," she said, closing the door behind her, padding down the hall in her slippers, while he stood there listening to her steps disappear in the distance.

That wasn't the end of it.

A few minutes later—he had closed his eyes, folded them shut, thinking of a movie he had seen a month ago of a lawyer on trial for the murder of a woman he had an affair with, had become obsessed with—his phone made a buzzing sound.

As he reached for the receiver in the dark, he said under his breath, Why does she want to torment me?

He listened dutifully to her silence.

Why call, he wanted to say, he almost said, if you have nothing to tell me?

When she had hung up, cutting him off at the very moment he was prepared to speak, he felt tears of anger rush to his eyes.

He put on his pants over his pajama bottoms and went out into the hall with a flashlight, went from door to door, looking for the right room.

The hallway turned, went down two stairs and up one, and the further he got from his own room, the more he despaired of finding his way back.

The last door was hers: Ms. Serena Swan.

He knocked once and then, embarrassed (what was he doing here so far from home in the middle of the night, in the middle of his forty-fourth year?) he reversed his steps.

Before he knew it, someone was pursuing him down the hall.

He had his key out, he found his room, he opened his door, he tried to pull it shut, an act that was resisted by the interposition of an arm.

"Are you mad?" she whispered, which made Wheeler smile.

"This isn't what you think it is," she said, squeezing by him into the room.

Wheeler crossed his arms in front of him, said, "What isn't it?"

Serena curled up in the nearest chair, yawned, said, "If you're going to say you started it, which is what I imagine you saying in my head, there's no point in either of us ever talking to the other again."

Wheeler studied her face before speaking, muttered in a barely intelligible voice, "You started it."

She frowned, nodded to herself in justification, closed her eyes and in a moment or two appeared to be asleep in her chair, her rosebud mouth ajar, her faint snoring adding itself to the otherwise distant voices of the night.

Wheeler watched her from his bed, unable to give up consciousness, afraid of what she might do if he weren't there to watch her do it.

2.

In his third week at the villa, in love, Wheeler rediscovered the rationale for his book on domestic violence. Pages emerged each day from his IBM Selectric, leaves of thought, accumulating from nowhere into a substantial pile.

Almost every night after the others were in bed, Serena came to his room and made love to him—

sometimes with apparent passion, sometimes as matter of ritual—with hardly a spoken word to acknowledge what was going on. When he woke at first light,
when he slept and woke, she was gone.

During the day, even on the rare occasions when
they were alone, she tended to ignore him, which
Wheeler accepted as an extreme version of discretion.
Only signor Antonelli, who would wink at him from
time to time, seemed aware of Wheeler's secret life.

One evening after dinner, Serena gave an exhibition of some of her work (a kind of high level show
and tell) for the assembled guests. The displayed art (an
odd collection of painted-on found objects), which she
described as conceptual, disturbed Wheeler with their
freakiness.

Later in bed after lovemaking, he made the mistake
of offering his uninformed opinions on her presentation
(she made the mistake of asking what he thought) with
only slight pulling of punches. Serena was outraged,
said she had known he was hostile but not that hostile,
put on her clothes and left his bed for her own.

What could he say by way of apology without compromising his integrity, he wondered in the wake of
her absence. He slept badly, dreamed several variations
of telling Serena he was sorry in various beseeching
ways which earned him without exception her silent
scorn.

He let the next day go by without approaching her,
then caught her smiling at him (or so he thought) from
across the dinner table but she did not appear in his
room that night which led him to read the smile in ret-
rospect as something else. In his dream, an abject Serena
apologized to him for being thin-skinned and insecure,
whispered in his ear the admission that a little hostility
was an attractive quality in a man.

The next morning Wheeler's mysterious low grade
fever, which had mysteriously disappeared for a week,
returned. He forced himself out of bed, dressed himself

in whatever was at hand and rushed to the villa terrace in the hope of catching Serena at breakfast.

The only one left at the table, which was otherwise cleared, was Michella Antonelli cracking the shell of one of three soft-boiled eggs spread out in front of her. "You are too late," she said to him, "but you are welcome, if you like, to share one of my eggs."

Wheeler settled for a cup of coffee and sat with his hostess while she excavated her eggs. "You seem happier now," she said, a woman who was nothing if not direct, "than when you first came, no?"

Someone had blown the whistle on him, thought Wheeler, letting a worst case scenario play itself out in his imagination. "It's only an illusion," he said, which made Michella laugh.

"The illusion in question is happiness in general or your own happiness?" she asked. A few minutes later, she excused herself and left the table.

Wheeler continued on the winding path that went by his studio with the idea of calming himself before starting work. He composed a letter to Serena in his head and when it was finished he found himself at the ruin of a medieval castle.

It was an undemanding climb and Wheeler worked his way to the top of the ruins, as if there were some secret that might be revealed by seeing things from the highest point of the grounds. As reward for his effort, he discovered the intriguing prospect of a cave—not mentioned in the guidebook—about a hundred yards to the right.

It wasn't really a cave, he discovered, when he found his way there, and left the early afternoon light for the shadowy dark, but a tunnel. He heard someone (something?) in the shadows ahead of him and he waited with his back to the wall for whatever it was to reveal itself.

Later, when he was back in his room at the Villa, he tried to assess what had happened to him. Something had touched his shoulder in the dark and he must have fainted because the next thing he knew he was lying on the ground near the exit, thirty—five minutes of his life lost to him.

His fever had gotten worse and he lay in bed, unable to focus, leaving his room again and again only to find himself in the same place. Eventually it was time for dinner.

Eventually it was time for breakfast. The phone rang intermittently and he didn't answer and then he did, but afterward he had no recollection of what was said to him or what he said in return if anything.

They brought him food which he tried to eat and couldn't and at some point an Italian doctor arrived to examine him. When the doctor in broken English asked how he was feeling, Wheeler said "Not at all."

When word of his illness got out, most of the other scholars made pilgrimages to his room to see how he was getting along. Serena was among the handful that, for one reason or another, didn't show up.

3.

The antibiotic the grave doctor gave him reduced Wheeler's fever to its previous inconsequential state, and the next day, feeling barely better, he was attending meals as before. There was much solicitude. Even Serena, who maintained her practiced silence, looked at him with what he took to be concern.

The doctor returned three day's later for a follow-up visit, seemed insufficiently pleased at Wheeler's progress, suggested he come to the hospital in Milan for tests. When Wheeler said he was all right where he was, the doctor let the issue drop. The fever continued, flickered on and off, as if the condition of health had been shorted by some loose wire in his system.

He was having a fever dream when Serena knocked at his door with her mildly insistent double tap. When he opened the door (his dream erection preceding him) she came in without a word of explanation—her pre-fuck silence—and sat down possessively on the side of his bed. "I'm back, Oh Henry," she said.

She instructed Wheeler to lie on his back and not worry about a thing, she would do the work, slapping his hands out of the way when he grabbed at her. She didn't want interference, she said, wanted things her own way for a change. "I love you, Serena," he said while she was riding him, which to his surprise brought tears to her eyes and broke her habitual silence.

The next morning when he woke up, she was still in his bed, cuddled against him, her arms sashed around his waist. He felt elated that she was still there, though later when she insisted on appearing at breakfast with him—"we have nothing to hide," she said—he felt as if some basic freedom had been abridged. Instead of going to her own studio, she accompanied him to his, visiting with him for over an hour, sitting on his desk with her legs twirled around his neck.

The period of subterfuge was over. She made a point of sitting next to him at lunch, her thigh touching his under the table. Unable to finish her gnocchi with pesto, she spooned her leftovers onto his plate, an intimacy which attracted a few amused stares.

Antonelli left a note for him in his mail box the next day, requesting a meeting, and Wheeler knew or thought he knew what was coming. He showed the note to Serena, whose only reaction was a shrug. "If it were about us, they would have sent me one too," she said, "no?"

4.

Wheeler decides that if they ask him to leave (or ask him to stop seeing Serena), he will politely refuse. He feels at home at the Villa, has never been happier anywhere.

He will not defend his actions or excuse them. Who knows better than the Italians that passion is its own justification.

In Wheeler's dream, Antonelli warns him to stay away from Serena, that she is disturbed and possibly dangerous. "I can handle it," he boasts, but the outcome of the dream belies his bravado. In the actual meeting, Antonelli tells him almost the same thing though not directly. Serena, he learns, had been institutionalized as a teenager for killing her mother's lover.

The next night when he knocks on Serena's door and she is slow to answer, he realizes—he hears a voice, a man's voice—that someone is in bed with her. He knocks again, banging his fist against the door in outrage. Eventually the door opens just enough for Serena's face to appear. When Wheeler forces his way in, he sees Antonelli in a white silk bathrobe, facing away, standing like a shadow at the window.

5.

The next time he sees Serena, she shows him the gun, a pearl-handled 22 caliber pistol the size of a cigarette lighter, she had used on her mother's lover. "Why are you showing me this?" he asks her. "If you have to ask," she says, winking, "I guess I'm not getting my message across." Wheeler notices that she is pointing the gun in his direction. "Hey, that's not funny," he says.

When her attention is distracted, Wheeler wrestles the gun away from her. He is surprised at how little resistance she offers. "Big strong man," she says. "It's not even loaded, you asshole." Wheeler winces under her verbal assault.

Serena comes to his studio the next morning to make amends, brings him a letter that had been sitting in his mail box for days. It is from Flora and he folds it in half and stuffs it in his pants pocket. "You can open it now," she says. "I'll turn my back while you read. There are no secrets between us."

Is it always that way? When you have wanted something badly and then no longer want it, it tends to come to pass. Flora, who is to be in Italy for unlikely reasons, asks if she may come and visit him. "You may not believe this," she writes, "but I've missed you." Serena reads his face with a troubled glance as he reads his wife's letter.

The best of times pass more quickly than the worst. Wheeler wakes up one morning with the awareness that in two short days he will have to leave Mondare and return to the world. How could his time have passed so quickly? He remembers arriving—the difficulties of that first day—and the day Serena left without saying goodbye and little else. He remembers writing to Flora, asking her not to come to Mondare.

There is a knock on his door while he is still in bed. The limousine, which has come to take him to the airport, can only wait five more minutes. "I'm not ready," Wheeler says. Later that day, Marco Antonelli visits him in his room. "We need your room for another scholar," says Antonelli in his mild, reasonable, slightly ironic voice.

When Antonelli leaves, Wheeler locks the door to his room and returns to bed. In his dream, Serena arrives with two policeman who forcibly enter his room and, wrapping him in his blankets, take him from the Villa. They board a ferry, smuggle him aboard as if he were cargo. "To live in the world," Serena tells him after they stuff him in a barrel in the hull of the ferry, "you must learn to give up the world." "Last call for Magenta," the captain calls and a new group of passengers (after a period of hectic comings and goings) replace the old.

He goes without food, refusing to respond to the impre-
cations—the insistent knocking and officious chatter—
at his locked door. When he feels strong enough, he
wedges the heavy wardrobe against the door. He showers off the sweat and dresses himself in his gray suit,
which hangs on him. Antonelli calls him on the phone
to ask him to let the doctor visit him. If the doctor says
he is too sick to leave, Antonelli assures him, they will
let him stay until he is better.

Can he trust them? Wheeler wonders. The gardener, who killed his wife in a notorious case ten years ago,
says he will give Wheeler an interview if he opens his
door. "I thought you spoke no English," says the suspicious Wheeler, who at the same time is not unappreciative of the significance of the offer. "If they knew I
speaka de English," says the gardener, "do you think
they would a letta me go?" Wheeler says he will submit
a list of ten questions to the gardener and if the first
two are answered to his satisfaction, he will unlatch
the door. The gardener says something in Italian, which
Wheeler takes for agreement.

The chef appears at the door with a bowl of Wheeler's
favorite soup—chicken soup with stars Mondare style.
It has been so long since Wheeler has eaten anything,
the idea of food repels him. "Leave it outside if you
don't mind," Wheeler says. "It is meant to take warm,"
the chef says ruefully. Wheeler imagines he hears the
chef carrying the soup away, though also dreams opening the door to find the bowl of steaming soup awaiting
his reluctant pleasure.

6.

Somehow Flora is produced, or is it merely Flora's
voice on tape outside his locked door. "Honey," she
says, "this has gone much too far. Let me in, okay? I'll
look after you as I used to. You know you need me

to look after you, you know you know that. I do love you, Henry."

7.

Dressed in his gray suit, Wheeler sits on his terrace and studies the world at large. A crowd gathers. When people wave at him, he accepts their homage with an almost imperceptible military salute. After awhile a succession of unmarked police vans drive up, arrange themselves in a semi-circle in the courtyard below. Marco Antonelli is talking to the driver of the first van. Wheeler can tell they are talking about him because Antonelli points in his direction from time to time. So many people have gone to so much trouble on his account, Wheeler thinks, which is more burden to him than pleasure.

8.

When the sun goes down, he returns to his room. The phone has been ringing for several minutes before he troubles himself to answer. It is his father on the line, calling from Seattle, Washington. "Henry," the old man says in his booming voice, "Flora called to tell us what was going on and I want you to know your mother and I are a hundred percent behind you. If you're in the right, you stand by your guns." Wheeler, conserving his energy, merely nods in response. "Right or wrong, we're proud of you," his father says. "Now this is costing some money, so I'm going to sign off. Just to say your mom and dad's thoughts are with you in this your hour of need."

9.

Days pass. The appeals to reason have fallen off, he is considered a hopeless case. The carbinieri wait outside his balcony in military formation, pass the time spitting, smoking butts, and shooting at random birds. The one time Wheeler ventures on to the balcony to get some air, a stray bullet nearly takes his head off. No, thank you. So he stays in the room, conserving his strength, getting weaker, occasionally pacing back and forth. He thinks of agreeing to leave in exchange for a meal, but he wants the other side to make the first offer of conciliation. He calls the office and asks to speak to Antonelli. The secretary he speaks to, a young woman named Francesca, says signor Antonelli is not available.

10.

This morning Wheeler unlatches his door, and leaves it ajar. A cleaning woman comes in to change his sheets, but no one else comes his way. Though he feels light-headed, his legs feathery, when the time is right he saunters to the dining room for lunch. The strangers around the table nod to him in greeting as if he were a new arrival. Names are thrust at him. It is like his first day at Mondare the second time around. He notices the waiters looking at him askance, talking in whispers among themselves, the occasional finger pointing in his direction. Afraid that they won't serve him, afraid that he will have no appetite, he eats ravenously—two packages of breadsticks, a salad of sundried tomatoes and mozzarella, two helpings of linquini with sea food. He lingers over coffee and desert, is the last one to leave the table. Michella Antonelli, wearing her rueful sympathetic smile, seems to be waiting for him as he leaves the dining room, motions him to follow her to the library. When they are alone, she outlines a plan for his escape, warning him that if he returns to his room, the carbinieri have orders to shoot him on sight.

11.

Disguised as a woman, carrying a gun in his purse, Wheeler boards a ferry at Tuamo. It is his plan to take the bus at Terrarossa to Switzerland and from there, after an overnight stay in Zurich, fly back to America. His problem is this. He is identified as a man on his passport so he needs to get out of his female disguise and back into men's clothes before he reaches the Swiss border. He goes into the Women's Room on the ferry to make manifest gender change, but the ferry docks before he can complete transformation and he has to hurry—the door sticks a bit—to get off the boat before it takes off on return trip to Tuamo. As soon as he is on dry land, Wheeler realizes that he left his purse with his passport in it in the bathroom on board so he jumps over the chain as the ferry is pulling out and twists his ankle in a clumsy sprawl. And then the purse isn't in the Women's Room where he left it but has been removed to the Captain's quarters, which means (he hardly knows what it means) he will have to explain his unlikely predicament in guide book Italian. Fortunately, the captain speaks some English and he hands over the purse with no questions asked, all the time staring at Wheeler, his woman's make-up askew from prior attempt to remove, as if he were some kind of pathetic freak. Two policemen board at Tuamo and elect to sit on the bench directly behind Wheeler. If they wanted to arrest him, they could have taken him in at Tuamo. He hums to himself some long forgotten jingle his mother used to sing to him as a child.

12.

He is on a crowded bus among mostly German-speaking tourists heading toward Switzerland. A mile or so from the Swiss border, the bus is stopped by an unmarked black car. Two uniformed officials board and walk down the aisle while Wheeler looks out the window—a gray stone wall the only vista—as a way of disguising his presence. A man two seats behind Wheeler is removed by the two uniforms. "What's that about?" he asks the stout woman next to him. "I don't know," she says in foreign English, "but I would guess that he's the child rapist they've had an all points alarm out for." The bus moves into switzerland without further incident. He rents a car in Lugano in conjunction with his companion from the bus, who is from England, her name Gretchen, and drives to the airport in Zurich. They spend the night in an airport hotel in adjoining rooms. When Wheeler wakes at 5 a.m., he discovers that Gretchen has gone and all his cash except the twenty dollar bill he keeps in his shoe for just such emergencies, has gone with her. At the Zurich Airport, after waiting in line for forty minutes, he discovers (his frustrations multiplying) that all the flights convenient to his stateside destination have been over-booked and the only available flight back is by way of a two-hour stopover at Milan, which is the last place he wants to go. Rather than spend two more days in Zurich, which is the alternative, Wheeler takes his chances with Milan, figuring the Italians may have forgotten their grievances toward him by this point, hanging out in a booth in the Men's Room to make himself unapparent during the hiatus between flights, eavesdropping on a drug deal between two men dressed as priests in the adjoining booth. The trip back to Boston, except for some minor turbulence, is uneventful. On his return to Earth, his estranged wife, Flora, and two editors from Houghton Mifflin, eager to publish the completed manuscript of his seminal book on domestic violence in mostly primitive cultures, greet him at the arrivals gate at Logan Airport like a returning prisoner of war, his wife holding on to him as if he might float away into the ether, lost to the world of ambition forever, if not pressed to earth by love's embrace.

II. From *Babble*

Drool

There is at the moment a baby with bowlegs standing on my lap. *Quelle chance!* He has been in the same position for hours, tilted forward like a figurehead. It is what he likes to do, and I am not, though my knees begin to ache, unappreciative of the honor. "Don't you have anything else to do?" I ask him. The question slides by him like a greased pig. I was meditating when he arrived, trying to come to terms with feelings of failure and emptiness, and have lost concentration, have fallen into vagueness. Why don't I lift him off my lap and return him to the floor? It hurts his feelings. And he is tenacious and will, if removed, find his way back.

Mostly, he just stands there, flexing his knees a bit, looking ahead. He is no trouble, not much, a good boy, self-sufficient and forward-looking. I suggest that he go to the corner and see how the weather bodes. He turns his head to see if I mean what I say, a pained quizzical look on his face.

Nothing frets as much the spirit in my business (meditating) as time wasting. I haven't thought a thought worth thinking since he climbed on my lap.

Look, I say in desperation, I enjoy having you on my lap but I need a little time by myself and perhaps you would like some time by yourself. He takes the hint and climbs down. "Bye bye," he says wistfully. Two minutes later he is back.

I am in the early middle of a thought when he returns to my lap, so ignore him briefly which is what he is used to. He digs his heels in as if getting ready for a long siege. "Wipe my drool," he says, "and I'll tell you a story." It is the most words in sequential order I have heard him speak. I pretend not to be astounded so as not to upset his equilibrium, wipe his drool with a yellowing handkerchief.

For an infant, he tells an excellent story. I won't recapitulate it all for you here, but will try to limit myself to the high points. The central figure, not unexpectedly, is a baby.

The storyteller apologizes for his choice of hero. His choice is limited, he explains, by his tender years.

At the start the baby says goodbye to his father and goes out into the world, seeking adventure. The father pleads with him to stay another year, at least until he is toilet trained, but the baby is impatient. Why postpone living? The father holds philosophically that a child should be free to make his own mistakes.

THE BABY'S ADVENTURE (A SAMPLING)

A woman, hanging out clothes in her front yard, invites the baby in for soup. Another time, the baby says. The woman says the soup will get cold if the baby doesn't drink it and will not accept refusal. It is a thick, nearly impenetrable pea soup the woman has to offer which in truth is not the baby's favorite. To be polite he has one spoonful on which he gags through no fault of his own. Throwing the bowl off the table, he gets up to go. The woman, almost as wide as she is tall, imposes herself in the doorway. You can't leave, she screams, until you finish your soup.

Meanwhile, a woodcutter chancing through the neighborhood hears the woman's screams.

"What's the trouble, madam?" he asks, breaking down the door with his axe.

"This baby," the woman says, pointing, "has just been horrible and won't finish his soup."

The woodman, moved by the lady's tale, raises his axe over the baby's head as if to split him in half.

"I beg of you, woodman," says the lady, "spare that baby's life." She throws herself on her knees and weeps on the woodcutter's shoes, which makes it slippery for him. "Please. Please. Please."

The woodcutter is a simple man, he says, unused to pleas of mercy. Once his axe is raised it is harder to withdraw than to strike the necessary blow.

The lady offers her hand in marriage to the woodman in exchange for the life of the child. The woodman says he will think about the lady's offer and return in one day with his decision.

"Are you grateful?" the lady asks the baby when the woodcutter is gone. She kisses his face a hundred times. The baby says that he'd like to continue his journey.

"All I want is a little show of gratitude," the lady says, weeping at the humiliation of her position, "and then, all things being equal, you can go."

The baby shows gratitude—he will do anything for his freedom—at which time the lady reneges on her promise. What good is gratitude, she asks herself, without the continuing presence of him who is grateful. She proposes to put the baby's gratitude on display in the kitchen window so that the casual passer-by can see what kind of a woman she is.

The baby takes back his gratitude; the lady screams; the woodman returns with his axe, making a striking appearance.

"I've brought you my decision," the woodman says. Baby doesn't wait to find out what it is but runs through the woodman's legs and out the door and out into the street. He will not be persuaded, he thinks, to stop for another bowl of soup. Then he thinks what will happen to the lady in his absence. She will bawl her heart out, no question, the poor lady. One day he will return with an axe of his own and make her proud.

In the course of his travels, the baby falls into despair, and missing the people he has left behind, considers aborting his journey. People are either the same everywhere, he decides, or not the same anywhere, merely seem the same to one whose eyes are inexperienced with distinctions.

There are certain functions the baby requires others to do for him, which cuts into his independence of action. His diaper, for example. He scours the city for someone who will change his diaper without asking in return an excess of gratitude.

He leaves a notice in the Personals column of an underground newspaper. "Groovy baby, Capricorn, interested in meaning of life, seeks mature gentle couple for intimate exchange."

A gray-haired woman, a former mother, says that there is nothing in the world she would rather do than change a baby's diaper. Her husband adds, "My wife's an angel when it comes to children. She spoils them silly."

The baby puts himself in her hands. She is a bit clumsy from being out of practice, but there are certain things, as she says, that you never forget. When she pins the diaper to his flesh he lets out a howl which causes several fire trucks to come rushing in their direction. Done (the mistake corrected), she hugs him and says, "You poor baby, did your mum and dad desert you, sweetheart?" She hugs him breathless.

When she releases him, the husband unplugs the baby's thumb from his mouth. "Now you look like a big boy," he says.

When he is by himself again the baby returns thumb to mouth.

The mature couple insist on buying the baby a gift, something useful yet out of the ordinary, to remember them by. "What do you need, sweetheart?" the woman asks the baby. "Give us some idea what you want."

"A cookie would be nice," says the baby.

"Babies never know what they want," the husband says.

"You give them something and then they want it. Sometimes they don't want it just because you give it to them."

After long discussion, the couple decide on buying the baby a giant piggy bank to teach him the value of savings. The husband removes the baby's thumb from his mouth. "With a bank like that you don't need to suck your thumb." The baby goes off without the piggy bank—it is too heavy to carry—and the police are called, the couple heartbroken.

"All we want, officer, is to give this baby this token of our affection. After that you can do what you want with the young fellow. "

"Who does this baby belong to?" asks the officer.

The streets of the city are filled with people who have no answer to the policeman's question. "If he belongs to no one, we'll have to run him in." There are a few who laugh; others go about their business buying Christmas presents or not buying them.

The piggy bank and baby are taken to the station for questioning. The mature man and woman come along as material witnesses.

Someone is guilty, the chief of police says. The diaper the lady changed is brought in on the end of a long stick as evidence. "The odor," says the chief, "does violence to the air." Everyone in turn has a sniff before the diaper is sent to the lab for testing.

The husband and wife turn out to be undercover police, revealing themselves in a startlingly personal moment. "Though we love him," they say, "he's been a handful."

The police ask the baby a number of difficult questions.

"Where do you live, baby?" "Where did the stuff come from?" "Who put you up to it?" They give him a lollypop to loosen his tongue and take turns saying kitchy koo which is routine procedure with babies.

Unable to understand his answers, they let him go with a warning to keep his nose clean.

"Nose?" he asks.

"It's just an expression," they tell him.

The baby is followed by a detective disguised as another baby, a deception that fools no one. The detective's outfit is transparently inauthentic, out of style, unlived in. The point of his gun in fact sticks out from under his diaper. He drools to excess.

It is no fun for him being followed. To lose his shadow the baby slips into a movie theater and sees his first film. The enormous heads of a man and woman are kissing when the baby comes in. It is the only thing he can see in the dark, two enormous mouths. Thinking the seat is empty, the baby crawls into someone's lap. "I don't allow strangers in my lap," she says. The baby apologizes, is about to change his seat when he notices the baby-disguised detective coming down the aisle in his direction. In danger of being caught, his comprehension of the law limited by his youthfulness, he asks his companion if he might hide in her purse a few minutes. There is no time to wait for an answer. He opens the snap—it is a soft leather bag, big enough for him if he folds himself over—and crawls in. "Don't disturb anything in there," she says. "I'll tell you what's happening so you won't miss the picture."

The detective takes the seat next to the girl in whose purse the baby is hiding. His suspicion is aroused when he sees her talking to her purse. The smell of his cigar advertises him. While he is in the seat next to them, the baby has to stay put in the purse. Powder spills on him. His image in her compact mirror is smaller and whiter than he remembers. The air is thick with sweet powder.

With the detective close by, watching her lips, the girl neglects to tell him what's happening in the movie.

The baby closes his eyes and dreams his own very different version of the movie. Just when he is about to come to an interesting part, the girl snaps open her purse. She is crying, and the baby in sympathy cries too. The woman on the screen, wearing a flimsy bathrobe, is also crying. Everyone in the movie house appears to be crying except the detective, disguised as a baby, who is smoking a cigar and sleeping.

The movie is very sad, says the girl. The woman in the movie has an incurable disease, which no one knows about except the woman herself and her doctor, who dies just when he is about to discover a cure. Meanwhile the man she loves, and has sent away, is fighting in a war in some obscure part of the world.

The baby is halfway out of the bag when the girl pushes him back in. The detective has woken in a suspicious mood. "May I pway wit you pockeybook," he whispers to the girl in fake baby talk.

The tears on the purse block the air from coming through the soft leather. The baby learns that it is next to impossible to revisit old haunts. Using a nail file that he finds among assorted paraphernalia, he cuts a hole in the bottom of the purse just large enough for him to slip through. A clatter of odd objects follows, but the baby is away, crawling under seats. An enormous screen is facing him, the oversized heads of a man and a woman kissing, which is where he came in. The closer he is, the more frightening the picture. He has never seen lips so large or so red. When the large woman face cries, her tears are like a waterfall. He thinks he will never get out from under them.

He is hungry, he announces, brushing away a small tear with the back of his fist, climbing down.

"Bye bye," he says, waving as he does with both hands. He patters into the kitchen and while a random thought or two crosses my mind, I hear him ask his mother for a cookie.

"And one for me too," I call after him, flexing my legs to restore circulation.

"If you get your father," she says, "we'll all have our dinner together."

Spooky in Florida

"Batman," says the baby in my ear, "used to be called Bathman, did you know that, until something happened to him that changed his name."

We are walking along the Boardwalk, the baby on my shoulders, his right hand around my neck, when he imparts this information.

"Bathman flew to Florida with his son, who wasn't called Robin in those days, and when he got there Florida was closed. OPEN ON WEDNESDAYS, the sign said. Florida was nice, but a kind of spooky place. The sign said, CLOSED ON MONDAY. That was spooky. Bathman fell into the water and got his hair wet. Then he lost his pants and changed his name to Buttman."

I feel old holding him on my shoulders while we walk as if his weight were added years, a salt spray covering us like that invisible net women used to spray on their hair. "Batman fell into the ocean?" Such news is hard to assimilate.

"Not Batman," he protests. "Bathman. That was when he was still Bathman. After he drowned, he came out of the water and changed his name. Florida was closed when he got there because it was the wrong day for Florida."

It is as if he is rehearsing the fragments of a story, trying them out in various configurations to see which way they make the most satisfying pattern.

Bathman's sidekick (the baby continues), whose name was something like Peter or Pener, something like that, said, "Bathman, I mean Father, could we go to Florida tomorrow, sir?" And Bathman said, "Son, I'll have to look at the calendar and see if we have any crime-fighting scheduled for that day. No. Tomorrow is all right, son."

Florida was owned by a cleaning lady named Doris and sometimes called Mrs. Woo, who took a vacation with her father. That's why Florida was closed. One thing Bathman didn't like, it was his secret weakness, was to get his hair wet. When his hair was wet he didn't look like himself. When you look like someone else, sometimes—the storyteller gets a wistful look when he reports this—you really are someone else. "You're all wet, Bathperson," the cleaning lady said when she got back from her vacation. "Is that your little son Pener there with you? I wouldn't have recognized him he's grown so much or maybe what it is his clothes have gotten smaller." She gave Bathman a funny looking towel with long-necked birds on it and when he dried himself with it his hair came off. Bathman was so embarrassed he wore a hat all the time after that, even when he slept, even when he went BM which were his initials. "Don't be angry, Father," his son said to him. "Mrs. Woo was just teasing. I have a suggestion. Why don't you change your name so people will think someone else is bald and not Bathman. How about Buttman? Or Captain of the World?"

Bathman's secret identity was crying secretly under his mask. "Bathman and I have shared the same mailbox for so long, we're like two peas in a pod. I wouldn't know who I was with a different name."

The Cleaning Lady, who was in the refrigerator cleaning the food, said in an icy voice, "Some people I know think Bathman is the funniest thing they ever heard."

When she said that about his name being funny Bathman got so angry he said, "Come on, Pener. We're not staying in Florida another minute."

Here the story seems to stop—the baby looking off into the distance, which is one of his ways of terminating things—and I ask him if the story is over.

"Can I have something to eat?" he asks. "After lunch I'll tell you the rest of the story, which is also about Kitwoman though I haven't thought of that part."

He has already had his lunch, but since he is hungry or thinks he is—the odors of food in the air hard to resist—I say he can have one of anything he wants. It is of course the wrong tack. He says that he will have two of what he wants or he won't have any.

He crosses his arms in front of him, an indication of immovable conviction. "Mommy lets me have two," he whispers, no argument, merely a gesture toward breaking impasse, the introduction of another opinion.

THE CONTINUING STORY

When Bathman got angry at the Cleaning Lady, Mrs. Woo, he picked his son up like a suitcase and they flew to London.

The remainder of the baby's story, except for an occasional flashback, takes London as its setting.

When Pener wakes he sees the shadow of a moose on the curtains of his London room, which frightens him momentarily.

Later, Bathman comes in and says "Superheroes don't give way to tears," and Pener says I'm sorry. "And what about you, sir? In Florida..."

"Sometimes superheroes have to cry in Florida," says Bathman in a contrite mood, "I hate, as you know, to get my hair wet. We all have our character failings. It's just that we adults make the rules and even if we don't always live by them ourselves, we don't want to see you up and coming superheroes learn our bad habits."

The narrator wishes to remind his listener at this point that this is the story of how Bathman and Kitwoman got together and came apart.

The Cleaning Lady asked Bathman if he would take out the garbage and Bathman said taking out garbage was not something superheroes did.

"You superheroes are a lot of junk," she said, "when it comes to doing a little help around the house. What's the matter you're not strong enough to lift that can?"

"You know what's the matter," said Bathman.

"You're embarrassed, is that it? Dignity undermined? I have a suggestion. Why don't you walk backwards when you put the garbage out so that people will think you're going the other way."

They got into a fight in which Mrs. Woo stuck a pot on Bathman's head and Bathman dumped Mrs. Woo in with the garbage. At first Pener thought it was funny, but then he said, "Stop it. You're making me angry." To make things all right, he took the garbage out himself, forgetting that the Cleaning Lady was in the can.

"If you do that again," she said to Pener, "I am going to have to send you away to school."

It was after that that Bathman and his sidekick Pener decided to fly to London.

"Can we take the Cleaning Lady with us?" Pener asked. "Please. She's not so bad when you get to know her. I mean one thing about her she knows how to keep a place clean."

"London's already as clean as it can be," said Bathman who was thinking of changing his name to Boatman and making a fresh start.

All the trouble started when Bathman and Pener flew to Florida.

The Cleaning Lady didn't like the two superheroes to sit at the dinner table with their masks on. "It's my opinion," she said, "that at mealtimes the business of the day ought to be set aside. It makes me feel as if the food I put on the table for you is some kind of crime."

When the two superheroes arrive in London the rumor is that the pound is falling. Boatman and Pener ride down Fleet Street looking in vain for evidence of fallen pounds.

"Can Boatman fly?" Pener asks the original of that name.

"If that's what he wants to do," says the authority, who seems to have some unspoken doubts. "Mostly the Boatman likes to travel by Boatplane or, if the Boatplane is in the shop, by Boatmobile or Boatship."

It strikes Pener, who hides his disappointment behind a cough, that it might take awhile for a new superhero to discover the activities that characterize his superiority.

Boatman, soon to change his name unofficially to Bloatman for reasons of added poundage, moves in with his former arch-enemy Kitwoman, also known (it is her English name) as Churlgirl. Churlgirl's favorite trick is kissing and Pener thinks of her, dreams of her, insofar as dreams admit to recollection, as the Kisswoman.

In the morning before breakfast Bloatman and Kitwoman kiss. It is reported under Miscellaneous Theatrical Events in the Nicholson's Guide. At lunch time, if you can believe the *News of the World*, they kiss twice, Bloatman a creature of habit. And then after lunch more of the same. They kiss on the average of eleven or twelve times a day.

"Ugh," Pener says, for weeks his only conversation with the others.

"Did you say something, lad?"

Pener doesn't remember if he did or not. "I'm sorry, Bloatman. I'm very angry. You said we were going to do some crime-fighting when we got to London, but all anyone does around here is kiss.

"Oh you've noticed the kissing," says Bloatman. "Well, I'm on a case right now, which I can't tell you about until you're older. Give me a little more time, okay?"

"A little more," says Pener, holding up thumb and fore-finger in indication of the limits of his already over-extended patience.

Pener is not old enough to go out crime-fighting on his own. "How old am I?" Pener wants to know. Every time he asks he seems to get a different answer.

"You're getting to be a big thing, ducks," Kitwoman says, kissing him.

Pener Has a Dream:

He wakes up in his dream bigger than Blatman, his former sidekick, father and friend. Pener has grown during the night and/or the father has shrunk. (Has the other's name changed again, he wonders, or is it just another way of pronouncing it?) Blatman, when he wakes (in Pener's dream), is as much smaller than Pener as Pener, before going to sleep, was smaller than Blatman.

"It wasn't my idea, little fella," says Pener. "What a bore! We'll probably have to change our names."

Blatman stands on his toes and says, "There must be an explanation. Think, Pener. Did we eat anything out of the ordinary? The capers from Fortum and Mason's perhaps."

To accommodate their reversal of stature, the two super-heroes change their names to Peeman and Blatter. Peeman moves into the big bedroom with Kisswoman while Blatter, as the smaller, makes do in the little room in the little bed.

So this is what I've been missing, thinks Peeman, lying next to the warm-sided Kisswoman who has a tendency to take more than her normal share of the blanket.

"Which of my two men is it?" the cunning Kisswoman asks. "My big or my little?"

"I used to be the little, which you probably didn't notice, though now I'm the bigger."

She kisses him all over his face, starting with the eyes, extending to the ears and working down to the chin. UmmUmmUmmUmmUmmUmmUmmUmmUm mUmm UmmUmmUmm...

"Superheroes don't like to be kissed or fussed over," he says. "In your case however, since no one told you before, I'm willing to let it pass as a misunderstanding."

"You're so misunderstanding," she says teasingly, "I'm going to eat you up."

Feeling pieces of himself disappear—sometimes jokes turn out to be true—Pener cries out in his sleep and wakes up for real.

When he wakes up his bed is wet, which is mysterious. Kitwoman is in the next room, purring sweetly in her sleep. Blatman is in the bathroom peeing, which is something that people who don't know superheroes imagine they never do. "Is that you, sir?" asks Pener. "It's just the rain," says the other.

Blatman has six croissants with strawberry preserves, a poached egg and two blood sausages for breakfast. He has gotten fatter since his accident in Florida and his eyes have gotten red. "What do you say we do a little crime-fighting before lunch, son?" he says, lighting up a cigar.

Pener is overjoyed and does a somersault on the kitchen table, knocking over a cat and a pint of milk. "Do you mean it, sir? Will it be like old times?"

"Get your mask and cape on, Wondrous Boy—I'm going to call you Wondrous Boy from now on—and we'll knock 'em dead."

"Wait a little minute," says Kitwoman, kissing them one at a time. "Do I understand that you plan to leave me behind like an old shoe?"

"We don't want to see you get hurt," says Blatman.

"Close your eyes," says Kitwoman.

"It might be different if the crooks were midgets or only had one arm," says Pener.

Kitwoman laughs her Kitwoman laugh. "The two of you have so many Band-Aids and bandages on, I have the impression that a strong wind will blow you apart."

"Those Band-Aids are part of our disguise," says Pener.

"We'll be home for dinner, honey," says Blatman. "Don't worry about us."

"Look, forget it. You're not going to go without me." She steals Blatman's belt and the crimefighter's pants, unsustained, fall to his knees.

"I can see your butt, man," says Pener.

Buttman's face under his cowl and mask turns a deep shade of embarrassment. "We're superheroes, honey," he says. "You have to understand that that's our job."

"Ha!" says Kitwoman. She gives him a playful punch in the stomach, which doubles him over.

"If there's one thing superheroes don't like," says Buttman, holding up his beltless pants, "it's to fight over nothing."

"Am I nothing?" says the Kitwoman, getting down on all fours. "Am I beneath notice? Is the Churl person beneath the attention of the illustrious superheroes?" Her sarcasm is silken.

After a terrible fight—Pener covering his eyes to avoid taking sides—the Kitwoman leaves through a secret passageway.

Word gets back to the two superheroes that the Kitwoman has become the biggest crook in all of London. Wherever she goes she does something of noteworthy and record-breaking badness.

"How could she do this to us, Pener?" says the larger of the two superheroes, looking for a place to change into his new costume, the bathroom door unaccountably locked. The bathroom, under ordinary circumstances, is Buttman's favorite place to change identities.

While waiting for Pener to come out of the bathroom, Buttman notices the Wondrous Boy sitting in the kitchen sucking his thumb. "If you're not in the bathroom, Pener, and I'm not in the bathroom...it must be someone who is not either of us."

"Maybe it's my secret identity," says Pener.

The toilet flushes with a roar.

When they force open the bathroom door the room is empty and the commode and shower are missing. They find a note where the toilet used to be. *Call me Cutperson*, it says.

"I think she means Catperson!" exclaims Pener.

"Think, Pener," says his mentor. "If you were the Catperson, where would you go?"

Pener thinks..."If I were the Catperson, I'd go to the Tower of London," he says.

"That's the very place," says the other. "That's where I would go if I wanted to tower over former friends."

The superheroes, with not a moment to lose, get stuck in London traffic and are forced to abandon the Buttmotor at Picadilly Circus. Somewhere along the way they get on the wrong queue and find themselves trapped in a tour of Westminster Abbey. It is educational, though not what they had in mind for the day. When the pair finally arrive at the Tower of London there is a sign on the door saying Closed for Repairs. It is the Florida situation all over again.

"If we had only known," says Buttman, "we could have completed the tour of Westminster Abbey and maybe even have gotten a look at the Houses of Parliament."

They wait impatiently for days, it seems, for the Catperson to appear, sleeping among German tourists on stone floors, experiencing boredom and hunger.

"What has she done that's so bad?" Pener asks. Buttman looks like he has an answer but it stays inside his mouth.

Just then Catperson and her henchpeople, disguised as knights in armor, sneak in without waiting in line and steal everything in sight including Buttman's pants.

They are in for a surprise, Buttman is wearing another pair of pants under the first pair. Taking a lance from the Tower wall, he knocks over Catperson's false knights like a row of toy soldiers. At the same time, or moments later, Pener captures the escaping Catperson by the tail. "Got you," he says.

"It's me who's got you," she says, holding the arm that's holding her tail.

"That's not the way the game is played," says Pener.

"I'll give you a kiss if you let me go," she says, and not waiting for his answer gives him a Catperson kiss. "I have a terrific idea, ducks. Why don't we team up. Catperson and Pener. C and P. We'd knock 'em dead, luv."

Pener is tempted but sees in her offer a potential conflict of interest. "What about Buttman?" he asks.

With a roar of laughter Catperson escapes her captors. The two superheroes follow her, but she is always a step or two ahead. They follow her through Lillywhite's which she cleans out in a pillaging spree and into the lower reaches of Marks and Spencer's basement. "I have nothing to wear," she says wherever she goes.

"Why are we following her?" Pener wonders.

"Because she's running away," says Buttman. "What's your opinion?"

"I think it's because she's running away," says the other. The two superheroes like to agree with each other and do it at every opportunity.

"Copy cats," says Catperson, sneaking by in her velvet tiger boots.

"Well, you're a Catwoman copy," says Pener, "or a copy Catwoman."

"Am not," she says. "I won't let you be my sidekick if you call me that."

"He's my sidekick," says Buttman.

"He can be mine if he wants to be."

They can't make up their minds and pull on the Wondrous Boy—one on each arm—until he almost comes apart.

Later, everyone says I'm sorry. "Tell me about Florida," says Catperson.

"Florida was closed," says Pener. "It was spooky in Florida."

"That's where the story ends," says the storyteller. "Do you want to know what happened next?"

"I thought you said the story was over."

"That's what I said. This is what happens *after* the story is over. Pener wanted to stay with Buttman who used to be Bathman before he fell into the ocean and he wanted to go with Catperson who used to be Kitwoman before she changed her identity. He wanted to stay, you see, and he wanted to go to a different place. Well, he flew to Florida and fell into the ocean and died."

I take him off my shoulders and we sit down on a bench overlooking the ocean. He elbows me in the side to gain my attention. "When Pener came out of the water he was allowed to eat three of anything he wanted."

The terms of things have changed again. "I thought Pener died."

"He did, but then Bathman and Kitwoman got together and pulled him out of the mouth of a giant fish and took him to London. That's a different story. That's not really what happened. That's what he was thinking would happen." He leans his head on my shoulder and closes his eyes. "I'm hungry," he whispers. In a few minutes he is asleep.

The Fell of Love

"I think you ought to know I'm not going to marry you," I hear the baby, who is no longer quite a baby, say through the closed door of my study. "Marie and I are going together."

Who is Marie?

"So you and Marie are going together," she says a thin note of pain breaking through the coolness of her tone.

"One of these days we might get married," he says.

A few minutes later the baby's mother comes into my study and asks if she might interrupt my unproductive self-absorption for a few minutes.

"I feel rejected," she says, laughing in a way that implies she thinks she ought to be amused but isn't. "Our baby's got another woman."

"The worst of it is that the woman he's infatuated with,—Marie, you may remember her, that streaky stacked blonde that sat for him a couple of times—won't have anything to do with him. Yesterday, when I asked her if she could baby-sit Friday night, the truth came out. She said she's no longer interested in babies, that they have nothing to teach her."

"Did you tell the baby what she said?"

"He's been so miserable as it is, moping around the house and sighing in his pathetic way, I couldn't make it worse. Will you talk to him man to man?"

"I'm not very good at that."

She blows me a kiss. "I was only kidding, you know, about the unproductive self-absorption. I think your self-absorption is as productive as anybody's."

Moments after she leaves, almost as if it's been rehearsed, the baby takes her place in the room.

"When you're married," he asks after a point, "does that mean you have to sleep in the same bed as the other person?" He asks the question with both hands over his face, one eye peering through the slats of his fingers.

"Only if both people want to," I say. "Well, both people do want to," he says, "and that's final." He does a parody of his father storming furiously out of a room.

He returns. "What about love?" he asks.

"What about it?"

His thumb, as if it were just passing by, finds its way into the tunnel of his mouth. It is apparent after a while that neither of us, with all good will, can think of anything to say. The word "love" has come between us. We study the silence for clues. Before I can put my thoughts into a sentence, he is gone.

Later that day, or possibly the next day, I get a phone call from a young woman who calls herself Marie.

"Your little son has invited me to share his bed," she says in a voice that strives for outrage.

"I've heard something about that," I say.

"Have you? In the last house I worked the father used to come into my bed at night, pretending to be the son. As you might imagine, such a deception couldn't go on for long."

I say something to the effect that I can't imagine how such a deception could go on even once, though my remark, like the father she cites, seems to pass unnoticed.

"I'm prepared to give it a trial run, if you want me," she says. "My boyfriend's moved back in with his wife, and I'm at loose ends."

"It's the baby who wants you," I say. I am about to say something about talking it over with my wife, when the woman on the phone overrides me again.

"I get that," she says. "I only hope he's not too de-
monstrative. I really love babies, I really do, if they
don't expect too much from you. I have a lot to give,
you know, if not too much is asked."

An appointment is made for an interview.

2.

Two weeks have passed since Marie has become a part
of our household. The baby, whom I've hardly seen
since the girl has come to live with us, comes glumly
into my study and sits down on the floor with his back
to me.

"Is something the matter?"

"Nothing's the matter."

"Are you sad because it's Marie's day off?"

He treats the question as if a reply were too self-
evident to deserve notice. "Do you know what?" he
says. "Marie won't sleep in my bed."

"She won't?" He has caught me, as he often does, in
a moment of distraction.

"Maybe she will if I ask her. Will she? Tell her she
has to, okay? Tell her if she doesn't...if she doesn't, she'll
have to sleep with the dog and we don't even have a
dog. Okay?"

I indicate, which is something we've been through
before, that it's not within my power to compel Marie
to sleep in his bed.

He is unconvinced. "I am angry at you," he says,
"also disappointed. And I'm not going to tell you the
story I was going to tell you unless you say to Marie,
'Marie, you have to sleep with the baby. That's the
rule.'"

"I'll tell her that you would like her to," I say. "How's
that?" He shakes his head in an aggrieved manner. "If
you wanted her to sleep in your bed, I would tell her
that she had to."

I lift him in the air and hug him, to which he offers an obligatory complaint. When I put him down, though he insists he is still angry with me and still doesn't like me, he offers me the story of what may have been his last night's dream. What follows is the baby's account.

THE STORY OF MY DREAM

The baby is in the bathroom taking off his overalls when a woman he's never seen before walks in, carrying a baby about his own size.

"Is it my brother?" the baby asks her.

She doesn't say anything, a reproachful quality in her silence, and puts the other baby, who may or may not be the baby's brother, in the baby's place on the toilet.

"Isn't he a little prince!" the lady says.

The baby holds his nose politely, doing the best he can to ignore the foul air of the other.

A big dog comes into the bathroom, not the dog the baby doesn't have but another one, a large white pig-faced dog with flower-like spots. The dog sniffs the room, then in one large bite eats the other baby, toilet seat and all.

The lady is very sad. The baby tells her not to cry, but she is too busy crying to listen.

"We were going to be married," she says. "Why did that monstrous dog have to eat him?"

The baby sits on the toilet the way the other did, but fails to make the same kind of splash. Nothing he does seems to please the lady, who is moaning and blowing her nose.

In a voice that makes the windows rattle, the baby orders the dog to return the baby he swallowed. At that moment, a lion comes in and eats the dog.

"Take me away, sweetlove," says the lady, "before something really bad happens. I like you better than that smelly baby."

She says her name is Marie, though she is a different Marie.

The baby reaches into the lion's mouth and pulls out the dog, then reaches into the dog's mouth to pull out the other baby, who seems a little smaller for having been eaten.

The lady is so overjoyed she announces that both babies can sleep in the same bed with her if they promise not to kick or wet. When they all go into the lady's room, they discover that someone has eaten her bed.

3.

Marie requests a private interview. It comes in the form of a note delivered to me by the baby.

I tell her as soon as we are alone that I don't like her using the baby as a go-between.

"I make such a mess of things," she says. "I'm terrible. I really am. I really am terrible."

"No, you're not."

"Oh yes. It was a terrible thing to do. I'm always doing terrible things."

"No."

"Yes."

"Let's agree to disagree."

"Oh you're cruel." She laughs with self-mockery, offering one or two jewel-like tears. "The baby, you know, your baby, like, doesn't dig me any more. I told him yesterday that in my opinion it would be to his benefit to have more peer group experiences, and now he won't talk to me and he won't even look at me."

"He doesn't like to be pushed into anything. Which doesn't excuse his being rude. If you like, I'll talk to him about it."

She throws back her head in a melodramatic pose. "You people make me so angry. No offense. But a baby needs some kind of structure from his adult models. You can't just let him do whatever he wants to do... Now I've said too much and you're going to ask me to leave." Her face turns a deep red.

I indicate that we're receptive in this house to differences of opinion.

"He's really a love," she says. "He really is." She gets down on her knees and pleads with me to change my approach.

Her zealousness is hard to resist. "Have you talked to my wife?" I ask.

"I've always had more success with men," she says.

ANOTHER VERSION OF THE SAME STORY

The baby tiptoes into Marie's room while she is sleeping or, in any event, giving the impression of being asleep, and asks her if she'd like to hear the story of the Sleeping Beauty. She's heard it too many times, she murmurs, for it still to be fresh and exciting for her. Besides, she's still, ummm, asleep. "This is a different Sleeping Beauty," says the baby. "This Sleeping Beauty is awake." Awake? The idea seems to interest the baby-sitter for a moment or two before it slips away into the dead spaces of unrequited loss. "She's not really awake," says the baby, improvising. "I just said that to make the story sound different. Well, I'll tell it to you in a very low voice. Okay?"

The baby-sitter seems to agree to this compromise though she falls asleep in the middle of the story. When she wakes up—it is at the most surprising part of the story—she is in a bad mood and says that the baby has no business being in her bed. "Only people I ask to come into my bed are allowed to be there," she says. "Now go away."

The baby is tenacity itself, refuses dismissal, buries

himself under the covers, attempts to charm.

Marie rolls him over the edge of the bed, like a sausage, tumbling him to the floor with a bang.

"I won't tell you any more stories," the baby says, refusing against disposition of habit to let her see the pain she has brought to his life.

When the baby takes himself away, Marie comes after him, saying she's sorry, inviting him back. "I'm always like this in the morning, baby. When I'm fast asleep, I can't bear to be touched. I'll tell you a story if you come back."

"Well, I'm not coming back," says the baby.

All day he refuses to look at the baby-sitter and he refuses to talk to her.

The next morning the baby forgets that he is angry with his baby-sitter and he asks her if he can sleep in her bed.

"Why don't you go out and play?" she says, turning her back on him.

The baby will not. The baby will not do anything she asks of him.

4.

Contemplating the nature of things in the bathroom that adjoins my study, I overhear this exchange between the baby and Marie.

"Do you love me?"

"I love you."

"Do you really love me?"

Kissing sounds, or what I imagine to be the sounds of kissing, follow. Moments after that I hear the door to the baby's room click shut.

Hours pass. Sibilant whispers snake through the house like a gas leak from some indeterminable quarter.

I am, for no reason I can explain to myself, disturbed at the behavior of baby and baby-sitter. It is just not polite,

I tell myself, for the two of them to stay by themselves all day in a closed room. It is also, I should imagine, not particularly healthy to be locked in that way. After a point, as an act of responsibility, I knock gently on the baby's door. "Is everything all right in there?"

I am answered by giggles, which I find not a little shocking under the circumstances.

I mumble something about it perhaps not being a good idea, not being exactly healthy, spending a lot of time in a closed room, do you think? More giggles. Some boos.

"It happens to be a beautiful day out," I say, and when I get no further answer, go out for a walk to prove my point.

My wife returns from shopping late in the afternoon, laden with packages. She laments the difficulty of finding anything in the stores she really likes. Everything is not quite right, has been created with someone else in mind.

I make no mention of the baby and Marie.

After my wife shows me the things she's bought, including a pair of socks and a tie for me, she asks if anything interesting happened while she was gone.

"Nothing interesting," I say.

She calls the baby, singing out his name and gets no answer.

"Did they go out?" she asks.

"They're in his room."

"Are they?"

She is about to raise an eyebrow when Marie and the baby glide into the dining room, holding hands, the baby's face aglow. At the dinner table, they exchange secretive smiles, which do not, of course, escape notice. The baby sings to himself as he eats, his mother observing him with pained concentration.

After dinner, baby and sitter mumble their excuses and disappear upstairs.

"They seem to be hitting it off," I say to make conversation.

"Do they?" my wife says. She presses her face into my shoulder and holds on.

The next day, when the baby comes into the study to borrow my typewriter, I ask him what he does in his room with Marie when they have the door closed.

He shrugs. "Things," he says.

A certain awkwardness appears to have come between us. I inform him, looking out the window as I deliver my obligatory speech, that his mother and I would prefer him to keep the door slightly open when alone in the room with his sitter.

When he is gone, I regret having yielded to what seems to me unexamined impulse. I call him back. "Just because it disturbs us," I say, "it doesn't mean necessarily that it's wrong."

"If the door is open," he says, "someone might come in and someone might go out. We do Batman, Batwoman and Batbaby in the room and if the door is open, the baby could run away."

We punch each other gently and hug, having come to a better understanding of our respective situations.

5.

"The Sleeping Beauty doesn't marry the prince that kisses her awake," says the baby. "She marries a different prince."

The baby comes into my study—Marie away on an emergency day off, her father sick—to tell me a new story.

In this story, when the Sleeping Beauty is awakened by the prince, she is angry at him. "Why won't you let me sleep?" she says. "If I wanted to be kissed, I would have told you I wanted to be kissed."

"You looked so nice sleeping, I couldn't help it," the prince says.

"I hate you," she says. "Ohhhhhh!"

The prince, who knows how the story used to end, asks the Sleeping Beauty if she'd like to get married.

"Are you kidding, prince?" she says. "I'm not going to marry someone who wakes me up when I'm trying to sleep."

The prince regrets having wasted a kiss on a lost cause. He asks the Sleeping Beauty to marry him one more time in case she didn't mean her first refusal of him. The Sleeping Beauty says if there's one thing she can't stand it's a man who doesn't take her at her word, which is no.

The prince says that though there may be other Sleeping Beauties in his life, he'll always love this one the best. Then he goes away. The Sleeping Beauty is sad when he is gone but after awhile she falls asleep and dreams of a prince who will never wake her up.

6.

"He kisses too much," Marie complains to me. "I don't like so much kissing."

"You don't have to go into his room with him and close the door."

A small glint of surprise animates her otherwise impassive face. "If I had known that, I wouldn't be in the present predicament." She stands with her back to me. "I hope you won't hate me when I tell you this? There's another man in my life."

"Another man?"

She nods, lets out an exhausted sigh. "My boyfriend is insanely jealous. About little things. I had to tell him what was going on, and now he wants me to give up the job. He even talks of punching the baby in the nose."

"He sounds unbalanced to me," I say. '"

"He's a little unsure of himself," she says. "Like, he's had a difficult life. His real mother gave him up and he was brought up by foster parents, both of whom happened to be blind. It gave him a suspicious view of life. He wants to marry me."

"Your boyfriend?"

"The baby. For my boyfriend's sake, I think it would be best if I gave up the job."

For the baby's sake, I press her to reconsider her decision. Couldn't she stay until he got over his crush?

Again we misunderstand each other. She furrows her brow, a pucker of tension in her forehead. "My boyfriend?"

"The baby."

"And what about me, what about my feelings? The baby will grow up and find someone else. I'm twenty-two. In eight months I'll be twenty-three." Tears fall. I put an arm on her shoulder.

There's a knock on the door. We freeze, unable to speak, watching the door slowly open.

"Oh my God," she whispers. "What should I do?" She panics and rushes to my closet, opening the door and flinging herself in.

"Where's Marie?" the baby asks.

"She's hiding," I say. "See if you can find her."

He punches me in the side, a gesture more of impatience than of anger, the intent symbolic rather than violent. "I don't want to play that game."

I nod my head in the direction of the closet, give Marie away in silence.

"If you see Marie," the baby says in a loud voice, "tell her I'll be in my room with Polly."

The baby-sitter comes out of the closet. Loose pages from an unpublished manuscript of poems follow her in profusion. "So young and so unfaithful," she says, hurrying out, turning to give me a sharp look as if I were implicated in some deception practiced against her.

Crashing noises assail my concentration. The baby, red-eyed, furious, returns, saying, "I'm going to tell. Marie is throwing things at me."

"He started it," she says, following him in. "He called me a name. You tell him to stop calling me names."

"She tore up a picture I made of Polly and broke the arms off my Spiderman model."

Their grievances against the other extend and intensify, a competition of complaint, painful to witness. I stand between them, a truce team to defend against further outbreak of violence.

"You ought to punish him," says Marie. "I think at the very least his television privileges ought to be taken away."

"I think her television privileges ought to be taken away," says the baby.

"I don't watch television that much," says Marie, looking at me as if I were the one who would deny her. "Still, I don't need to be told things like that. That's no way to treat someone who lives in your house. I'm not going to stay like that."

The baby goes with Marie to her room to help her pack. Forty minutes later, she emerges with a valise under each arm, the baby at her side carrying one of her plants.

"I don't want her to go," says the baby after they've kissed goodbye two or three times.

"I don't want to leave my baby," she says. Her momentum apparently a determining factor, she moves irresistibly to the front door. "I'll come back and see you," she says.

"Will you come tomorrow?" the baby asks.

"I'll try," she says in a voice that acknowledges the odds to be prohibitively against succeeding. "I'm going to miss him."

"I don't want her to go," the baby says.

They say goodbye several more times, and when it seems that the procedure might go on indefinitely, Marie rushes out as if weeks late for an appointment she still hopes to keep. The baby waves and calls to her, banging on the window to catch her fleeting attention. We watch Marie walk away with her head bent slightly forward as if she braces against a hurricane. In the distance, she seems almost as small as the baby himself.

"'I think she was waving," the baby says, "but I couldn't see it because she was turned the other way." His thumb eases its way into his mouth.

7.

A week without word of her has passed since Marie's departure. The baby keeps an optimistic vigil on a footstool at the window. He pretends he is studying the weather for signs of change. Her name is not mentioned.

Occasionally, he sings the name to himself. "Marie marie marie...marie marie marie...marie marie marie... marie marie marie."

The day the baby stops watching for her at the window, Marie calls. Her voice is so low that I think at first she is calling from some great distance.

"Where are you?" I ask.

"Here," she says.

"Are you in the country?"

"I'm just a few blocks away." Her voice fading out. "Does he remember me?"

"Of course he remembers. Should I put him on?"

"I don't know. My head's so untogether. I'm such a mess. Maybe I'll come over and see him."

"Why don't you come over tonight and have dinner with us. Look, he'd love to talk to you."

"He would? If he does it quickly, maybe it'll be all right. My boyfriend's in the bathroom and he'll be out, unless he gets into what he's doing, in about five minutes."

I call the baby to the phone. "Is it anyone I know?" he asks, wary about taking the receiver, a stranger to its pleasures.

I step outside to give him privacy, and light up a

cigar I was saving for a special occasion. Five minutes later, the baby comes out of my study walking backwards. "Why did you give me the phone?" he asks.

"Didn't you speak to Marie?"

"I spoke to Marie," he says, "but it was a different Marie, not the Marie that was my baby-sitter."

"It's the same Marie," I say.

"It's not," he says.

The next evening when the phone rings and the baby answers it, whoever it is says nothing or hangs up on hearing the baby's voice. The same circumstance repeats itself the next evening.

One day the baby and his grandmother walking in the park—this reported to my by the baby—see a young woman pushing a stroller who looks like Marie or who is Marie. The baby calls to her.

(What he is about to tell me is true, the baby says, though it may also be dream.)

The presumed Marie turns her head in the direction of her name, appears to see nothing (or everything) and then goes on, somewhat more quickly than before.

The baby calls Marie's name again and gets no reaction except that a dog, apparently named Marie or something like it, comes running toward him.

The misinformed dog knocks the baby over and licks his nose. When the baby is restored to his feet, the other Marie is a distant shadow of her former self.

The baby continues his pursuit, stopping every once in a while to pick up his fallen grandma or to call out Marie's name. Each time he calls her name, she seems to increase her pace as if—is it possible?—she is actually running away from him.

Does she think he is someone else? Who could he be if not himself?

It is only me, he wants to say, but finds himself restrained by doubts.

His pursuit takes him through places he has never

seen before outside of books and postcards.

After hours of relentless chase—the baby too tired even to call her name—he arrives at the stroller he saw Marie with, now deserted.

There isn't another baby in the stroller (as he might have expected) but a large stuffed bear with a note pinned to his chest.

To my darling darling baby.

Love, Marie

P.S. As soon as I have the time, I'll come and visit you.

"That's the end of the story," the baby says.

"Does she come and visit?" I ask.

"Does who come and visit?"

"Marie."

"When I'm older," the baby says.

III. from *The Return of Service*

The Traditional Story Returns

Too many times you read a story nowadays and it's not a story at all, not in the traditional sense. A traditional story has plot, character, and theme, to name three things it traditionally has. The following story, which contains a soupçon of mood in addition to the three major considerations named above, is intended as a modest "rearguard action in the service of a declining tradition."

The plot is this: A woman of good family (we won't say just how good the family is) marries a man of means. They live together in uneventful happiness for seven years until their love runs out. Then they split up but not before some bad times that leave scars of bitterness. Afterward, the bad times remain, particularly for the woman, and the good times are dashed on the rock of negligent memory, which is one of the themes of the story. Bad times in a marriage erase all memories of former happiness. The name of the woman of better than average family is Eve. What more is there to know of her? The answer to that question is the character part of the story.

Eve was born in Asheville, Ohio, to, as I said before, though it bears repeating, a good family. (On the night she and her husband, Fairlie, separated, the Yankees lost to the Milwaukee Brewers, ending a seven-game winning streak which had catapulted them to within eight games of first place.) She had a younger brother who died as an infant. Eve five at the time. After her brother Townsend's death, she had her parents to herself, although they were by nature busy people, occupied by one remote grief or another—I'm speaking of the mother now. The father had his work. Eve was a shy, frail, long-legged girl, skittery as a deer, with a hockey mistress manner and a fierce intelligence. When nervous she talked a streak, an articulate, charming prattle song, much admired by her teachers, which, if you listened to it whole-heartedly, had a desperate pleading note. *Stay with me.* it said, *love me. There is a princess beneath the manner and I am smart as hell and loyal and passionate and brittle as kindling.* She attended a girls' school in the East—one of the seven sister colleges, Smith or Wellesley. Smith, I think, though it doesn't matter to the story. Wellesley will do, or Holyoke. Not Vassar, of that I'm sure. In her second year she met the man she was going to marry, a pre-law student at Amherst or Yale. At the time she was in love with someone else or, which is almost the same thing, had given her heart away. Not much is known about it. She was given to self-conscious romantic poses during that period, took entranced walks in the woods, wrote obscure poems, would break off sometimes in the middle of her own chatter and get a misty, faraway look.

She thought Fairlie Robinson "a perfect bore" when she met him, which was what she told her roommate. Eve sometimes spoke with an English accent or used old-fashioned phrases to disguise her sense of the inadequacy of language to convey the ineffable. Her roommate, who tended to sensible questions, asked Eve how come she continued to see Fairlie if bored by his company. She knew what he was like, she said with affected cynicism as if she had practiced the answer to herself in anticipation of the question. Someone else might be worse.

When Fairlie Robinson first laid eyes on Eve he liked what he saw. He was a man, even then in his fourth year at Yale, who knew what he liked. She told him, to be honest and fair with him, that he was not her type. Nor could he ever hope to be, she said with sibyl's tongue. Fairlie liked a girl with spirit.

Eve was surprised when on their second date Fairlie parked the car and grabbed at her.

I don't do that kind of thing, Eve said. Fairlie thought that she might make an exception in his case, but Eve said exceptions were out of the question.

Nevertheless he continued to do what he was doing and seemed to have more hands, Eve told her room-mate, than an octopus.

It doesn't surprise me in the slightest, the room-mate, who spoke from firsthand experience, said. And then what happened?

What did happen? I've heard several versions of the incident, all of them agreeing on certain details and dis-agreeing on others.

I let out a stream of vile invective, Eve told Allison, which I don't wonder must have burned his ears. That's what Eve says she said. Allison's recollection was some-what different. She became absolutely rigid, she told me, like an alabaster statue, which served its purpose.

What was the purpose it served?

To get him to stop, silly. What a question.

Eve loved college, though tended, her class corre-spondent reports, to seem unhappy, a flower pressed between pages before its time.

Sometimes it was hard not to want to scream. Although a grabber—with experience would come savoir faire—Fairlie had the reputation of being a brick. It was that she admired most in him, his brickness, no mean quality.

When he broke off with her she had a feeling of heartbreak from which she thought she would never recover.

One day they were married. The heartbreak con-tinued, which had its reassuring aspect. It was no fly-by-night fatal wound. They had seven idyllically happy years of marriage, but afterward the bad times covered over the good like a fat kid sitting on top of a skinny and she could hardly remember one good time. He had when making love, she remembered, more fingers than a centipede.

Here the story takes a surprising turn.

The war was over. The returning soldiers lined the streets looking for work.

When Eve left her husband—truer to say they left each other—we lost sight of her.

Only scattered reports about Eve since her breakup with what's his name. Fairlie A. Robinson, Jr.

Some notes about Fairlie's character. It is true that in his younger days he had the habit of grabbing at women in parked cars. There was more to him than that; that wasn't the whole story about him.

Before he met Eve, Fairlie used to ride around with a reckless friend. When in the course of their dalliance a woman (or women) crossed their reckless path, Fairlie would pull down his pants and show his bare behind. It was called mooning and had a brief vogue at eastern men's colleges in the late fifties. Otherwise, he was kind, industrious, cheerful, thrifty, vaguely dishonest, and a moon among bricks.

During the second year of their marriage, two Jehovah's Witnesses came to their door, one a good-looking blond man in a sport coat and tie, the other a nondescript the blond introduced as his wife. They were very polite, asked if they might come in for a few minutes to share with the Robinsons a message of the utmost importance. They couldn't have been nicer, but Fairlie sent them packing.

We have our own religion here, he said.

What religion do we have? Eve asked later when there were no Witnesses. What religion did you have in mind?

Fairlie was watching (at the time of Eve's question) the NBC Game of the Week. Idol worshipping. How's that?

The next time the Jehovah's Witnesses came by, Fairlie invited them in for "a little comparative religions talk," slapping backs to show there were no hard feelings. The Witnesses, who were former thieves, reconverted after an hour's dull debate, bound and gagged the Robinsons and robbed them blind.

That was how Fairlie and Eve got religion if the truth be known. They went out together as a team a few times, proselytizing in strange neighborhoods, but it didn't seem like much of a profession for college graduates. It was on the whole more satisfying to tell the story at parties, where everyone laughed fit to be tied.

Wherever they went people would say, oh tell us the story of how you kids got religion.

Eve didn't particularly like the way Fairlie told the story, which was one of the side effects of the incident. It seemed unfair, since it was her idea to have the Witnesses in the first place, for him to tell the story more than she got to tell it. I mention this to indicate that even during their happy times the seeds of dissension were being sown.

Shortly after they were robbed blind, Fairlie got a job with his father's firm, clipping coupons. His mercurial rise was a legend in its own time. While he was away transacting business, Eve pursued her own interests.

One morning they woke up to find themselves in a bed of suffering married seven years. Then it was all over but the recriminations.

Eve put it down to a learning experience, though couldn't articulate what it was she had learned that she hadn't already known from the word go.

A record of their next to last fight follows.

Fairlie: (Striding into the room) Eve, I'd like to talk to you.

Eve: (Feeling trapped by his presence, playing nervously with her hair, moving it back and forth across her shoulder) Please don't. If you go away for an hour, it doesn't matter to me where you go, I'll be gone when you get back.

Fairlie: (Offering a view of his erection in profile, wanting to grab her, graciously) Why should you be the one to have to leave?

Eve: You asked me to leave, damn it, didn't you? (Thinking of smashing him on the head with a bat, hitting him over and over, arm weary from her labors, until his head was pulp, body looped over stiffly like celluloid.)

Fairlie: After you, Eve, it will be hard to find someone who measures up. (When the fastball is gone, you must learn deception to stay in the big leagues, changes of pace, artifice, screwballs and knuckleballs, tricks of dispassion.)

Eve: (Made ashamed by his compliment, touched to deeper rage) I'd like to finish my packing if you don't mind.

Fairlie: (Promising himself that he will not grab at her no matter what, grabs her arm) Look.

(*The end*)

From another source we learn that Eve punches him in the stomach, Fairlie laughing holds her by the wrists as if two snakes in his hands, Let's go to bed, he whispers, Let's.

She would go, she thinks, if he would ask in a way that would permit her to, says, Under no circumstance whatsoever my god will I ever let you stick that thing in me again. Smells whisky on his familiar breath, bourbon or Irish, when he lifts her from behind and thrusts her out of the apartment without her suitcase.

I'll make a scene, she says softly, if you don't let me in this instant. Her breath coming heavy as it does in panic. You mucky bastard.

In her suitcase, finishing her packing for her, Fairlie finds a photo of another man. He studies it for some time. It's not even anyone I know, he says. It seemed unfair.

Eve comes back in say ten minutes to finish the fight. At least give me my purse, she says mournfully at the door. I don't have a cent, not a cent.

That's your tough luck, he says.

He unpacks her suitcase looking for clues. Something about her has always eluded his grasp, not everything of course—he has known her in and out for seven years.

Eve threatens to bring the police if not admitted.

It is a forefinger of fiction that you find what you're looking for, when not aware in advance of the hidden purpose of the quest. What Fairlie finds is an old letter—the condition of the paper indicates its age—written by Eve, apparently unsent, to someone named Harris.

Dear Harris (So the letter begins),

It is difficult for me to write your name, a totemistic superstition no doubt. I am embarrassed that you will read the "dear" as literally as it sounds in my head when I write it. I know, though I would like to be wrong, that you will think this letter indulgent, or, worse, school-girlish. But I want to break through to you—is there any way to do that?—to tell you who I am. God, doesn't that sound pretentious. If one day I ceased to exist would it, dear Harris, affect your life in the slightest?

When Eve let herself in with the key she had gotten from the super she discovered Fairlie reading her letter.

Please give that back to me, she said.

He ripped the letter in half and handed it to her.

It was as if he had torn her in two. If she had had a gun, she would have killed him without a qualm. Giddy, lightheaded, she whirled around and around in her imagination on perfect point, folded the two halves in half and ripped the letter evenly in quarters, then in eighths. When it was like confetti she sprinkled the pieces at Fairlie as if blessing him with holy water. Still, some part of her, though she had never felt so light before, was deeply offended. She felt like a flower opened beyond any further opening, inviolable. Her sense of her own power astonished her. It was as if she were a laser beam and could burn him to dust (the thought itself erotic to her) by the merest touch. When she came toward him he actually flinched, putting his hands in front of his face. She grabbed him. What do you think you're doing? he said. She tumbled him to the floor and though Fairlie was not indifferent to the opportunity, took her pleasure by force as if it were a debt he had for seven years refused to pay. Fairlie's view of it was somewhat different. As he saw it, what seemed like mysterious behavior on Eve's part had, like all things, a perfectly simple explanation. Eve had let herself go because he had showed her he cared for her by destroying the letter.

You couldn't go two steps in any direction without becoming aware of the general decline in cultural standards. Where would it all end?

He thought afterward that they might make it up, but she was afraid of the violence of her feelings (or so he interpreted her behavior) and moved out some minutes after their bout of love on the floor.

Her leaving as she did—the peculiar timing of it—embittered him, made him feel cheated. He said some nasty things about her to friends, tried unsuccessfully on more than one occasion to get her to come back. She would always hold a special place in his feelings, he thought. Was there another girl in the world like her?

They had one more fight but there was no heart in it and then by accord, perhaps merely by drift, went through with the divorce.

The Adventures of King Dong

The trip to the island takes longer than one might expect. The head of the expedition, a famous impresario down on his luck, keeps a journal of the voyage. *Nothing much happened today*, he writes each day. At night he is unable to sleep, made anxious by the dark, tormented by impotence. His dreams of failure waft like smoke before our eyes. Apparently, no one knows of his affliction, not even his beautiful assistant, the touching and vulnerable Lola. A run of unseasonably bad weather, most of it fog, puts the expedition a week behind schedule. Bad omens are in abundance. The rats leave in an unprecedented hurry. There is talk of mutiny among the crew, savage whispers of discontent.

Pages and pages of journal are written before the island is sighted. It is none too soon. The journal entries have become increasingly bleak. *Rations are low*, Commander Buck writes in his journal. *We are reduced to eating the bread of affliction*. And then the fog lifts to reveal the uncharted island Hong Dong ("Mysterious Expanse" in English) like a small black cross in the distance. That night, the impresario calls a meeting of the crew to reveal the mission of the voyage. "I've kept you buzzards in the dark for a reason," he says. "We've come to Hong Dong to bring back the thirteenth wonder of the world."

There are some murmurs of disbelief, but as one of the crew, an old-timer, mentions, Commander Bill Buck has a reputation for unearthing the inexplicable.

That night there is an unanticipated full moon. A muted eeriness pervades the restrained shipboard celebration. Nothing out of the ordinary happens except for three separate attempts by drunken crew members to interfere with Lola, who, as it happens, is the only woman aboard. She is saved from these unwanted attentions by the intercession of the handsome First Mate, who has appointed himself, for whatever reasons, her protector. Lola, at this point, seems indifferent to rapists and protectors alike.

The island is just as we imagined it, an ominous and impenetrable place, majestic and uncivilized. There is something erotic in the very atmosphere. Lola remarks on it to Commander Buck, who says that there is a legend to that effect. The deeper one penetrates into the heart of the island, says Buck, the more potent the erotic influence.

One of the party is bitten in the leg by a snake, and Lola, who has had some training as a nurse, draws off the poison with her mouth.

Lola and the First Mate embrace in soft focus behind the screen of a waterfall. "I don't want this," says Lola. "This is not what I had in mind."

"Sometimes we answer to a power larger than ourselves," says the Mate.

Moments later, the entire expeditionary force is surrounded by a band of savage pygmies. The pygmies speak a primitive squall, a dialect (explains Commander Buck) that has remained unchanged for thousands of years. Buck converses with the group's leader, mixing language with gesture to make himself understood. The diminutive savages are intent apparently on taking Lola as their white queen. A queen of opposing color has been a long-standing tradition in their country. Odd growling sounds like some monumental indigestion seem to come from behind the high walls of the fortress and send tremors of fear through the populace.

Buck translates the conversation to the others, says the pygmies will allow them to return to their ship if they hand over Lola. There are murmurs of dissent. Lola is a great favorite among the men. Buck says that the wisest thing to do at this point is to pretend to leave and then come back, under cover of surprise, and rescue Lola. The First Mate is dead set against the plan, indicating that Commander Buck has a reputation for being a dissembler. Lola intercedes in the argument, saying that she welcomes the challenge of a new job, that her background and training have prepared her for a position of authority among backward peoples.

Lola is turned over to the pygmies and the small band of adventurers, under the leadership of Commander Buck, retrace their path (or seem to) back to their ship. A tracking shot, delineating each of the men in turn, reveals that the First Mate is not with the others.

The Mate, we discover, has followed the pygmies back to their encampment. Hiding himself in the tall grasses on a cliff overlooking the pygmy settlement, he is witness to the following scene.

Lola, who has been stripped to the waist and garlanded about the breasts and neck with chains of red flowers, is recumbent on a hammock like throne. One by one each of the males of the tribe pays obeisance to her. The ceremony is odd—its particulars difficult to follow—and has something to do with shooting sperm in the air (over the queen's navel) like a fireworks display. It is the tribe's primitive way of paying homage.

Meanwhile, Commander Buck and his men are lying in a field of yellow flowers, enervated, lost to the world of responsibility. Buck, rousing himself briefly, reminds the men that they have made a promise to Lola to return. "We will," they say. "Give us time." Buck tells them of King Dong, the object of their quest, and we cut away from the small band of white men to a huge black hand. The hand reaches over a wall and lifts the queen from her primitive throne.

The pygmies seem unsurprised at the theft of their white queen and go about their business—chanting and darting back and forth in their ritual manner—as if nothing more exceptional than a change in the weather had passed.

"Dong," the natives chant. "Dong. Dong. Dong."

Dong has taken Lola to his cave, which is strewn with the broken bodies of other "brides."

The giant ape holds her in the palm of his hand, studying her, an impassive expression on his wizened face.

"Me Lola," she says, pointing to herself. "You Dong."

The giant ape nods in apparent understanding, though it may only be a circumstantial gesture. Abruptly, his face is transformed. He is moved by Lola's beauty and vulnerability, her sexuality and innocence. It is as if nothing in his life mattered until this moment. The sigh that passes from him is almost human. He strokes Lola's long blond hair with his giant finger, moving down to touch a breast.

From Dong's finger we cut to Commander Buck's pen as he writes in his journal. *Once we commandeered the poppy field, we lost all ambition to rescue Lola or indeed even to return to our ship but lay in the field in a stupor of pleasure. Some pygmy girls joined us after a while—a gift apparently from the chief—and although we still intended to rescue Lola, the days passed without a single gesture in that direction. There is something in the atmosphere of this island, some unseen power.*

From the point of Buck's pen, as if emerging from it like a spurt of ink, we cut to the First Mate rushing pell-mell through the maze of the jungle. He follows Dong's enormous footsteps, stopping from time to time to call out Lola's name, the sound echoing back. Impelled by the erotic pull of the landscape, he embraces a tree in desperation. All sense of proportion is lost.

We discover Lola asleep on a mat of grass at the foot of Dong's cave. Dong himself is sitting up, though he seems quiescent, on the verge perhaps of going to sleep himself. We see him glance over lovingly at Lola before closing his eyes.

Lola wakes to find Dong asleep, snoring gently, a complacent hum. What to do? She kisses the sleeping ape on the top of his head, then scratches a note in the ground with a stick, unable to walk out of Dong's life without some parting communication. "Dear Dong," she writes, "We are worlds apart." The message is not quite what she means to say and she erases it and starts again. Her name is called, startling her. It gives her pleasure to have her name in the air, a sense of belonging.

Lola looks around, unable at first to determine where the voice is coming from, discovering finally the First Mate on the edge of a promontory perhaps a hundred yards away. He signals her to join him. "I can't," she mouths.

Going down the side of a mountain, Lola trips over a root and falls headlong. Fragments of her immediate past flash before her eyes. When she regains consciousness the Mate is holding her head in his lap. "Ambivalence got the better of me," she says. "I couldn't bring myself to leave him."

Dong lets out an enormous roar of anguish when he discovers Lola has gone. When he comes upon her with the First Mate his grief turns to anger.

"Leave him to me," says Lola, interposing herself between her two suitors. "Hide behind something until I tell you to come out."

Dong lifts her in his hand, squeezing her just enough to let her know that he is a monster of displeasure.

"You are making me regret my affection for you," she shouts at him.

Dong shakes his head, a tear (perhaps a drop of moisture in the air) poises in an eye. He mumbles something almost human, struggles to make himself understood.

While Lola tames the beast, soft-talks and scolds him into docility, the Mate looks on from behind a rock.

When Dong seems no longer murderous, she introduces him to the Mate. "This is my brother," she says to Dong. "This is King Dong, the thirteenth wonder of the world," she says to the Mate. Dong probes the Mate with a finger, knocking him back and over, laughing apishly.

Lola establishes an uneasy truce between them, a grudging accommodation. "I want you two to be fast friends," she announces.

Some time passes—we see pages of calendar flutter in the wind—before we return to Dong, Lola, and the First Mate (Tex) living together in domestic compromise in Dong's lair.

Lola sleeps with Dong in the main quarters while the Mate sleeps by himself in a corner on a pallet of leaves.

"I can't stand to see you with him," Tex says to Lola when Dong is away on an errand. "I've made up my mind to leave tonight. Whether you go with me or not is up to you."

She is torn by his request, agrees to leave with him, then reneges. "I can't leave King Dong," she says. "No matter how it seems, there is something between us. He befriended me at a bad time in my life."

"If you stay with him out of pity, you'll end up hating each other."

Lola slaps his face, they fight; he pins her to the earth, they kiss. "You're beautiful when you're angry," he says. We see the lovers bathed by sunlight screened through the high trees. We see them in long shot in a variety of attitudes like paintings of Adam and Eve in the Garden of Eden.

"That's the best it's ever been for me," says Tex.

She pleads with Tex to stay a little longer, promising to make a choice between her two lovers as soon as she knows her own mind.

Tex agrees grudgingly, though confesses not to understand her relationship to Dong. Sex, he would suppose, is out of the question.

"Not so," says Lola, looking off into the distance.

Tex presses for an explanation. Dong, confides Lola, has a disproportionately small member, which is why he tends to prefer human females to the women of his own species.

"It's barely bigger than yours," she tells the Mate.

"Is that so?"

"It is the reason he is so unsure of himself."

This conversation is interrupted by the arrival of Commander Buck and his men. Buck has come, he announces, to take Dong back to the States to make a film star out of him. Lola is at first opposed to the idea—the removal of Dong from his homeland might create an ecological imbalance, she says—but the impresario is a fast and persuasive talker. "I want to do what's best for all concerned," says Buck. "Dong will make so much money in films, any lifestyle he wants will be available to him. I don't think it's fair to deny him this opportunity. Do you want to be the one to deny him?"

Lola makes conditions. She will help Commander Buck capture the giant ape on the grounds that if things don't work out with Dong's career, or if Dong is unhappy in his new life, Buck will see to it personally that Dong returns to his island.

"If that's the way you want it," says the impresario, "that's the way it will be."

On shipboard—Dong in captivity in the hull of the ship—Commander Buck strides the deck with uncharacteristic swagger, a swagger stick under his arm. When Lola comes by he signals her with his head to follow him. He takes her to his quarters and orders her to remove her clothes and position herself at the foot of his bed. She can see from his obsessive manner that there is no arguing with him. She manages to divert him from his purpose by telling him a succession of stories.

In another part of the ship, Dong weeps and moans under the burden of his chains. Civilization has already begun to change him. He has taken to smoking a pipe, a comfort to him in his isolation.

There has been a breakdown in discipline, Buck writes in his journal. To avoid mutiny, I've had to put half the crew in chains. The choice of who to chain and who not has been wholly arbitrary. All week I've been crazed with sexual longing. I hear whispers of mutiny in my sleep.

The First Mate, who has been put in irons for insubordination, has fantasies of murdering Commander Buck and taking command of the ship. Lola visits him and encourages him in his ambition to make something of himself.

In captivity, Dong takes up with the two men who bring him his food, a sublimation of unfulfilled desires. He keeps a picture of Lola on his wall, a pin-up from her modeling days before she got her advanced degree in Anthropomorphology.

I've done what I've set out to do, writes Buck in his journal. *Who can say it hasn't been worth it?*

True to his promise, the impresario stars Dong in a motion picture treating in a semifictional way the ape's early life on Hong Dong Island. The audience at the premiere gives the film a prolonged standing ovation. King Dong is launched on a brilliant career.

Commander Buck arranges for the construction of an extraordinary house for Dong overlooking the Pacific Ocean. The interior decor simulates the landscape of Hong Dong Island, and Dong, although puzzled by the unfamiliar similarities, accepts the gift gracefully. Lola lives with him as friend and advisor and there is some gossip in the prints of a secret marriage.

In real life, however, Lola has become tired of living with someone unable to share the same intellectual interests. She keeps to herself, wears dark glasses, is seen reading difficult books or walking along the ocean's edge, looking bored and feckless.

Success has gone to Dong's head and he has of late become extremely careless of Lola's feelings. Other women, starlets and would-be starlets, the famous and the infamous, come to the exotic Malibu residence at all hours of the day and night to pay homage to the beast. Lola keeps his appointment book and warns him of the implication of social diseases.

Dong had a certain integrity when they found him, a kind of primitive innocence, while now he is a creature governed solely by his pleasures.

Montage of Dong on his back like a fallen colossus being licked in a variety of formations by five or six starlets at once, his small hairy tower smoldering like some apprentice volcano.

Dong growls and beats his chest, his eyes rolling out of his head in ecstasy. Lola stands on a parapet, overlooking the scene, her hand shielding her eyes from the full brunt of her naked sight. When the starlets (or whoever—it is rumored that the daughter of a former President is one of the ape's visitors) are gone, Lola chides Dong in a gentle voice. "If you keep this up, you'll ruin your health," she says.

It goes on this way for a while. The more successful Dong's public life becomes, the more vile is his private behavior. For those who love him for himself, there is nothing but ashes and grief.

Dong does not seem particularly happy with himself and is short-tempered and sulky, prey to every passing vice. Sex, marijuana, amphetamines, cocaine, heroin, alcohol—a classic downfall. Dong drinks heavily, downing gallon bottles as if they were shot glasses. The beast carries it well, but is always a little out of focus these days, his eyes exceptionally glassy.

At Lola's urging, Commander Buck has a fatherly talk with Dong about his unacknowledged drinking problem. Dong has a way of going *non compos mentis* when there's something he doesn't want to hear, his normally intelligent face lapsing into bestial stolidity. The impresario warns Dong that unless he shapes up, he will sell his contract to the syndicate and go off on another expedition. "I made you," says the impresario, "and if I have to, I can unmake you."

When Lola threatens to leave Dong, the beast turns maudlin, moaning and weeping in a heartbreaking way. Lola says she will continue to live with him if he promises to give up boozing and womanizing. The ape agrees or seems to, but we can see it is only a ruse to get her to stay.

Dong becomes increasingly temperamental at the studio, refusing to shoot certain scenes when not in the mood. One director quits the picture rather than be undermined by his erratic star. In a fit of pique—one or two details not to his liking—Dong tears down a million-dollar set.

Lola has to plead with the studio head to take him back. Only if she agrees to appear with him in the picture, says the head, will he work with Dong again.

Lola keeps Dong in line for the completion of the film, and just as it seems as if things are working out in their lives, Dong learns that Lola has gotten the lion's share of the press—she has become a star in her own right—and he hits the sauce again.

One day, working in his first B film, Dong collapses on the set and has to be taken home and put to bed. The studio doctor comes to examine him and we can see from the doctor's face that there is something gravely wrong with the ape.

"Is it very serious?" Lola asks.

"I assure you that I'll do the best I can," says the doctor. "New discoveries are being made every day. The important thing is that he want to live. Without the will to live, there is nothing that modern medicine can do for him."

After the doctor leaves, Tex comes to the house to renew his plea to Lola to run off with him. He has become a successful Hollywood writer (five straight hits in a row, including Lola's latest picture) and can offer Lola everything she wants.

Lola looks away, unable to speak, but we can see (or sense) that she wishes she were free to go.

"I want you to tell me that you don't love me," says Tex. "I want to hear you tell me that from your own lips."

"I don't...," she says, but can't finish the sentence. "I don't love you."

They come together irresistibly. We see their love-making in slow motion through a dark red filter; it is as if they were dancing at the center of a fire.

Some intuition (or perhaps it is the noise) wakes Dong from his stupor and he staggers to his feet. He knows something is wrong, but is unable to perceive what it is. We notice the naked figures of Lola and Tex in reflection in the overhead mirror moments before Dong himself becomes aware of them.

Dong overhears the following conversation. "You don't love him, do you?"

"I pity him," she says. "He had the world in his hand and threw it away. But I can't leave him, Tex, not while he's ill I can't. I'll nurse him back to health and then when he's on his feet again tell him about us."

We see the dawn of comprehension on the stricken gorilla's face. He mouths Lola's name—it is almost as if he could speak it—and stumbles wearily from the house onto the terraced beach that leads to the ocean.

In four steps he is at the water's edge. And then, hesitating a moment—perhaps only to locate his desti-nation—he enters the water.

Inside Dong's palatial Hollywood estate: Lola has just discovered that the giant ape is missing. She goes from room to room looking for him, overrun by pan-ic. Tex tries to calm her but she pushes him away and rushes from the house.

"Dong," she calls, but he is already several miles out into the ocean, shrinking as he moves further and fur-ther from our view.

"Dong," she calls, running to the water's edge. "It's Lola, honey."

"He's going home," Tex says. "Let him go."

A helicopter circles over Dong's head and he swats at it as he would a large fly.

"Come back, Dong," Lola calls. "Please come back."

If he can hear her, he gives no indication of it, continuing determinedly on his way, a relentless figure.

A second helicopter joins the first and lets out a stream of machine-gun fire, kicking up the water around Dong.

Lola and Tex stand at the water's edge, looking out at Dong, who is now almost imperceptible in the distance, a shadowy head above the waves.

A crowd has gathered. Concessionaires have sprung up like a plague of weeds.

A silver-gray limousine drives up. Commander Buck and the head of the studio that owns Dong's contract get out of the car.

"Where the hell is he?" says the studio head.

A bystander, an Oriental boy about seven years old, points toward the ocean.

"He's gone," says Buck. "I can feel his loss as if some piece of me had gone with him. That ape brought the gift of love to this town."

"I'm out a million bucks," says the studio head. "That's the last ape I ever put into pictures at your advice."

The limousine drives off as precipitously as it had arrived.

The sun is setting. Onlookers leave in groups or one at a time, some lamenting the loss of Dong, others looking for a new thrill, anything to deflect the boredom and emptiness of their lives.

"Let's go home," says Tex.

Lola pushes his hand away when he tries to move her. There are tears in her eyes. "I'll see you at the house," she says.

It is almost completely dark now, the moon a knife slash in the gray flesh of the sky, Lola is alone on the beach. She reels with exhaustion, falls, staggers to her feet.

She is lying in the sand, weeping bitter tears.

She is sitting up, her hands covering her face, a reprise of voices in her memory. The chanting of pygmies. *That ape brought the gift of love to this town.*

The night is black like an ape. Lola perceives Dong coming to her in the night, her arms out, her legs apart. Whatever it is—the night, an imagined lover, a dream— it takes her by force, enters her. A groan of acceptance or pain. She takes him to her. "Dong," she is heard to cry. The lovers thrash in the wet sand, barely illuminated by the slash of moonlight. Dong is with her; she is alone. It is being filmed by a giant camera.

The great ape has left his footprint on the imagination.

The Fields of Obscurity

His wife was the first up that morning. She looked at him asleep and said, "Oh Rocco, my sweet man, if you don't go after what you want, you're never going to get past first base."

On the field, waking or sleepless, picking his nose under cover of glove, he would hear or remember it, the same touchingly useless advice.

"Okay," he said or he said nothing.

"You don't mean it," she said. "If you wanted to be successful, you would be."

"Yes," he said. "Okay."

He had married a thin pretty woman who kept the world from moving too quickly by having a theory for everything. "You get what you want," she would say when he complained about not getting what he wanted, "and if you don't get it then you don't really want it."

He had difficulty, which kept him from rising to the top of his profession, making contact with the low curve ball on the outside quarter of the plate.

She would not make love to him, she said, perhaps implied rather than said, unless he demonstrably wanted what he said he wanted. She had come from two generations of failed perfectionists and had no patience with anything more or less.

Her love denied him, the fast ball also tended to elude his stroke. That's the way it was.

And when he didn't get good wood on the fast ball, he either warmed the bench or was sent to the minor leagues for what the management called seasoning. He had had, to the point where this account begins, an up and down career. It was written about him in *The Sporting News* that Lawrence Rocco Kidd spent his early years toiling in the fields of obscurity.

Some days he thought, *Is it that I'm not good enough?* But when he was going good he was hard pressed to imagine anyone being better.

"You see," she said, "you can hit the curve ball when you want to hit the curve ball."

"They just didn't get it on the outside corner today," he said, too pleased with himself to admit his pleasure.

"You don't want to succeed, do you? You just want to be right. That's why you'll never be first rate at what you do."

He had wanted to marry a woman smarter than himself and he had, although not without occasional regret for having wanted what he had gotten.

Sometimes he thought (whenever he gave himself to thinking) that it wasn't that she was really smarter but that her intelligence, unlike his, presented itself in words.

She occasionally went to see him play, liking the game in the abstract but considering it dull to watch. Whenever she went, she took a book with her to read or something else (like knitting if she knitted which she didn't) so as not to be without occupation. It embarrassed her, she said, when he struck out and the fans booed and he lost his temper and flung his bat. She closed her eyes when that happened and pretended to be somewhere else.

One time, misconceiving the distance of a long fly ball, he made a leaping catch, somersaulting over backward with the ball sticking delicately like a pocket handkerchief out of the corner of his glove. The crowd stood up and screamed its admiration, almost everyone on his feet screaming and clapping and slapping each other. When he came home that night and asked her what she had thought of it she said she had been reading her book (something called *The Golden Notebook*) and hadn't noticed until she heard the man in back of her mention his name.

If she wasn't going to watch, he said, he didn't want her there not watching. It was to please her that he devised his heroics. If she wasn't there, if he knew that she wasn't, he would have just run back and caught the ball in its course.

"I think you know me better than that," she said. "I prefer substance to style, except in films and literature. That's the way I was brought up and that's the way I am."

After that she stopped coming to the games except for those times when she did. It used to be the exception when she wasn't there. Now it was the exception when she was, although in terms of actual appearances at the ball park things remained about the same.

Before the game, the manager called Rocco into his office and asked him if he had any problems that were getting in the way of his ball playing. Pop, or Boss as the players called him, liked to talk to the men about their problems.

For a while Rocco couldn't think of any problems he had, which was one of the problems he had when anyone asked him. The only thing, he said, which he didn't want to make anything of since it wasn't *much* of a thing, was that he was not getting enough playing time. His was the kind of game that thrived on hard work.

"I like a man who wants to play," Pop said angrily. "The only place I can think of you getting more playing time, Rocco, to be frank, is at our farm club, Vestal, in the Postum League. You don't hit for average and you don't hit consistently for power. What else can I tell you? On no team that I managed has there ever been any problems with the way I do things."

The next day, without prior warning, Rocco found himself in the starting lineup at left field. What did it mean? He tried to catch Pop's eye during batting practice to say thanks or something else, but the doughty little manager seemed whenever Rocco looked at him to be looking on the ground for something he had dropped.

A telegram came for him as he was stepping into the batter's cage to take his swings.

Last chance
It's make or break
Hang loose
—An Admirer

It was only the third telegram he'd ever had in his life. The fourth was delivered to him by the bat boy at his position in left field. *Far out.* he thought, after getting two telegrams the first thirty years of his life to get two more on the same day.

This one, it was clear, was from his wife (the signature blurred by tears), with whom he had had.a falling out before coming to the ball park.

Have had offer to go off with another
Will make decision by nightfall.
Love etc.

He had had enough messages for one day. Worried about losing concentration, once lost it could take years to recover, he thought about a movie he had seen the other night at Venestra's urging, rehearsed the plot line to himself. In the movie, which was in French, this man and woman were living together when this woman's former boyfriend showed up. The guy she's living with gets jealous and then it's only a matter of time before she runs off with the old boyfriend. After she leaves the old boyfriend—or he leaves her—the two men move in together.

The game was being played miles away from the mind's resting point as if he were on a hill looking down at the lights of a city in the distance.

The first pitch he looked at was called a strike, to which he had no valid objection, a fastball or slider on the inside corner of the plate. He had been anticipating a breaking ball on the outside, so he had been unable to take advantage of a pitch he usually liked to stroke. What was the pitch most likely to come next? If he were the pitcher, putting himself in the other's place, he would throw himself a curve or slider on the outside of the plate or, the deception of the obvious, the same pitch in the same place.

He guessed the same pitch and was right, though the second was not quite as far inside as the first and was, at quick estimation, three inches higher. Rocco triggered the bat, his anticipation a fraction of a second ahead of an ideal meeting, exhilaration frightening him as the ball jumped from the bat.

All was ruined, he let himself think, his best hopes shot to hell, but the ball danced along the foul line crashing the wall inches fair.

The applause sung to him as he stood on second base regretting his failure to do more. He wondered if there was anyone in the stands who really liked him for himself as opposed to the disguises of accomplishment.

In the fourth inning, moments after he had dropped an unimaginative fly ball hit directly at his glove, he got a Special Delivery letter from an anonymous fan, which read (in its entirety), "You have disappointed our best hopes." There was nothing you could do to please them, he thought.

He struck out swinging in the fifth and got hit in the face by a tomato. That didn't seem right.

In the eighth inning, after hitting a home run with two men on to put his team in the lead, he received in the mail several offers of marriage from grateful fans of both sexes.

After the game the television announcer asked him what was the pitch he had hit so prodigiously and he said he thought it was a fastball on the inside of the plate or a slider right down the middle, one or the other. When they watched the replay on the television the pitch looked like a low curve on the outside corner.

"How does it feel to be a hero?" the announcer asked him.

"I can take it or leave it," he said. "Tomorrow if I do something wrong, they'll be booing me again. I mean, you can't live with people like that."

"They're the ones that pay our salaries," said the announcer.

"You know where they can stick their salaries," said the player. Whatever his public reputation, he envisioned himself as a credit to the game.

"That's no way to make friends," his wife said to him when he came home. "That was a very destructive thing to do."

"That's the way I am."

Pop called him on the phone that night. "I don't know how to tell you this, Kidd, because I know how much it means to you, but you're going to have to give back that home run you hit yesterday."

"How come?"

"That thing you said on the television. The commissioner made a ruling on it last night after the mail went twenty to one against you. They're giving the game-winning home run to Hatchmeyer whose place you took. It's a real good break for the rookie who I understand is your best buddy on the club."

Rocco was almost too disturbed to complain, the news fulfilling the worst of his life's prophecies.

"It doesn't seem fair," he said.

"You have the right to file a petition of appeal to the commissioner's office, which is the league rule."

"The commissioner was the one, you said, that took my homerun away. What would be the good of appealing to him?"

"No good. No way. I'm just telling you what your rights are in case you want to make use of them. Okay, son?"

"Okay, Pop."

The next day he wasn't in the lineup, nor was he the day after.

On the third day it rained.

"You have only yourself to blame," his wife said, holding out her arms to him in comfort. "What did you do it for?"

Why did he do it? It did itself. He kissed his wife's neck, lifted her off the floor, and carried her into the bedroom. "I prefer substance to style," he said.

Stripped of his home run, his name not in the lineup for a whole week, Rocco fell into a severe depression, began to drink heavily, became the bloated substance of his former shadow, gave way to greater and greater distraction.

One day he was on the bench watching a game and he day-dreamed that he was in the clubhouse watching a movie of a game played the day before. It might even have been an old game, the cinematic representation of former glories. When you weren't playing, and even sometimes when you were, one game could seem very much like another.

He was trying to remember whether he had gotten into the game he was watching when Pop said to him, "Rocco, get up and swing a couple of bats, why don't you?"

Had he done it already or was it something he still had to do?

On the third pitch he swung under the ball and hit a major league foul that the squat catcher caught between first and home, staggering jelly-assed under his burden. When Rocco went back to the bench he asked the manager what he had to do to get that taken from his record.

Pop said, "Do you know what the trouble with you is, Kidd, the trouble with you is you think you're too good for this game."

Always the curve ball sliding away from the bat, sliding obliquely down and away almost as if it were insubstantial, the faded recollection of a pitch. Always in his dreams the snakelike pitch eluded the expectation of his club.

"If you admit to him you were wrong," his wife said to him over the phone, "maybe he'll let you play again."

"What did I do that was wrong?"

"Just tell him that you sincerely regret what you did and that you won't do it again."

"Won't do what again?"

"You know. Why do you always pretend you don't know when you do?"

It may even have been a replay of an earlier conversation, the filmed highlights, his nonplaying time given over to a study of the real and imagined past. Untouched by education, Rocco had never lost his faith in it.

He used to consider Slaughter Hatchmeyer, whom he roomed with on the road, his best friend on the team, but since the other had acquired Rocco's home run it made him angry just to look at the long-haired rookie. When Hatchmeyer came into the room, Rocco would find some excuse for leaving it.

"Cool," said Hatchmeyer, an easy-going type oblivious to slight. "What do you say later, man, we go out for a couple of steaks and catch a flick?"

When Rocco came back from the road trip he found Hatchmeyer in his apartment having dinner with his wife.

"What's he doing here?" he asked.

"I thought you invited him," said his wife. "We've been talking about you. Slaughter thinks you have an extraordinary natural talent. "

"I'd like you to clear out," he said to Hatchmeyer. "I'd like a little time alone with my old lady if you don't mind."

"I'd like to oblige you, man," said the imperturbable Hatchmeyer, who in the off-season studied self-oblivion in an Adult Education Program in his home town, "but I've already asked Mrs. Kidd, I mean Venestra, to run away with me."

All eyes, including in a manner of speaking her own, were on Venestra.

"I have nothing to say," she said, opening the second and third buttons of her blouse.

"Man, I was seeing the ball good today," said Slaughter. "Some days you see it big as a balloon, Venestra, and some days, it's like a pimple on a cow's ass. Right, Rocco?"

Rocco wasn't hungry and he didn't want to talk, particularly not to his roommate and former friend, so he sat in the living room and collected himself while they ate.

The phone rang.

"How you doing?" a familiar voice asked. "Your arm still hurting?"

"Nothing wrong with my arm," said Rocco. "Anyone tells you there's something wrong with my arm is in the pay of a foreign power."

"Sure. What I called to say was that I want you to think of yourself as the regular left-fielder until I tell you different."

"Yeah?" He had the impression that someone was playing a joke on him, although he couldn't imagine who or why.

"I want a man to know a job is his so he can have the confidence to go out and do a good job. You really made good contact out there today, which is what I like to see."

"Look, I didn't get in the game today. *Who* is this?"

"This is Pop. Who is *this*?"

Rocco announced his name in a fierce whisper though not before hanging up to protect himself from the embarrassment of being discovered an imposter in his own house.

He returned to the dining room, swinging a weighted bat he kept in the closet for training purposes, to catch his wife and Hatchmeyer like a commercial between bits of movie finishing up their salad.

"Who was it, dear?" she asked her husband. There were four buttons open now on her blouse.

"It wasn't anybody."

Hatchmeyer was eating Wheat Thins with brie, stuffing them into his jaw three at a time. His large face diminished, though swollen, by a crossing thought.

After a moment Rocco said what he had planned not to say. "Why the hell don't you get out of here, Slaughter? Take as many crackers as you like."

"I think it's good that you can express your anger," said his wife. "You usually just deny what you're feeling."

"Cool," said Hatchmeyer, nodding benignly.

It was his own place no matter what was going on in it. He could swing his practice bat any place he liked in his own house. He could even, if that's the way he felt about things, bring it down like a sledgehammer on the dining room table inches from Hatchmeyer's plate, precipitating a shift in the balance of objects and some broken wooden boards.

"This time you've gone too far," said Venestra. "Expressing your anger is one thing, dumping it on others something else altogether."

Hatchmeyer collected his double-breasted red jacket from the closet and looked around the room for a way out. "One of us is going to have to be traded," he said. "I mean that sincerely, man."

The deposed left-fielder took a practice swing and caught his replacement in the side of the knee with the weighted end of the bat. Now he had gone too far.

"I'm sorry as hell, Slaughter," he said, the suspicion of a smile emerging in the teeth of his regret.

They put him to bed, the crippled starting left-fielder, in the room they had set aside for the children they had never had.

His wife explained herself when they were alone. "Slaughter and I experience an attraction for each other which is hard to explain."

"Cool," said Rocco.

The next day, wearing the rookie's uniform, which was a little tight in the waist, he took Hatchmeyer's place as the temporary regular left-fielder. Rocco thought to fail—it was his game plan—as a means of winning back his job under his own name. His second time up, the first pitch looked so sweet he hated to pass it by so he laid his stick on it as lightly as a kiss just to prove to himself that he could make contact if he had to. Somehow the ball got between the outfielders and Rocco wound up on third, running as slowly as he could.

The more he didn't try—he also didn't not try—the more success he seemed to have. It was the uniform, he thought, or the number or the dumb luck of the former tenant of that uniform. After getting three triples in one game, he went up with his eyes closed and knocked the ball over the fence.

It went on for days, his not trying—his not not trying—with disturbing, really crazy success.

Rocco wore a false mustache and a long-haired wig doing Hatchmeyer, which he took off when he played himself. In his own right, under his own name and number, the old bad luck continued to plague him.

For the first few days he came home to his own apartment where his wife and Hatchmeyer were now living, but after a while it was simpler to stay in Hatchmeyer's hotel room as if he were in fact the very man he pretended to be.

One day his wife called and asked him over for lunch, the other Hatchmeyer being away at a doctor's appointment.

Wherever he went reporters followed him, asking impertinent questions. Rocco did everything he could think of to elude them, disguising himself once as a woman, and another time as a black man, several times going in the wrong direction, but no matter what you did you could only fool them on essentials.

Venestra, who had her blouse buttoned to the neck when he came in, kissed him on the forehead. It was all she had to do.

He undressed her like a baby. In bed, under the gun, she said, "Lover, what do you call yourself these days? Is it Slaughter or Rocco?"

He had to check his uniform number, which was on the floor next to the bed, to make an accurate determination.

"What name has he been using?" he asked.

She shrugged. "I mostly call him Teddy Bear."

"Teddy Bear?"

"Sometimes Pooh-Pooh with an h. He's really very sweet in his pea-brained way. Why is it, honey, that all your friends are so stupid? Do you have any idea?"

He thought about it until he got distracted, then thought about something else. "Search me," he said.

"Do you know the kind of thing he does? Rocco reads to me from the paper about you hitting a grand-slammer or something as if it were about himself."

"I'm Rocco," he said.

"I mean Slaughter," she said, "though he calls himself Rocco for the sake of the neighbors. I kept telling him that it's pea—brained to identify with the achievements of someone else. And he says, 'they use my name so it must be about me.' He actually believes, though he can barely walk on his banged-up leg, that he's the one that's been doing all the exploits he reads about in the paper. Anyway, we're both proud that you're doing so well."

"The crazy thing is, I haven't even been trying."

She nodded sympathetically the way she used to before they were married. "I can understand that," she said.

They were still in bed when the original Hatchmeyer let himself in with his key. He had brought some steaks home which he thought to chicken fry, he said, ignoring his replacement, who was lying there with his eyes closed and his hands behind his head.

"Anything you want to do, Rocco, is all right with me," she said.

While they were making dinner plans, the other Rocco, the original of that name, got himself out of bed and dressed. "I have to get to the stadium for batting practice," he announced. "If you're late, the manager fines you."

"Have a good game, honey," Venestra said.

He got a hero's welcome at the ball park, American Legion bands, fan clubs, Shriners, confetti, baton twirlers, a twenty-one-gun salute, singing prisoners of war, a religious leader to throw out the first ball. He was awarded a slightly used Plymouth Duster and had to listen to four or five speeches lauding Slaughter Hatchmeyer as a fine athlete and a credit to the game.

His first time at bat he received a standing ovation and heard the fans chant... Hatchmeyer... Hatchmeyer... Hatchmeyer... Hatchmeyer... Hatchmeyer...

The chant made him slightly sick, an experience comparable to watching a movie made with a hand-held camera. "I'm not Hatchmeyer," he called back, though nothing was made of it. His protests were taken as modesty. Suddenly, he dropped the bat he had been swinging and pulled off his false mustache and wig in full view of the thirty-eight thousand home fans and countless numbers of television viewers, although on television the camera immediately cut to a commercial.

A groan from the great crowd and then what he thought of, hard to define otherwise, as a stunned silence.

In the next moment they were applauding madly again, tears on everyone's face who had eyes to cry.

It was like a movie he had once seen or had had described to him by a parent in exceptional detail. Perhaps he was watching that movie on television at this very moment.

Taking a few practice swings, he stepped into the box to face the opposing pitcher. It looked like the same pitcher he had faced yesterday, a curve ball artist who had the look of a lonely man perpetually in mourning. He remembered the first pitch as it came breaking toward him, watching it as he had the day before, not trying to hit it, watching himself watch it. The crowd as always was full of itself.

As the bat came around, repeating the past, he could see his wife Venestra in the stands behind a book called *What Comes Next*.

The fans scream his name as Hatchmeyer punishes the curve ball with his long-handled bat for all the bad times it had given him.

The Return of Service

I am in a tennis match against my father. He is also the umpire and comes to my side of the court to advise me of the rules. "You have only one serve," he says. "My advice is not to miss." I thank him—we have always been a polite family—and wait for his return to the opposing side. Waiting for him to take his place in the sun, I grow to resent the limitation imposed on my game. (Why should he have two serves, twice as many chances, more margin for error?) I bounce the ball, waiting for him—he takes his sweet time, always has—and plan to strike my first service deep to his forehand. And what if I miss, what if ambition overreaches skill? The ordinary decencies of a second chance have been denied me.

"Play is in," says the umpire.

The irreversibility of error gives me pause. It may be the height of folly to attempt the corner of his service box—my shoulder a bit stiff from the delay—and risk losing the point without a contest. The moral imperative in a challenge match is to keep the ball in play. If I aim the service for the optical center of his box, margin for error will move it right or left, shallow or deep, some small or remarkable distance from its failed intention. Easily enough done. Yet there is a crowd watching and an unimaginative, riskless service will lower their regard for me. My opponent's contempt, as the night the day, would follow.

I can feel the restiveness of the crowd. The umpire holds his pocket watch to his ear. "Play is in," he says again. "Play is in, but alas it is not in."

It is my father, the umpire, a man with a longstanding commitment to paradox.

Paradox will take a man only so far. How can my father be in the judge's chair and on the other side of the net at the same time? One of the men resembling my father is an imposter. Imposture is an old game with him. No matter the role he takes, he has the trick of showing the same face.

I rush my first serve and fault, a victim of disorientation, the ball landing two, perhaps three, inches deep. I plan to take a second serve as a form of protest—a near miss rates a second chance in my view—and ready myself for the toss.

The umpire blows his whistle. "Over and done," he says. "Next point."

This one seems much too laconic to be my father, a man who tends to carry his case beyond a listener's capacity to suffer his words. (Sometimes it is hard to recognize people outside the context in which you generally experience them.) I indicate confusion, a failed sense of direction, showing my irony to the few sophisticates in the audience, disguising it from the rest.

My latest intuition is that neither man is my father, but that both, either by circumstance or design, are stand-ins for him, conventional surrogates.

I protest to the umpire the injustice of being allowed only a single service.

"I'm sorry life isn't fair," he says.

I can tell he isn't sorry, or if he is, it is no great burden of sorrow.

The toss is a measure low and somewhat behind me. Concentrated to a fine degree, I slice the ball into the backhand corner of my father's box. The old man, coming out of his characteristic crouch, slides gracefully to his left and though the ball is by him, he somehow manages to get it back. A short lob, which I put away, smashing the overhead at an acute angle, leaving no possibility of accidental return.

A gratifying shot. I replay it in the imagination. The ball in the air, a lovely arc. The player, myself, stepping back to let it bounce, then, racket back, waiting for the ball to rise again, uncharacteristically patient, feeling it lift off the ground, swelling, rising, feeling myself rise with the ball. My racket, that extension of myself, meets the ball at its penultimate height as if they had arranged in advance to meet at that moment and place, the racket delivering the message, the ball the message itself. I am the agent of their coming together, the orchestrator of their perfect conjunction.

I didn't want to leave that point to play another, hated to go on to what, at its best, would be something less. I offered to play the point again. There was some conversation about my request, a huddle of heads at the umpire's chair. The crowd, in traditional confusion, applauded.

The decision was to go on. My father advised, and I appreciated his belated concern, against living in the past.

What a strange man! I wondered if he thought the same about me, and if he did—strange men hold strange opinions—was there basis in fact for his view of my strangeness?

We were positioned to play the third point of the first game. It was getting dark and I expected that time would be called after this exchange or after the next. If I won the first of what I had reason to believe would be the last two points, I was assured of at least a draw. Not losing had always been my main objective. Winning was merely a more affirmative statement of the same principle. I took refuge in strategy, thought to tame the old man at his own game. (I kept forgetting that it wasn't really him, only somebody curiously like him.)

I took a practice toss, which drew a reprimand from the umpire's chair. I said I was sorry, mumbled my excuses. It's not something, the toss of a ball, you have any hope of undoing when done. "This is for real," I said.

My credibility was not what it had been. I could feel the murmurs of disbelief whistling through the stands, an ill wind.

"Let's get the road on the show," said the umpire.

My service, impelled by anger, came in at him, the ball springing at his heart, requiring a strategic retreat.

I underestimated his capacity for survival. His return, surprising in itself, was forceful and deep, moving me to the backhand corner, against my intention to play there, with disadvantageous haste. "Good shot," I wanted to say to him, though there wasn't time for that.

There's hardly ever time, I thought, to do the graceful thing. I was busy in pursuit of the ball (my failure perhaps was compliment enough), staving off defeat. Even if I managed the ball's return, and I would not have run this far without that intention, the stroke would not have enough arm behind it to matter. It would merely ask my opponent for an unforced error, a giving up of self-interest.

There were good reasons, then, not to make the exceptional effort necessary to put the ball in my father's court, and if I were a less stubborn man (or a more sensible one), I would not have driven myself in hopeless pursuit. My return was effected by a scoop like shot off the backhand, an improvised maneuver under crisis conditions. Wherever the ball would go, I had done the best I could.

My father tapped the ball into the open court for the point. His gentleness and restraint were a lesson to us all.

I was more dangerous—my experience about myself—coming from behind. Large advantages had always seemed to me intolerable burdens.

The strain of being front-runner was beginning to toll on my father. His hair had turned white between points, was turning whiter by the moment, thinning and whitening. I perceived this erratic acceleration in the aging process as another one of his strategies. He was a past master in evoking guilt in an adversary.

The umpire was clearing his throat, as a means of attracting attention to himself. "Defecate or desist from the pot," he said, winking at the crowd.

Such admonishments were intolerable. He had never let me do anything at my own time and pace. As if in speeded-up motion, I smashed the ball past my opponent—he seemed to be looking the wrong way—for the first service ace of the match.

There was no call from the umpire, the man humming to himself some private tune. We looked at each other a moment without verbal communication, a nod of understanding sufficient. I was readying the toss for the next serve when he called me back. "Let's see that again," he said.

Why again?

"Didn't see it. P'raps should. However didn't. 'Pologize." He wiped some dampness from the corner of his eye with a finger.

I could see that he was trying to be fair, trying against predilection to control all events in his path, to perceive history as if it were the prophecy of his will.

I said I would play the point over, though under protest and with perceptible displeasure.

"I will not have this match made into a political spectacle," the umpire said. He gestured me back to the deuce court, world weary and disapproving, patient beyond human forbearance.

I would only accept the point, I said, if it were awarded to me in the proper spirit. I had already agreed to play it again and would not retract that agreement.

The umpire, my father, crossed his arms in front of him, an implacable figure. "Are we here to argue or play tennis?" he asked no one in particular.

I started to protest, then said "Oh forget it" and returned to the court he had gestured me to, embarrassed at getting my way.

I was about to toss the ball for the serve when I noticed that my opponent was sitting cross-legged just inside his own service box.

I asked the umpire if time had been called and he said, "Time calls though is almost never called to account," which made little sense in my present mood. My father, I remembered, tended to treat words as if they were playthings.

"Are you ready?" I shouted across the net. "I'm going to serve."

My opponent cocked his head as if trying to make out where the voice was coming from.

"I'm going to count to five," I said, "and then put the ball into play. One..."

There was no point in counting—the old man had no intention of rousing himself—though I was of the mind that one ought to complete what one started. I wasn't going to be the one to break a promise.

I finished counting in a businesslike way and served the ball. "Indeed," said my father as it skittered off his shoe. The point was credited to my account.

My father stood in the center of the court, arms out, eyes toward the heavens, asking God what he had done to deserve ingratitude.

I would not let him shame me this time, not give him that false advantage.

The umpire coughed while my father got himself ready, dusting off the seat of his shorts, combing his hair.

I hit the next serve into the net cord, the ball catapulting back at me. I caught it with a leap, attracting the crowd's applause.

"Deuce," said the umpire with his characteristic ambiguity.

I had lost count, thought I was either ahead or behind, felt nostalgic for an earlier time when issues tended to have decisive resolutions.

I suspected the umpire not of bias, not so much that, no more than anyone's, but of attempting to prolong the match beyond its natural consequence.

The umpire spoke briefly, and not without eloquence, on the need to set our houses in order. "Sometimes wounds have to be healed in the process." He spoke as if the healing of wounds was at best a necessary evil.

My opponent said the present dispute was a family matter and would be decided at home if his prodigal son returned to the fold.

What prodigal son? I was too old, too grown up, to live with my parents. I had, in fact, a family of my own somewhere which, in the hurly-burly of getting on, I had somehow misplaced. "Why not stop play at this point," I said, "and continue the match at a later date under more convivial circumstances. Or..."

"What alternative, sir, are you proposing?" said my father from the umpire's chair, a hint of derision in the query.

I had planned to say that I would accept a draw, though thought it best to let the suggestion emerge elsewhere.

"I will not be the first one to cry enough," said my father. "Don't look to me for concessions. On the other hand..."

The umpire interrupted him. "The match will continue until one of the contestants demonstrates a clear superiority." His message was announced over the loudspeaker and drew polite applause from the gallery.

My plan was to alternate winning and losing points. There was nothing to be gained, I thought, in beating him decisively and no need to take the burden of a loss on myself.

If I won the deuce point, I could afford to give away the advantage. I could afford to give it away so long as I created the illusion that it was being taken from me.

"Can't win for losing," I quipped after the second deuce. "Deuces are wild," I said after the fourth tie.

These remarks seemed to anger my adversary. He spat into the wind, sending some of it my way, swore to teach me a lesson in manners. When he lost the next point after an extended rally he flung his racket and threw himself to the ground, lamenting his limitations and the blind malignity of chance.

I turned my back, embarrassed for him, and kicked a few balls to show that I was not without passion myself.

I had served the last add point into the net and assumed a repetition of that tactic would invite inordinate suspicion among an ordinarily wary and overbred audience. My inclination was to hit the serve wide to the backhand, an expression of overreaching ambition, beyond reproach.

A poor toss—the ball thrown too close—defeated immediate intention. I swung inside out (as they say in baseball when a batter hits an inside pitch to the opposite field), a desperation stroke whose only design was to go through the motions of design. (Perhaps this is rationalization after the fact. The deed, of course, manifests the intention.) The ball, which had no business clearing the net, found the shallow corner of his box, ticking the line. As if anticipating my accidental shot, he came up quickly. He seemed to have a way of knowing what I was going to do—perhaps it was in the blood—even before I knew myself. He was coming up, his thin knotted legs pushing against the artificial surface as he drove himself forward. There was a small chance that he might reach the ball on its first bounce, the smallest of chances.

His moment arrived and was gone.

My father swung majestically and connected with space, with platonic delusion, the ball moving in its own cycle, disconnected from his intention.

Game and match to the challenger. My father came to the net on the run as is the fashion, hand outstretched. We never did get to shake hands, our arms passing like ships in the night. "I was lucky," I said. "That serve had no business going where it did,"

He looked through me, said in the iciest of voices, "I'm grateful for your lesson," and walked off.

Murmurs went through the gallery, an ominous buzzing sound. I asked one of the linesmen, a sleepy old man with thick glasses, what the murmurs signified.

"Well, sir," he wheezed, "this may be out of line, my saying this, but there's some feeling among the old heads that your final service was not in the best traditions of fair play."

I was perfectly willing to concede the point, I said, an unintentional ambiguity. "Why don't we call the match a stalemate."

The old linesman said that it was not within his authority to grant such dispensation. He suggested that I talk directly to my father.

"If I could talk directly to my father, if either of us could talk to the other, we would never have gotten into this match." (That wasn't wholly true. Sometimes you said things because they had a pleasant turn to them.)

"Sir," said the linesman, "a broken heart is not easily repaired,"

I walk up and down the now-deserted corridors of the stadium, looking for the old man. He is, as always, deceptively difficult to find.

Someone comes up to me in the dark and asks if I'd be interested in a match against an aggressive and skillful opponent,

I say that I am looking for my father; perhaps another time.

"Hold on," he says, holding me by the shoulder, "What's this father of yours look like? An old dude passed here maybe ten minutes ago, tears running down his ancient face."

"The old man was crying?"

"Crying! Jesus, the falls of Niagara were nothing to those tears. I mean, it was not a good scene."

I try to get by, but my companion, a younger man with a vice-like grip, holds fast. "Excuse me," I say.

"After we play, we'll talk," says my companion. "I want to show you my new serve."

I am in no mood to look at serves and say so in a kind way, not wanting to hurt his feelings or not wanting to hurt them to excess.

"I may be your last chance, pal," the kid says in his brash way. "To count on chances beyond the second is to live a life of un-reproved illusion."

His remark, like most nonsense, has a ring of truth.

I return to the playing area alongside my insinuating companion.

We take our places on opposing sides of center court, though I have not at any time, by word or sign, agreed to play him.

My father, or someone like him, is again in the umpire's chair and announces, after a few preliminary hits, that the match is begun.

It is the moment I've been waiting for. "I have not agreed to play this young man a match," I say. "This is not a contest for which I feel the slightest necessity."

My refusal to play either comes too late or goes unheard. My opponent has already tossed the ball for his service, a brilliant toss rising like a sun to the highest point of his extension. The meeting of racket and ball resounds through the stadium like the crash of cymbals.

The ball is arriving. Before I can ready myself, before I can coordinate arm and racket, before I can coordinate mind and arm, the ball will be here and gone, a dream object, receding into the distance like a ghost of the imagination. The first point is lost. And so the game.

And so the match. Waiting for the ball's arrival—it is on the way, it has not yet reached me—I concede nothing.

IV. from _The Life and Times of Major Fiction_

Familiar Games

Every family has its games. Ours were in the service of an ostensibly competitive hierarchy. We had to defeat our mother—the game was basketball in those days—before we got to play our father. Not that we got to play him after that either, but if we were ever to play him, the obstacle of our mother had first to be set aside.

Our mother was usually too busy to play, and sometimes too busy to discuss her busyness, though one supected that she practiced on the sly. If her form was wanting, or subtly underdeveloped, she had an uncanny knack for putting the ball through the hoop from the oddest angles. She played, whenever she could be enticed into a game, in an apron and slippers, and at times, when coming directly from the kitchen, in rubber gloves.

She gave advice while we played, suggestions for improvement, a woman with a pedagogic bent. The game I most remember is not one of mine but a game my younger brother played against Mother. Phil had challenged me first, but for some reason—perhaps because I thought he might be able to take me—I declined the contest. Having limited natural ability, Phil practiced at every opportunity, studied self-improvement. One could wake up at two a.m., look out the window, and see him taking shots in the dark. His tenacity awed me.

Our mother was not awed. "This will have to be quick," she said, making the first basket before Phil could ready himself on defense. "There's something in the oven that needs basting."

"Did that count?" Phil asked, withholding strenuous complaint, not wanting to provoke her into resigning from the game, one of the lessons by example she occasionally offered.

"I'll do that over," Mother said. "You weren't ready." Phil insisted that it was all right, that even had he been fully prepared he couldn't have stopped her shot.

Phil took the ball out at the crest of the driveway, which was approximately thirty-five feet from a basket hung on a wooden backboard from the top of our garage, dribbled to the left, then to the right, then to the left again, proceeding by degrees to an advantageous spot. Our mother waited for him, unmoving, at the foul line, her arms out.

Mother blocked Phil's first shot, knocking it behind him. Phil ran down the ball and resumed his pattern of moving ostentatiously from side to side. He told me later that his idea was to get Mother to commit herself.

It was Mother's policy to treat Phil's feints and flourishes as invisible gestures. The more Phil flashed about, showcasing his skills, the more unblinkingly stationary Mother became. Phil's brilliant maneuvering tended to cancel itself out and he invariably ended up coming right to Mother, shooting the ball despairingly against her outstretched hand.

"That's not getting you anywhere," she told him.

That knowledge had already inescapably reached Phil, and one could tell he was planning new strategy, though at the same time he also wanted to demonstrate that his original plan of attack was not without merit. He was down three baskets to none before he decided to relinquish his exquisite shuffle and shoot from the outside.

Phil sinks his first long shot and Mother's lead falls to two.

I've neglected to mention procedure, assuming mistakenly that we all play this game in the same way. In our rules, the player that has been scored upon gets the ball out, which tends to keep the games closely contested. Not always. If Phil is to catch up, it will be necessary for Mother to miss at least two more opportunities.

It is Phil's strategy to force Mother to shoot her odd shot from just beyond her range. He presses her when she takes the ball out, swiping at it repeatedly, on occasion slapping her hands.

"I don't enjoy that," she complains. "I don't think it's very nice."

Phil apologizes and steps back, giving Mother the breathing room she needs to launch her two-handed shot. One of its peculiarities is that when it leaves her hands it never seems to be moving in the direction of the basket. In its earliest stages, the poorly launched missile seems fated to fall short and to one side, an embarrassing failure. Halfway in its course, the ball seems buoyed by an otherwise unnoticed wind and accrues the remote chance of reaching the front or side of the rim. The shot outlasts expectation, gains momentum in flight, and instead of touching the front of the rim, lifts over it, ticks the back rim, echoes off the front, and drops through. For an opponent to watch the flight of one of Mother's shots is to risk heartbreak.

Phil has seen Mother's game before and is no longer as vulnerable to the disappointment that comes of false expectation.

"That's a terrific shot," says Phil, hitting one of his own as Mother basks in the compliment.

Unharried by Phil, Mother misses high off the backboard, the shot extending itself beyond the call of accuracy. Phil takes the rebound and dribbles into the corner.

"That must be very tiring," says his stationary opponent. "I don't think you ought to waste so much motion."

Phil takes a jump shot from the corner and cuts the deficit to one. It is a shot he has rehearsed, though he shakes his head as if blessed by undeserved fortune.

"That was a beauty," Mother says, pretending as she does disinterest in the outcome. She shuffles into position to launch her shot, Phil crowding her, waving his arms. Suddenly, accelerating the pace of her shuffle, she goes by him, a move neither Phil nor I have witnessed before. She lays the ball in off the backboard, though it characteristically revolves around the rim a few times before dropping.

Phil, one can tell, is dismayed, has his mind on defending against Mother's next shot instead of readying himself for his own. A halfhearted jump shot falls short and rolls out of bounds. Mother's ball.

Leading six baskets to four, Mother refuses her advantage, or gives that appearance, hefting her odd heave with more than usual indifference, the ball missing long and to the left. "What was I thinking of?" she says to herself.

One is never sure whether it is generosity or tactic.

Phil matches Mother's indifference with a shot even further off the mark than its predecessor.

"Are you letting me win?" Mother asks.

It is only after Mother hits her next shot, a casual two—hander that bounds in off the backboard, that Phil is able to regain his touch.

"You may have made that one, but you're rushing your shot," Mother tells him.

Phil says it's not so.

"Believe what you like," says Mother. "I'm only telling you what I know to be true."

"Why don't you give me the credit of knowing what I'm doing?" says Phil.

While this argument is going on, Mother sinks another long shot, increasing her lead to three baskets.

Showing off, Phil dribbles under the basket and lays the ball in from behind his ear.

Our mother claps her hands in appreciation. "That maneuver, if maneuver is the word for it, took my breath away," she says.

The score at this point—I am serving as scorekeeper for the match—is eight baskets for Mother, six for Phil. The first player to reach twelve, while being at least two baskets ahead, is the victor.

Although comfortably in the lead, Mother appears disconsolate, nudging the ball in front of her with the toe of her slipper.

"What's the matter?" Phil asks her.

"Who said anything was the matter?"

Phil is momentarily defeated by Mother's question, gives his opponent considerable space for her next shot.

She takes her time, holding the ball out toward Phil, teasing him with its proximity. "Aren't you playing?" she asks him.

"Take your shot, okay?"

"I'm waiting for you, big shot," she says, dandling the ball. "You're not guarding me the right way."

Phil inches closer, waves an arbitrary hand in the direction of the ball.

And still Mother refuses to launch her shot.

"What have I done wrong?" Phil wants to ask. I know the feeling, have been trapped in similar mystifications.

Mother sits on the ground, her arms crossed in front of her. Phil, not to be put in the wrong, follows suit. The progress of the game has been temporarily halted.

Mother gets up after a while and announces that she is willing to continue if Phil is willing to apologize for his misbehavior.

Phil says he's sorry, says it two or three times since, as it appears, he has no idea what for, and gets to his feet.

Mother scores on a long, unlikely shot that angles in off the backboard. Phil shoots before readying himself and misses to the right, rushing to the basket to retrieve his own rebound. Unguarded, he scores on a lay-up and receives some brief applause from his opponent.

"Thank you one and all," he says, mocking himself, flipping the ball behind his back to our mother.

"I hope you're not trying to impress me," she says, nullifying his basket with one of her own.

Phil dribbles behind his back, through his legs, whirling and turning, exhausting his small repertoire of tricks before kicking the ball out of bounds.

When in the course of her deceptively effective performance Mother reaches eleven baskets, needing only one more to claim victory, she hits a cold spell and misses on her next five attempts. Phil, more by attrition than escalation of skill, gradually edges to one basket behind.

The association comes unbidden and without rational cause. I was in the garden with my mother. We were weeding, or she was; I was watching the process or looking for something to do. There were children in the next yard playing. I could see them, just barely, through the spaces between the slats in their high fence. The game they were playing was like no game I had ever seen before.

There were two of them—at first I thought there were four—a boy and a girl, my age or a year or two older. The girl was taller than the boy and more obviously mature, but girls tend to be more advanced at that age. The reason I didn't know them was that they were new to the neighborhood, their parents—I'm assuming they were brother and sister, though perhaps not—had just bought the house next door.

Did they think the high fence of their garden screened them from the eyes of outsiders? I couldn't imagine what they thought. It may have been they were unconcerned with the opinions of others.

The top half of the girl, at least that, was uncovered

and one of her budlike breasts available to my limited perspective. The other breast, insofar as I could tell, was covered by the back of the dark blond head of the boy. The girl's long hair, raven black, glistening in the sun like wet tar, covered much of her face. The boy seemed to be pecking at her small breast in imitation of a chicken. The girl was laughing, though without sound—at least I heard no sound—her wide mouth appearing periodically through the waterfall of her hair. The boy danced up and down, moving from one foot to the other.

I felt something stiffening against my leg and turned away, turned in a way that protected my secret from the possibility of Mother raising her eyes. The price of my reticence was to give up my view of the game on the other side of the fence. I sensed that Mother was watching me, that she would look up from time to time to see what I was doing, though I never caught her in the act.

When I cautiously returned to my vigil, the picture had changed, took some moments to assimilate in its new form. I blinked my eyes, sucked in my breath.

"What was that?" my mother asked without raising her eyes.

"It wasn't anything," I think I said, not wanting to be heard, not by them, thinking the words rather than saying them.

The first thing I saw was the girl's naked behind thrust out like a thumb, her long hair screening it from full view. She was standing with her legs apart, knees bent, leaning forward. The boy was not where I could see him, not at first. Momentarily, the girl jumped forward, legs askew, as if imitating a frog. Then the boy— he had been somewhere else in the yard—performed a similar jump. I assumed they were playing Follow the Leader or some game of similar principle. It seemed innocent enough except for them both being unclothed and except for the apparent excitement in the air, the sense that they were doing something in violation of the rules. When the girl hopped on her left foot the boy recorded the gesture with his own. Then she hopped on her right foot, as did the boy. Then she did a tumble in the grass, a forward somersault of no special difficulty, though done with exceptional grace. The boy leaned forward to do his, then apparently decided against it. The girl stamped her foot in mock anger, a hand on her hip.

"If you won't do it, you'll have to pay the penalty," I think she said. "And you know what the penalty is, don't you?"

In the next moment she was chasing him around the yard, calling out some threat I couldn't quite hear and was unable to imagine. The word *penalty* was part of it. I could only make out their relative positions when they crossed my line of vision. The boy kept dodging her, putting himself in peril then slipping away.

I heard my mother groan with exhaustion, an oblique request for aid. I was afraid she would see what I was looking at, so I withdrew my eyes, pretended to study the ground.

I went down to my knees, staying as close to the fence as I could without creating attention, and dislodged a handful of weeds and grass.

I was about to glance through the slats when I saw my mother standing over me, her huge shadow preceding her. "Make sure you get the roots," she said. She was there to offer instruction.

While she was there, more shadow than substance, I didn't dare look through the spaces in the fence, though the temptation was extreme. What was the penalty the girl whose name I may have known and have now forgotten intended to exact? My life, I thought at the time, depended on such knowledge.

I pulled the weeds as she advised, thinking if I did it right, she would go away, but she continued to watch and to instruct, though there was no longer any point to her instruction, no longer the slightest need.

"You're doing very nicely," she said, "except some of what you pull out aren't weeds."

"It's like having someone read over your shoulder," I said. "You make me self-conscious. I know what to do. You don't have to watch."

"I know I don't have to," she said. "I'm watching because I enjoy watching you weed."

The only way to get her to move away, I thought, was to stop weeding, which I did, announcing I was bored, lying on my back in the grass with my arms out. The sun was hot and I could feel my face burn.

Nothing I did or didn't do would get her to leave. Something astonishing was going on on the other side of the fence, and I was missing it because of Mother's lingering presence. I mentioned that I heard the phone ringing in the house but that didn't move her. I weeded in another part of the garden, thinking she would follow me there to see how I was doing. I was sick with desperation.

She didn't follow, remained standing with her back to the neighbor's high fence, surveying her garden with benign indifference, a permanent obstruction to my hopes.

When Phil tied the game at eleven all, Mother broke her fast and scored on a towering set shot that bounded in off the back rim, the ball in flight for the longest time, seeming to hover over the basket awaiting official clearance to land.

Mother's sudden resurgence of skill seemed to discombobulate Phil who disguised the tension he felt, the sense of impending failure, by becoming silly. He wriggled with mock arrogance as he took out the ball, whistling over and over some mindless jingle from a detergent commercial. You could see he was afraid to let the ball out of his hands. Though our mother gave him ample room, he withheld his shot, edging the ball closer to the basket by degrees. Mother stepped away at his approach, bided her time. I would have called to him to shoot—it was hard to resist—but it wasn't my part. Greedy for better position, Phil forced his way closer, Mother acceding step for step. When he decided he was close enough—he was already under the basket—and sought to reclaim his dribble, the ball glanced off his *foot* and went out of bounds.

"What bad luck," Mother said.

Phil kicked the ball before turning it over, said he would never play this effing game again, not if his life depended on it.

Mother reprimanded Phil for his poor sportsmanship, said it didn't matter who won, it was the fun of the game and what you learned from it that counted.

Phil said if there was any fun in losing, none of it had ever come his way.

Although Phil had in effect conceded defeat, the game had its course to run. Mother had a habit of keeping things going beyond their normal duration.

Clenched with mock determination, Phil crowded Mother as she put the ball in play, waving his arms in her face, goading her with childish taunts. He would not give up the last basket, he was letting us know, without the formality of a struggle. One could see that Mother disapproved of the tactic, thought it excessive or in bad taste. At one point she put down the basketball to shake a finger at him. "Don't make me lose my temper," she warned him.

Phil, his face red, said he was only doing his best and no one could be faulted for that, could they. Could they? Mother thought this assertion unworthy of a reply. "Are you ready?" she asked him.

"If you're ready, I am," he said. "I got your number, lady."

In deliberate fashion, Mother feinted to the right and side-stepped to the left, hip to the right, step to the left, shoulder to the left, sidestep to the right.

Phil grudgingly yielded space, sidestep by sidestep, the court shrinking on him, his balance confused. Still, he would not let her have her way, not then, not for a moment.

The repetition of her movements would only take her so far and just when we thought she had nowhere to go she surprised us again. In the next moment, or the next, she appeared to take flight, spinning in the direction opposite from the one she had been going, rising from the ground, lifting the ball over her head with two hands as she flew. Neither of us believed what we saw, required at the end the corroboration of the other's witness. Mother, in her apron and house slippers, taking flight, rising to the height of the basket, suspended like disbelief in air, slipping the ball through the rim like a gift, like a secret. Phil stood at her feet and waved, a belated farewell, his mouth agape.

In later years, if one of us derogated her ability, the other would bring up the recollection of her glorious moment as reproof. Mostly, it was as if it had never happened.

Mother circled the basket, keeping her observers in momentary suspense, before donating the ball to the charity of her triumph.

When she returned to the ground she apologized for letting herself get carried away.

Phil fought back tears, offered the hand of a graceful loser.

Mother enthused over the improvement in Phil's game, said that in truth she had been lucky, that Phil would surely win the next time.

Phil, you could tell, was willing to believe her. He was young enough then to trust forever in illusion.

Who Shall Escape Whipping

Wednesday, 5 October: *Film Staff Meeting at 4. Don't forget flowers. Call L.*

The same cryptic note—Call L—recurs on Thursday, October 6, which opens certain speculations. Did I miss contact with L on Wednesday, or did I simply not get around to calling? The likelihood is that I didn't call, had second thoughts, or was too busy, too involved in my work (I was writing a screenplay, as I remember) to get to the phone. (I've been going through the pages of a 1977 desk calendar, revisiting the events of that year through what seems at times an impenetrable code. I was intending to employ the base for the 1981 filler, but once into 1977 I couldn't turn away.)

It doesn't follow. If the call was important enough to note on the calendar, I would have found the time to bestir myself. It would help, of course, in making sense of what happened if I could remember who L was. I suffer like most people from selective amnesia, forgetting those things that are no pleasure to remember.

There are (or were) thirteen people in my life whose first or last names begin with L. Eight are women; two are former wives.

I remember an occasion when a theater manager whom I considered a friend turned down a play of mine for production, citing reasons that were virtually incoherent. I was driven to call the man up and ask him what he meant by his incomprehensible note. I planned to phone him at his office the next day and perhaps even wrote it down on the calendar as a reminder to myself. The call, despite its reasonableness, embarrassed me, and I put it off, each day's delay increasing my anger, for a period of weeks. When I finally got on the phone, I was so angry I could barely make myself understood. I found myself overstating my case so as to make it impossible for him to take it seriously. "You can't read a word," I shouted at him, and, mortified for us both, he said it was altogether possible that I was right.

Friday, 7 October: *Radio Interview at 12:30. Don't forget to pick up gloves and scarf. Dentist at 3:00.* There is no mention of L, which might mean that the call had been concluded the day before.

There are no pressing obligations on Saturday, 8 October, just the inexplicable message: *Fantasies in present tense like color in a black and white movie.*

I am reminded of a story I had heard about a woman who one day, without apparent warning, asked her husband of sixteen years to move out. She was tired of him, she announced. He cluttered the air with irrelevancies. The man, who couldn't bear to be discarded by his beautiful, celebrated wife—she had a small reputation as a painter of erotic landscapes—offered to change his ways. A truce was negotiated. The woman would see if she could remake this unacceptable husband into the man she imagined she wanted. One of the woman's whims was that her husband dress in woman's clothing before lovemaking. An ordinarily timid man, the husband tended, under provocation, to excessive behavior. After reluctantly taking on his new role, he was continually turning up in some bizarre new costume, offering himself to his wife like a parody of a gift. The woman was moved, despite her contempt, by this new aspect of her husband. She found him more beautiful in his feminine disguise than she had ever thought him before. His nature seemed to redefine itself. He had that insistent glow that many pregnant women have in the early months. His undisguised neediness sometimes brought tears to her eyes. She sketched him, wearing one of her bathrobes, frolicking among goats. Afterward they made love—his reward—on a couch in her studio. Her pleasure in the charade began to stale after a few weeks. There was, after all, something freaky about having a husband disguised as a woman, something deeply unacceptable. And when it came down to it, he was as unimaginative as a woman as he had been as a man.

The husband, whose name I can't remember, whom I think of as H, lamented his failure to please, said he was willing to take full responsibility for the needless disrepair of their marriage. What else might he do to regain his place? he asked.

The woman said she was open to suggestions, though said it in a way that indicated that she couldn't imagine H offering an idea that could possibly engage her. The husband wondered if they couldn't carry their recent experiment one step further as a means of furthering mutual understanding. They would this time move beyond the exchanging of clothes to the transference of identities. He was very sincere about his idea, and the woman, although dubious about the success of such a regimen, consented to try it out for a few days. She didn't want to seem a bad sport, she reported.

It didn't work. They couldn't very well switch identities. At best they played in a superficial way at being the other and in short order the woman renewed her request that H take his tiresome presence elsewhere. If she were going to be a husband, she decided, the man she lived with was not the role model she wanted to emulate.

Not everything has been tried, said the resourceful H, some stones that might have been turned remain unturned. The woman was dubious, was ready for a change in her life, but out of guilt or habit (perhaps even love or its memory) offered her husband one last chance to prove himself.

I am trying to understand why in 1977 I was unable to complete a call to someone referred to only as L for a period extending at least a week and probably longer. It might have been that my phone was on the blink. The slightest storm tended that year to put the phone's nose out of joint, though that hardly seems a suitable excuse. The evidence suggests that I resisted making this call, was ambivalent about its necessity.

When I was a kid of sixteen or seventeen, I had great difficulty phoning some girl I hardly knew for a date. I tended to hang around the phone, working up my courage, sometimes dialing all but one of the digits before returning receiver to cradle in defeat. I think it was the prospect of the call that bothered me more than the call itself, the artificial chatter, the inescapable preliminaries. Even then I had no small talk. Sometimes, to avoid embarrassment, I would write out the dialogue in advance, anticipating the girl's responses or overriding them. More often I postponed the call, held onto it for weeks awaiting the propitious moment, which sometimes never came.

I still have difficulties making phone calls to people from whom I want something, resist them tenaciously.

Was the mysterious L expecting this call, anticipating it with pleasure, dreading it? If I knew L were expecting to hear from me, if I were absolutely sure of that, I wouldn't have postponed the call for as long as I had. The prospect of having to identify myself fills me with anxiety.

I am tempted to call the woman with the partially discarded husband, L, which is not her real initial. This somewhat celebrated artist, whom I present in the disguise of L, gives her unsatisfactory husband one final chance to regain his lost tenure in her life. "I'm listening," she says, hands on hips. He will do absolutely anything she asks of him, he says, *absolutely* anything. It takes a while for the implications of this to register.

"This is laughable," she says, not so much laughing as smiling broadly, fingering the idea in her imagination. "Even if I were willing to go along with the idea, which I happen to think is obscene, how can such an arrangement be enforced?" H has an answer to that too. She can whip him if he fails to carry out the least of her directives. He throws open the foyer closet door to reveal what looks like a coiled snake.

L says she will stay with H for a trial period if he will agree in writing to be ruled by her decisions. If he fails to obey her, or fails to please her by his obedience, he is to be punished at her whim. They giggle like witches around a cauldron as the agreement is drawn up. "I think I might begin to love you again," she says.

Would she really have the nerve to whip him, L wondered, if H did something that displeased her? How could he avoid it? It was in her nature to be easily displeased.

For a time, to threaten him with the whip, to tickle his back with its tentacle was sufficient retribution. H would cower and cringe with exaggerated dismay. And L would extort a promise from him not to displease her again. "You know what's going to happen to you if you do it again," she'd say. It was hard to make these solemn threats while keeping a straight face, though L had a certain self-control. Only an occasional giggle would escape like a hiccup or a belch. H, on the other hand, would be overwhelmed with hilarity, crying and laughing and pleading for mercy all at once. It was a heady game for a while.

L has gotten bored with the unimaginative quality of H's servility. It has become necessary for the life of the senses to draw a little blood. One evening after he has broken a dish cleaning up, L cuts her husband's face with the whip. H cries out in real pain, his hand over his eye.

The celebrated painter of erotic landscapes is all repentance and tears. "Let your mistress kiss it," she says. "Oh my sweet thing, my dearest, my darling."

Tenderness moves up or down the scale (depending on your measure) to passion. They make love on the dining room floor with a clamor that causes a hand-painted plate to fall from the mantle. "You can't make a marriage without breaking a few plates," says H. It is the kind of dense remark that makes the woman want to whip him again and again.

I have gone another week without calling the L on my calendar, have forgotten L or renounced the idea for unremembered reasons. On October 19, it says: *Don't forget tense shift*. It was a note to myself about a story I was in the middle of writing, a reminder to put fantasies in the present tense. If I can trust my recollection on the matter, I rejected that advice to myself and kept fantasies and nonfantasies alike in the conventional past. The advice was written on the calendar not to be taken but to be exorcised as a possibility. Maybe the charge to phone L had a similar intent. Maybe the repeated reminder was a way of canceling out the necessity of the call, a game I played with myself on some unconscious level.

And why should I have wanted to avoid calling? The same question repeats itself. The same answer comes to mind: I was protecting myself from some form of rejection. Even now, three years later, the idea of being refused by L enrages me. It follows, I suspect, that the reason I can't remember L's identity is that I can't forgive her (his?) probable rejection of my request. What an agony of unresolved obsession. Unable to ask for something I want, I blame the person I am too reticent to approach for an uncommitted slight.

There it is on Tuesday, November 1. *Call L*. More than three weeks have passed since its first appearance on my calendar, and the need for communication with L persists like an unhealed sore.

The other L was upset with herself for letting H provoke her into violence. "I won't whip you again," she told him, "not until I recover from the sense of revulsion I have at my own behavior." H sulked at the rebuke, broke another dish, seeking to provoke. "You bastard," she whispered to him. She considered asking him to leave, though thought the timing inappropriate.

They didn't talk through dinner, barely looked at one another, and afterward sat apart in the living room reading separate copies of the same book.

"You're being terribly provocative," she whispered. "You know what you can do," he said, pointing to the whip, which was lying on the rug like a coiled serpent. "Never again," she said.

H removed his Italian shirt and tossed it on the floor.

L sighed. "You have a beautiful back," she said as a matter of unassailable fact. "It was never your back that displeased me."

He wore the shirt over his shoulders like a cape, then slipped it off in slow motion as if he were doing a burlesque number. "It awaits your pleasure, mistress," he said. L returned to her book.

H had the sense that she was watching him while pretending to read. After a while he took off his pants and folded them neatly over the arm of the couch on which L sat with an open book in her lap.

"I wish you would stop whatever you think you're doing," she whispered, regretting the remark the moment it was spoken.

He had difficulty reading her, though pretended to impressive self-assurance. "Is that an order or a suggestion?" he asked.

She was tempted to pick up the whip and lash him for his dullness, but instead stifled a yawn.

"I give you fair warning I'm not going to stop," he said.

It was not what she wanted—how tiresome everything was!—though she was intrigued by the tenacity of his failure. H was touching in his foolishness. She glanced up from her book, paid brief notice to his position in the room. As she had no response to him, none large enough to matter, she felt constrained to invent one. "You promised to do anything I asked," she said. "Isn't that so? Absolutely anything and without question."

H stood alluringly in his shorts, hands on hips. "Have I been unfaithful?"

"I don't want to see you again for the rest of the day," she said. "I want you out of my sight."

He looked injured, though offered no argument, no request for reprieve. He picked up the whip, wrapped it around his neck like a scarf and left the room with as much dignity as a man dressed solely in undershorts and socks could affect.

His absence brought tears to her eyes, a combination of shame and anger. Who was he to walk out on her that way? Her heart was beating violently. She thought how awful she had been to him and how awful he was to have allowed her to be so awful. She thought of going after him and saying she was sorry and ordering him to return. I'm guessing at her thoughts. The fact is, after a suitable hiatus, she got up from her place on the couch and went looking for her exiled husband. She found him sitting in a yoga posture in front of the cat's dish. "How terrible I've been to you," she said, and knelt next to him. It was as though the cat's dish were some kind of sacred object to which they both paid obeisance. Eventually, they moved into the babysitter's narrow bed and made love with what L refers to as "heartrending tenderness." Details are left to the imagination. What we do know is that H achieved a temporary restoration and that L grieved for several days at the treatment the man had suffered at her hand.

On November 2, I note that I finished Nabokov's *Despair*. I started the book in 1975 at the recommendation of a former editor, read twenty-five pages, then succeeded in losing the book on the subway. A woman dropped a glove on my lap without my noticing. When she reclaimed the glove in a hurried gesture she picked up the book, which was under it, stuffing both in her purse and rushing out of the train. That's my story about *Despair*.

There it is on November 3: *Don't forget to call L!* As if a failure of memory were the issue. Anyway the warning was there. I was not to forget. How did I get around calling this time. I called when L was out, got a message that she was not at her desk, did not leave my name, said that I would call back. My obligation to myself not to forget is concluded.

The other L lived in relative tranquility for another week with her soon to be ex-husband. His almost endless capacity for abasement charmed her. He slept at the foot of the bed except on those occasions when it suited her to invite him under the covers.

He would make a noise to claim her attention and she would ask, "Who is it?" And he would announce himself as one of her lovers (she had a few months before confided her adulteries to him in novelistic detail), or present himself as some noted actor, or as a character out of a novel or film. If he chose someone she had in mind (or came reasonably close), she would hold out her hand to him. Sometimes she would hold out both arms.

One time when she asked him who he was he said, "Bela Lugosi. I've come to check out your precious fluids, my dear."

She was about to invite him to bed when the telephone interrupted them. A woman friend she hadn't seen in five years was on the phone, someone she could remember having missed. L invited her over, said to her missing friend, Natassia, that she had been about to embark on a liaison with Bela Lugosi when she called.

"I've had enough bloodsuckers in my life," said Natassia. When L got off the phone she asked her husband (calling him Bela) if he objected to having new blood around.

H, in one of his swaggering moods, said that he had no objection to entertaining both women. L said that she didn't know that that was in the cards but that she would give him his cue if and when the time came.

When Natassia arrived the two women embraced while the man of the house, costumed as a vampire, hung back in the shadows. L gushed at how unexpectedly terrific her friend looked, how radiant with health. "Don't you think so, Bela?" she asked her husband. They had been smoking dope awaiting Natassia's arrival. H, dressed in black cape, bowed formally, said in bogus Eastern European accent, "To see the blood in your beautiful cheeks warms my heart."

What did Natassia, a no-nonsense, cerebral type, make of such behavior?

"Tell us what you've been doing with yourself," L said, passing around a joint. "We want to hear absolutely everything."

Natassia talked dispassionately of the recent dissolution of a love affair, a virtual marriage, that had lasted five years. The thing was, she said, she could feel nothing at all about the loss, or the man for that matter, neither regret nor exhilaration. In the past several months, she had become estranged from her feelings.

L said that sometimes people live with you for extended periods, and when they go you discover that they've taken up no real space in your life. They pass through your life like wisps of smoke. (She is ingesting smoke when she says this, so laughs self-consciously.) H twinkles at Natassia.

Natassia has more to say, though is not given the chance. "Isn't it marvelous to smoke again with old friends," said L with characteristic irrelevance.

"That is exactly what I wanted to say," said the serious Natassia, still musing apparently about the unaccountable muteness of her feelings.

They talked about going out for Chinese food but discarded the idea after making a meal of the discussion. Smoke becalmed appetite or increased it, did whatever you imagined it was doing.

The question came up. "Isn't Bela beautiful when he smokes?"

There was no way for Natassia to deny it without being rude, without abusing the rules of hospitality.

H brought a book into the room (an untranslated collection of Italian poems) and read to the women in a naive approximation of the language on the page.

Natassia made no sense of the words so assumed she was losing her mind. "He reads so nicely," she said to no one.

"When you don't know what the words mean," L said out of some pocket of memory, "you get much closer to the music of the language."

H continued to read aloud after the two women, by silent arrangement, had quit the living room. It was an aspect, L would have said, of an underrated integrity. H finished whatever he started no matter the inappropriateness of the context. He read for another fifteen minutes, with increasing stridency, to the empty room.

When the poems had run their course, H searched for the two women, found them in the master bedroom, asleep together, angled apart like an inverted Y, on top of the lavender-striped sheets of the queen-sized bed. It was not easy to know what to do next. He kissed his wife on the lips and heard her murmur another's unintelligible name, then he did the same to Natassia who put her arms around his neck. "I love you," he said to her.

"Don't say it, darling," Natassia said, putting her finger over his lips. "Don't say a word."

L woke to find her husband and friend in the first throes of the sexual act. Whatever else was happening, it was clear that penetration had been made. L had an extended moment of outrage to which she gave no voice.

The least they could do, she thought, the very least, was to invite her to join them. She put her arms around them both, the position awkward and unpleasurable, though she was unable to wrest either's attention from the other.

I could understand what L was going through. Without prefiguration or warning, she had lost control of the world. The music she had been conducting so artfully had decided to take off on its own course, to conduct itself. A resourceful woman, L made a few phone calls to former lovers but could roust no one to take a fourth hand in the present game. I was one of the men she called, though I had never been her lover, had been merely someone she kept in mind for a rainy day or a dry month.

When she returned to the bedroom, Natassia and her husband were still making love, though at a retarded almost imperceptible pace. Their lethargy seemed positively comic, as if, literally, they were going through the motions. She wondered how to include herself, sat poised on her side of the bed, staring into space. "Why don't you join us?" one of them whispered, or perhaps she imagined the words in the rustle of breathing. A previously uncharted impulse governed her. Her affection for them both vanished like a fever, and she announced in a loud voice, "I want the two of you out of here. Immediately. Out of here."

No one protested. H and Natassia stopped what they were doing, dressed themselves with the same dreamy slow motion of their lovemaking, put on coats and hats, said goodbye to L, and left the apartment.

The next day, or perhaps even the same night, she called all her dearest friends to say that she had thrown her husband out and was now to be thought of as an unencumbered woman. To some others, usually the wives of former lovers, she simply said that H had moved out, said it in a choked voice to make it seem that she had been the mistreated one. She didn't know in truth who had mistreated whom, occupied herself with the sound of her voice telling the story of the last days of her marriage again and again to forestall an inevitable sense of loss.

So far, December has fewer cryptic notations than the preceding months. There has been no further mention of L, no exhortation to call for almost a month. *Buy gifts*, it says on December 10 and again on the 12th and 13th. Apparently to get anything done, I had to remind myself of the obligation more than once.

On Friday, 23 December: *Funeral, 10 A.M., Riverside Chapel*. It was not L's funeral, not L who had been married to H or the L I had been hesitant to call. It was the funeral of a former therapist who had died unexpectedly of a heart attack. He was an abrasive man, competitive, sometimes arrogant, always impatient with the least of my self-deceptions. Although I had never told him so, I felt indebted to him for whatever ability I had to move sanely in the world.

It makes me sad to see 1977 thin down to a few remaining leaves of calendar. I feel myself losing the year all over again, passing through it in accelerated time, rushing toward oblivion.

On December 29, among a list of pre-New Year's resolutions, there it is again, number five in order of priority: *Call L*. Is it a new call, about some different matter, or has the advice to myself of two months before been neglected this long? I regret the unconcluded call, rue it like some failure of character I can never hope to correct.

There are a number of discrepancies in the story of L's marriage to H. One of them stands out in particular. There is mention of a narrow bed belonging to a babysitter, but there are no babies in evidence in the story, no babies and no sitter.

At the funeral: Friends of Kurt Mannheim were invited on stage to give personal testimony about the dead man. Two older men had already spoken at length when I felt compelled to get up. Despite my usual reticence—I've always distrusted exhibitionists, have held them in contempt—I went on stage as if I had something of unusual moment to say. Looking into the faces of the mourners, none of whom I really knew, I felt embarrassed and self-conscious. His wife, or a woman I assumed was his wife (I had never met her except in fantasy), was staring at me with what I took to be encouragement and sympathy. "I don't know why I'm up here," I started out saying. "I'm not, strictly speaking, a friend of Kurt's. I never saw him socially or met any of his family or friends, and to be honest, I was aggrieved with him more than half the period of our acquaintance. He once said to me—I can actually hear his voice at the moment—that I would never get up spontaneously before an audience because I had some stake in remaining aloof, that I was frightened to death of revealing myself as human (therefore mortal) like everyone else. He made that observation to me in the second year of what was to be a six-year therapy. Who the hell did he think he was to tell me that?" It was as if I were waiting for an answer. My throat constricted. Tears pricked my eyes. When I could speak again, I mumbled the following, "I've gotten up here to make a fool of myself because it was something Kurt wanted me to be able to do. This..." I was unable to finish the sentence and have no recollection of getting off the stage and back to my seat. There was neither applause nor derision for my gesture (I had imagined applause), though Mrs. Mannheim came up to me after the ceremony and thanked me for my statement.

The sentence I didn't complete might have gone as follows: "This is to affirm, Kurt, that I am as mortal as you are." I don't know. I might have had something else in mind, something more appropriate and less self-concerned.

I remove the last two pages with some reluctance, pinch out the clips and insert the 1981 filler, giving me the illusion of having moved more than three years in the space of a few hours. So this is the present. It's nothing new.

When I get L on the phone she doesn't say, "Hello," but "Who is it?" as if accusing me of being an imposter. To protect myself, I give her a false name, say "This is Harold."

"Harold? Harold?" she says querulously in her hoarse voice. "Are you sure you have the right number? I don't know any Harolds outside of my father. You're not my father, are you?"

It strikes me that under a false name I am free to be more like myself. "Are you interested in going to a movie with me, Friday night?" I ask.

She gasps with what I take to be pleasurable surprise. "I'm dying to meet you, Harold," she says, "but I have this rule whereby I never go on dates with strange men."

I try to persuade her of my familiarity, but she is adamant about not violating her rule.

"Then there's no more to say," I say. (I knew it was a mistake to call, another occasion for humiliation.)

"Wait a sec, Harold," she says. "Don't go away, baby. I just had this overwhelming perception that I know you from somewhere. Weren't we once an item? Weren't we once, under different names, an official couple? I have the idea that we have a lot of lost time to reclaim."

I didn't go away or hang up but in a moment or so we seemed to disconnect, a busy signal rising between us, then dead space. I would have called back, but I couldn't remember her number, couldn't find it listed in any of my address books.

I had lost her, I remember thinking in the dream, lost her without hope of recovery, emerging slowly from the bottom of some dark pool, waking open-mouthed, barely able to breathe, in an empty room in a silent house.

Passion?

1.

A man I know, a longtime sometime friend, recently left his wife and three children because he had fallen in love with another woman. Such news has a disquieting effect on our crowd. Henry is the most domesticated and repressed husband among us, the most devoted of fathers. If Henry, our moral light, is capable of such anarchic behavior, it strikes us that almost anything is possible. Surmise, however, is not the business of this report. What I mean to do here is to separate the knowable evidence from unwarranted conjecture. I mean to investigate the mystery of Henry's inexplicable act as though I were a detective tracking down a criminal.

2.

Henry was barely twenty-four when he married Illana. They had met at college, had started going together when Henry, who was a year or so older, was in his sophomore year, though they had known each other casually (or such is the story one pieces together) from childhood. There were times, says Illana, when each was the other's only real friend. Her remark is not surprising. Henry and Illana had always seemed, to those of us who thought we knew them well, exceptionally close. They had grown over the years of their marriage to seem like mirror images of one another. One breathed in, we supposed, and the other breathed out. They saw themselves, and we tended to confirm that view, as a perfect couple.

3.

The year before he married Illana, Henry, then a Rhodes scholar, started work on a novel about a young intellectual affianced to his childhood sweetheart who falls in love during a summer abroad with a French woman twelve years his senior. He wrote 126 pages of this book before giving up, and the manuscript apparently still exists in its first and only draft. It was, insofar as anyone knows, Henry's only attempt at prolonged fiction.

4.

In the second year of their marriage, their first daughter, Natalia, was born. Henry and Illana were extremely serious about the responsibility. Shortly after that, Henry, an up-and-coming editor, moved to a job in another publishing house that paid twenty dollars more a month. Illana also was working, and they had a live-in maid to look after the child. Henry announced, we all remember, that Illana's working was a temporary arrangement, that it was the preference of both of them that she stay home with the child. Illana said that she and Henry on that matter were in thorough agreement. She made this assertion, as I remember, with surprising passion.

5.

Henry was under a great deal of pressure at work and went into therapy to avoid, as he said, breaking down altogether. He had a dream—his therapist had been after him to write down his dreams—in which his father, whom he hadn't seen in ten years, came to him and said that there was evidence that someone was shooting at him, and he wondered if it were Henry. Henry said that he admitted to being angry at his father for having walked out on his mother, but that he had no recollection of trying to kill him. The father said if thoughts could kill, Henry would have to be number one suspect. Thoughts don't kill, said Henry. Well, how do you explain the bullet in my stomach? said the father.

6.

About that time Henry reported to friends that he and Illana were reading to each other in bed at night. "We are going through the entire canon of Dickens," said Illana, "one chapter a night." "How long will it take to do all the novels?" someone asked. Henry, figuring to himself, a private smile on his face, said nothing. "We'll do it until we decide not to do it," said Illana.

7.

Illana had written a children's book in her spare time. Henry agented it for her, showing it to children's book editors at two other publishing houses, avoiding his own as a matter of moral discretion. Illana and Henry had always taken impeccable moral positions. And though they didn't presume to judge others, one sensed a certain discomfort with the unscrupulous or over-weaningly ambitious. Illana withdrew the book at some point, indicating that she had no great desire to make her work public.

8.

I spoke to Henry at the hospital after the birth of his second daughter, Nara. He said, although he and Illana had wanted a boy, they were not in any way disappointed. Illana said the same thing to my wife in almost the same language, impressing on us (was it meant to?) how together they were, how intimately allied. A week later, when we visited them at home, Henry in Illana's presence made the same speech. When we got home my wife said, "Perhaps they protest too much," and I said, no, I thought they meant it. "It's the same thing," she said.

9.

We all admired the seeming ease with which Henry rose in his chosen profession. What was most impressive was that his ambition, which evidence suggests was considerable, was never aggressively displayed. He had never, not to our knowledge at least, advanced his career at the expense of someone else. We had almost never heard a bad word of him. Yet at the same time, we felt that Henry's full capacities were not being realized. What we meant by that was not at all clear.

10.

What do we know about Illana? When friends of Henry's and Illana's get together, the question tends to come up. What has she had to say for herself in all the years we've known her? We thought of her as taciturn, though not unfriendly, a bit formal in manner, a woman who spoke her opinions as if they were national secrets. She had a way of looking after her children—this was when Henry was there to help—without making it seem, as do some mothers, that the job was overburdening her. We can enumerate her qualities with no strong sense of knowing the person who contains them.

11.

This is Henry's story mostly. It is Henry who announces one day, while Illana sits at the kitchen table with the baby on her lap, that he has fallen in love with someone else. "You have?" Illana is imagined to have asked. "What does that mean in terms of our marriage?"

"I don't know," said Henry. "It's too new to me."

"You don't know?" The question asked with some manner of skepticism. "What do you want to do?"

"What do you want me to do?"

"Well, naturally," Illana said softly, "I'd like you to break it off if you can."

"Out of the question," said Henry.

"I didn't realize that it..." said Illana, a small crack of panic in her usually impassive face, swallowing her words as though ashamed of their inadequacy.

"It happened," said Henry. "I didn't mean it to, but it did. I'm terribly sorry."

12.

After that first confession, Illana becomes a tacit partner, an accessory after the fact, in Henry's double life. Henry works out a regimen, accommodating both worlds. He has dinner with Illana and the children, helps put the children to bed, leaves afterwards to spend the night with Patricia, returning by taxi at five a.m. to be present when the children awake. It is important to him to have the children perceive their world as intact. (Also important perhaps to keep up appearances in front of himself and Illana, a way of deflecting awareness.) "I want you to do what's best for you," Illana is reported to have said to Henry. "I don't want to leave you and the children," said Henry, "and I can't give up Patricia." If this assertion wounds Illana, there is no visible evidence for it. After breakfast, Henry takes the oldest daughter, Natalia, to school, as he has always done, before going off himself to work.

13.

The vice president of the government foundation at which Henry worked had been having an affair with the wife of one of the board of directors, and word of it—one wondered why the news had taken so long—finally reached that lady's husband. Scandal ensued and the notorious editor had no choice but to resign in favor of a slightly higher paying job in the private sector, leaving in his wake a vacancy at the top. It was rumored that Henry was in favored consideration for the post. Who knows where such rumors start? Henry, at the time, was the youngest and ablest associate director at the foundation, and it was more than possible that his well-wishers, wanting the rumor so, presumed its likelihood. Henry, taking nothing for granted, went to see the president of the foundation to indicate his interest and availability. Whatever Henry's boss said to him—the account given to me was notably short on specifics—Henry appeared hopeful in his guarded way. "Frankly," he said, "I have no reason to expect anything."

14.

Illana said, out of Henry's hearing, that she thought Henry was setting himself up for a fall. "You think he won't get the job?" asked her confidante, who in this case was my wife Genevieve. "I think his chances are not as good as he thinks they are," said Illana, according to my source. It was the first any of us had heard Illana express an opinion at sharp variance to Henry's. "Of course, he deserves the job," she added. "I just don't think he's in line for it." Something odd was going on between them, we thought. Why hadn't Illana, who was the epitome of loyalty, offered this perception to Henry?

15.

One day my wife asked me if I found Illana sexy? Sexy may not be the word she had used. "Attractive" or "beautiful" is more likely. I don't remember what I answered. "Uhnrr," perhaps. Something that cancelled itself out, I suspect. What's that about? I thought, though let it slide by at the time. About a week later, something else bothering me, I asked her why she had asked about Illana. "Oh," she said, "someone else was saying, I don't remember who, that Illana was the most beautiful woman of his acquaintance and I wondered if you thought the same thing." I said I didn't even think Henry thought that. "That's an odd thing to say," she said. "Well, she's beautiful in a conventional way," I said, "but there's something glacial about her as if she weren't quite alive."

16.

Why do I remember my wife's question about Illana and my answer, and what do they have to do with the larger questions under investigation in this study? I think that we both felt that there was something invisibly wrong with Henry and Illana's perfect marriage, though we were not in touch with that perception. And why should we have been? Why should we have thought of Henry and Illana at all? I ask the questions merely to ask them. Illana was not the issue of my wife's question as it turned out, merely the displaced occasion. I had heard the question she had asked, but not the unspoken confession it contained.

17.

Two days after Henry's son was born, he got word that the job he had coveted, had come in fact to count on, had been given to someone else. The news arrived, as it tends to in Henry's profession, by way of rumor, and Henry, as angry as he ever remembers himself, went to see his boss to check it out. "Don," Henry said, "I've heard some disturbing news." Don took his glasses off to listen, lit a cigarette, though he had given up smoking a week ago this day. "Well, what have *you* heard?" he asked. (His tone suggested, Henry reported, that there wasn't any rumor around he wasn't prepared to deny.) "I had heard," said Henry, "that *you* had made a decision on Calvin's replacement." "Oh that;' said Don. "You said you would let me know as soon as *you* came to a decision," said Henry. "Did I say that?" said Don. "Frankly, I don't remember making any such promise. The feeling was, and as *you* know I queried opinions from all directions, that you could have done the job adequately—no one had anything negative to say about your capabilities—but that..." Henry had no recollection of how the sentence was completed.

18.

Henry, it was reported took his disappointment with extraordinary grace, which was our idea of Henry. "That's the way it goes," he said, defending the qualifications of the man chosen in his place. "What I have to do is reevaluate my commitment to my job." Illana seemed emotionally drained. We perceived it as a form of loyalty to Henry and admired them both—this special couple—all the more.

19.

The following account has been confirmed by two sources and so it is included here despite my own tendency to disbelieve it. The time was about four weeks after Henry had learned that he had been passed over for the promotion he had anticipated. The affair with Patricia, if it had already started, was some two months shy of becoming public news. Henry and Illana were at a party hosted by Henry's employer. It was a cocktail party held in some east side apartment to honor the grant recipients of that year and the living room was crowded to the walls with the mostly uninvited. Some bearded middle-aged composer, congenitally sour, took it into his head to assail Henry over the granting policy of the foundation that had just passed Henry over for promotion. Henry was polite at first, said he was not responsible for the choices of committees on which he hadn't served, then proceeded, which is typical of Henry, to defend the foundation's policies unequivocally. The composer kept after him, finding fault with one choice after another. When he could take no more—one can imagine the complication of his feelings—Henry turned his back on him. Illana, who happened to be on the periphery of the small group listening in, was heard to whisper to Henry, "Why didn't you answer him?" Henry, usually under control, lost his temper and shouted at her, "Why didn't I answer him? Why didn't I? I didn't answer him because the son of a bitch is not listening to anything I say." It is reported that Illana's face reddened and that she apologized to Henry's adversary for her husband's behavior.

20.

Even after Henry moves in with Patricia, Illana continues to pretend to the children that she and Henry are
together as before. "Why are you doing it?" my wife
says to her when she comes to visit with the three children, who range in age from six months to six years. "If
I were you, I'd tell him to fuck off." Illana, who rarely
smiles, smiles at that. "I would if I felt that way," she
says. "I'm not angry at Henry. I want him to be happy,
and if he's happy this way, then that's the way it has to
be." When Illana is gone my wife says to me: "One of
these days she's going to realize how angry she really is.
And then..."

21.

A call from Henry this morning at work. He wants us,
he says, to be the first of his friends to meet Patricia.
An appointment is made for dinner at a Chinese restaurant called Hunan Feast. My wife says, when she
hears of the arrangement, that she won't go, that it is
a disloyalty to Illana even to meet Patricia. I mention
that Henry is also a friend and that there is no reason
why we have to take sides. "I can't forgive him," she
says. "He may be a friend of yours, but he's no friend
of mine."

Patricia seems as nervous to meet us as we are to
meet her, and the experience reminds me of the blind
dates of my adolescence. None of us seems able to strike
the right note. "What do you think?" Henry whispers out
of earshot of the women. "I think she's..."— I search for
the word—"fine," I say generously. My answer seems to
disappoint him. "Is that all?" he asks.

22.

"What do you think of her?" my wife asks when we're in bed that night, the first either of us has risked the subject. "She's different from what I imagined," I hear myself saying. "I don't know what you mean by that." A note of irritation in her tone.

"Does that mean you don't like her?" I ask.

"It's not a question of liking or disliking her. She's nothing. She's a blank. Didn't you see that?"

My silence offers denial.

"My God, Joshua, I've never seen anyone with less personality. She's pathetic."

"Well, what do you think she has for Henry?"

"I haven't the faintest idea. What do you think?"

"Well, she's not unattractive," I say.

"Not unattractive? She's the most ordinary looking woman I've ever seen in my life."

23.

Henry is on one of his periodic diets; we go to a health food restaurant for lunch and have a couple of shredded carrot sandwiches. Our conversation is correspondingly low on calories. "Patsy liked you and Genevieve," he says a few times, rephrasing the remark so as not to seem to repeat himself. "She felt the two of you accepted her." "She seemed extremely nice," I say. "Very..." The word eludes me. "Lively," he says. "Lively," I repeat. "In that way, she's the opposite of Illana," he says. "Do you think you'll stay with her?" I ask. He becomes thoughtful, which is a form of reprimand with Henry, an indication that you've overstepped yourself. Then he says with a forgiving smile: "We take every day as it comes." It goes like that until later in the meal when Henry says, "Illana and I still love each other. The situation hasn't changed that."

"Then you are thinking of going back to her?"

"It's impossible," he says, smiling enigmatically. "We're both happier this way."

"Both of you?" My incredulousness seems to escape notice.

Henry eats his yogurt and nuts with a beatific smile.

"Is it sex?" I ask, expecting no answer.

"Never been so good," he says.

24.

"It's not sex," says my wife. We are still trying to understand our friend Henry. "Or sex is merely an excuse for something else."

"If Henry says their sex is good, why should you doubt him?"

"Henry," says Genevieve, "is trying something out. He wants to see how far he can go, how outrageous he can be, before Illana will say no more."

"That leaves out the implication of Patsy altogether," I say.

"Patsy doesn't count. Don't you see that?"

"If you ask Henry, Patsy is the only one who counts." Our conflicting views of the reality abrade against one another, strain the limits of our friendship.

"Why are we fighting over Henry and Illana?" my wife asks.

The continuing argument becomes its own answer.

25.

Henry and Patricia have been living together for six months. Henry visits with the children on weekends and sometimes comes over in the evenings to put them to bed. Illana, although she sees other men, appears to work at it as if a recommended though pointless exercise, remains in her heart faithful to the Arrangement. How do I know this? Illana tells us or tells Genevieve, which comes to the same thing. Genevieve becomes increasingly impatient with Illana's stance, though talks to her almost every day on the phone, gauging her emotional temperature from the evidence of the unspoken. "She has no idea how angry she really is," says Genevieve. "Her calm is a form of self-oblivion. Meanwhile she won't allow herself to get interested in any of the men she sees. I can't stand it."

26.

My wife says, apropos of my arm around her, "You're behaving like Henry."

"What does that mean?"

"Henry and Patsy, as you know, behave like teenagers in public, but they have an excuse. They're new to each other."

Her rebuke turns into a fight. I recall my arm and take refuge in another room.

She follows after a moment. "Don't you see what you're doing?" she asks. "You're jealous that Henry has another woman."

"Maybe I am," I say.

27.

I overhear Genevieve complain to Illana on the phone about me, her way, I think, of criticizing Henry indirectly. All of our men are unreliable, says her tone. And what have I done? Whatever it is, she refuses to forgive me. "I am not Henry," I say to her.

"You wish you were," she says.

I call Henry from work, but he is not available for lunch that day, which is too bad. He is precisely the person I need to talk to in my present mood. An odd coincidence: I run into Illana at lunch; she is with another man, I am with another woman. We hail each other across the restaurant. At first I didn't recognize her—how absolutely smashing she looks!—was staring at her in admiration. "We'll have to talk some time," I say to her. She says, "Yes, yes."

28.

Have I drifted from the subject of this investigation? The subject itself drifts. To tell someone's story is to identify, to some extent, with the inner life of that person. In explaining Henry, I explain myself; in explaining myself, I explain Henry. Although not influenced by Henry's behavior—I am convinced that he is not my example—I have just split with my wife of ten years. My situation differs from Henry's in certain definitive ways. I haven't (at the time, at this time) fallen in love with anyone else. Genevieve and I weren't getting along, were fighting too much, were making each other unhappy. I realize this sounds evasive, but the disrepair of our marriage is too immediate for me to see it with any clarifying distance. It is easier, if not altogether more edifying, to talk about Henry and Illana. Henry continues to live joyfully, passionately, with Patsy, who is neither more nor less beautiful than his wife and who, despite apparent differences, resembles her more than not. Illana continues to make do and to accept her husband's manifest disaffection with public and private grace. I envy them both. My situation is neither pleasurable in itself nor might engender the admiration of others.

29.

Tonight I have dinner with Illana and the two older children, sitting at the table with them in their makeshift living/dining room as I had times before in significantly different circumstances. Illana prefers, she says (the evening's arrangement is her idea), to eat with the children like a family. After dinner, I help her put them to bed, a chore of some complication. "How do you manage by yourself?" I ask. "Henry usually comes by to help," she says. "But since you were coming, I told him there was no need for him to bother." I indicate some surprise that she had mentioned it to Henry. "We have no secrets from each other," she says with that seriousness characteristic of them both.

"What now?" she asks.

The question is not meant to be answered. We sit on the sofa, holding hands, talking about nothing. At one point, she says—we have just kissed somewhat awkwardly—"Joshua, do you think of me as a cold person?" I reserve answer, kissing her again as if that urgent gesture (is it really as urgent as it seems?) were a response to her question. And yet what I think one moment ceases to be true the next. She is passionate yet remote, as if her passion were a private wellspring separate from her day-to-day nature.

30.

I return to my hotel room at four in the morning and have barely dropped off when the phone rings. "I want you back," the voice says. It is odd that I am unable to identify or rather confuse the identity of that voice. I finesse my confusion. "At this moment?" I ask. "As soon as you can," says the voice. (I will know in a minute who it is, I think. Keep her talking and she will reveal herself.) "Why do you want me back?" "Oh, God! Do you have to ask? If you don't come to me, I'll come to you." She hangs up abruptly though soundlessly, fitting the phone like a piece of a puzzle into the base. Three hours later (all time is an estimate here), a knock on the door wakes me from an erotic dream.

"Who's there?" I ask the nurse in my dream. The knock repeats, replays itself. I put on a bathrobe and stagger to the door, bumping invisible furniture en route. "Do you mind my coming to your room?" she asks, stepping in, locking the door behind her. Perhaps she says nothing at all, and the voice I quote is out of the interrupted dream. There is no time for questions and explanations; there is barely even time to kiss. Coupling is impersonal and urgent like some natural disaster. "Who's with the children," I ask later.

"Never mind," she says. "The children are well looked after."

31.

Henry seems unusually jaunty when we meet after work at O'Neill's for a drink. I am not eager to talk to him, would have avoided this meeting if I hadn't felt obliged to face him. It takes him two drinks to get to what's on his mind. "I don't know that I like what's going on between you and Illana," he says casually and then again with added weight as if he hadn't heard himself the first time. "I've always liked Illana," I say. He nods. "She's a terrific person, and I don't want to see her hurt." Although expecting something like this—Henry is one of the most consciously moral people I know—I can think of nothing useful to say. "Are you in love with her?" he asks. "Henry, come on," I say. His face clenches and for a moment, just for a moment, he is so pissed off he can barely keep himself together. "I feel very close to Illana," he says softly. "I appreciate that," I say. His glass overturns, and the bartender comes over to mop the counter. "It's all right," he says. "I'm not angry with you." The conversation seems to repeat itself. "I don't understand what you're asking," I hear myself say perhaps for the third time. "I don't want to see Illana hurt, that's all," Henry says once again.

"Are you asking me to stop seeing her?"

"I don't think I have the right to ask you that," he says.

32.

Illana seems to call at least once a day, which is all right, though sometimes I wish it were Genevieve, who never calls. One night at her place, she says, "I really want a husband, not a lover."

"You have both," I say.

"I have neither," she says. "Joshua, I'm opposed to disorder."

"I'm not sure it's over with Genevieve," I say.

Illana laughs. "She says it's over. We talk about you on the phone."

That night after the children are in bed and we have made love with our customary hunger, rushing through the act as if it might be taken from us if we waited, I have an odd perception. "You would take Henry back, wouldn't you, if he was ready to come back?" She thinks about it and thinks about it. "I would," she says finally, "but afterward I'd be sorry."

The Dinner Party

I have a rule, one of few—perhaps my only rule—that I never discuss work in progress. To talk about something not fully born is to risk, as I see it, unspeakable loss. So when at a dinner party this youthful, gray-haired woman on my right, Isabelle something, some other man's discontented wife, asked me what I was working on, I hedged my answer. This is what I said. I'm working on a novel about a marriage in the process of invisible dissolution. Isabelle gave me an odd, almost censorious look and returned to the business of eating. Had I said the wrong thing? Did she think I was telling her something about her own life? I had said more than I wanted to say, though perhaps less than she felt it her right to know.

The loss of my audience so early in the proceedings seemed a depressing omen. It provoked me to want to regain her attention. It is a mistake to let yourself get challenged like that at the house of strangers.

For three consecutive nights Joshua Quartz had dreams that included the appearance of his estranged wife, Genevieve. Six months had passed since their separation, and he had considered himself free of her until the dreams presented themselves like undiscovered evidence with a significant bearing on the case. There was a progression in the dreams, as if they were installments in some larger yet undefined unit.

"Isn't there anything else you'd like to know?" I asked, trying to make a joke out of a serious question. She was chewing her food—her turkey or chicken—and couldn't find her way clear to making an answer. She held up one finger as if to say, Give me time. I waited, looked around the table and realized there was no one I knew well at this party. The Garretsons, friends of my former wife, had invited me out of some misplaced idea of kindness. For some reason, I was the only one at the table—there were fifteen guests in all—who had not yet been served. Isabelle turned to me and said, "Of course I want to know everything. Do I dare to ask?"

In the first dream, Joshua was in a small bedroom talking to a man—his father? brother? a doctor acquaintance?—about problems he was having with his back. The door to his bedroom was open, offering him a partial view of a long hallway. His wife, Genevieve, was on the phone at the furthest point of his vision. She was talking to an unnamed man, her current boyfriend, whom she referred to from time to time as darling. He felt the inappropriateness of the endearment in its present context and was more amused than pained by it. The man in his room continued to talk—something about wrapping the back in Corning's fiberglass—but his attention was on Genevieve. She turned to see if he was there, and their eyes met. She seemed to smile at him. As a matter of choice, he declined to smile back. She continued to watch him while she talked on the phone.

I felt a kick under the table and moved my leg away, thinking it an accident. The second kick suggested intention, a statement of presence from the woman on my right. I returned the kick or perhaps kicked someone else, a few heads raised from their plates, a few pained looks here and there. "Consider it a down payment," said the woman, Isabelle something, putting one of her braised potatoes on my plate. "This is a novel about two people, two wary romantics, with unrealistic expectations," I said. Then I ate the potato the woman had given me. It created a desire for more, and I stared longingly at the three other potatoes on her plate. "Sometimes I just want to scream," Isabelle said. She speared one of her potatoes and held it to her lips, held it suspended in air while she considered its fate. "What you're giving me is what I could get from the dust jacket," she whispered. "Aren't you being just a little bit evasive?"

In the second dream he had come home to his new apartment to discover several radical changes in his absence. For one, the lace curtain on his door had been replaced by a white apron. He knew what it meant, knew instantly that Genevieve was somewhere in the house and that the apron was her calling card. He admired the wit of the apron, though considered its presence inappropriate in a place a man lived in by himself. He planned to take it down at first opportunity. What was going on? His cleaning woman, Henrietta, was in the kitchen preparing a turkey, stuffing it with olives and apricots. The house was pulsing with preparations for some holiday dinner. He went back to the vestibule door and removed the apron, intending to replace it with the original curtain, which was not to be found. The door looked naked without a covering, suggested deprivation and loss. He worried that Genevieve would make a fuss about his removing the apron, would take it as a rejection of her gift. When he put it back he couldn't get it straight, so he left it hanging at an awkward tilt.

Joshua washed his hands, then went to the bedroom to change his clothes, saw Genevieve in the adjoining room at his desk. Nothing is said. He starts to undress, lifting his shirt over his head. He glances at her to see if she is watching him. It is hard to tell. The book she is reading covers her face. The title, he notices, is *The Curtain Falls*.

The hostess, Kiki Garretson, served me a bowl of shell-shaped pasta in a green sauce. It was not what the others had, but was certainly an acceptable substitute. I had a reputation when younger for preferring pasta to almost anything. Perhaps the Garretsons had made this separate dinner especially for me. Or perhaps they had run out of the main course and this was a leftover from another party. "What the people in your novel love," Isabelle whispered in my ear, emphasizing each word like a radio announcer, "is the idea of being loved. Isn't that the point?"

I chewed quickly, as quickly as the pasta, which was a touch crisp, allowed, not wanting to lose this audience. Her hand was on my knee, a gentle weight. "Yes and no," I said. I looked around the table to see if anyone was watching us. "They are both married to others when they fall in love. Their relationship begins in passion and ends in anger and insentience. Ends in the death of feeling." My neighbor nodded her head in acknowledgement, confirmed in some private unhappy truth. "There's nothing worse than the death of feeling," she said, giving me the last and largest of her potatoes. We exchanged sad smiles.

The third dream was the most elaborate. He was with her in an underground parking lot, collecting their car. They were going somewhere together, the destination urgent though obscure. It was as if they were a team of some sort, detectives like Steed and Mrs. Peele or Nick and Nora Charles, a partnership that had survived other disaffections. In this case, they both knew too much. This too much knowing, this excessive knowledgability has put them in a kind of danger, a danger that offers more thrill than anxiety, a danger without menace. The fact is, they are having fun, pursuing or being pursued. Affectionate wisecracks are exchanged. They get into a waiting taxi, and Genevieve says to the driver in a perfunctory voice, "Follow that car." In the next moment they are pursuing a Lincoln limousine, tearing around corners as in movie chase scenes, going through stop signs, riding on sidewalks. They hear the squeal of brakes as they flash through an intersection, but there is no sign of other cars. The canopy of a fruit stand collapses, oranges and apples roll into the street. It's just like a movie, he thinks, which is what he hears himself saying. "Who's with the children?" she asks him. "I thought you were," he says. Talk of the children deflates his exhilaration. It is too serious a topic, too rueful and painful a topic in light of their present roles. The limousine they have been following stops in front of an Italian restaurant called Pasta Mia. No one emerges from the limousine, and they wait expectantly in their cab for some further revelation.

The shells on my plate were not sufficiently cooked, crackled when chewed, though I said nothing, letting the crunching sound speak for itself, not wanting to seem ungracious. "I've been holding my breath waiting for you to continue," said my neighbor on the right. "I hope you don't mean to disappoint me." I was reluctant to continue but felt I owed her a few more details, having already taken her this far. "They can't keep apart," I said, "so hate the other for the loss of freedom and self-respect. They agree to stop seeing each other, which only intensifies irrational necessity. It goes on this way for a while, the resolution not to see each other, the breaking of the resolution, false endings, new beginnings, guilt, regret, passion, unforgivable recriminations." When I looked down I noticed another potato on my plate, smaller though more perfectly formed than either of the first two. It was gemlike, this potato, and I had not noticed it on her plate before. I ate it slowly, sensuously, holding it on my tongue for a time before swallowing it in two bites. "And what kind of credit does that get me on the literary market place?" she said.

They tell me my paralysis is a state of mind. I don't move because no matter what I say to the contrary, I don't want to move. This is not something I'm willing to believe. They carry me from bed to chair in the morning. How do I start? They bring me my food. Sometimes they—one or the other of them—feed me. Sometimes they leave the food for me on a black plastic tray, and when they're out of the room I feed myself. I can only move my arms when no one is watching. Not everything I say is true. My memory is short.

Taylor Garretson came by and filled my wine glass, asked if everything was satisfactory. My plate, I noticed, was the only one around the large table that still had food on it. "I've been talking too much," I said. I studied the food on my plate with apologetic regret, took a small forkful of the brittle shells. My companion on the right, the one who had given me her potatoes, Isabelle something, winked at me. The woman on the left, who had hardly noticed me before, turned her head in my direction. In fact, everyone at the table was looking at me with apparent curiosity. I held up my wine glass. "To a better year than the last," I said. The others joined me in the toast, all but the woman on my left, who had turned her head away.

Joshua departs the cab and enters the restaurant while his estranged wife stays behind. There is no one inside Pasta Mia that he knows or has even seen before, though they are almost all indefinably familiar. It is a family restaurant and everyone there is sitting at the same table. Joshua asks to speak to the owner. When the owner wearing a chef's apron comes out from the back, Joshua can't remember what it is he is supposed to ask. His wife comes in, takes his arm, says this is the wrong place, darling, we haven't a moment to lose. Some cliché like that. They run together for a few blocks, Genevieve glancing behind her to check on the distance of some apparent pursuer. It strikes Joshua that the owner of the Pasta Mia was the man in the limo they had been following, that the apron he was wearing had been put on as a disguise. "Who's behind us?" he asks. "Never mind," she says. Joshua is thinking that this experience with his estranged wife requires further definition. "It's been the man in the apron all along," he says, "hasn't it?" The intimacy of being pursued together touches him. Genevieve makes no comment. They arrive at their former apartment where he drops her off. "Are you going to be all right?" he asks. "Let's do this again sometime," she says. Joshua is trying to find a language for his feelings. Genevieve hesitates at the door, thinks perhaps of inviting him in. They neither embrace nor shake hands. She goes inside

"I don't have the whole picture," Isabelle said to him. "Something crucial has been left out. I hope you're not one of those writers who leaves things out in order to be obscure." I was playing with the remainder of my shells, crushing them with my fork into a greenish powder. "Did I tell you how they met?" I asked. "I don't remember," she said. I didn't remember whether I had either. "They met in a mixed doubles game at The Wall Street Racquet Club," I said. She shook her head, pointed her finger at me. "You know that's not true," she said. I felt the detail was wrong and I wondered how I could take it back without destroying my credibility with her. "The tennis game was in an earlier draft," I said. "In a more recent version, they meet in an analyst's office. She has the appointment before him. They nod to each other for months before they begin to talk. What's important is not how they met but the intuitive sympathy they felt for each other." My plate was removed with the others, and I felt a sudden gnawing hunger. "Yes?" she said.

Let me start again in a more direct and honest vein. I can stand if I have to. I can walk. I can feed myself as ably as the next person. I walk from bed to door and back again, go the whole route. Most of the time I lie in bed with my hands under my head, thinking about getting up and walking around the room. The door is locked. I am a prisoner in my own room. They bring me my meals on a black plastic tray three times a day. Perhaps the meals arrive no more than twice a day. I tend to exaggerate for effect. My memory is a string of broken connections.

"She was crying one day when he arrived late for his appointment, crying and putting on her coat with no success. Her grief moved him. He helped her with her coat. She took it as her due, thanked him without saying so. When his own session was over she was still in the waiting room." The salad course was served. The woman on my left addressed me directly for the first time. "My husband hates salad," she said. "The children, particularly the older boys, won't touch it with a pole. I think that's a shame." I smiled politely, took a forkful of leaves. "I've come to salad late myself," I confessed. "But now I can't get enough of it, particularly when it's good." "You have a good attitude for a man," she said, "but in my unsolicited opinion"—she lowered her voice—"there's more to salad than leaves."

I felt a pinch from the other side and turned toward Isabelle. "He was helping her on with her coat," she said. "They were in the waiting room of his shrink. It was the first time they had talked." The woman on the other side was also saying something, my attention divided. "He invited her for coffee," I said, then turned to the salad woman to see what she wanted.

Joshua called Genevieve the morning after the third dream. He didn't know what he wanted to say, let the conversation unfold to no purpose. Finally, he mentioned the dream, the first of the three. "I haven't dreamed of you at all," she said with what sounded over the phone like regret, as if she had failed to honor her part of the bargain. "I haven't even thought about you," she said, "though I like hearing your voice over the phone."

The dessert was some kind of berry cobbler—boysenberry was my guess—with a white sauce. As we were waiting to be served, Isabelle said in a somewhat plaintive voice, "What have you and Desiree been chatting about?" Desiree? "You know who I mean," she said, indicating with her eyes the woman on my left. "Nothing of consequence," I said. The salad plates were being retrieved, and it came to my attention that I had eaten only two leaves. "In their first few years together, they were obsessively jealous of one another, the woman perhaps more than the man. Because they had started out illicitly, they felt increasingly uneasy as a legitimate couple, feared betrayal." "Wait a minute," Isabelle said, "they're still in the therapist's office, they've just begun to talk, he's holding her coat for her." "If I get too specific, I'll never be able to tell you the gist of the story." "What's the matter with people?" said Isabelle, aggrieved. "Why must they ruin everything?" My neighbor on the left was saying something about leaving my salad in the lurch. "After what you told me, I was hoping you would set an example for my husband." The hostess had started to serve the cobbler when she realized she had forgotten an intervening course and so she collected the plates and returned the dessert to the kitchen. We were crestfallen as a group. The delay seemed intolerable.

The door to my room is not really locked or is only locked from the inside when it suits me to lock it. In truth, my legs are tired. My back is bad. I have no inner life. I sleep half the day. When I leave the room, which is rare, I go directly to the kitchen to get myself something to eat. I go from my room to the kitchen and then from the kitchen directly to my room. Sometimes I walk into the closet and stand among the shirts and jackets, as if I too were something inanimate, something to put on and take off.

"He invites her for coffee after finding her in the waiting room when his own session is finished. She thinks of all the reasons she can't go or shouldn't and offers them with her apology for refusing him. They are only words, and once they are out of the way she gladly goes along. They talk for several hours, find themselves of like mind on a number of subjects. It becomes a ritual, this after-therapy assignation, and both look forward to it, both thrive on it. It is the talk that does it. They are both verbal people. Words fly between them like kisses. They are in love before they make love. And then it takes three years for them to disentangle from other relationships." I stopped for breath and Isabelle said, "You don't have to say anymore." The host and hostess, I notice, are huddled together in the doorway between kitchen and dining room, planning some new strategy. In a moment, the hostess goes back into the kitchen and returns again with cobbler. She wears an apologetic smile. "I'm not a dessert person," Desiree says to me. "I'm going to give you mine." Isabelle says something of the same. New possibilities for my story dance in my head, and I long to try them out on Isabelle, though I wait for the plates of dessert to be passed around.

I have an antique rocking chair in my room where I take comfort in moments of panic. The rocking of the chair stimulates recollections of sweeter times. I sit and rock until the circulation stops in my left leg then I get up, force myself to get up. I shake my frozen leg until it unnumbs itself. The shaking of the leg tires me. I am in the business of conserving energy, storing it up like food in wartime for a crisis even more unimaginable than the present one. If for some reason I leave the room, I am filled with uneasiness, as if the air that sustains were no longer available.

I had two plates of cobbler in front of me. The woman on my right, Desiree, had given me hers after I'd already taken one for myself. When I returned her dessert, Desiree refused to accept it, slid it back toward me. "Please," she said. "It makes me happy for you to have it." Meanwhile, Isabelle had pushed her plate toward me from the other side. So: I had three plates of boysenberry cobbler with *creme anglaise* in front of me. "She doted on him in the beginning," I said to Isabelle. "It was too much. It left no place for their romance to go." "Did she?" said Isabelle in a dreamy voice. "What a coincidence." They were short a dessert on the other side of the table and I gave over one of mine, the one that had been intended for me. I still had the two gift desserts, though I wasn't sure where to start, not wanting to offend either of my companions. "If you're not going to eat it..." Desiree said and reclaimed her cobbler. Isabelle was chipping away at the other one with a spoon. As I took my first bite, her spoon brushed my fork. "Why didn't you keep yours if you wanted it," I asked her. "It's better than I imagined," she said, "and what's more I wanted to share it with you. If you had taken Desiree's and not mine, I would have been heartbroken." Her husband, or the man I thought was her husband, was watching us from the other side of the table.

I walk a block from the house after breakfast and then, as if invisible chains pull me back, return to my room. In the street, sometimes I pass a woman walking a small terrier, and we nod to each other. Sometimes she makes a comment on the weather, an innocuous, impersonal comment. Like: Not so cold today, is it? I share her pleasure in the weather's improvement. I think of things to say to her, variations on our usual exchange. I work up conversation in my hermetic room, rehearse it in the mirror before going out. This is what I will say to her.

There was, as it turned out, another course brought belatedly, out of traditional sequence, to the table. A broccoli soufflé with a plum glaze. "This is Bozo's dish," the hostess said. (Taylor's nickname is Bozo.) Taylor stood, bowed, shook a fist in triumph. Desiree whispered: "He's a terrible cook, you can't imagine." I was the only one at table who ate Taylor's dish. Except for the fact some of the broccoli was still frozen, it was not so bad, not as bad as advertised. Desiree, I noticed, had covered her plate with her napkin, apparently unable to bear even the sight of the dish. I said to Isabelle, "In the beginning they talked like angels to each other. After they made love, there seemed nothing else to say." "It makes me sad to think about it," Isabelle said.

There was a cheese course next, followed by coffee, followed by glasses of some green liqueur. During all this, Isabelle and I held hands under the table. From time to time, I felt compelled to throw out morsels of my novel in her direction, whatever came to mind. I was aware that the party would be over soon, that someone would get up to leave, and that the others would follow. An intense sadness overwhelmed me.

Genevieve called Joshua in the middle of the night, waking him from a restive sleep. "I want to tell you that I've been dreaming about you," she said, "Look, I'm sleeping," said Joshua. "Why can't you call in the morning like any sane person?" "My dream," she said, "concerned a dinner party at our old house on Watkins Place." She laughed to herself. "Everyone around the table was naked. You were the only one with clothes on, the only one. I was disappointed in you at first. I thought, how gauche to stand out like that, to not get in to the spirit of things. Then I thought, what terrific integrity. You retained your dignity, your propriety, while others had yielded to some pointless fashion."

Joshua thanked her for the compliment.

"That's not the end," she said. "I went upstairs to get dressed to show the others that I was on your side in this. When I got back to the dining room, you had gone off with someone else."

"I hate to say good-by to people I like," Isabelle said. "Someday you'll have to tell me how your novel ends. Perhaps I'll see it in the window of a bookstore and go in and buy a copy."

"I told you all I know," I said. "At this point, you know about as much as I do."

"I don't believe that," she said. "How can you possibly say something like that? I think you've been trying to pique my interest. Yes?"

I had nothing to deny. The telling had neglected the structure, of course, the formal concerns, the flashes of language, the urgency of experience. The transitions. What had been left out, when I thought of it, was everything. The rest had been devalued by recitation, had slipped away into the smoke.

I held her coat for her. "The next time I see you, I'll have more to tell," I said. We shook hands in a businesslike manner.

"Until then," she said, following her husband out the door and into the night.

The Life and Times of Major Fiction

1.

It wasn't that he was a great reader as a child but that he hardly read anything, hardly even cracked a book until he was in his mid-twenties. At least that's the story he told me. He told other people other stories, which is their business and only of peripheral concern in this report. Once he discovered books, he told me in one of his side-of-the-mouth confidences, he couldn't get enough of them. "It was like," Ernie has been quoted in print as saying, "coming of age in Samoa," though in fact he was stationed in Japan at the time, a supply sergeant in Special Services during the last months of the Korean War. Once he discovered books he wondered where they had been all his life and why no one had ever told him how astonishing they were. It was as if it were some kind of unspoken secret, he said, and those on the inside weren't generous enough to share it with those on the out. Ernie took it on himself to spread the word in a way that would make people pay attention.

2.

"He was a real-life Gatsby," my friend Jack said about Ernie, "except that it wasn't a woman that inspired him to reinvent himself but a literary ideal he only partially understood." Ernie read voraciously, read everything that came into his hands, yet we wondered, we couldn't help but wonder—he was always there talking about who to read, who we *had* to read—when he found the time. There was something of the con man about Ernie, but we trusted that it was mostly an act, a facade under which sincerity and sensitivity kept unannounced watch.

3.

The first fan letter he wrote, the first time he put his feelings about a book down on paper, he was embarrassed to have the author, whom he admired beyond words, read his "pathetic attempt at appreciation." Despite such misgivings, he posted the letter. "That took real guts," Ernie confided. "I thought, let the guy think I'm some kind of unwashed schmuck. I loved the man's books, and I was going to tell him regardless of the impression it made." Jack told me that Ernie sent fan letters to two writers at the same time, commending each as the most important influence in his life. Neither writer answered him, not at first, and the silence on the other end, which was how he experienced no answer, saddened Ernie. He would have answered gratefully, he told us, if someone like himself had written an admiring letter to him.

4.

Then there's the story, which only some of us credit, of how Ernie, when in the service, had an extended affair with an English nurse. They were wild about each other, we heard, but various obstacles—the war not the least of them—kept them apart, intensifying the romantic aura of their feelings. Finally, tenacity was rewarded, and they lived together in idyllic circumstances for several months. The woman was pregnant with Ernie's child and Ernie was overjoyed at the prospect of being a father and spending a life with this woman. Then something terrible happened, the kind of thing that warns you against exhilaration. There were unforeseen complications in the delivery. Neither mother nor child survived the birth. The news devastated Ernie, though he made no complaint, walked around in the rain as if he were composed of a thousand fragments held together by lacings of glue.

5.

He wrote a second and third time to one of the writers, a recluse who hadn't published a book in eight years, and the third letter elicited a two-line response. It was typed like a ransom note.

If My Books Please You, Fine.
If They Don't, That's Also Fine.

The signature was illegible, or almost illegible, but there was no question whose fine literary hand it was.

Ernie put the letter behind a plastic sheet in a photograph album, though he was unaware at the time that it was the beginning of a collection. Ernie wrote letters of admiration to other writers and began to accumulate over a period of months a handful of answers. When he got a letter from one of his writers—he couldn't help but think of them as his—it brought tears to his eyes. If he admitted it to anyone, he said, admitting it to everyone, he'd become a laughing stock. So please don't tell anyone, he told us all.

6.

For a while he lived with a woman who had been a writer, who had in fact published two novels in the distant past, though had written nothing for several years, had reached a point where she could barely get a sentence down on paper she might be willing to acknowledge. "Just think what you're denying the world," Ernie would say to her, closing her in a room with a typewriter for four hours a day. Her name was Zoe. He called her Zo Zo, which occasionally sounded like So So.

Sometimes she would complete a sentence in her four hours of exile, sometimes a half page of x's, an unseen text buried beneath.

Ernie bullied her and shouted at her, but she seemed not to mind, laughed good-naturedly at his excesses.

One day she came out of her prison with a completed story, a vindication of Ernie's regimen for her. He read the story with unqualified admiration, although he had (truth to tell) some minor reservations about the ending. She said she would change a line or two if it would make him happy. "I'm happy with things as they are," he reported himself saying. "It's the opinion of posterity I'm concerned about."

7.

Another time Ernie fell in love with a woman whom he used to see every morning on Broadway walking her dog. Ernie tended to walk along with the two of them, paying the dog attention, which ingratiated him with the woman. They had a brief affair, then broke up when it got serious—the woman dependent on her husband in childish ways—then came together again. Their time together was mostly disappointing, informed as it was by regret and the prospect of impending separation.

They consoled themselves with the illusion that one day they would live together as an acknowledged couple. It was one of those relationships that never ended, that continued to beguile itself with hope, though Ernie and the woman saw each other less and less. And then not at all. There was a rumor that the woman threw herself under a train or took an overdose of pills, though I suspect it was untrue, had grown out of a wish to give the story a more conclusive ending.

8.

It was hard to keep track of the jobs Ernie held before his rise to celebrity. In a sense certainly, they were all the same job. He started out selling aluminum siding at carnivals, then after a brief stint as a radio actor, he emerged as a book traveler for a textbook firm in Boston, which kept him away from home somewhat more than he liked. He worried, from all accounts, that Zoe would leave her room in his absence to talk on the telephone or to smuggle food from the refrigerator, temptations difficult for her to resist. Once seduced from her task, she might never return to it.

What he liked about the job was that it provided occasion to meet some of the writers whose books he admired. Beyond a few obligatory visits to the colleges in his terrain, he could use his time as it pleased him. As a matter of discretion he only looked up those writers who had answered his correspondence. He didn't court rejection, he told us, but on the other hand, he didn't let it get him down, never thought of it as personal.

9.

After a whirlwind visit to the University of Maine—"I'm in and out," Ernie liked to say—he decided to look up

Jason Honeycutt, who lived somewhere on the border between rural Maine and New Hampshire. The reclusive novelist had no phone, so Ernie waited for him outside the Deerfield general store, where Honeycutt, so said an informer at the university, did his shopping every Friday.

Ernie has told this story differently to different people, but I've pieced together the following account.

Ernie introduced himself to Honeycutt when the man came out of the store, offered to help him carry his groceries, which seemed to overburden the writer. Honeycutt mumbled something unintelligible and walked off to his oversized station wagon.

"I know what your privacy means to you," Ernie shouted after him. "I have no intention of imposing on you."

10

"Your books are very special to me," Ernie said. They were standing in front of Honeycutt's sprawling farmhouse, a box of groceries on the ground between them. "I just want to say that a single line of yours moves me more than the collected works of just about anyone else."

Honeycutt took a deep breath, a sigh of impatience or resignation. "All right, what are you after?" he asked.

Ernie came away from that visit with Honeycutt's avowed friendship and a signed first edition of one of the early novels. Given Honeycutt's reputation for turning away intruders, Ernie's success is all the more mystifying and impressive. The joke was, and Ernie told it on himself, that Honeycutt had bought his departure with that gift. Which didn't explain the literary correspondence that followed and Honeycutt's professed admiration, in several of his letters, for Ernie's understanding of his work.

After Ernie had won over the legendary Honeycutt, the other writers he pursued seemed to fall in line. After a point, it became a symbol of achievement to receive a letter from Ernie Sommer. Almost no writer of any distinction was ignored by him.

"They were very generous to me," Ernie has been quoted as saying. "I might have been the literary equivalent of a mass murderer for all any of them knew."

11.

Ernie was extremely attached to his mother, I'm told. His father did some kind of physical labor, which seemed to use him up, shuck him of all vitality and hope. The rare occasions he spent with the family, he was often drunk and sometimes violent. Disappointed with her husband, Ernie's mother, who was artistic, turned to Ernie for consolation. Ernie took sustenance from his mother, became dependent on her affection and approval. He showed some talent for painting as a child—it was his mother's idea for him—but then he gave it up. At some point, he realized that he had to get away from his mother to survive. As he got older, he took on something of his father's manner, some of the gruffness and swagger, though he remained, even after her death, essentially his mother's son.

12.

When Ernie became a literary editor—eventually he started his own publishing company, Cervantes & Sons—he took his writers with him in surprising numbers. By this time Ernie was almost as well known (his picture on the cover of *People* magazine) as the most celebrated of his writers. Ernie made light of his success, liked to say it was a case of "importance by association." "The other guys wrote these books and all I had to do was get the word around." Ernie's authors didn't tour the provinces promoting their books. He saw the practice as demeaning to serious artists so he went himself, stood in for his authors on talk shows, made public appearances at bookstores, seemed everywhere at once, developed a reputation for saying the most provocative thing that came to mind. That was when he was starting out as a publisher, the first two or three years. In the third year of his publishing venture—things came apart after that—his writers were as dedicated to him as he had been (and maybe still was, though it was no longer easy to tell) to them.

13.

What went wrong? When a group of Ernie's writers get together at one of the traditional watering spots that question invariably comes up. The answers tend to be provisional and dogmatic. The favored position is that the culture tends to destroy its heroes to make room for new ones. The rival position, which had almost equal claim, is that Ernie self-destructed. The more celebrated he became the more outrageous he got. He took to referring to the audience—the first time in a radio interview in Las Vegas—as "those unwashed illiterate peckerheads out there." That didn't ingratiate him a whole lot, I suspect, or maybe it did until his listeners realized the "peckerheads" he was talking about were themselves. According to Jack, Ernie destroyed himself by trying to educate an audience that was wholly content being insulted.

14.

Despite the critical success of the books Cervantes & Sons produced, the company, owned in partnership with two traditional types, managed to lose money or make so little, given the favorable attention it attracted, that it seemed like loss. Ernie was advised by his partners to practice greater economy, particularly in regard to his authors. Ernie's answer, he had told us each separately in private unrepeatable confidence, was that he practiced all the time though never seemed to get it right. One of his partners told me that after the first six months or so Ernie lost interest in the running of the firm. "He was more concerned with his own celebrity," the man told me, "than with the nuts and bolts of the business." On the other hand, Ernie had equally harsh things to say about his partners, whom he took to calling Heckyl and Jeckyl. Heckyl, he said, couldn't read and Jeckyl could but didn't.

15.

We backtrack a bit here. Ernie is still on the rise, an ascending star in the lit celeb firmament. A collection of his correspondence called *Heroes and Heroines* is about to be published. As soon as he signs the contract for the book, Ernie regrets having made "my private obsession public." He insists that the book is incomplete and initiates new correspondence with a variety of international figures, forestalls publication date, dreams a letter from Tolstoy that he publishes in an obscure literary quarterly. Ernie denies that he is himself a writer. He is a longstanding appreciator of writers, an avaricious reader who is serious about what he reads, and perhaps (evidence the Tolstoy letter) a medium for literary voices. "Do you mean to say," the interviewer asks him, "that you didn't actually write the letter from Tolstoy?" "What can I tell you?" Ernie says. "I've never written anything, have never shown the slightest talent for writing. You could look it up. The 'C' I got in freshman English at the University of Pennsylvania was a generosity from the instructor. Tell you the truth, I don't know how the

Tolstoy letter was written. It came to me in a moment of pure light. I think it would be ungracious of me to question the source."

A letter from Sophocles followed, though was never released for publication. Ernie himself questioned its legitimacy. "The man dictated it," he said, "but to tell the truth most of it was Greek to me."

16.

Ernie was so self-important, one of his partners complained to me, that he would scotch film deals by abusing the person who wanted to buy the rights to one of his properties. He reputedly asked for a written critique from an independent producer who was after Jack's absurdist novel about Auschwitz. The man said that what interested him most about the novel was its wellspring of humanity. Ernie, according to the partner, told the man not to come back until he read the book word for word and had some idea what he was buying.

Whether Ernie was subversive of his own business is a moot issue. Ernie said not to believe it, that he only interfered when negotiations became wearisomely protracted. Besides, he added, he thought it immoral to sell the books he loved as if they were underarm deodorants.

Whatever the case, Ernie's partners offered to buy him out by paying him, according to the partner I interviewed, twice what his share in the firm was worth. Eight months after Ernie left, the company, in order to survive, sold itself to a conglomerate and both surviving partners, in due course, were forced out of the business.

17.

Ernie had a friend, a psychologist, who ran an experi-
mental clinic which took on only patients that had
been previously diagnosed as incurable. One of the
friend's incurable cases was a beautiful schizophrenic
seventeen-year-old girl, who had had real or imagined
relations with her father when she was twelve. When
Ernie visited the friend at his clinic in California, he
was moved by the girl's intelligence and courage and
spent some time talking to her. Later they exchanged
letters—her letters full of remarkable perceptions—
and Ernie found himself longing to see her again. The
doctor encouraged the relationship—Ernie's friendship seemed to have a salutary effect on her condition—while warning Ernie not to let himself get too
involved. The girl might improve, he told Ernie, but
there would be inevitable relapses; she would never be
able to lead a wholly normal life. Ernie threw himself
headlong into the relationship with the girl and an odd
turnabout took place. As the girl made an astonishing
recovery, Ernie began drinking to excess, seemed to
come apart. When the girl no longer needed him, she
rejected Ernie for a man who seemed more confident
of himself. After that Ernie went through a period of
bad weather, was drunk more often than not and got
into a succession of pointless brawls. Eventually, the
experience toughened him, made him more attentive
to the demands of self.

18.

Women. That's another story, though also inextricably
connected to the story of Ernest Sommer's rise and fall.
At a certain point in his life, women became almost
as crucial to Ernie as books. Their pursuit, their affection, their approval conferred status on him. He was

suddenly important enough to be loved for reasons other than himself.

I remember a lunch we had together when all Ernie wanted to talk about was "this absolutely gorgeous lady" who had come to his office to interview him for some magazine. "I said to her," he told me, "that all she had to do was say the word and I'd run off with her to some edenic spot on the other side of the globe and she says, looking directly at me, and this is a gorgeous lady, What word is that, Mr. Sommer? I told her I was serious and she says, this dazzler, the kind of lady that never would have looked at me twice outside of this book-lined office, I think you're a beautiful man, Mr. Sommer."

"I said to myself she had to be kidding. Smart, I may be. Beautiful I ain't. But she meant it and after the interview was concluded—I mean she was there to do a job—she demonstrated her sincerity. You know what I'm saying?"

How could he continue living with one woman when almost every desirable woman he came in contact with was available to him. "I can't handle it," he said whenever the subject came up. It was more of a boast than a self-deprecation, though the remark was not without some regret.

19.

Zoe put up with Ernie's womanizing for a time—he would get over it, she must have thought—but then they had a fight at a party over the attention Ernie paid some starlet or princess and everything that had been kept inside came out.

Ernie professed shock at Zoe's abrupt explosion. "How can someone you lived with for twelve years treat you that way?" was his constant question.

Whatever happened next happened quickly. Zoe moved out, took the child, accused Ernie of promiscuous adultery, and sued him for two-thirds of his recorded income.

According to Jack, nothing hurt Ernie more than Zoe's disaffection. After she left him his confidence began to erode.

Ernie is reported to have thrown himself at Zoe's feet in the lobby of her apartment building in an attempt at reconciliation. He apparently begged her to come back to him, using all his powers of persuasion.

20.

"He hated more than anything not to get his way," Zoe told us. "He absolutely refused being turned down, though he would say—it was one of his favorite lines—that he never wanted anything for himself, that he could survive on nothing if he had to.

"I told him several times to let go of my ankles, that he had no business keeping me from my appointment. When he released me, I said no hard feelings and walked out on him."

"You didn't kick him as he claims?"

"Kick him?" The question seems to amuse her. "I didn't kick him, if that's what he says—he would say that—which is to say it wasn't my intention to kick the son of a bitch. When I saw blood coming from his lip I felt awful, was ready to drop everything and look after him for as long as he needed me. I've always felt that way about Ernie. Let's just say that whatever happens, Ernie and I will always be friends. "

"Did she really say that?" Ernie asked me. "That's unbelievable. That lady has class."

21.

A former acquaintance of Ernie's, an author who had not written anything in years, showed up one morning at Ernie's door to accuse Ernie of having ruined his life. The man was unpleasant but also in need—broke and broken—so Ernie, who was temporarily living alone, let him stay over for a couple of nights. The former acquaintance read the gesture as an admission of Ernie's guilt and became even more demanding and abusive. It was the man's idea that Ernie was part of some kind of Jewish establishment that controlled who got published and who didn't. In his crazed view, Ernie had cut off all avenues of publication to him because he had once made an anti-Semitic remark in Ernie's presence. As a consequence of Ernie's perceived treachery, the man had lost the will to write. Although he despised the intruder, Ernie suffered his extended visit, felt in some inexplicable way obligated to the man. The man became fixated with Ernie, dressed in his clothes, imitated his voice on the phone, wrote letters in which he signed himself Ernest Sommer. One night Ernie woke to see his other self lighting a fire in Ernie's bedroom. The attempted murder released Ernie from any feelings of obligation. He threw the man out of his apartment and then subdued the fire. Ernie was burned, we understand, though nothing serious.

Ernie thinks of himself as rising from the fire like a phoenix.

22.

The day after Ernie separated from the publishing house he had imagined into existence, it was as if he had never been there. When I called to speak to him—it was how I had learned he had gone—his former employees seemed unable to remember his name.

I was shunted from receptionist to receptionist, was kept waiting for ten minutes, then found myself holding a dead phone. Ernie will be furious at such incompetence, I thought, or else get a good laugh out of it. Colonel Fiction, as we sometimes called him, tended to complain in a seemingly parodic way at the quality of the help. If the gossip can be believed, he once asked a pompous young editor to sweep out his office and polish his desk. The editor quit (a week after he had both swept and polished) and Ernie is reputed to have said, "If you can't last fifteen rounds, there's no point in fighting for the championship of the world."

The second time I phoned, some assistant told me that Ernie was no longer employed at Cervantes & Sons. I thought of saying that a company doesn't employ its owner, but let it pass. I asked to speak to one of the partners. Both were in conference at the moment and were not expected to be free to come to the phone for an indefinite period of time. I left my name in that void, expecting it to disappear as heartlessly as Ernie had.

I called Ernie at home later that day and got no answer. And then, involved in my own work, I didn't concern myself with Ernie for a few days—maybe it was a few weeks—let the issue of his apparent disappearance slide. The next time I called his apartment his phone had been disconnected.

A few days after that, Jack told me Ernie had moved out of his loft and no one, at least no one Jack had talked to, knew where he had gone. Traces of him remained in the atmosphere like the fragments of an exploded meteor.

23.

Time passes as we wait for Ernie to surface. Zoe publishes a novel centered around a character that resembles

Ernie Sommer. This Ernie, called Howard Swift in the novel, is a heavy drinker and semi-heavy womanizer, a man unable to control the least of his desires. (By the time the book came out, Zoe had married her therapist from whom, one imagines, she had gotten her license to kill.) There is some sympathy for Howard/Ernie in the book, though it relies for the most part on the heroine's willful generosity, the object of it beyond redemption.

It was not a heroic portrait; it was not a portrait of the man we thought we knew as Colonel (sometimes Major, sometimes Captain) Fiction. Howard Swift is a nightclub comedian who becomes a talk show host, becoming more ruthless and exploitative (and sexually bizarre) with each new success.

"Perhaps it's not meant to be Ernie at all," Jack suggested. "The character of Howard Swift may have no prototype in the real world but cliché."

I wrote Zoe a long letter protesting the book's portrait of Ernie, but then misplaced it among my papers or threw it out accidentally.

24.

A story circulates—it is one rumor among many—that Ernie cut himself off from his old friends in order to pursue his own writing. I tend to accept rumors that have a poetic rightness about them even if their source is less than authoritative. I imagine Ernie writing in longhand on loose-leaf pages, working all day and into the night, drinking bourbon and pacing the room, an obsessive figure capable of the most extreme vices and the most intense virtue.

When will we hear from him again? I sit patiently at my desk and put down words, fragments, sentences, paragraphs in what seems to me a telling order. As I write, I glance over my shoulder from time to time (I'm speaking figuratively of course), looking for Ernie, imagining myself as Ernie, wanting to be greeted by my friends as I emerge from obscurity.

25.

I am at my desk trying to imagine the next stage of Ernie's career, trying to create an imaginary history more substantial and valid than the real one. Who is Ernie after all?

There are a number of possible conclusions to his story, none absolutely right, almost all with some claim to verisimilitude. I put them down in longhand on the loose-leaf sheet in front of me.

A pseudonymous manuscript of over 1200 pages shows up (delivered by messenger) in the office of an editor of some power and authority. It is accompanied by a note from the reclusive writer, H, commending it to the editor. The book is published, gets mostly excellent if uncomprehending reviews, sells modestly, is almost sold to the movies. At some point Ernie lets out in an interview that he is the actual author.

Ernie produces a best seller of little or no literary value, talks in interviews about the importance of reaching a large audience. Established as a public figure, he laments the plight of celebrities, says all he wants is to be left alone to write his books.

Ernie reemerges as the editor-in-chief of a new incarnation of a once prestigious men's magazine, which in its bid for trendiness had lost its identity. He calls a press conference to announce that the magazine will publish the best writing in America and the world regardless of mass market appeal, that its only aim is to be first rate. The opening issue sells out; the second issue does almost as well; the third sells half as many as the second.

Ernie leaves his post after ten months to write a memoir of the experience.

Unable to write at the level of his aspirations, Ernie gives way to depression, drinks heavily, turns himself into a clinic for rehabilitation, writes the story of his breakdown and recovery.

Ernie writes versions of the books he's admired, publishes them under pseudonyms, lives modestly out of the public eye. Most of us never see him again, though over drinks we share anecdotes about his career, keeping Ernie afloat in the collective imagination like a character in a novel.